# ZERO HOUR

# BOOKS BY JAMES REASONER

THE LAST GOOD WAR
*Battle Lines**
*Trial by Fire**
*Zero Hour**


*Manassas*

*Shiloh*

*Antietam*

*Chancellorsville*

*Vicksburg*

*Under Outlaw Flags*

*The Wilderness Road*

*The Hunted*


*denotes a Forge book

# ZERO HOUR

## THE LAST GOOD WAR
### BOOK III

# JAMES REASONER

A TOM DOHERTY ASSOCIATES BOOK
NEW YORK

ZERO HOUR

Copyright © 2003 by James Reasoner

Edited by James Frenkel

This book is printed on acid-free paper.

A Forge Book
Published by Tom Doherty Associates, LLC
175 Fifth Avenue
New York, NY 10010

www.tor.com

Forge® is a registered trademark of Tom Doherty Associates, LLC.

Library of Congress Cataloging-in-Publication Data

Reasoner, James.
    Zero hour : the last good war : book 3 / James Reasoner.—1st hardcover ed.
        p.  cm.
    "A Tom Doherty Associates book."
    Sequel to: Trial by fire.
    ISBN 0-312-87347-6
    1. World War, 1939–1945—South Pacific Ocean—Fiction.  2. World War,
1939–1945—Africa, North—Fiction.  3. Americans—South Pacific Ocean—
Fiction.  4. Americans—Africa, North—Fiction.  5. South Pacific Ocean—
Fiction.  6. Africa, North—Fiction.  7. Oceania—Fiction.  I. Title.
PS3568.E2685Z33 2002
813'.54—dc21

                                                                    2002014586

First Edition: April 2003

Printed in the United States of America

0  9  8  7  6  5  4  3  2  1

For Livia, Shayna, and Joanna

# ACKNOWLEDGMENTS

Special thanks to Tom Doherty, James Frenkel, Martin Greenberg, John Helfers, Larry Segriff, Ed Gorman, Larry Richter, Morgan Holmes, Leo Grin, Gerald W. Page, Robert Sankner, Dobie Reasoner.

And to Livia for going way beyond the call of duty.

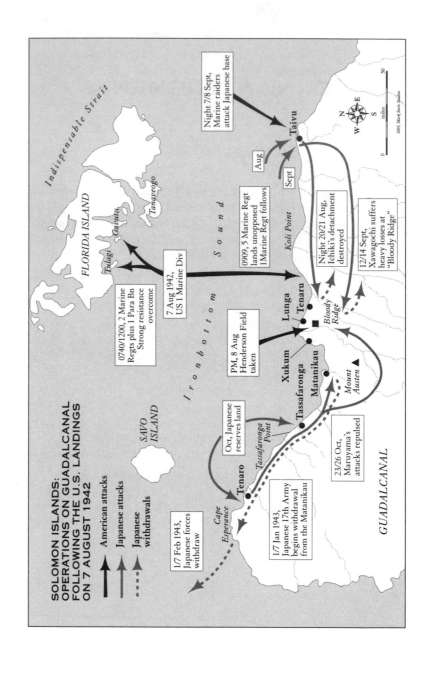

SOLOMON ISLANDS:
OPERATIONS ON GUADALCANAL
FOLLOWING THE U.S. LANDINGS
ON 7 AUGUST 1942

American attacks
Japanese attacks
Japanese withdrawals

Indispensable Strait

FLORIDA ISLAND

Tulagi
Gavutu
Tanaveogo

Sound

Ironbottom

SAVO ISLAND

Cape Esperance

Tenaro

Tassafaronga Point

Tassafaronga

Matanikau

Xukum

Lunga

Tenaru

Bloody Ridge

Mount Austen

GUADALCANAL

Koli Point

Taivu

Night 7/8 Sept, Marine raiders attack Japanese base

Aug

Sept

Night 20/21 Aug, Ichiki's detachment destroyed

12/14 Sept, Xawagochi suffers heavy losses at "Bloody Ridge"

0909, 5 Marine Regt lands unopposed 1Marine Regt follows

7 Aug 1942, US 1 Marine Div

0740/1200, 2 Marine Regts plus 1 Para Bn Strong resistance overcome

PM, 8 Aug Henderson Field taken

Oct, Japanese reserves land

23/26 Oct, Maruyama's attacks repulsed

1/7 Jan 1943, Japanese 17th Army begins withdrawal from the Matanikau

1/7 Feb 1943, Japanese forces withdraw

N
W    E
S

0          miles          50

2005, Mark Stein Studios

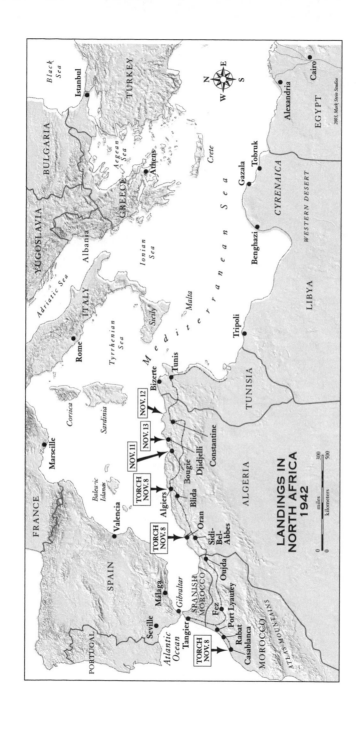

# ZERO HOUR

# ONE

Dale Parker wheeled the jeep up to the oasis, brought it to a stop, looked around and said, "Where's Rudolph Valentino?"

"Who?" Bert Crimmens asked. "Oh, you mean the American movie star."

"Well, I'm not so sure he was American. He always looked kind of foreign to me. The women sure did go crazy over him, though." Dale waved at the cluster of palm trees around the small pool of water in the middle of a vast expanse of burning sand. "This looks like just the kind of place he'd ride up to on a camel, wearing that sheik outfit."

"I believe you're thinking about Arabia," Bert said with a frown. "This is Libya."

"Oh, yeah."

On the far side of the oasis, which had no name as far as Dale knew, a dozen tanks were parked in the circular formation known as leaguer. Though they belonged to the British Eighth Army and were part of the Third Royal Tank Corps, the tanks were American-made, the M3 model they called the General Grant. The British tankies were so taken with the M3s that they referred to the tanks as Honeys. The name had originated the previous autumn when the 3RTC had been using the earlier model General Lee tanks during Operation Crusader. When the Grants had arrived in December 1941 and January 1942, the nickname had been transferred to them.

Dale Parker was American-made too, a tall, blond young man from the South Side of Chicago. He wore the uniform of a sergeant in the United States Army, and a member of the Army Services

13

Force that had come here to North Africa along with the General Grant tanks, to serve as instructors for the British. Today, since he was on the front lines in Libya, he wore a steel helmet instead of a fore-and-aft overseas cap.

He swung his long legs out of the jeep and stood up, stretching weary muscles. It was a long drive from Tobruk down here to this oasis near Bir Hacheim, the southernmost end of the Gazala Line. The British had been dug in along this defensive front since the spring, when they had stopped the advance of General Erwin Rommel and his Deutsche Afrika Korps. The line stretched from east of the town of Gazala, on the Mediterranean coast, south to Bir Hacheim, and then curved back to the north in a fishhook shape. East of the line, also on the coast, was the stronghold of Tobruk, which really wasn't all that strong from what Dale had seen of it during his brief visit there the day before. The British had held off Rommel once before by forting up inside Tobruk, but Dale wasn't sure they'd be able to do it again.

He followed Bert toward the circle of tanks. Bert Crimmens had been a good friend to Dale and his brother Joe ever since all of them had been at the British Armour School at Bovington, south of London. That was where Dale and Joe and the other American instructors had begun teaching the British tankies how to operate the General Grants. Dale was an expert on the tanks' engines while Joe knew everything there was to know about the radios (British Wireless Set No. 19) that were installed in the M3s. They had learned all about those things during their training at Camp Bowie, Brownwood, Texas, during the spring and summer of '41.

They were a long way from Texas now, a long way from their home in Chicago. A long way from the United States, period. Just going to England had been quite an adventure, and now they found themselves in Africa, lending a hand to the British Eighth Army. President Roosevelt had started the Lend-Lease program to help out the British, back in the days before the Japanese attack on Pearl Harbor and the United States's entry into the war itself, so Dale supposed he was on loan to the Brits. Or maybe they were leasing him. He wasn't sure which.

A rugged-looking, brown-haired man came out from the tanks

to greet Dale and Bert. He wore laced-up boots, khaki shorts, and a sweat-stained khaki shirt with pips on it indicating that he was a captain. The brown hat on his head had the left side of the brim pinned up. He was an Australian, though officially he was a member of the British Army.

"There you are, Bert," he said. "I was afraid you weren't going to make it back in time."

Bert came to attention, clicked his heels together, and saluted. "Corporal Crimmens reportin' for duty, sir," he said, then added in a less formal tone, "In time for what, sir?"

"To go foxhunting," Captain Neville Sharp replied.

Dale and Bert glanced at each other. They both knew what Sharp was talking about: General Rommel was known as the Desert Fox.

"Goin' on patrol, are we, sir?"

"That's what we're here for." Sharp looked at Dale. "And why are you here, Sergeant Parker?"

"I'm just a taxi service today, Captain," Dale replied. "I ran into Bert in Tobruk and he said he needed a way back out here, so I volunteered to bring him."

"I see. The possibility that you might wind up in the turret of a tank again never occurred to you, I suppose."

Dale grinned. "Well, not really, sir. But you never know what might happen."

"Don't get your hopes up," Sharp said. "Much as I appreciate what you did last time, Sergeant, I believe I'll command my own tank today, thank you."

"No problem, sir."

A couple of months earlier, during another visit to the front, Dale had happened across Captain Sharp's tank and had taken command of it when he found that Sharp had been wounded and knocked out during a fight with a German armored car. The rest of the crew—radioman Bert Crimmens, gunner Jeremy Royce, and driver Tom Hamilton—had been doing the best they could, but they were lost and probably would have been easy prey for the Panzers clanking across the desert if Dale hadn't stepped in to help. While he was in command of the tank, they had traded shots with and ultimately destroyed one of the German behemoths. Dale hadn't been able to claim any credit for his actions because as an advisor he wasn't supposed to be anywhere near the front lines, but the members of the British tank crew knew what he had done. He suspected that Captain Sharp—Hell-on-Treads Sharp, as he was known in the Royal Tank Corps—had had something to do with the promotion to sergeant that he had received soon after that, but Dale couldn't be sure.

"My God, who's that?"

Dale turned to see a rawboned, dark-haired man walking back toward the tanks from the pool at the center of the oasis. He had a wet shirt in his hands. Dale assumed the man had been washing out the garment. He said, "Hello, Royce."

Jeremy Royce grunted. "Can't we get rid of you? I thought all you bloody Yanks were back in Cairo."

"You've got a couple of tanks in Tobruk that your mechanics couldn't fix," Dale said. "The brass sent me over to take care of them for you."

Royce glared and said, "Should've sent me back there. I know more about those engines than you do."

"Everything you know about those engines you learned from me," Dale pointed out. "And you're such a good mechanic they made a gunner out of you."

Royce took a step toward Dale, his hands bunching into fists as he held the wet shirt. Sharp moved between them, saying, "That'll be enough of that, you two. You can refight your old wars some other time." He turned back to Crimmens. "Bert, how's the leg?"

"Dandy, Captain. The medical blokes at hospital sewed up that gash and pumped me full of sulfa. I've got the all-clear to return to duty."

"Good. We can use you." Sharp clapped a hand on Bert's shoulder. "We're pulling out in ten minutes."

"What about me?" Dale asked.

Sharp shrugged. "You can drive back to Tobruk, I suppose."

"It's eighty miles. I'm not sure I can make it before dark."

"Stay here, then, and start back in the morning."

Bert asked, "Are we coming back here, Captain?"

"Yes, I intend to make leaguer here again when we get back from our patrol. We won't be gone long. I just want to take a run down to that box manned by the Third Indian Motor Brigade and see how they're doing."

"I'll hang around, then," Dale said. "That'll give me and Bert a chance to visit some more. We didn't finish catching up on old times."

Jeremy Royce snorted. "Old times? It's only been two months since you saw each other. Gotten sweet on each other, that'd be my guess."

Bert's face darkened with anger. He faced Royce and said, "Shut up that bloody nonsense, Royce. I won't stand for it."

"I'm near twice your size," Royce said with a sneer. "What're you goin' to do about it?"

"*I'm* going to do something about it," Sharp said. "Royce, get back to the tank. That's an order. And both of you, can the chatter."

Dale grinned. "You're starting to sound like an American, Captain."

"If you're going to be insulting, you can just toddle on back to Tobruk, Parker."

Still smiling, Dale held up his hands, palms out. "No offense meant, sir."

Chuckling, he strolled over to the oasis while the British tank crews climbed into their tanks. With a rumbling roar, the engines started. Dale listened to the sound with a professional ear and was satisfied with what he heard. All the engines seemed to be running fine.

He sat down under one of the trees, reached into the pocket of his fatigue shirt, and brought out a candy bar. In this heat, the chocolate was soft, of course, but he unwrapped it and ate it anyway, licking the last of the sweet, sticky stuff off the wrapper. He watched the tanks disappear over a sand dune in the distance and wished he were going with them. He'd had a taste of combat, and while only a damned fool would ever say that he liked being shot at, Dale had found the whole experience exhilarating. He'd been scared when that Panzer was chasing them, sure. His heart had pounded like mad and his shirt was soaked through with sweat by the time the brief fight was over. But he had accomplished something that day, and he was proud of it.

Late afternoon was the hottest time of the day here on the edge of the great Western Desert. As the air grew hotter, Dale found himself nodding off. He shifted around a little, getting his back into a more comfortable position against the trunk of the tree, and he tilted his helmet forward to shade his eyes from more of the sun's glare. He'd been in the army for more than a year, and he had developed the same skill as most soldiers had: He could fall asleep quickly, just about anywhere, and snatch a few winks whenever possible.

He wasn't sure how long he slept, but he knew what woke him. It was the rumble and clank of tank treads. Captain Sharp's squadron was back already, he thought as he sat up and rubbed his eyes. He turned around and looked toward the approaching tanks, realizing only then that the sounds were coming from a different direction than they should have been. Sharp's squad had gone the other way when it left the oasis. That meant—

Dale shot to his feet as four German Mark III Panzer tanks rolled into view, topping the crest of a sand dune.

# TWO

The thud of Dale's pulse was so loud in his ears that he could hear it over the rumble of the German tanks. The Panzers were bearing down on the oasis. The jeep Dale had used to bring Bert Crimmens out here from Tobruk was parked on the far side of the trees from the Germans, so maybe they hadn't noticed it yet. Dale considered making a dash for the jeep and getting out of here as fast as he could.

But movement would just draw the attention of the Krauts, he told himself, and no matter how much speed he was able to coax out of the jeep, it wouldn't be enough for him to outrun a shell from a 75mm-cannon like the ones mounted on the turrets of the Panzers. If he stayed where he was, though, the Germans would either find him when they stopped at the oasis or spot the jeep if they drove on past.

Either way, he was screwed, blued, and tattooed, he thought.

In the back of his mind, he wondered what the Germans were doing here. They were supposed to be a few miles away, on the other side of the Gazala Line. Everyone seemed to think they would launch an attack sooner or later, but no one knew when.

He knew now, Dale thought. Whatever the Germans were doing, he was smack-dab in the middle of it.

Lowering himself into a crouch, he put the tree trunk between as much of himself and the Germans as he could. In the olive-drab fatigues and the steel pot on his head, he wouldn't stand out too much from the varying shades of brown that made up the ground here in the oasis. The trees gave him added camouflage. Maybe the Germans wouldn't notice the jeep. Just keep going, he urged them silently. Drive right on past.

Instead, the tanks ground to a halt on the far side of the oasis. Dale grimaced and sank lower to the ground as he peered around the tree trunk and saw the massive metal monsters slowing and then stopping. The drivers didn't cut their engines, just idled down. Over the racket, Dale heard soldiers shouting orders in German.

They were going to refill their canteens and water cans, Dale thought. In this arid wasteland, water was precious, more precious than anything except maybe gasoline and ammunition. No one with any sense passed up a chance to replenish his water. And say what you wanted about the Nazis, they weren't fools. They hadn't conquered most of Europe and half of North Africa by squandering opportunities.

Dale had a Model 1911A1 Colt .45 ACP automatic pistol holstered on his right hip. The magazine in the pistol grip held seven shots, and another thirty rounds were tucked away in a box in one of his pockets. He wasn't sure how many men were in the crews of those Panzers, but there had to be at least four for each tank. That meant if he put up a fight, he would be facing at least sixteen men. Those were flat-out lousy odds, no matter how you looked at them.

He couldn't run, and he couldn't fight. That left surrendering as his only option. But even as the thought crossed his mind, the sick feeling in his stomach told him he couldn't do that. The United States had barely gotten its toes wet in this war. American sailors and Marines had fought the Japs in the Pacific, at Wake Island and the Coral Sea and Midway, and U.S. advisors here in North Africa were helping out the British. But that was it so far. Dale felt certain that something else was coming, something big, and he wanted to be part of it. He couldn't spend the rest of the war languishing in some Kraut POW camp. That was what would happen to him if he surrendered now. *If* he was lucky and the Germans didn't shoot him just so they wouldn't have to bother with a prisoner.

Running, fighting, and surrendering were all out, then. Dale was starting to understand that old saying about being between a rock and a hard place.

He heard the Germans talking about *vasser*. That was *Deutsche* for "water," wasn't it? He risked another glance around the tree trunk and saw several men making their way through the trees toward the pond, carrying five-gallon cans.

They knelt at the edge of the water, unscrewed the caps on the cans, and started filling them, holding them under the surface of the pool so that water flowed in and air bubbled out. The Germans were turned so that they weren't facing Dale straight on. He started edging backward, hoping the bubbling from the water tins would cover up any little sounds he might make. From the other side of the trees, he heard laughter. A whiff of cigarette smoke drifted to his nostrils. Except for the men filling the water cans, the Krauts were taking a break. Maybe they wouldn't be paying as close attention to their surroundings as they should be.

Dale reached the jeep and bellied down in the sand on the far side of it. He looked over his shoulder and tried to judge the distance to the nearest dune. It was about forty yards away, he figured. If he could start the jeep going one way and decoy the Germans into following it, he might be able to dash back over that dune and out of sight before they noticed him. He would be on foot, in the middle of the desert, miles away from any help, but at least he would be alive and free. A look at the sky told him it would be dark in less than an hour. It got cold out here at night, but he figured he could stand it. He was pretty good at navigating by the stars too. He would head north, and sooner or later he would run into a squad of British tanks in leaguer or one of the heavily fortified boxes that made up the Gazala Line.

No sooner had the elements of the crude plan lined up in his mind than he was reaching up to the dashboard. The key was still in the jeep's ignition. He twisted it into the ON position then reached over to press down the starter with the heel of his hand. The engine turned over.

The Germans still hanging around the tanks wouldn't notice the sound of the jeep over the tank engines. But the Krauts at the pool might. Using his hands instead of his feet, Dale fed the jeep some gas. The engine caught. Dale reached down to his right foot and yanked his boot off without bothering to untie the laces. He jammed the boot against the accelerator, wedging it against the floorboard so it would stay down. Then he hit the clutch with one hand, slapped the gearshift lever into first with the other, and threw himself away from the jeep and onto the sand as the vehicle lurched into motion.

Dale rolled over several times, hearing shouts from the oasis as he did so. As he surged to his feet he looked back and saw the Germans who had been at the pond running out of the trees to stare after the jeep, which was trundling over the sand toward a dune. One of the Germans jerked a Luger from its holster and started blasting away at the jeep. He probably thought one of the Tommies was lying down on the seat and driving the thing. That was just what Dale wanted them to think.

He sprinted toward the dune in the other direction. His gait was awkward because he wore a boot on only one foot. If he got away, he could take that boot off and walk in his socks. But first he had to get away . . .

The slope of the dune rose before him. He didn't waste time looking back. If the Krauts were about to riddle him with a machine gun or blow him to smithereens with a 75mm round, Dale didn't want to know about it. He would rather die in ignorance. He started running up the dune. The sand dragged at his feet and slowed him down so that it seemed as if the top of the dune was still as far away as when he started climbing toward it. Hot air rasped in his throat, and blood pounded inside his skull.

Suddenly he was at the crest. He threw himself over and landed in a diving roll that carried him several yards down the far slope. He slid to a halt, his legs half-buried in the soft, yielding sand.

Pistols still cracked on the other side of the dune, but the Germans hadn't brought into play the machine guns and cannons mounted on the Panzers. No doubt they were confused by the jeep's sudden appearance and the apparent fact that it was moving without a driver, but they must not have considered it much of a threat.

Dale crawled back up the sandy slope until he could peer over the top. What he saw made him groan in despair. The tracks he had left in the sand as he climbed the dune were so visible they could be seen without any trouble if the Germans bothered to turn around and look. The wind that blew almost all the time was filling in and covering up the tracks, but at such a slow pace that it would take hours before they disappeared. By then, the Germans would have discovered that the jeep was a decoy, and they would follow the tracks right to him.

The jeep was still moving, but as it reached a dune and started up, it slowed and its wheels began to bog down in the sand. As Dale watched, it came to a stop. He could hear the engine racing and knew the transmission must have slipped out of gear. Half-a-dozen Germans in peaked caps and green *Afrika Korps* uniforms approached the now-motionless jeep, Lugers drawn and leveled.

Now was the time to beat a retreat if ever he was going to. He took off his left boot, slid down the dune, and came up running. The heat from the sun that the desert had soaked up all day came through his socks and seared the bottom of his feet, and the tiny pebbles mixed in with the sand gouged at his soles. He ignored the pain and kept running as best he could. Sweat bathed his face.

When would he learn? How many messes had he gotten into in his life because he didn't think before he jumped into something? He had been told to go to Tobruk to fix a couple of tanks; that was all. He'd hitched a ride there with a convoy of supply trucks, done the job he'd been given, and had been ready to head back to Cairo when he'd run into Bert Crimmens leaving the field hospital the British army had set up. Bert had a long, deep cut on his leg that he'd gotten when he slipped and fell off the tank, and the medics in his unit had decided that it would be better to send him back to hospital in Tobruk. He would have hitched a ride too, but Dale had the jeep that the Eighth Army had put at his disposal while he was in Tobruk, so he hadn't hesitated in volunteering to take Bert back to his squadron. Hell, he thought, it would only make him a couple of days late getting back to Cairo. The brass wouldn't squawk too much about that—he hoped.

Now, instead of having to worry about some officer giving him an ass chewing, Dale had a bunch of Krauts in Panzers after him. That was worse. One hell of a lot worse.

He had run up and down several dunes before he heard the roar of engines growing louder behind him. They were after him now. They had found his boot in the jeep and figured out what had happened. A man could outrun a tank for a short distance—but this was a long-distance race, and one that Dale was doomed to lose.

He was panting for breath already. A man wasn't made for running around in blazing sun and blistering sand. The only ones who would do that were lizards and idiots. Or was it mad dogs and Englishmen? As the thought crossed his mind, he realized he was getting a little light-headed. If he fainted, the Germans would catch up to him in a matter of minutes.

They might anyway, he told himself as he slowed even more. The engines were getting louder all the time. In fact, they were so loud he was confused. It sounded now like the tanks were in front of him, but he knew that wasn't possible. The Germans hadn't had time to circle around and come at him from the front.

A second later, he knew they were still behind him, because one of the Panzers topped a dune and he saw it as he glanced over his shoulder. He saw the flames lick from the muzzle of its turret-mounted machine gun as well, though the flash was washed out in the late afternoon sunlight. Sand spurted into the air to his right as the bullets dug into the desert floor. Dale veered to his left, away from the machine-gun slugs.

That was just what they wanted him to do. With a whip-crack of sound, the Panzer's cannon blasted. The shell slammed into the ground ahead of Dale as the Nazi gunner led him a little too much. The concussion was strong enough, though, to pick him up and fling him backward like a rag doll. He was half-senseless as he came to a stop on his belly after rolling over half-a-dozen times.

Groggy from the blast, he lifted his head and shook it, trying to clear away some of the cobwebs around his brain. The explosion had deafened him, but he could still see all right even if he couldn't hear anything. He saw that he was lying at the foot of a dune. About fifty yards away, across a stretch of open ground, another dune rose, and as Dale watched in horror, two of the Panzers rolled over the top of it and started down the near side.

Toward him. Right toward him.

The ground shook underneath him. At first he thought the approaching German tanks were causing the vibrations, but then the shuddering got worse, and something made him look up toward the top of the dune that rose above him. The first thing he saw was a long metal cylinder thrusting out beyond the crest of the dune. After a second he recognized it as the barrel of a 75mm-cannon. A moment later the rest of the tank followed the cannon into view. It was a General Grant. Two more were right behind it.

Dale jerked his head the other direction and saw that the other three Panzers had joined the first one. They were slowing to a stop now at the sight of the British tanks. The General Grants were coming to a halt too. It was a standoff, Dale thought as he laid there, his head swiveling back and forth. The four Panzers faced the three General Grants across that narrow strip of intervening ground, and it was likely that any second the air would be filled with the hellish thunder of the tanks' cannons.

Dale Parker realized that he was trapped right there between the two armored forces. He looked back and forth again and expressed that realization with a fervent "Oh, shit!"

# THREE

After lying there frozen for a moment, Dale let his instincts take over. If you were in the middle of a big mess, the thing to do was get the hell away from it. He rolled several yards to the side and sprang to his feet, breaking into a run. He had gone only a couple of steps when his left leg went out from under him and pitched him forward on his face.

Agony shot through his knee. He figured he had twisted it when that shell blast picked him up and flung him to the ground. With sweat running from him like a river, he pushed himself up and started running again. This time when the pain hit his leg, he was ready. He forced himself to ignore it and stay upright. He kept running.

The cannon on the General Grant that was in the lead erupted in noise and flame. An instant later, all three of the British tanks lurched into motion, heading down the slope. Dale threw a glance over his shoulder and saw that they were weaving back and forth, moving with a grace that seemed out of place in such massive metal contraptions.

One of the Panzers fired its cannon. Sand and rock geysered next to one of the General Grants, but the blast didn't slow it down. Machine guns began to chatter.

Not all the German bullets were aimed at the British tanks. Some of them chewed into the ground near Dale's feet. He ran harder, the twisted knee forgotten now, all the pain washed away by the adrenaline and survival instinct coursing through his body. Something slammed against his helmet in a glancing blow, either a rock or a partially spent bullet. The impact was enough to knock him down again. An anvil chorus played inside his skull. His hearing was coming back, and he almost wished it wasn't.

He lifted his head and shook it, hoping that would make the terrible din stop. It didn't help the noise any, but he saw that he had fallen in a shallow depression in the desert floor. The little dip didn't offer much protection, but any old port in a storm . . .

Dale lowered his head and pressed his face against the sand. He put his hands over the back of his neck, though what good that would do if a 75mm-shell landed on him he didn't know. Making himself as small a target as possible, he lay there in the depression and listened to the roaring and thundering of the cannons.

A huge explosion shook the earth and assaulted Dale's ears. He risked a glance and saw that one of the Panzers had blown up. A lucky shot must have found its ammunition stores. The Mark IV had lurched to a halt. Flames licked out through its turret and slots, and a cloud of thick black smoke poured from the destroyed vehicle.

The wind carried that smoke toward Dale. As it billowed over him, he scrambled to his feet again and lunged out of the depression, running at right angles to the battle in hopes that he could get out of the line of fire before he was blown to bits.

This time luck was with him. He covered five yards, then ten, then twenty. Behind him in the little valley formed by the two dunes, the British tanks and the remaining German tanks continued maneuvering and firing. The odds were even between the two sides now.

But really they weren't, Dale knew. The Panzers were more heavily armored than the General Grants. Rounds from the 37mm-cannon mounted on the turrets of the British tanks were ineffective against the Panzer armor. Trying to fight off the German tanks with genuine Red Ryder BB guns would have made just about as much sense. Even shots from the 75s sometimes didn't penetrate the armor. Sure, the General Grants were faster and more maneuverable than the massive Panzers. But that advantage in speed didn't mean anything as long as the British guns couldn't hurt the Krauts.

Those thoughts went through Dale's head as he raced away from the battle. He knew the Tommies had saved his life by showing up when they did, and he felt guilty that he couldn't help them. But there wasn't a damned thing he could do. If the General Grants were outgunned and out-armored, a lone man on foot didn't stand even a chance in hell of doing any damage against those Nazi monsters.

He ducked around a shoulder of rock that jutted out from one of the dunes and shielded him from the sights of the combat. Not the sounds, though. The blasting of cannon fire was still almost loud enough to be deafening. Dale bent over, rested his hands on his knees, and tried to drag enough air back into his lungs so that the choking sensation in his chest would go away. He was sick at his stomach too, and fought down the urge to retch.

Somewhere in the confusion, he had lost the other boot he had been carrying. He stared at his feet, clad only in socks that were now ragged from the punishment they had taken over the past hour. He leaned against the rock and lifted one foot, looked at the sole and saw the dark blood stains on the sock where rocks had scratched and torn his foot. Then his knee twinged and he put his foot down to take some of the weight off his other leg.

He was still leaning against the rocks when with a growling roar, a jeep shot over the top of the sand dune to his right. It was moving so fast it was airborne for a second before crashing down to earth. Sand and gravel spit from under its screeching tires.

Dale's head jerked in that direction. He recognized the British jeep he had used to drive Bert Crimmens back to the oasis. Now, however, the man behind the wheel wore the uniform of the Deutsche Afrika Korps. The German skidded the jeep through a turn and gunned the engine, sending the jeep straight at Dale.

With a startled yell, Dale flung himself to the side as the jeep raced past him. He heard its brakes squeal as he landed on the ground and rolled over. As he came up on his knees, he saw the German soldier turning the jeep around for another run at him.

Dale's hand went to the holster on his right hip. With all the running and falling and jumping around he had been doing, he wouldn't have been surprised if the .45 was gone. But the holster's flap was still snapped down and the pistol was there. Dale jerked the gun from leather as the jeep shot toward him again.

The Colt jumped in his hand as he squeezed the trigger three times. Brass glittered in the late afternoon sunlight as the slide snapped back and forth and spent cartridges were ejected into the air. Dale saw the jeep's windshield shatter. The vehicle veered off to the left. It came to a stop, throwing up a cloud of dust.

Dale ran toward the jeep, hoping one of his shots had tagged the driver. As he came closer, he heard a crack and saw a muzzle flash. Something whipped past his ear. Recognizing the sound of a hand-gun firing, he tried to stop, but his momentum carried him forward. As the dust thinned a little, he saw the German clambering out of the jeep. The left shoulder of the man's uniform was covered with blood, and his left arm dangled at his side.

But his right arm was still just fine, as he proved by firing another shot at Dale with the Luger in his right hand. Dale ducked and threw himself forward in a flying tackle. His arms went around the German's waist, and the man crashed backward against the jeep.

Both of them fell to the ground. Dale wrestled his way on top. The collision had jostled the Colt out of his hand. The German still had the Luger, though. Dale grabbed the wrist of the man's gun hand and hit it against the sand, trying to knock the weapon loose. The German held on to it with fierce determination. With his other hand, he clawed at Dale's face. Dale twisted his head to the side to keep the Kraut's fingers away from his eyes. Broken fingernails scratched and scraped at his cheeks.

Dale dug his good knee into the German's midsection, pulled it back, drove it forward again. The German was still trying to bring his gun to bear. Dale held it off. Both men were sweating, and their lips were drawn back from their teeth in fierce grimaces. Dale stared into his opponent's face from a distance of no more than a foot. It was a lean face, with leathery, tight-drawn skin, the skin of a man who had spent months in the desert. Drops of sweat had cut trails in the thick coating of dust on the man's features, so that his face looked like it had stripes on it. The crazy thought that it looked like a tiger's face crossed Dale's mind.

Forcing the wounded arm to work, the German hit him in the belly. Dale cried out in pain. He tried to knee the man in the groin but missed. Dale felt his strength ebbing. He'd had plenty of training in hand-to-hand combat, but this was the first time he'd had to fight for his life at such close quarters. When Captain Sharp had been wounded and Dale had taken command of the tank, his life had been in danger during the battle with the Panzer that had pursued them, but that had been different. In that fight, life and death had been dealt at a range of hundreds of yards, with layers of thick armor plating between the combatants. Now all that separated Dale from his enemy was a few inches of air. The German was stronger, more experienced, and as they struggled, Dale saw the knowledge of impending victory creeping into the man's eyes. The German knew he was going to kill this enemy. All he had to do was move the barrel of that Luger another three or four inches, and then a shot would ring out . . .

Dale didn't think about what he was doing. If it didn't work, he'd be dead too fast to worry about it. He kept hold of the German's wrist but stopped pushing against it. The Luger swung toward him. Dale's other hand shot across his body and grabbed the German's wrist too, pulling instead of pushing. Before the man could pull the trigger, Dale wrenched the gun down so that the Luger's barrel gouged into the German's throat, just under his chin.

The man's eyes widened in horror as he realized what Dale was doing. Dale slid his right hand over the German's hand where it was clenched around the butt of the pistol. He used his weight to keep the barrel pinned against the man's throat. The German bucked and writhed in desperation, but before he could throw off his opponent, Dale had slipped a finger into the trigger guard. There was barely room for it since the German's finger was already there. All it took was a little pressure to make the gun go off.

The explosion was so close to him that Dale gave an involuntary, incoherent cry. He squeezed his eyes shut as blood spattered his face. The German heaved up off the ground and then fell back as all his muscles went slack. The gun came loose from his fingers. Dale ripped it away and pushed himself off the man. He scooted backward on his knees, reversing the Luger so that he could point it at the German. The gun shook a little as he held it in one hand and used the other to paw the blood out of his eyes. Blinking, he saw that the German was no longer a threat. The 9-millimeter bullet had slanted up through the man's brain and burst out the top of his head, taking half the skull with it. The internal pressure of the wound had made the man's eyes and tongue bulge grotesquely. A sheet of blood covered his face.

Dale kept moving back, still on his knees, until a wave of weakness hit him and he collapsed on his side. Again he wanted to retch, and again he suppressed the urge. He had to get up, had to take a look around. Where there had been one Kraut, there could be another. He reached out with his free hand to grab hold of the jeep's fender. Using it for support, he pulled himself to his feet.

The battle was still going on; he could hear the engines of the tanks and the explosions as they fired at each other. But Dale and the dead German were the only ones over here in this little pocket of ground removed from the rest of the fight. Dale turned slowly, still leaning on the jeep, and checked a full 360 degrees around him. Nothing was moving except the endlessly walking hills of sand, driven ever onward by the wind.

He became aware of the vibration against his hand. The jeep's engine was still running. The windshield was busted, but other than that, the vehicle seemed okay. He could get in it, Dale thought, and drive like blazes away from here. If any of those Panzers got away from the British tanks, he could outrun them easily in the jeep.

Only it wasn't a case of the Germans getting away, he reminded himself. It was much more likely that the British tanks would be destroyed. Then the Panzers would continue their deadly hunt.

Those Brits had put their lives on the line for him, Dale thought. Well, not for *him*, exactly. They would have fought the Germans whenever and wherever they'd run into them, whether some Yank was there where he shouldn't be or not. But still, they had saved his life. There was no getting around that fact. As Dale stood there next to the idling jeep, he knew he couldn't just hightail it and leave them there.

He lifted the Luger in his hand and looked at it for a second. Then he tucked the German pistol behind his belt and looked around for the Colt he had dropped earlier. His eyes tried to avoid the corpse with its destroyed head. He spotted the Colt lying a few feet away on the sand and went to pick it up. A check of the barrel told him it hadn't been fouled. He worked the slide, ejecting the round that was in the chamber and catching it in midair. The slide worked just fine. Not too much grit had gotten into it. Dale thumbed the button that released the clip, put the bullet back into it, and dug out more ammunition to replace the three shots he had fired. With the heel of his hand, he pushed the clip back into the butt of the gun.

Now he had two pistols and a jeep. He wasn't sure what he could do with them against a trio of Panzers. Probably not a hell of a lot. Probably he was just wasting his time and risking his life in a futile attempt to help the British tankies.

But one thing was for sure: Whatever he did, the Krauts wouldn't be expecting it.

# FOUR

It all came back to him in a rush. The feel of the steering wheel in his hands, the sense of power that flowed from him through the gas pedal and into the engine, the wind in his face, the feeling that gravity was only barely holding him to the earth as he whipped through a tight turn and the outside wheels lifted a little into the air . . .

Dale laughed. It was just like racing again. For a second, he might as well have been back on one of those dirt tracks in the Midwest, where he had had the only brief tastes of glory in his life, those fleeting but heady moments of triumph when he had sped across the finish line in front of all the other drivers.

But he was in the desert wastes of North Africa, not a racetrack in Illinois or Indiana or Ohio. No one was cheering him on here. No Harry Skinner, who had rebuilt his car's engine with him. No Joe or his friends Adam Bergman and Catherine Tancred. And no Elaine. That bitch. He missed the others, but not her. Never her.

Except sometimes in the middle of a dark and lonely night he couldn't sleep, and he found himself remembering the sleek warmth of her bare skin and the way she clutched at him and cried out as he moved inside her. Yeah, he'd miss the hell out of her now, if she hadn't turned out to be a lying slut with a rich, vengeful husband.

Dale shoved those thoughts out of his head. He had bigger fish to fry, more important things to worry about, like the Germans and those damned big Panzer tanks they were driving.

He had circled around, following the valleys between the dunes so that he was behind them. Now he pointed the jeep toward the sounds of battle and pressed down on the accelerator. The jeep leaped ahead, climbing a shallow dune.

When he reached the crest of the sand hill, Dale could see the

Panzers in front of him. To his left, one was clanking along on a damaged tread, smoke coming from it. Like a wounded animal, it was still dangerous, though. Its machine gun was firing, and the 75 on the turret swiveled toward the British tanks, trying to draw a bead on one of the General Grants. The other two Panzers looked undamaged.

One of the British tanks was a motionless, smoldering husk, obviously the victim of a direct hit. The other two were still all right. They had split up, one going right, one going left, so that they were attacking the Germans from the flanks now.

Dale took all that in in a split-second as he sent the jeep racing down the slope toward the two Panzers in front of him. They had stopped, secure in the knowledge that their armor was superior to that of their enemies. Their turrets rotated slowly as they tried to bring their cannons to bear on the British tanks. That was another advantage the Panzers had. Their heaviest gun was mounted on the turret instead of the tank's hull, so the entire tank didn't have to be moved to bring the 75 around. Somebody needed to point that out to the guys who had designed the General Grant, Dale thought as he floored the gas, jerked the wheel around, and sent the jeep skidding through a wide turn that took him in front of the Panzers.

He hoped like blazes none of the British gunners picked that moment to fire and came up a little short on their aim. He'd hate to get blown to pieces by guys on the same side as him.

With that ironic thought echoing in his head, Dale slammed on the brakes and brought the jeep to a rocking halt. He could just imagine the startled exclamations coming from the Germans inside those tanks. The Panzers were all buttoned up, so their crews couldn't have seen him coming.

But their drivers had to have a slit to look through, and that was where Dale aimed as he lifted the Colt and pointed it at the nearest tank. The opening was narrow, but at this range Dale thought he could hit it. From the corner of his eye he saw the barrel of the Panzer's machine gun start to swivel toward him. He ignored it as he fired off all seven shots as fast as he could squeeze the .45's trigger.

Then his foot tromped on the gas again and he was off, rocked back in the seat by the speed of his acceleration. Driving left-handed, he dropped the Colt on the floorboard and jerked the Luger from behind his belt with his right hand. He had never fired one of the Kraut pistols before, but he figured it was simple enough. Point and pull the trigger. That's what he did, and the gun bucked against his hand as he fired.

He didn't slow down to aim this time, just raked his fire across the front of the second undamaged Panzer and hoped that one of the bullets found a vulnerable spot. Even if it didn't, he was serving as a distraction, and that was what the British tankies needed now. While the Germans were looking at the madman in the jeep in front of them, the gunners inside the General Grants could be drawing a bead. . . .

That was what happened. The cannons on the British tanks belched fire, and both shots scored direct hits, spiraling in where the turrets were attached to the Panzers' hulls. Smoke poured from both tanks. One of them managed to get off a final shot, but it missed the General Grants.

That left the damaged Panzer. Knowing that he was now outnumbered and in a bad position, the German tank's commander must have ordered his driver to get out of there. The tank tried to swing around as it increased its speed. With a noisy clatter, the damaged tread came off, and the tank lurched to a stop.

The Panzer might be disabled, but its crew wasn't giving up the fight. As Dale turned the jeep so that he could see the battle again, the Panzer fired its cannon toward one of the British tanks. The Grant was already moving, though, and the round exploded behind it without doing any damage. Sparks flew in the air around the crippled Panzer as both Brits poured machine-gun fire in at it. Dale brought the jeep to a halt and sat there watching in awe.

The remaining two General Grants had the Panzer in a cross fire. Their gunners lined up their shots, and as if one man was operating both guns, they fired at the same time. The twin blasts sounded like one. Both high-explosive rounds slammed into the Panzer, and under that terrible onslaught, the German tank had no chance. A fireball erupted, engulfing the tank. Dust, sand, and debris were flung high into the air. Some of it was thrown so far it pattered down like molten rain around Dale's jeep, more than a hundred yards away.

For a long moment, the tableau held: the five burning tanks, four German and one British, scattered around on the sand; the two surviving British tanks, guns still trained on the blazing ruins of the Panzers; the lone American sitting off to the side in a jeep with a broken windshield. Then, slowly, one of the British tanks began to move. It turned away from the battlefield and rolled toward Dale.

He killed the jeep's engine and climbed out to wait for the General Grant. The tank came to a stop about ten yards away, its engine idling down. After a moment, the hatch on top of the turret lifted, and a man climbed out. He wore the leather helmet of the RTC, but he had taken off the headphones. Dale recognized him right away as Captain Neville Sharp. He hadn't realized that the tank squadron's commander had been in the thick of the battle, but it didn't surprise him. Sharp had a habit of being where the fighting was.

Dale realized that the same might be said of him. He wasn't sure whether he liked that or not.

"Sergeant Parker," Sharp said. He pulled off the helmet, revealing sweat-matted brown hair. "What in the name of all that's holy was that you were doing?"

"I, uh, wanted to get in on the fight, sir." Dale couldn't decide if Sharp looked amused or infuriated.

"By taking on a pair of Panzers in a bloody jeep!"

Definitely infuriated, Dale thought. He shrugged and said, "Well, sir, I thought at least it might buy you a little time."

Sharp stared at him for several seconds and then surprised Dale by laughing. His annoyance seemed to have vanished. "It bought us some time, all right," he said. "I'm sure the Jerries were busy staring at you and thinking that you were bloody insane. I know I was."

"You got over it quick enough to put those rounds into them, though," Dale pointed out.

"Yes, that's true. But what the hell are you doing out here? You're supposed to be back at the oasis where we were in leaguer."

Without much embellishment, Dale explained how the German tanks had rolled up to the oasis, forcing him to try to flee. "They would have had me cold if you hadn't shown up when you did, Captain," he concluded. "But what were they doing over here in the first place? I thought all the Krauts were on the other side of the Gazala Line."

Sharp's face was grim as he replied, "They were until today. Rommel made his move this morning. He flanked us to the south of Bir Hacheim and then turned north. That put him in our rear. He went through the Third Indian Motor Brigade without too much trouble."

"You were going to check on them," Dale said.

"That's right. But we saw the smoke from the battle and then got the word of the attack over the wireless, so we turned back to establish a new defensive line." Sharp waved a hand toward the destroyed German tanks. "I'd say that was a forward-ranging patrol. The bulk of Rommel's force is still to the south."

"But they're coming this way."

Sharp nodded. "Aye, that they are."

Dale thought about what that meant, then said, "I've got to get back to Tobruk!"

"If you want to reach Cairo anytime soon, that would probably be a good idea," Sharp agreed, his voice dry.

Another figure climbed out of the British tank. Bert Crimmens called out, "Dale! I thought that was you." He dropped to the ground and hurried over to join Dale and Sharp, hesitating only as he came up to say, "With the captain's permission . . ."

"Granted," Sharp said.

Bert grabbed Dale's hand and pumped it up and down. "You saved us again, you did!"

"Hold on," Dale said as he tried to work his hand free from Bert's grip. "I think it was the other way around this time. You guys saved me."

"Not at all. I never saw anything like that. One man in a jeep, fighting two tanks with handguns! Remarkable! Brilliant!"

"More like stupid," Dale muttered. "I just couldn't think of anything else to do."

"You seem to have a flare for the unexpected, Sergeant Parker," Sharp said. "I hope that continues to stand you in good stead."

"Yeah, I guess." Dale looked around. "Where's the rest of the squadron?"

JAMES REASONER

"Spreading out in that defensive line I mentioned."

Dale nodded. "I guess I'm part of it, for the night anyway. That is, if you'll have me."

"I suppose we'll have to put up with you," Sharp said, but a smile took any sting out of the words. "In the morning, though, I want you to take that jeep and get back to Tobruk."

"Don't worry about that," Dale said. "I'll be hotfooting it out of here."

Bert said, "In the meantime, Captain, is it all right if we brew up?"

"Of course."

Bert took hold of Dale's arm. "Come along, Sergeant. I'm sure you could use a nice cup of tea."

He would have preferred a good stiff drink, Dale thought as Bert led him back to the tank. It was almost dusk now, and a dark haze from the smoke of the burning tanks hung over the desert. Dale had a feeling there would be plenty of smoke in the air before the battle for this wasteland was over.

He summoned up a smile for Bert and said, "A cup of tea would be just fine."

# FIVE

A hot breeze swept over the terrace of Shepheard's Hotel in Cairo this evening, bringing with it a mixture of smells from the Egyptian bazaar that seemed quite exotic to Joe Parker. He was more accustomed to the smell of the Chicago Stockyards. Joe's father had worked in those stockyards for years, until an accident had ruined Sam Parker's leg and ended his career, such as it was. The stench of blood and shit had clung to his clothes every day when he came home from work, and when the wind was right, the foul odor from the stockyards themselves washed over the working-class neighborhood where the Parkers lived.

Funny the things you missed when you were a long way from home, Joe thought as he lifted a bottle of beer to his mouth and took a long swig. The beer was cold and good, a lot better than the warm, bitter stuff he and Dale had drunk while they were in England, stationed at the Armour School.

Wicker armchairs surrounded dozens of small, square tables that were scattered around the hotel's terrace. A piano stood in the midst of the tables, and at the moment a balding, blond-haired major from the Eighth Army was perched on the bench pounding away at the keys, trying to make up for with enthusiasm what he lacked in talent. A sallow-faced man in a dark suit stood not far away, looking on with a frown of disapproval on his face. He was an Egyptian, the musician who usually played the piano here at Shepheard's. Tonight, however, the major had asked to be allowed to "tinkle the old ivories," as he put it, and he hadn't been willing to take no for an answer.

The major launched into an awkward rendition of "The White Cliffs of Dover." People at the surrounding tables, mostly British officers and a few Englishwomen, began to sing along. As their voices rose, they made the piano-playing sound better. The emotions they felt were so genuine that Joe found himself moved. He would have sung along with them, but he felt it wouldn't be proper for him to do so. He was an American, after all, not British. They didn't need a bloody Yank joining in.

Well, not with their singing, anyway, Joe told himself with a faint smile. If the Americans hadn't joined in the war effort, the British would be in even worse shape than they were now. Not that things looked all that good. For the past couple of weeks, ever since General Erwin Rommel had attacked the Gazala Line, the situation in the desert had gone from bad to worse for the Eighth Army. Rommel had driven up the line, destroying the British fortifications known as boxes. In the south, defenders in the city of Bir Hacheim had held out for a while, putting up a stubborn resistance, but a couple of days earlier, Bir Hacheim had fallen too. The only good thing about it was that most of the troops there had managed to evacuate before the Germans stormed in and took over. In the north, Rommel was closing in on Tobruk. The year before, the British had forted up in Tobruk and held off an assault by Rommel. They might not be so lucky again. Joe's brother Dale had returned from there not long after Rommel's new offensive began, and he told Joe that the city was not equipped to withstand another long siege.

Joe was just glad that Dale had gotten out of there when he did. As usual, Dale had gone off and gotten into trouble while he was away from Cairo. At least, that was the story Dale told, all about fighting Panzer tanks in a jeep. Joe supposed he believed him; Dale didn't have the imagination to come up with a yarn like that on his own. As a writer of stories for the pulp magazines, Joe was the member of the Parker family who had been blessed with a vivid imagination. Joe figured Dale had embellished the story to make himself sound like more of a hero, though. He told himself that he would get the straight poop the next time he talked to Bert Crimmens or Captain Neville Sharp.

Assuming he ever saw the two men again, Joe thought as he took another pull on the beer bottle. Along with the rest of their tank crew, they were out there somewhere in the desert, trying to turn the tide of the German onslaught. They might be dead by now, for all Joe knew. He hoped not. He had few enough friends here in North Africa.

The major at the piano finally stood up and turned the instrument over to the Egyptian. He came across the terrace, pulled back the wicker chair opposite Joe, and sat down. Raising his hands, he wiggled his fingers. "Haven't lost the old touch, eh?"

"I was hoping you'd play 'Boogie-Woogie Bugle Boy,' " Joe said.

"Eh? What's that?" Major Colin Richardson asked.

Joe waved off the question with the hand holding the beer bottle. "Never mind, Major. It's not important. What I'd really like to know is why you asked me to meet you here tonight. I don't think you just wanted to pad the house for your little concert."

Richardson signaled one of the white-jacketed waiters to bring him a drink, then clasped his hands together on the table and leaned forward. "Not at all. I find myself in the position of needing your help again, Sergeant."

Months earlier, not long after Joe and Dale had come to Egypt, Joe had stumbled across a robbery in progress in a Cairo alley. He had pitched in to help the victim, who had turned out to be Major Richardson. The major was involved in the British intelligence effort, and on a couple of subsequent occasions, he had dropped hints that he wanted to get Joe mixed up with that spy stuff too. The idea was intriguing, to say the least, but Joe wasn't sure he was suited for work like that.

"Look, Major," he said, "I appreciate the fact that you seem to trust me, but I don't think—"

"You've put your finger on it, right there," Richardson broke in. "Do you know how difficult it is to find anyone in this town who can be trusted?"

"What about all the other officers you work with?"

Richardson waved a hand. "They're known to the enemy. Make no mistake about it, Sergeant; Cairo is swarming with Nazi agents. A lot of these wogs don't like having us here, you know. They can't wait to cooperate with the Germans. They'll find out what a mistake they've made if those filthy storm troopers ever come marching in here and take over. I'd almost like to see that happen, just so those treacherous curs would see how bloody foolish they were to trust the Jerries."

Joe looked across the table at Richardson, thinking about what the major had said. After a moment, he said, "So you need somebody to do something who isn't known to the Germans as an intelligence agent."

"Precisely."

"In that case, Major, it probably wasn't a very good idea to meet me here." Joe looked around the crowded terrace and added in a low voice, "There might be a dozen Nazi agents in this room right now."

"Quite probably," Richardson agreed, seeming unconcerned by the possibility they were being watched by German agents. "But you see, I didn't invite you here tonight to recruit you as an agent."

"You didn't?"

"Not to any watching eyes, at any rate. As far as they're concerned, I had another purpose entirely."

Joe frowned. "And what was that?"

Richardson opened his mouth to answer, then looked across the room and said instead, "Ah, there she is now."

*She?* Joe turned his head to follow Richardson's gaze and found himself looking at a young woman who had just come onto the terrace through the doors leading from the hotel's lobby. She wore a yellow, short-sleeved dress and a hat with a broad, floppy brim. Thick auburn hair fell to her shoulders. She carried a large purse made of tightly-woven straw. Richardson lifted a hand to wave to her, and when she spotted the major, a broad smile lit up her face. She came across the terrace toward the table where Joe and Richardson sat, and Joe couldn't help but admire the smooth play of muscles in the calves visible under the dress. She was an attractive young woman, but for the life of him, Joe couldn't figure out what she had to do with him.

Both men rose to their feet as the woman came up to the table. "Hullo, Major," she said, her accent definitely British.

Richardson took her hand. "Melinda, my dear. I'm glad you could make it."

"Oh, I wouldn't have missed it! A chance to meet a real, live author!" The woman turned to Joe. "And this must be him!"

Joe knew he was staring, but he couldn't help it. The woman's green eyes were large and luminous and filled with excitement.

"Indeed," Richardson said. "Melinda, I'd like for you to meet Sergeant Joseph Parker. Sergeant, this is Miss Melinda Thorp-Davies. Melinda works in my office."

"I see," Joe said, even though he was as confused as ever. He shook hands with Miss Thorp-Davies and summoned up a smile. "I'm pleased to meet you."

"The pleasure is all mine, I assure you, Sergeant." She let go of Joe's hand and reached into her purse. "I know this may be an imposition, but . . . would you mind terribly?"

She pulled out a copy of a magazine and thrust it at him.

Joe knew right away from the garish colors on the cover that it was a pulp. Melinda looked so eager, so expectant, that he reached out and took the magazine from her. As he did, he saw that it was an issue of *Exciting Western*. He recognized the cover and knew that he had a story in this issue, a short under his own name. When he looked up at Melinda, she said, "I just *adore* American cowboy stories. I can't believe Major Richardson actually knows a famous cowboy author. Would you mind?"

"Would I mind what?" Joe asked, knowing he sounded silly.

Melinda pointed at the magazine. "Why, signing your story for me, of course!"

"Oh. Oh!" Joe understood now, though the request took him by surprise. So few people had ever asked him to sign something he'd written that the idea hadn't occurred to him.

"Why don't we all sit down and have a drink?" Richardson suggested. He took a pen from his pocket and held it out to Joe. "In the meantime, you can sign that magazine for Miss Thorp-Davies."

"Sure," Joe said as he took the pen and uncapped it. He started to sit down, then realized that he ought to be a gentleman and hold Melinda's chair. She smiled at him as he did so, fumbling with the pen.

"My, aren't you sweet."

Joe didn't feel sweet. He felt foolish and a little tongue-tied. He sat down and put the magazine on the table in front of him. He didn't remember exactly where his story was, so he opened it and checked the table of contents, then turned to the right page. There it was, all right, "Pistol Pandemonium" by Joseph Parker.

"Could you sign it *To my dear friend Melinda, with love and kisses?*"

"Uh, I suppose so," Joe said. He wrote what she had requested and then signed his name. The cheap paper soaked up the ink and made the writing fuzzy. He blew on the ink to dry it before pushing the magazine back across the table to Melinda. "I'm afraid it probably went through to the page behind it."

"Oh, I don't care about that. I'll treasure this forever."

The waiter brought fresh drinks, including something pink and frothy for Melinda. She sipped the drink and beamed at Joe. He was getting uncomfortable now, and he could tell by the unnatural warmth of his face that he was blushing. This was crazy, he told himself. He shouldn't be feeling this way just because some dizzy English dame was gushing over him.

Richardson smiled and looked at them like some sort of benevolent uncle. "I'm certainly glad I was able to get you two together. When I mentioned that I knew a chap who had written stories for the American magazines, Melinda insisted that she had to meet you. I hope that's all right, Sergeant."

"Of course," Joe said. He could at least be gracious, even though he wasn't accustomed to such adulation. Pulp writers had their fans, sure, but it wasn't like he was Ernest Hemingway or somebody like that. From the way Melinda had been carrying on, that was what anybody watching would have thought.

And as that thought crossed his mind, Joe understood. He remembered what he had been saying to Richardson just before Melinda arrived, about how it didn't make sense to meet him here at Shepheard's if the object was to recruit him for espionage work. After the little show Melinda had put on, any Nazi agents in the room would think Richardson was just playing Cupid for one of his secretaries.

So that was the way it was. Joe nodded to himself. He would play along.

For the next twenty minutes, Joe sat there while Melinda went on about how she adored American Westerns. She mentioned several other stories he had written, referring to the titles and discussing enough about the plots so that he knew she had read the stories. Richardson had coached her well, he thought. Melinda's voice was loud enough to be heard without much trouble by anyone who wanted to eavesdrop, and her enthusiasm as she spoke drew the attention of everyone around her. She was quite an actress, Joe decided. She sounded like she meant every word she was saying to him.

After a while, Richardson said, "Well, I have to be toddling along. Sergeant, would you do me a very great favor?"

"I'll try, Major."

"Would you see that Miss Thorp-Davies gets back safely to her flat?"

Joe looked at Melinda. She gave him a coy smile. *Don't overdo it,* he thought.

"All right. I suppose I can do that." Turning to Melinda, he said, "It would be my pleasure."

Richardson scraped back his chair, stood up, put on his cap, and dropped a bill on the table to pay for the drinks. "Splendid." He handed Joe another bill. "Take a cab. On me."

Joe accepted the folded bill. "All right." As he tucked it in his pocket, he wondered if there was a secret message hidden inside the bill. He couldn't very well unfold it and look right here in the middle of Shepheard's terrace, but when they got in the cab, he would check it out.

Richardson's smile was positively avuncular as he looked down at the two of them. "I'm so glad you've hit it off," he said. "I thought you would. Good night, Melinda."

"Good night, Major," she said.

Richardson weaved through the maze of tables and went into the hotel through the lobby doors. Joe stood up and held Melinda's chair for her again as she rose.

"It's so nice of you to see me home."

"Not at all. I'm glad to."

Melinda looked around the room. "I love Cairo. It's so . . . exotic. Not at all stodgy, like London. But at night . . . Let's just say that I'm so very pleased to be escorted by a strapping American soldier. I feel positively safe as houses."

"I'm not all that strapping," Joe said. "You ought to see my friend Adam. He used to play baseball for the University of Chicago."

"I'm sure he's not half as handsome as you, Joe." She tucked her hand around his arm. "You don't mind if I call you Joe, do you?"

"No, that's fine." He put on his overseas cap and led her out of the hotel.

There were plenty of taxis in front of Shepheard's, most of them old British vehicles. Joe and Melinda got into one of them, and Melinda gave the driver an address that didn't mean anything to Joe. He knew his way around Cairo well enough to get where he needed to go, but he wasn't familiar with many of the streets.

The Egyptian driver knew where he was going. He drove fast enough so that he reminded Joe a little of Dale, but he handled the cab with enough skill to avoid all the obstacles in the crowded streets. Cairo was a modern city, but even so, there were hand-drawn carts in the road, along with lorries and cars. No camels, though; Joe had been a little disappointed the first time he realized that camels didn't wander around loose over here, at least not in the cities.

Melinda sat close to him in the rear seat of the cab, but not indecently so. Close enough, however, that he could feel the warmth from her body. She chattered on about cowboy stories, but Joe didn't pay much attention to what she was saying. He slipped a hand into his pocket as unobtrusively as possible and slid out the bill Richardson had given to him. Holding his hand down at his side, he unfolded the bill. He expected to find a note inside it, but instead, there was nothing. It was just a folded-up Egyptian banknote. Joe glanced down at it as the cab passed through a cone of light from a street lamp, hoping to see a message scrawled on it, but again there was nothing unusual about the bill. Frowning, he slipped it back into his pocket.

A short time later, the cab reached its destination. Joe used the bill Richardson had given him to pay the driver. It was good for that, at least, if nothing else. Joe started to tell the driver to wait until he'd seen Melinda to her door, but then she said, "I was hoping you'd come in for a drink."

Ah, of course, Joe thought. Once they got inside Melinda's flat, she would give him the details of what Richardson wanted him to do. Either that, or the major himself would be waiting in there for him. He nodded and said, "All right."

The building where Melinda lived had been a private residence at one time, Joe thought. It had been split up into several apartments. She took him up a flight of stairs, fished a key out of her purse, and unlocked a door. When she led him inside and turned on a light, Joe saw that the flat was decorated in Egyptian fashion, with low, heavy furniture and beaded curtains over the doorways. It was a one-room apartment with a tiny kitchen tucked into an alcove in a rear corner. The air inside was hot and a little stale. Melinda said, "Just let me open a window."

When she had raised a window, a faint breeze came into the room but did little to relieve the heat. It was a bit fresher, though. The place was far enough away from any of the neighborhood bazaars so that there was no smell of spices and rotting meat.

Joe saw several magazines lying on a table and moved closer. They were all American pulps, all Westerns. Maybe Melinda really did like cowboy stories. That much might not have been an act.

She took off her hat and tossed it on the table with the pulps, then held out a hand. "Come sit with me," she said. "Unless you want that drink now."

"No, later will be fine," Joe said, meaning after she had talked to him about the assignment Richardson had for him. Since the major wasn't here, that must mean that Melinda would fill him in. Of course, there was the question of whether or not he could accept an assignment from British Intelligence. After all, he was an American soldier, a GI. He was supposed to cooperate with the Brits, but that didn't mean he had to place himself under their orders . . .

"Later, is it?" Melinda said. "My, aren't you the naughty one?"

Joe's head jerked a little in surprise at the seductive tone her voice had taken on. He said, "I'm sorry, I didn't mean—"

"No need to apologize, love." Somehow she had gotten very close to him, and he was aware that her face was only inches from his. He felt the warm pressure of her breasts against his chest as she leaned even closer. "I was hoping you'd get the idea."

With that, she put a hand on the back of his neck and lifted her face to his, bringing her mouth against his lips in an urgent kiss. Joe wasn't shocked. He had kissed girls before. But never one whom he had expected to talk to him about Nazi spies and secret plots . . .

A moment later, Melinda broke the kiss and smiled at him. This time, Joe *was* shocked as she moved her other hand downward and caressed him. "Well, what do you say, Sergeant Parker?" she asked. "Shall we have a go?"

Joe hardly recognized his own voice as he said, "Whatever you want, Miss Thorp-Davies."

# SIX

It wasn't like Joe was a virgin or anything. He had gone out with Marguerite Hillman back in high school, and everybody knew that any guy who dated Marguerite more than once was going to get to third base at least, and maybe more. Joe had gotten more, one spring night in the backseat of Marguerite's dad's Studebaker. He had believed that it was never going to happen, that Marguerite was going to stop him after he'd kissed her and felt her up for a while, but then she had said something about F. Scott Fitzgerald and Joe said he had read all of Fitzgerald's novels and even some of his short stories in *The Atlantic* and *The New Yorker* at the public library, and Marguerite said that she had too, and then she reached down and groped him and said, "You're such an intellectual, Joey. Let's do it, okay?"

Joe hadn't been about to say no.

For the next three weeks they'd had a passionate affair, discussing literature and going at it like minks every chance they got. Then Marguerite had broken up with him so she could date Ted Keeler, who was two years older and already in college. Joe was brokenhearted for a couple of days before realizing that he had learned more about love from Marguerite than she had learned about books from him. He supposed it was a fair enough trade.

So he'd had some experience. He'd been around the block a few times. He was a GI, for Christ's sake, a man of the world, even if he didn't whore around like his brother and most of the other soldiers.

Still, Melinda Thorp-Davies did things to him that night he hadn't even dreamed a man and a woman could do. And Joe had responded, using that imagination of his to guide him until Melinda cried out and clutched at him and shuddered underneath him.

Marguerite would have been proud of him.

Hours after Joe and Melinda had reached the apartment—surely it had been hours, Joe thought—they lay snuggled together in the narrow Murphy bed that pulled down from a recess in the wall. Joe's arms were around her, and Melinda's head rested on his shoulder. Both of them were covered with a fine sheen of perspiration from their exertions.

Melinda stroked her fingertips over Joe's belly. "That was smashing," she said. "Utterly smashing."

Joe couldn't help but grin in satisfaction. "Yeah, it was pretty good, if I do say so myself."

"I can't think of anyone better qualified to judge."

He reached over and cupped her breast, rubbing the nipple with his thumb. "You don't want to talk about F. Scott Fitzgerald, do you?"

She lifted her head to look down at him and frown. "What?"

"Never mind." He moved his hand to the back of her head and brought her lips to his. Their tongues met, slick and hot and slippery. Melinda slid her hand down his body. The palm of her hand was hot against his flesh. Joe groaned.

"He's an insatiable little lad, isn't he?" Melinda whispered. "That's one thing you never read in those Western stories, all about the cowboys going at it with the schoolmarms, eh?"

"You've never read any of the Spicy pulps," Joe said.

"Ooh, spicy, is it? I don't think the newsagents in England carry them."

Joe kissed her again. "I'll have to send you some . . . after the war."

Then he had hold of her hips and was lifting her, positioning her over him so that she could lower her hips onto his taut body. She made a little whimpering noise, and for a second he thought he had hurt her. She began to move, and he knew she was all right.

As for him, he was more than all right. Meeting Melinda was the best thing to happen to him since he had come to Egypt. Hell, she was the best thing since he'd joined the army and left home. Maybe the best since Marguerite Hillman and her dad's Studebaker . . .

He had forgotten all about Major Richardson, and espionage

was the last thing on his mind. A little while later, when he dozed off
with Melinda in his arms, he still hadn't thought about it again.

*    *    *

He woke up with a start. The room was dark except for some faint
light that came in through the window. Joe had no idea how late it
was. He felt a surge of near panic. He was supposed to be back at the
barracks by 2200 hours. Fumbling on the floor next to the bed, he
found his wristwatch and brought it close to his face, squinting as he
tried to make out the time. The room was so dark he couldn't see the
hands on the watch. Carefully, he moved his other arm out from
under a sleeping Melinda and sat up. He angled the watch so he
could see it better. A sigh of relief came from him as he realized it
wasn't quite 2130. He scrubbed a hand over his face. Lord, it seemed
like it ought to be later than that! He felt like he had been here with
Melinda for four or five hours, instead of the two it had really been.
He swung his legs out of the bed.

She stirred and reached out to touch his naked hip. "Love?
Where are you going?"

Joe turned on the edge of the bed to look over his shoulder in her
direction. "I have to go," he said. "I have to be back at the barracks in
a half hour."

She stroked his flank. "You're not going to get into trouble
because of me, are you?"

"No, I still have time to get back. But I have to get moving."

"My cowboy . . ." she murmured, still caught up in half-sleep.

Joe didn't bother correcting her. He wrote about cowboys sometimes, but that didn't make him one, any more than his other stories
made him a private detective or a pirate or a space explorer. He
leaned over, felt around on the floor until he'd found his clothes, then
stood up and started getting dressed.

He was hurrying so much that he didn't think about anything
other than getting his clothes on, getting out of the building, and
finding a cab that would take him back to the barracks. When he
was dressed, though, he paused long enough to step over to the bed,

rest a knee on the mattress, and bend down to give Melinda a kiss. She held the back of his head for a moment and pressed her mouth hard to his. "I'll understand if you don't want to see me again," she said in a quiet voice.

"Of course I want to see you again," he said. "We never had that drink you offered me."

"Come back and I'll fix you some supper to go with it."

"It's a deal," Joe said. He kissed her again, then turned and hurried out of the apartment.

As he emerged onto the street and started looking around for a taxi, a car across the way started up. Joe didn't think anything of it, since there was still quite a bit of traffic around. But then the car, an old sedan, pulled out and made a U-turn so that it came around beside him. He saw the glow of a cigarette hanging from the driver's mouth.

"Get in," Major Colin Richardson said through the open window.

Joe stared at him for a moment without moving.

Richardson took one hand off the wheel, used it to take the cigarette out of his mouth, and said again, "Get in. I'll take you back to your barracks."

The events of earlier in the evening came back to Joe. He was more confused than ever now. He had been convinced that Melinda was some sort of secret agent working with Richardson, but he had forgotten all about that once she kissed him. Melinda had had plenty of chances to pass along a message or instructions from the major, but she hadn't done that. Instead she had taken Joe to bed, like the sweet but obviously loose-moraled young woman she seemed to be. Now here was Richardson again, showing up out of nowhere.

"You're going to be AWOL if you don't snap it up, Sergeant."

Joe reached for the door handle. "Yeah, I guess you're right." He got into the car, and it pulled smoothly away.

After a few moments of silence, Richardson said, "I suppose you must be curious."

"Yeah, you could say that. What the hell's going on here, Major? I thought Melinda was going to give me some sort of message, but instead—"

Richardson held up a hand, palm out toward Joe. "No need to

tell me what she gave you, my boy. I think I can make a fairly good guess. Melinda is a dear and quite a good secretary, but she succumbs easily to the temptations of the flesh."

Joe's eyes narrowed. "I suppose you've had her too." He tried not to sound bitter, but he wasn't sure if he succeeded.

"As a matter of fact, no. She has an inviolable rule about consorting with the people she works for. Not that I haven't given the matter a bit of thought." Richardson shook his head, keeping his eyes on the road. "But that's not important now. What's important is that I've changed my mind."

"About what?" As he asked the question, Joe had a tense, sick feeling in the pit of his stomach.

"I've seen Melinda reading those magazines many times, and it occurred to me that she would probably enjoy meeting someone who writes her beloved cowboy stories. That led me to consider what a good cover it might possibly be. If I introduced her to you, our meeting at Shepheard's would seem to be completely innocent."

"I figured out that much," Joe said. "That's why I was expecting her to give me a message from you, or instructions for an intelligence assignment, or something."

Richardson sighed. "That would have required darling Melinda to possess enough intelligence of her own to be trustworthy. I'm afraid she's lacking in that area, if not in others. No, the more I thought about it, the more I've become convinced that the entire idea was a bad one. I want you to go back to your barracks and forget that tonight ever happened, Sergeant. At least . . . forget about the parts relating to you and me and any ideas you may have had about working with us."

Joe stared at Richardson in the dim light coming from the dashboard instruments. "You mean you want me to forget about being a spy?"

Richardson smiled. "You Yanks do like to phrase things in melodramatic terms, don't you? Yes, that's exactly what I mean. I like you, Sergeant Parker . . . Joe . . . and I do trust you, but as for you assisting us . . . it would never work out."

Joe leaned back against the cushion of the car seat, an angry frown on his face. He was feeling more than anger; disappointment gnawed at him too. Maybe Richardson was right. Maybe he did look at life sometimes like it was a story from a pulp magazine. But he was still convinced that he could have been a good agent.

The whole thing was crazy, though, and a part of Joe's brain had to admit it. He was just a dogface, a sergeant whose job was to teach a bunch of British dogfaces how to use the radios in their tanks. That was all. Asking him to get mixed up in high-level espionage was like asking a sandlot pitcher to strike out Ted Williams. He would have been out of his league.

"All right," he forced himself to say. "If that's the way you want it, Major. But . . . can I still see Melinda?"

"I can't imagine why not." Richardson chuckled. "The two of you hit it off well, I suppose."

"Smashing," Joe said.

"I must say, that's one reason I've decided to withdraw my offer to you. I have a great deal of affection for Melinda. I would say that she's like a daughter to me, but I'm not quite *that* pure and wholesome. A favorite niece, perhaps. I'd like to see her be happy." The major looked over at Joe. "You won't do anything to make her *un*happy, will you?"

"I'll try not to," Joe said, and meant it.

They had reached the camp on the outskirts of Cairo. The guard at the gate waved the car on through, and Joe knew there must be some sort of insignia somewhere on the plain-looking sedan to indicate that it belonged to an officer. A couple of minutes later, Richardson brought the car to a stop in front of the barracks where Joe and Dale were staying along with the rest of the Army Service Forces detachment.

"I suppose we'll be seeing quite a bit of you around the office, now that you and Melinda are a—what do you Yanks call it—an item?"

Joe nodded. "I suppose so, sir."

"Good night, then."

Joe got out of the sedan and saluted. "Good night, sir."

Richardson gave him a casual salute, turned the car around, and drove back toward the camp entrance. Joe stood there for a moment, trying to sort through everything that had happened tonight.

"Parker! Is that you?"

The harsh voice, stripped by anger of its usual southern drawl, belonged to Master Sergeant Henry Garmon, the noncom in charge of the American instructors. Garmon had been at Camp Bowie, where Joe and Dale received their initial training, and he had come to England and then Egypt with them and the other American soldiers in the detachment.

Joe turned and saw Garmon standing in the doorway of the barracks, wearing his uniform trousers and an undershirt. Garmon put his fists on his hips and said, "I thought I was goin' to have the pleasure of reportin' you AWOL, Parker. Wouldn't have been as much fun as reportin' that goldbrickin' brother of yours, but it'd do."

"No, Sarge, I'm here on time." Joe glanced at his watch in the light coming through the barracks door. "It's only twenty-one fifty-eight."

"Well, you're a lucky bastard, I'll say that for you."

Joe thought about Melinda and couldn't disagree with Garmon's statement.

"Where've you been, anyway?"

"Sarge," Joe said, "if I told you, you wouldn't believe me."

Garmon stared at him for a few seconds, glowering, then said, "Lord help us, Parker's fallen in love! I recognize the dopey look."

Love? That couldn't be true, Joe thought. He had just met Melinda tonight. Lust, yeah, sure, he felt that for her. Plenty of lust. But love was something completely different . . . wasn't it?

He stepped past Garmon, saying, "Good night, Sarge."

"Yeah, yeah, good night . . . you lousy Romeo." Shaking his head in utter disgust, Garmon followed Joe into the barracks.

# SEVEN

On 1 February 1941, the Second Marine Brigade was redesignated the Second Marine Division and formally activated. Made up of the old Sixth and Eighth Marine Regiments, along with the Tenth Marines, an artillery regiment, the Second Division had a proud heritage beginning with the famous bayonet charge at Belleau Wood during the Great War, the War to End All Wars, the conflict that had been, as was now becoming obvious, the first but not the last World War. Once the brigade had become a division, the Sixth and Eighth Regiments each gave up a battalion, and the Second Regiment was formed out of those battalions. The Second of the Second, it was called.

Unit nicknames were common. The Sixth Regiment was known as the Pogey Bait Sixth because of a legend that had sprung up while the outfit was on its way to China during the thirties. Supposedly, during the overseas voyage, the Sixth had consumed thousands of bars of candy—"pogey bait"—while the bars of soap in the ship's stores went unused except for a couple. The Marines who were members of the Sixth took pride in the name.

Then, in May of 1941, the Sixth was dispatched to Iceland to make the Nazis think twice about expanding in that direction. Half a year later, following the Japanese attack on Pearl Harbor, the Second Marine Brigade was reorganized, taking in the Eighth Regiment, the 1st Battalion of the Tenth (Artillery) Marines, B Company of the 2d Tank Battalion, B Company of the 2d Engineer Battalion, B Company of the 2d Service Battalion, B Company of the 2d Medical Battalion, and C Company of the 2d Medical Battalion. In January 1942, the Second Marine Brigade sailed from San Diego, bound for American Samoa in the South Pacific, though only the officers knew their destination.

That left the Second of the Second behind in California, and thus its nickname was born: the Home Guard Second.

Adam Bergman hated it every time he heard someone say that. Guarding the American homeland was all well and good, but somebody else could do it. He was a Marine, by God, and Marines existed for one reason and one reason only—to fight!

So it came as no surprise to him when he heard that his friends Ed Collins and Leo Sikorsky were in the brig again, picked up by the Shore Police for brawling in a San Diego bar.

Adam's face was grim as he climbed out of the jeep in front of the building that served as SP headquarters and lockup for the sprawling naval base. He went inside and found a Chief Petty Officer on duty behind the desk. The chief seemed to be alone at the moment. All the other SPs were out looking for troublemakers in uniform. With all the sailors and Marines stationed at Dago, they wouldn't have very far to look.

"What can I do for you, Lieutenant?" the chief asked as he glanced up at Adam.

"You've got a couple of my wandering lambs," Adam said. "Corporal Collins and PFC Sikorsky."

The chief made a face. "Those two? You're welcome to 'em, Lieutenant. The fat one's snoring so loud he's keeping everybody else awake, and the skinny one gripes so much he gets on everybody's nerves. And you can imagine how much gripin' that takes around a bunch of sailors and leathernecks."

Adam made an effort not to grin at the description of Ed and Leo. The CPO had summed them up pretty well.

Adam followed the chief into the cell block. It stunk of urine and vomit and the ugly green paint that had been slapped on the cinder-block walls not long before. Some of the prisoners started to hoot and yell when the cell-block door swung open, but they fell silent as they saw the tall, muscular lieutenant following the chief. He didn't look like someone who was brimming over with mercy and the milk of human kindness. Adam kept the stern expression on his face as he surveyed the prisoners. About three-fourths of them were sailors, the rest Marines, including the two in the far corner of the big holding cell.

Ed Collins was still asleep, sitting with his legs stretched out in front of him and his back against the wall. His chin was on his chest. Great rumbling snores rolled out from him as he slept. The scarecrow-like figure of Leo Sikorsky hunkered on his heels at Ed's side. He dug an elbow into Ed's ribs and said, "Hey, wake up, you tub o' lard. Adam's here."

Adam's jaw tightened. He wished Leo hadn't referred to him by his first name.

Ed snorted, sputtered, and finally lifted his head. A grin spread across his round face. "Hey, Adam!" he called. "You come to get us out o' this stinkin' place?"

The chief turned his head and frowned at Adam. "Begging your pardon, Lieutenant, but are you sure you're really a lieutenant?"

This situation was about to slip out of control, Adam sensed. Which meant that as an officer, he had to take control of it, right now.

In hard, icy tones, he said, "If you doubt it, Chief, I suggest you call the XO at Camp Kearney. Better yet, why don't you call the commander? I'm sure he'd be glad to vouch for me."

The chief glanced at the clock on the wall and saw that it was almost eleven o'clock. Nobody at Camp Kearney would appreciate a call at such an hour, especially the CO. He said, "That won't be necessary, Lieutenant. I'll be glad to release those two into your custody." He cast a baleful glance at Ed and Leo. "If you're sure you want 'em, that is."

"Whether I want them or not, they're mine," Adam said. "Let them out of there, and I'll sign for them."

Ed and Leo scrambled to their feet, eager expressions on their faces. Within minutes, they had been released from the brig. "Outside, you two feather merchants," Adam ordered. "And don't even think about doing any more mouthing off!"

Adam didn't say anything else and didn't relax until he was off the naval base and heading toward Camp Kearney, several miles away. It was the last week of June 1942, hot as usual in southern California. Adam thought maybe the breeze blowing into the open jeep would cool him off a little, but he was still mad and finally couldn't hold it in any longer. Without pulling his eyes away from the twin headlight beams that lit up the road, he said, "What the hell did you two knuckleheads think you were doing?" He was shouting by the time he finished the question.

"Hey, sorry, *Lieutenant*," Leo said. "Sometimes we forget you ain't one of us anymore."

There had been a time, back on Parris Island, when all three of them had been raw recruits together. Adam Bergman, the law school student from Chicago; Ed Collins, the farmer from Iowa; and Leo Sikorsky, from Brooklyn, unemployed until he'd joined the Marine Corps. Unlikely though it seemed, the three of them had become friends. Adam and Leo had at least had their Jewishness in common, and somehow Ed had wound up in there too. He and Leo were misfits of a sort, as if Stan Laurel and Oliver Hardy had enlisted in the Marines. To tell the truth, Adam had expected both of them to wash out in basic training. They had both made it, though.

After Parris Island, their assignments had split them up, Adam being sent to Wake Island, Ed and Leo going on to further infantry training. On Wake, Adam had been part of the gallant defense that had held off a far superior Japanese force for several weeks. Tapped to act as a courier by the island's commanders, Major James Devereaux and Commander Winfield S. "Spiv" Cunningham, Adam had left Wake Island on the last PBY headed back to Pearl Harbor. He had managed to have a brief but passionate reunion with his wife Catherine, a naval nurse stationed at Pearl, before being sent back to the States. He'd wound up at Camp Kearney as part of the Second Marine Division, which was training for island warfare in the South Pacific. Ed and Leo were also assigned to the SECMARDIV. They were in Adam's company, in fact, but not in the platoon he commanded.

Adam had been a sergeant when he arrived at Camp Kearney, but having applied for and been accepted to the accelerated Officer Candidate School being run at the camp, he had graduated at the top of his class and been commissioned a lieutenant, a "thirty-day wonder," another nickname he didn't like. Unlike most of the other members of the Second of the Second, he had seen actual combat, and plenty of it. Some of the officers and noncoms were career

Marines, of course, and had seen action in Nicaragua and China. Adam knew firsthand, though, what it was like to fight the Japanese.

"I should have let Nash come and get you," he said as he drove toward the camp. "He's going to be royally pissed when he finds out I got you off the hook with the SPs. He would have let you stew in the brig for a few days."

"Why'd you come get us, then?" Ed asked. He was sitting in the passenger seat, next to Adam.

Adam didn't answer for a moment. Then he said, "Because I know something Nash doesn't."

After a few more seconds of silence stretched out, Leo leaned forward from the rear seat and said, "Well, are you gonna tell us or not? Or is it some big secret that only officers can know about?"

"As a matter of fact, yes," Adam said.

Ed held up a hand. "Maybe you better not tell us, then. I appreciate you goin' out on a limb for us, Adam. You go spillin' the beans about somethin' you ain't supposed to and you'll be screwed for sure."

"No, that's all right. I trust you guys." Despite his words, Adam hesitated as instincts struggled inside him. He was a Marine, dedicated to duty and discipline and doing things the Marine way. That meant there was a wall between him and Ed and Leo, a wall made up of the fact that he was an officer and they were still enlisted men. But they were also his friends and had been for a long time, and the fact that they were fellow Marines created a bond that overrode any other consideration. He said, "Combat Team Two is shipping out tomorrow night."

Silence greeted the news. Finally, Ed said, "Well, shit, we been expectin' that for a long time. You know where we're goin'?"

Adam shook his head. "No. But I'd be surprised if it was anywhere except Samoa, or some other island in the Pacific."

"That's what they been trainin' us for," Leo said. "We been stormin' the beaches for weeks now."

That was true enough. The unit designated Combat Team 2 consisted of the Second Regiment of the Second Division, the 3d Battalion of the Tenth (Artillery) Marines, C Company of the 2d Tank

Battalion, A Company of the 2d Engineer Battalion, D Company of the 2d Medical Battalion, A Company of the 2d Amphibian Tractor Battalion, a platoon each from the 2d Special Weapons Battalion and the Service and Supply Company of the 2d Service Battalion, A Company of the 2d Pioneer Battalion (construction and engineers), and the First Band Section of the Division HQ Company. For weeks, they had made practice landings along the beaches at La Jolla, so it would take a damned fool not to have a pretty good idea what the future held for them. Besides, *combat* was even in their name.

"It's about time," Ed said. "I was beginnin' to think we'd never get our chance at them slant-eyed little yellow bastards."

"We'll get all the chances you want," Leo said. "And they'll be shootin' live ammo." Nerves made him start drumming on his knees. "Adam, are you sure about this?"

"I'm sure. I got the scoop from somebody in the CO's office."

"You trust him?"

"Yeah."

Ed looked out into the night. "Then we're really goin'. Goin' to war."

Adam nodded and said, "That's right." His hands tightened on the jeep's wheel as he realized they were sweating. After a moment, he took a deep breath and wiped first one and then the other on his trousers.

After that he was fine, and a faint smile even tugged at the corners of his mouth as he drove on into the night.

# EIGHT

The three ships that had served as transports during the mock invasions at La Jolla originally had been luxury liners belonging to the Matson Shipping Company. Named after presidents, the *Hayes*, the *Jackson*, and the *Adams* had been transformed into strictly utilitarian vessels. All their amenities and luxuries were gone, stripped away by the Navy. The brilliant white paint that had once adorned their hulls was now covered with battleship gray. Decorative trim had been replaced by stenciled numbers. And they flew the flag of the United States, rather than the Standard of the Matson Line.

Tonight, the ships were nothing more than dark, bulky shapes as they floated next to piers at the San Diego Naval Base. Blackout rules were in effect, which meant the Marines going aboard the ships cursed as they stumbled over obstacles in the dark. Two more ships, the *Crescent City* and the *Alhena*, had joined the convoy, but they were primarily cargo vessels and had been loaded earlier in the day. The troops of Combat Team 2, though, were going on board in the middle of the night.

Adam stood on the dock in battle gear: dark green fatigues, heavy boots, a knapsack strapped to his back, a Colt .45 1911A1 in a snap-flap holster on his hip, and a Springfield Model '03 rifle in his hand. The rifle, which despite its designation as the 1903 model had been manufactured in the United States armory at Springfield, Illinois, within the past two years, was .30-06 caliber and carried five shots in its magazine. Adam had learned to shoot quite well with it on the range Camp Kearney. He was proficient with the pistol as well. The fatigues were slightly different from those he had worn before. Another item that was new since Wake Island, though he had worn one here at Camp Kearney, was the helmet, rounded and close-fitting instead of the flatter, World War I–style helmets the Marines on Wake had worn. The helmet was heavy steel over a lighter inner liner. It protected more of the head, especially the back of the skull. Anything short of a direct hit stood a good chance of glancing off the steel pot.

Adam knew that, but somehow the knowledge was less than comforting. It meant there was also a good chance somebody might be shooting at his head.

He was in command of Third Platoon, C Company, 1st Battalion, Second Regiment, Second Marine Division. The company commander was Captain Everson Hughes. Third Platoon was made up of four eight-man squads, each commanded by a sergeant. There were four platoons in C Company, giving it a strength of 128 men, plus the four lieutenants, Captain Hughes, and his staff, bringing it to a full complement of 138 men.

Adam had most of his troops on board the *Adams* when he heard the thud of footsteps close behind him on the pier. A second later, a hand gripped his shoulder. "Bergman!" an angry voice said. "I want to talk to you."

Adam swung around and shook off the hand. Though the light was bad on the pier, he knew the man confronting him was Lieutenant Theodore Nash. Nash commanded the Second Platoon of C Company, and Ed Collins and Leo Sikorsky were in one of Second Platoon's squads. Adam didn't have any trouble figuring out what had made Nash upset. In fact, he had thought he might hear a complaint from Nash earlier in the day.

"What is it, Ted?" he asked, even though he already knew.

"I just heard that you got two of my men out of the brig last night," Nash said. "What the hell did you think you were doing?"

"A favor for you?"

Nash moved his head in a gesture of surprise and confusion. "How do you figure that?"

"You wouldn't have gone off and left them in the brig while the rest of your platoon sailed for the South Pacific, now would you? That would have left the platoon at less than full strength."

Nash had been in law school before the war too, like Adam. The difference was that he came from an upper-crust East Coast family and had a partnership in an old, distinguished firm assured as soon as he graduated. Without hesitation, he picked out the relevant information from Adam's statement.

"You knew," he said. "You knew we were shipping out."

Adam shrugged. "I heard some scuttlebutt. It turned out to be right."

Nash thought that over for a second and then said, "That still doesn't excuse what you did. Those two foul-ups are my responsibility, not yours. I know why you really did it. They're your friends, and you didn't want them to get in trouble."

Adam's jaw tightened. Ted Nash, given his station in life, had gone into Officer Candidate School as soon as he enlisted in the Marines. He hadn't come up through the ranks like Adam. And though he claimed to be Adam's friend, at times such as this the distinction between them rose to the forefront. Nash would never be able to forget that Adam had once been a lowly private just like Ed and Leo.

"I just thought I'd help you out," Adam said. "If I was out of line, I'm sorry, Ted."

"You were out of line," Nash snapped, "and you damned well knew it. My platoon is my business. Keep that big nose of yours out of it."

Adam's right hand tightened hard on the Springfield. Nash's reference to his nose didn't have to have anything to do with the fact that he was Jewish—but Adam would have been willing to bet that it did. Still, he didn't want to be like Leo and see slurs where none were intended. Maybe Nash was being just a jerk, not necessarily a bigoted jerk.

"Sorry," Adam said again, though the word cost him an effort.

Nash gave him a curt nod, then turned and stalked away. Adam watched him go. With a sigh, he turned back to the ship and returned his attention to the boarding of the troops under his command.

It wouldn't be quite as bad, he thought, if he didn't know that Nash was partially right. He *had* been trying to keep Ed and Leo out of trouble. He had hoped that the paperwork concerning their arrest by the Shore Patrol wouldn't catch up to Nash until after the ships had sailed for the South Pacific.

There wasn't anything Nash could do about it now. If he wanted to bother with it, he might be able to find a sympathetic ear among the brass and get a reprimand put into Adam's record. Given the circumstances, though, he was more likely to let it go. That had been Adam's thought when he decided to help Ed and Leo.

At the very least, it had cost him Nash's friendship. That might not be so much to lose, Adam told himself. But he regretted it anyway. Nash was a spoiled, pompous pretty boy, but he had the makings of a good officer . . . if he lived long enough.

That was true of all of them, Adam thought with another sigh. Before they could accomplish anything in this war, they had to survive.

*       *       *

Adam placed his cards faceup on the table and said, "Full house."

Across from him, Lieutenant Barney Gelhart grimaced and said, "Damn." His fingers tightened on the cards, and they were so soggy from sweat dripping on them that they crumpled in Gelhart's grip. He threw them on the table and exclaimed, "Now look what I've done! The deck's ruined!"

"Take it easy, Barney," Adam said as he raked in the pile of matches in the center of the table. "We've got more decks."

"Yeah, but sooner or later we'll run out of 'em, and then what'll we do?"

One of the other lieutenants in the cramped compartment said, "Don't worry about it, Barney, we'll probably be ducking Jap bullets by then."

"Oh, well, that makes me feel one whole hell of a lot better," Gelhart said.

He was from Oxnard, California, was twenty-one years old, and a year earlier had been working as the assistant manager of a movie theater. He had gone from passing out giveaway gravy boats to housewives on Tuesday nights to commanding a platoon of Marines that would soon be in combat against the Japanese.

Well, maybe not all that soon, Adam amended as that thought crossed his mind. It was a long way across the Pacific. He didn't know exactly where the Second of the Second was bound, but he felt certain it would be somewhere in the vicinity of the Solomon Islands. That was where the Japs had made their big push toward Australia, the push that had been blunted and then stopped by the valiant efforts of the United States Navy. But even though the Japanese were no longer advancing, they still held New Guinea, the Bismarck Archipelago, and the Solomons. As long as they were there, they would continue to pose a threat to Australia.

Everything had gone the Japs' way during the first few months of the war. It was time to start taking back some of what they had grabbed.

To do that, though, the American forces first had to reach the South Pacific, and that would take some time. Weeks, certainly. And the time would probably seem even longer to the Marines stuck here on what they had come to call "the unholy three."

Cabin walls had been knocked out on the ships to form larger troop compartments. Even so, the vessels were overcrowded. Ventilation belowdecks was bad, and the stifling heat never went away. Bedding was soaked with sweat all the time. The men could either lie there and be slowly pickled in their own brine, or they could prowl the decks and get in the way of the swabbies. Everybody was on edge. Card games often erupted into brawls. The officers had their hands full keeping everything under control. And when they weren't busy trying to keep their troops from killing each other, they didn't have it any better than the enlisted men. Officers' quarters weren't quite as cramped as the enlisted quarters, but they were equally hot and lacking in creature comforts.

And it had only been a week since the convoy sailed from San Diego, Adam told himself as he stood up from the card table. If it took a month or more to reach their destination, half the men would have melted away to nothing.

"I'm going topside for a breath of air," he said. "Anybody want to come with me?" He glanced toward one of the bunks, where Ted Nash lay reading an old copy of *Life* magazine. Nash paid no attention to him.

That didn't surprise Adam. Nash had been very cool toward him ever since their confrontation on the docks at San Diego, speaking to him only when it was necessary. It looked as if he wasn't going to get over what he considered Adam's unwarranted interference in matters concerning his platoon.

Gelhart pushed himself to his feet. "I'll go with you," he said. "I could use some fresh air."

"You won't find it up there," one of the other lieutenants said. "I think this whole damned ocean stinks."

Adam didn't agree with that, but he didn't bother arguing. He didn't mind the voyage, other than the heat and the nervous strain of knowing they were headed for combat. Some of the men were anxious to fight, or at least they claimed to be. But from time to time, almost everyone on board was struck by moments of silence, as they thought about what they might be facing. *It always happens to somebody else,* they thought. *Not me. I won't be one of the guys who gets it.*

But no matter how often they told themselves that, they knew deep down it was a possibility. The odds were that a lot of them would never make it home.

Adam and Gelhart climbed a ladder and emerged through an open hatch onto the deck. A few lights were burning up on the superstructure, but from this angle they sort of blended into the vast arch of stars that swept across the sky. A hot wind blew into their faces as Adam and Gelhart went to the railing and looked out at the ocean. There wasn't much to see. They could barely make out the waves rolling past.

"Hey, Adam—I mean, Lieutenant."

Adam turned his head and saw Ed and Leo slouching along the railing, easy to recognize even in the starlight because of their distinctive shapes. When they saw that someone else was with Adam, they straightened to attention and saluted.

Adam and Gelhart returned the salutes, and Adam said, "At ease."

"You know these two feather merchants, Bergman?" Gelhart asked.

"Yeah. We were at Parris Island together."

Gelhart's stiff stance unbent a little. He said, "Hello, fellas. How's it going?"

"Just fine, sir," Ed replied.

"If you two are old friends of Bergman here, you don't have to stand on protocol on my account. Take it easy."

"Thanks, sir." Both Ed and Leo still seemed a little wary, however.

Adam was glad to have a chance to talk with them. He had seen them during formations and drills, but he hadn't spoken to either of them since the departure from San Diego. He asked, "What happened after Lieutenant Nash found out about . . . well, you know."

"You mean about us gettin' tossed in the clink?" Ed laughed. "He gave us a good ass-chewin', that's for sure, and then our sarge did the same. But I reckon we survived, didn't we, Chopper?"

"Yeah, but the lieutenant's promised to make our lives miserable once we get where we're goin'." Leo gave a hollow laugh. "Like anything he could do to us'll be worse than what the Japs do."

Gelhart leaned against the rail and looked past Adam at Leo. "Why does your buddy call you Chopper? No offense, but I don't think the name really suits you."

"His name's Sikorsky," Ed said before Leo could respond to the question. His tone was matter-of-fact, as if Gelhart should understand what he was talking about.

After a moment, Gelhart said, "Yeah? So?"

"A Sikorsky is a kind of helicopter. Some people call them choppers."

"What's a helicopter?"

"A rotor-driven aircraft," Ed explained. "The first single-rotor helicopter was developed about three years ago by a Roosky named Igor Sikorsky."

"No relation," Leo put in.

Gelhart nodded. "Yeah, I think I know what you're talking about. I've seen pictures of contraptions like that. They look sort of like a giant eggbeater."

"That's them," Ed said.

"Ed's an aviation buff," Adam said. "I think he'd like to be a pilot."

"Not much chance o' that," Ed said with a laugh. He slapped his belly. "Can you just imagine a big ol' boy like me tryin' to fit in the cockpit of an airplane? That's a job for skinny little fellas."

"Well, you're a Marine," Gelhart said. "That's just as good."

"Maybe better. I get to kill my Japs close up."

# NINE

The dream was always the same. He was in the water, fighting against the terrible strength of the giant hand trying to pull him under. His head was splitting with pain, his body was numb from shock, and life was slipping away from him. There were only a few precious seconds left. *Might as well give up,* a voice taunted inside his mind. *You're going to die anyway. Why not give up, let yourself slide under the waves, and let it go ahead and happen? All you'll miss is a few more seconds of terror and hopelessness.*

That was when Lieutenant (j.g.) Phillip Lange, USNR, usually woke up. Sometimes he was screaming when he awoke, but usually his head just jerked up off the pillow and his breath hissed between tightly clenched teeth. He might have bolted upright in his bunk if not for the fact that his torso was covered with bandages and he was too stiff and sore to move that fast.

Tonight, though, the nightmare went on a little longer. Phil felt the warm, salty water of the Pacific come up and close over his head, trapping him in eternal darkness. He felt himself sinking deeper and deeper, until it would be impossible for him to reach the surface even if he managed to find the elusive cord and inflate the Mae West life preserver he was wearing. Again, he tasted salt on his lips.

That sensation made him rouse from the troubled slumber. He blinked his eyes open and looked up into the face of the young woman who was bent over his bunk. Her cheeks were wet with tears, and as Phil watched, another of them fell, landing beside the corner of his mouth this time instead of on his lips.

"Oh!" Missy Mitchell said. She straightened. "I didn't mean to wake you—"

"It's all right," Phil said, his voice little more than a whisper because he was still weak from the wounds he had suffered at the Battle of Midway. "Don't worry, Missy. But . . . what were you doing?"

She hesitated before she answered. "Watching you sleep."

A faint smile curved Phil's lips. "Well, you're a nurse. I suppose you could consider it part of your job to observe your patients."

She crossed her arms over her chest. "You don't have to be a smart aleck about it. I happen to be in love with you. I wanted to make sure you were all right."

"Haven't I been all right ever since I got here?"

"Here" was the U.S.S. *Solace*, an American hospital ship moored at Nukualofa, on the island of Tongatapu, the main island of the Tonga Group that made up the nation of Tonga in the South Pacific Ocean. While nominally a British protectorate, Tonga was for most purposes an independent nation ruled by the massive Queen Salote. Nukualofa was the port that the *Solace* had called home for the past few months.

Following the Battle of Midway, in which the United States Navy had suffered heavy losses but ultimately seized victory by sinking all four Japanese aircraft carriers it had faced, the sheer number of casualties had been staggering. Most of the wounded had been hospitalized at Pearl Harbor, but some had been taken to other medical facilities, including the *Solace*. One of those wounded men was Phil Lange, and by being assigned to the *Solace* to recuperate from his wounds, he had been reunited with Missy Mitchell, one of the nurses on the hospital ship. A few months earlier, Phil had fallen in love with her while he was there recovering from an ankle broken in a freak accident. Actually, Phil had fallen for one of the other nurses first, a cool, classy blonde named Catherine Bergman. When he found out that Catherine was married—and to a Marine, no less—he had transferred his affections to Missy, a brassy brunette who was Catherine's best friend on the ship. Of course, the whole thing had been Missy's idea, but Phil had gone along with her. It was hard to say no to Missy. He knew now that the fact he was on the rebound had made her hesitate, but once she made up her mind to go after him, she'd been impossible to deny. Typhoon Missy, he sometimes called her when she had her dander up about something. The original irresistible force, and he was far from an immovable object.

"I'm just trying to look out for you," Missy said. "You were shot up pretty bad, you know." She kept her voice low so she wouldn't disturb any of the other patients sleeping in the ward. It was late, after midnight.

Phil grunted. "Yeah, I know. I was there, remember?"

"I thought you were dead." Missy's voice shook a little as she said the words.

"So did I."

"Sometimes I still . . . I still have a hard time believing that you're here, and that you're going to be all right."

"You and me both," Phil said.

He didn't have any right to be alive. His buddy Jerry Bennett, who had been the observer and rear gunner in the Dauntless SBD-4 dive bomber Phil flew, hadn't survived the battle. Jerry had bought it when a Jap Zero riddled the Dauntless on its way back to the carrier *Yorktown*. Phil had downed the Zero, but not in time to save Jerry and not in time to save his own airplane. The Dauntless had gone into the drink. Phil barely made it out before the plane sank forever. Only half-conscious because of his injuries, he had almost gone down with it. But somehow he had managed to inflate his Mae West even as he was losing consciousness, and a rescue boat from an American cruiser that was in the area arrived a few minutes later to pluck him out of the hungry sea. Phil had made it, but his survival was just sheer luck.

Unless . . . unless there was something to what Missy said, all that stuff about fate and destiny and how the two of them were meant to be together. Phil couldn't rule it out. It was his nature to be hardheaded, to believe in facts and the scientific method. That was why he'd wanted to become a science teacher, a dream that had been postponed first by financial need and then by the war. But he had to admit that some things just couldn't be explained any other way than by faith.

How else could he explain the fact that he had been able to pull the cord on that Mae West when he would swear that he had been out cold at the time?

A bullet from the Zero had ripped through his upper left arm, just below the shoulder, but it had missed the bone. He had an ugly gash on his forehead, a result of the shrapnel flying around the cockpit when the Jap shot up the Dauntless's instrument panel. His right knee was badly wrenched, and two of his ribs were cracked. Phil wasn't sure when those injuries had occurred, but he supposed they had happened when the plane made its crash landing in the ocean. He hadn't even been aware of them at the time, hadn't known the full extent of his injuries until he emerged from the morphine-induced haze on the American cruiser. By the time he reached the *Solace* on a PBY from Midway, the corpsmen were still keeping him doped up enough so that he wasn't fully cognizant of what was going on. When he first woke up on the hospital ship and found Missy standing over him, he thought he was dreaming. All it had taken was a few careful but passionate kisses to convince him that she was real.

With soft, gliding steps, another nurse approached the bunk. Phil turned his head enough to recognize Catherine Bergman. She smiled at him and Missy both and said, "You'd better let Phil get some sleep, Missy."

"I know, I hover over him too much." Missy blew back a strand of curly brown hair that had escaped from her nurse's cap. "He's just so darned adorable that I can't help myself."

Phil had to laugh. "You're going to give me a swelled head if you don't watch out. And with this bandage around it, I can't afford that."

"I guess not." Missy reached out and touched his cheek, her fingertips brushing lightly against his face. "Go back to sleep. I'm sorry I bothered you."

"You could never be a bother."

Catherine said, "Oh, yes, she can." She took hold of Missy's arm. "Come on back to the nurse's station with me. There's plenty of paperwork to keep us both busy."

Missy made a face. "Oh, all right." She kissed a finger and touched it to Phil's lips. "Good night, sweetie."

"Good night," he said. He settled his head against the pillow and closed his eyes as Catherine led Missy away.

He touched the tip of his tongue to his lips. He might have been imagining it, but he thought he could still taste the salt of her tears.

\* \* \*

"I'm pretty silly, aren't I?"

Catherine shook her head in response to Missy's question. "Not at all. You thought you'd lost him. You still can't quite believe that he's here, and that he's going to be all right." She put down the pencil she had been using to make notes on a patient's chart. "When Adam was on Wake Island, there were plenty of times I convinced myself that he was dead, or at least that I would never see him again. But he came back to me, just like Phil came back to you. All the time Adam was at Pearl Harbor with me, I couldn't keep my hands off him."

Missy sighed. "That's the problem. You and Adam were able to hit the sheets. I can't do anything with Phil except kiss him, and I have to be careful about that."

Catherine shook her head and said, "I didn't really mean it like that. It wasn't about just . . . making love. I had to keep touching Adam to assure myself that he was really there, that I wasn't just imagining the whole thing."

"And then one thing led to another . . ."

Catherine felt her face growing warm. After all this time, Missy still had the ability to make her blush. "Yeah, it usually did," she admitted with a smile.

"Is he still in California?"

"The last I heard. Of course, it takes a long time for letters to get here."

"I hope they let him stay there until the war's over."

Catherine didn't say anything. She knew Missy probably expected her to agree with that sentiment, and a part of her did. As long as Adam was stateside, he was safe. He had done his part already, fighting the Japanese on Wake Island. It wouldn't be fair for the Marines to send him back to the South Pacific.

Yet she knew he wouldn't be happy sitting out the rest of the war. He felt an obligation to fight the enemies of his country. At first, it was his hatred for Hitler and what the Nazis were doing in Europe that had led him to enlist almost a year before the Japanese had attacked Pearl Harbor. His grandparents on his mother's side still lived in the Ukraine. At least, they had until Operation Barbarossa, when that part of the world had found itself in the path of the Nazi war machine. There was no way of knowing if they were still alive or not.

Figuring that joining the Marines would give him his best chance of helping to stop Hitler's blitzkrieg, Adam had joined up at the same time as his friends Joe and Dale Parker. But then things had gotten screwy. Adam had been sent to the Pacific, on the other side of the world from where he had hoped to end up. The foe out here was the Japanese, not the Germans and Italians. Joe and Dale were the ones who had gone east instead of west. The last Catherine had heard of them, they were in Egypt doing something with the British tank corps. Adam had gone to Wake Island, and then the Japanese came . . .

Adam was all right with that now. Catherine had talked about it with him while he was on temporary duty at Ewa, the Marine air base across the channel from the naval base at Pearl Harbor. The Japanese were Hitler's strongest allies. In this war that was spreading its tentacles around the entire world, the Nazis needed the Japanese effort to expand its Greater East Asian Co-Prosperity Sphere to be successful in order for the Third Reich to hang on to the territory it had seized. They were like two bullies standing back-to-back in a schoolyard. So every blow against the Japanese was also a blow against the Nazis, at least indirectly. Or as Adam put it, "Once we've polished off the Japs, then all of us can go after Hitler's goons."

Catherine hoped that came to pass, for Adam's sake.

She stood up from the tiny desk at the nurse's station. Missy asked, "Where are you going?"

"I thought I'd go up on deck for a few minutes. That is, if you don't mind keeping an eye on things down here."

"Sure."

Missy had agreed a little too quickly, Catherine thought. She said, "I don't mean go stand over Phil's bed. He needs his rest, and you have to keep an eye on the other patients too."

"I know that. Gee, you don't have to tell me how to do my job, Catherine. Remember, I've been a nurse longer than you have."

"You're right. I'm sorry."

"Ah, that's okay. You go on. I know you want to think about Adam."

Catherine looked at her. "How do you know that?"

"Hey, I'm a woman too. I know a lovesick gal when I see one. I look at one in the mirror every day."

# TEN

Mike Chastain was humming "I Can't Get Started With You" when he got out of the cab in front of the apartment building where he lived. He was a medium-sized, well-dressed man with sleek dark hair under the stylish black fedora he wore. The dark eyes in his lean face were always on the move and seldom missed anything. In the neighborhoods of Chicago where he had grown up, a guy who wasn't on the lookout sometimes didn't live very long.

Those days were behind him now, and so were those neighborhoods. From his penthouse, he could look out across the city and see some of those squalid areas, but that was as close as he ever came to them now. There was nothing there for him, no reason to ever go back, despite his roots. Whenever he needed to conduct some business with somebody from the South Side, the guy came to him, not the other way around.

As the cab pulled away, Mike paused on the sidewalk to light a cigarette. That gave him a chance to look up and down the street. His eyes narrowed as he spotted a familiar car parked on the other side of the street, about half a block up. A tiny red spot on the passenger side in the car's darkened interior marked the glowing coal of a cigar. That would be Bowden, Mike thought. The older cop was the cigar smoker. Which meant Corey was behind the wheel.

Did those dumb bastards know that he had seen them? Did they even care? They did such a lousy job of tailing him that he had almost decided they didn't care if he spotted them. They might even prefer it that way. They were so stupid they probably thought they were making him nervous enough so that he would slip up.

Fat chance of that, he thought as he dropped the match to the sidewalk and stepped on it. He walked up to the door, and the fancy-uniformed doorman opened it with a smile and a cheerful, "Good evening, Mr. Chastain. How are you?"

"Just fine, Benny," Mike said. "Couldn't be better."

He walked across the lobby toward the elevators, wondering how long the two cops would sit out there before they decided he was in for the night.

*　　*　　*

"This isn't going to get us anywhere, Carl," Pete Corey said as he used his right forefinger to push the heavy black glasses higher on the bridge of his nose. "That bastard's just laughing at us."

Carl Bowden drew deeper on the cigar clenched between his teeth, making its end glow cherry red. "Let him laugh," Bowden said around the stogie. His voice was like car wheels on a gravel road. "He'll wind up laughin' out his ass once he's behind bars. He'll make a mistake sooner or later. Hotshots like him always do."

"Yeah, well, I'm gettin' tired of tailing him. We've been at it for weeks now. We know he's involved with Hale. Hell, we know he's the one who got Hale patched up after that shoot-out on the South Side. Why don't we just bust into that fancy penthouse of his and beat the truth out of him?"

Bowden took the cigar out of his mouth and rolled it between his fingers. "We could do that," he said, "but if we did, Chastain would pay some shyster lawyer to get the case kicked out of court. He might even try to have our badges yanked."

"Fat chance of that."

"Stranger things have happened." Bowden put the cigar back in his mouth. "Better to let him stew in his own juices."

Corey thumbed his hat to the back of his close-cropped head. "You got more patience than I do, partner."

"That's because I'm older. I move slower these days, but I still get where I'm going."

Pete Corey looked up the street at the expensive apartment hotel where Mike Chastain lived. Carl could afford to be patient, he thought. Carl had lived his life, put in his time on the force, done the things he'd wanted to do. He had helped arrest some of the big shots, back in the days of Nitti and Capone. Hell, he'd even worked with Ness. Pete had been in high school then, a chunky, four-eyed loser who could only dream about being a racket-busting G-man. His dad, Patrick Corey, had been a cop, just like Pete's grandfather and great-grandfather. Pat Corey didn't figure his boy would ever be on the force, though. Pete's eyes were too bad, and he was too damned fat. When Pete came to him and said that he wanted to go to the academy, Pat had tried to talk him out of it. He might be disappointed in the boy, but he still loved him and didn't want to see him hurt. Pete had his mind made up, though, so Pat had fixed it so he could at least take the physical. Nobody was more surprised than Pat Corey when the boy passed. He made the weight limit by a couple of pounds after starving himself for nearly a month, and his eyesight without glasses was the absolute minimum. So Pete made it into the academy, but Pat was convinced he'd wash out before he graduated.

To tell the truth, Pete had been surprised too. He struggled with the physical aspects of the academy but had no trouble with the mental ones. He was smart as a whip; no one had ever said that he wasn't. And with time and effort, he got stronger, in better shape. He was still chunky and would probably always have to fight his weight, but when he put on the uniform he didn't look too bad. The main thing was, he was finally a cop. His old man could be proud of him at last.

Less than six weeks later, Pat Corey had dropped dead, his heart exploding in his chest one day while he was chasing a guy who had stolen some fruit from a stand. What a damned, stupid waste his death was, Pete always thought. If a cop was going to die in the line of duty, it ought to be while he was going after somebody who counted.

That was probably why he had taken the risks that he had. Nobody got away with anything on his beat, not if he could help it. He had shot it out with bank robbers, barely missed getting his belly opened up by a butcher knife when some guy started fighting with his old lady and went nuts, and busted up a couple of protection rackets even though the bozos running them threatened to have him rubbed out. After all that, the department had pinned a shield on him and told him he was now a detective and that everyone expected him to continue his sterling record as a law enforcement officer. Pete planned to do just that. He couldn't let the old man down, even now.

Then the damn war had come along.

Peter Corey was twenty-five years old. If his eyes were good enough for the cops, they were good enough for the army. When his number came up in the draft, as he was sure it would, he could try to pull some strings and get out of it because he was on the force, but he didn't know if he wanted to. With all the crap that Hitler was pulling in Europe, and after the way the Japs had bombed Pearl Harbor, Pete didn't know if he could turn his back on a draft notice. Somebody had to put things right in the world again, and it looked like it was up to the good old U.S. of A. If he were called on, he would have to do his part.

But he wanted to get the goods on Mike Chastain first. The black market ring Chastain ran with Roger Hale was the biggest case Pete had drawn as a detective. He wanted Chastain behind bars before he went off to the Army. He knew Chastain's type: slick, self-assured, confident that he would always come out on top. Pete would get a special pleasure out of seeing that smug son of a bitch behind bars.

A few days earlier, Roger Hale had surfaced again after being missing for weeks. Pete and Bowden had been convinced that Hale was dead. They knew he had been wounded in the attempted hijacking of a meat truck. When Hale was spotted making the rounds of the clubs again, just like the old days, they had moved in on him, pulling him in for questioning. Hale had lost weight, and his face had a pallor that said he had been cooped up somewhere for a while. He had gone to ground to recuperate from his wounds, Pete figured. But Hale had denied having anything to do with the hijacking, and he had an alibi. Of course, phony alibis were just about the easiest thing in the world for crooks to come up with, but they hadn't been able to shake Hale's. Pete wanted to rip the bastard's shirt off and expose the scars those bullets must have left on his torso, but Bowden stopped him. This wasn't like the old days, Carl said later. They had to follow at least some of the rules and could only go so far in questioning a suspect, especially one like Hale who could afford a good lawyer.

The whole thing was a bunch of crap as far as Pete was concerned, but he would try to be patient . . . for now.

"You need to relax," Bowden told him as Pete drummed his fingers on the steering wheel. He reached down to the radio knob on the dashboard. "Why don't we listen to some music, or try to find a ball game?"

"I just don't know why we're sitting here," Pete burst out. "Hale's not going to come along and go waltzing up to Chastain's penthouse. He's too smart for that."

Bowden switched on the radio and fiddled with the tuning knob until music came from the speaker. He left the volume low and said, "Maybe we're not waiting for Hale."

"Who, then?"

As another cab pulled up at the curb in front of the apartment building, Bowden pointed with his cigar. "Could be that's her right now."

*　　*　　*

Karen Wells knew she was making a mistake. The best thing for her to do would be to stay away from Mike. She had known that ever since they had walked into his apartment that night weeks earlier and found blood on the floor. A moment later, Roger Hale had come stumbling out of the bedroom, a gun in his hand, and collapsed in the hallway in front of them. Karen had walked out that night, unable to bear watching Mike turn back to the life of crime they had both thought he'd left behind.

If only she'd had the strength to not come back, she had thought many times since them. But she was weak. She told herself that Mike would come to his senses. He would get out while he still had the chance, and they could go back to the life they'd had before Roger Hale came along. Mike could gamble at the clubs; Karen didn't mind that. He didn't have to cheat at cards. He was good enough he could clean up even in an honest game. And she would go on singing, putting her heart and soul into the songs again instead of just going through the motions like she had been lately. Life could be good. She knew it could.

So hope brought her back here a couple of times a week. And so far, hope had let her down every time.

She leaned in through the open window of the cab and gave the driver a couple of dollars. He said, "Thanks, lady," and touched a finger to the brim of his cap. As the taxi pulled away from the curb and Karen turned toward the building, she heard someone call her name. She stopped in surprise and looked at the two men coming along the sidewalk toward her.

She recognized them right away. More than once, she had seen them talking to Mike at the Dells, the supper club on the outskirts of town where she sang. They were cops. Mike said they were stupid and claimed that they didn't bother him, but she knew better. She saw the way his face tightened up when they came around.

She was a little surprised it had taken them this long to talk to her.

"Miss Wells?" the older, gravel-voiced man said again. "Mind if we talk to you for a minute?"

"Not at all," Karen said. "I suppose you boys have heard me sing and want an autograph."

The younger one coughed. Karen wasn't sure, but she thought he did it to hide a grin that flashed across his face. At least one of them appreciated her wit.

"No, ma'am, we need to ask you some questions," the older one said. "We're from the police. I'm Detective Bowden, and this is Detective Corey."

Bowden looked like a cop. If Karen had seen Corey on the street, she would have thought he was an accountant or something like that. Corey said, "Do you know a man named Michael Chastain?"

Her voice was cool as she replied, "You know that I do, or you wouldn't be asking me that question."

"What about Roger Hale?" Bowden said.

"I know who he is. I've seen him around."

"We're going to arrest Hale for murder. There's a good chance your boyfriend will take the fall with him."

Karen shook her head. "I don't know what you're talking about. Mike doesn't have anything to do with Roger Hale."

"You didn't say anything about how Hale couldn't be guilty of murder," Corey noted.

"That's because I don't know what Roger Hale is capable of,"

Karen said. "You see, I don't know him well at all. But I know Michael Chastain, and I know he's not a killer."

Bowden gave her an ugly grin. "Sure of that, are you?"

"Of course." Karen's hands tightened on her purse. "Now, if you gentlemen are through wasting my time . . ."

She started to turn away. Bowden stopped her by placing a hand on her arm. His fingers were long and heavy, and their touch made Karen want to jerk her arm away. She forced herself to stand still and look at the detective with an impassive stare.

Bowden leaned closer to her, close enough so that she could smell pastrami on his breath. "Listen, lady," he said. "If you give a damn about Chastain, you'd better convince him to break off whatever he's got goin' with Hale. Hale's got a date with the electric chair, whether he knows it yet or not. If you don't want Chastain to wind up sittin' in his lap, you better listen to what I'm tellin' you."

Karen suppressed the shudder that tried to go through her. If she started to tremble, Bowden would feel it, and she didn't want him to know that he was getting to her. She said, "I don't know what you're talking about, Officer—"

"Detective," Bowden broke in.

"I don't know what you're talking about," Karen said again. "And I'd appreciate it if you'd let go of me."

Bowden lifted his hand from her arm. "Hey, nobody's holding you." He reached into his vest pocket, took out a fresh cigar, and put it in his mouth. "Just remember what I told you." He turned away, adding over his shoulder, "Come on, Pete."

"In a minute," Corey said.

Bowden just grunted and walked on. Corey waited until the older man was halfway up the block, then he said in a quiet voice, "I'm sorry about that. Carl's an old-timer. He gets carried away sometimes."

Karen gave him a faint smile and shook her head. "You don't really expect this to work, do you, Detective? I'm not going to fall for it."

Even in the dim light on the sidewalk, she could see his face darken. She couldn't tell if he was angry or embarrassed. "I'm not trying to pull a fast one," he said. "I mean it. I want to see that boyfriend of yours behind bars as much as Carl does, maybe even more, but that's no excuse for . . . Well, he shouldn't have grabbed you like that, that's all."

"Aren't you the gallant one?"

"Make fun of me if you want, Miss Wells, but before this is over, you're liable to need somebody on *your* side. You're not spotless in all this. If you want to save your own neck, you'd better start thinking about what you've heard tonight."

She stared at him. Somehow, it had never occurred to her that the police might come after her too. She had been convinced they were concentrating on Mike and Hale and didn't care about anybody else.

Corey started to walk after his partner. Then he stopped and looked back at her. "By the way, I *have* heard you sing. You're good, and you're one of the prettiest girls I've ever seen. I wouldn't mind having your autograph . . . if I wasn't afraid that I might have to arrest you someday." He shook his head. "I don't think I'd want to arrest somebody who'd given me their autograph."

This time he did walk away, leaving Karen to stare after him. He was just a cop, she told herself, a dumpy, stupid cop. Why should she care what somebody like him thought of her?

But what was that he had said?

*One of the prettiest girls I've ever seen . . .*

# ELEVEN

The sound of hammering filled the air as Dr. Gerald Tancred stood in the storefront and watched the work going on around him. Tancred, a tall, lean, distinguished-looking man with a neat Vandyke beard, didn't seem the sort to be doing carpentry work. His hands were soft, with long, slender fingers. Those fingers held surprising strength and dexterity, however. They were the hands of a healer. He raised his arms and looked down at his hands. For a long time now, ever since he and his family had immigrated from Germany and he had established his practice on the wealthy North Side of Chicago, those hands had been used mostly to pet rich, spoiled, middle-aged women who were convinced they were afflicted with mysterious ailments when most of them were really as healthy as horses.

What a waste of his talents, Tancred thought.

And yet, he didn't really believe that. Making a good living was not a waste of time or talents, and he had made a good living indeed for his family. His wife Elenore and their children, Catherine and Spencer, had never wanted for a thing. Instead of simply putting a roof over their heads and food on the table, Tancred had provided them with a very comfortable estate on Lakeshore Drive, maids to clean it, and cooks to prepare sumptuous meals. They drove only the most luxurious automobiles and wore the finest clothes. The children had had the best education money could buy. It had been a good life. A very good life.

But if that was true, Tancred asked himself at moments such as these, why did he feel so hollow inside?

Was it because his daughter had gone against his wishes and married a poor, struggling law student, and a Jew at that? Or because his son had proven to be a reprobate who had to be sent away to military school? Of course, Adam Bergman was no longer in law school. He was a soldier now, a Marine. And Catherine had gone off with him, joining the Naval Nurse Corps. She could have been a doctor herself, Tancred thought. She had the intelligence and the natural ability. Female doctors were uncommon but not unheard of. Catherine would have made an excellent physician. Now she was reduced to changing bandages and bedpans on some squalid hospital ship somewhere in the Pacific.

But at least she was alive, and that was more than he could say for Spencer.

"Where do you want this, Doc?"

Tancred gave a little shake of his head and looked around to see one of the workmen standing there with a medicine chest. "Put it in one of the examining rooms," Tancred said. "It doesn't matter which one." He stopped himself from making the acid comment that the man should have known where to put the chest. He had to be polite to these workers, even when it went against the grain for him. Without them, he couldn't finish the job of remodeling this empty storefront into a modern medical clinic. And without the Spencer Tancred Memorial Clinic to occupy her time and her thoughts, his wife would have no reason to keep her own demons at bay.

After all the trouble and heartache Spencer had caused, he had gotten it into his head that he could make up for everything by enlisting in the Navy. He had been sent to a naval base in the Pacific so that he could learn to fly airplanes and be an aviator. It was a place called Pearl Harbor, and Spencer had been there on the morning of December 7, 1941. A peaceful Sunday morning that had been Spencer's last day on earth.

His death in the Japanese attack had sent his mother spiraling into a mental and nervous breakdown. Part of the time, Elenore was all right, but she suffered from delusions that could overwhelm her with no warning. When that happened, she believed that Spencer was still alive. She retreated into a place in her mind where her son still lived, and when something happened to challenge that delusion, as it usually did, Elenore went into fits of screaming and hysteria, becoming so upset that she had to be sedated. Every such episode was like a knife in Tancred's heart.

So when she had come up with the idea of this clinic during one of her rational moments, he had at first tried to talk her out of it and then agreed to consider the idea. That was all it took. He had caused his wife so much pain that he could not refuse her anything that might make her feel better.

He had to admit that since then she had done much better. She had found a possible location for the clinic before ever approaching him. They went to look at the South Side storefront together, and Elenore had been bursting with ideas about how it could be made over into a clinic. The Spencer Tancred Memorial Clinic. That was the most important thing to her, that her son's name not be forgotten. But she wanted to help people too, and this clinic, which would bring free medical care to the poor neighborhoods of the South Side, would provide definite help to the people who lived there. Tancred had always given money to various charities—not a lot, of course, but no one could say he never contributed—and now he would be giving not only of his money but also his time and his skill as a physician. For the first time in years, Elenore seemed to be truly proud of him.

Tancred looked at his hands again and then went over to one of the workmen. The man was hammering a piece of Sheetrock into place against a wall. Another hammer lay on the floor. Tancred picked up the extra hammer and held out his other hand.

"Let me have some nails, and I'll give you a hand," he said to the workman.

The man turned a surprised frown toward Tancred. "You sure about that, Doc?"

"Positive."

"You ever put up Sheetrock before?"

"No," Tancred said, "but I believe there is an old saying about there being a first time for everything."

Kenneth Walker got off the El, walked along the platform to the stairs at the end, and went down them to the street. An old man ran a newsstand at the bottom of the stairs. Ken paused there and looked over the ranks of colorful magazines. He paid particular attention to the pulps as he searched for the name of his friend, Joe Parker, on the garish covers. Ken didn't read much fiction, but he made an effort to pick up Joe's stories. Of course, there wouldn't be very many more of them for a while, because Joe had been in the Army for over a year now. When he enlisted, he'd had quite a few stories "in the pipeline," as he called it, meaning they had been accepted for publication but hadn't appeared yet. Ken didn't know how many of those stories had not yet been published. Maybe not any of them. And Joe wouldn't know, since Joe was clear around on the other side of the world in Egypt.

Ken was a blond, handsome man in his early twenties, a former classmate of Joe and Dale Parker and Adam Bergman. He had been mistaken for a football player more than once, but not when he put on his glasses and a lab coat. He was doing postgraduate work in physics at the University of Chicago, or at least he had been until fate had tapped him for something else.

He was bending over and reaching for a copy of *Blue Book* when a voice asked, "Is that the new one?"

Ken turned his head and looked up at the young woman who had spoken. She wore a blue dress and a little blue hat on lustrous dark hair that framed a heart-shaped face. She had her hair pushed back behind ears that Ken thought stuck out just a little too much. When she smiled at him, her mouth had an odd quirk to it too. She wasn't really pretty at all.

But she was so beautiful Ken felt like he had just been punched hard in the chest. For a second he couldn't seem to get his breath.

He straightened, bringing the issue of *Blue Book* with him. Though it was hard to tear his gaze away from the girl's face, he looked at the magazine and checked the date. "Yeah, it's the new issue, all right," he made himself say.

"Good," she said. "There's a serial in it I'm reading." She started to step past him and reach down toward the bottom row of the rack.

"Here, take this one," he said, thrusting the magazine toward her.

"You weren't going to buy it?" She frowned slightly, and that expression was almost as fetching as her smile.

"I, uh, I don't know yet. I can get another one if I decide to."

"Well, thanks." She took the magazine from him and opened it,

92

flipping to the table of contents. "Yeah, there it is, part three of six. I hate serials, don't you?" Without giving him a chance to answer, she went on, "But that doesn't stop me from getting all caught up in them. I just have to find out what happens."

"Yeah," Ken said. He knew his conversation with her so far hadn't been very sparkling or witty, but there wasn't anything he could do about it. His heart was pounding so hard in his chest it was all he could do to get any words out, let alone be charming or amusing. "I . . . I know a guy who writes magazine yarns."

"Really? I'll bet that's a great life. Nothing to do all day but sit around and dream up stories and get paid for them. That would be grand." She laughed. "I'm sure it's better than working as a clerk in a dry goods store. That's what I do."

Ken wasn't so sure about that. He didn't know everything that Joe had gone through, but he remembered plenty of times when he'd been short of money. Joe had worked at a lot of different jobs too, including clerking in drug stores and hardware stores. It hadn't looked like such a glamorous life to Ken, although Joe had never talked about giving it up.

"What about you?"

Ken realized the girl was still talking to him. He said, "What about me?"

"What do you do?" She was still smiling at him, but there was a trace of impatience in her voice, as if she had realized she was talking to someone who was slow mentally.

"I, ah, work at the university. The University of Chicago."

"Really? That sounds fascinating. Are you a teacher?"

"No, not right now. I've been a teaching assistant before, but right now I'm, uh, I'm . . ."

He felt a surge of panic. What was he going to say now? He couldn't very well tell her that he was working on a top-secret project to split the atom and figure out a way to use the process to make the biggest, deadliest bomb the world had ever seen.

But that was exactly what was going on in the rat's warren of laboratories underneath the west grandstand at Amos Alonzo Stagg Field, on the campus of the university.

Ken had been working on the project, assisting Dr. Enrico

Fermi, a visiting professor of physics from Columbia University in New York, for months now. His involvement had been accidental at first, but once he knew of the work going on there, he'd had to either join the team or face being locked up for the duration of the war. The project was too important for the country, too important for all mankind, to risk it being compromised by a grad student.

There had never been a question of which choice Ken would make. He loved science and always had, as far back as he could remember. He had worked hard and gained the trust of Dr. Fermi and the other scientists working in the Metallurgical Laboratory, or MetLab as it was called. Even now, the atomic pile where it was hoped that the first controlled nuclear chain reaction in history would take place was being built in an abandoned squash court under the football field. Ken had been a part of that effort, and he was justly proud of his work.

But he couldn't explain that to this girl. Not without jeopardizing the whole project.

Of course, it wasn't like she was a Nazi spy or something. Ken could tell that just by looking at her. She was just a girl, a shop clerk. Totally harmless. But beautiful, very beautiful. And she was waiting for him to finish his sentence.

"Now I'm working with one of the professors," he said, knowing how limp it sounded.

"I'll bet he's got you grading his papers and stuff like that," she said. "Big shots never do their own work."

Ken didn't bother explaining that Dr. Fermi, Dr. Bohr, Dr. Szilard, and the other scientists working on the project put in longer, harder hours than any of the assistants. Again, that was something he just couldn't go into. He would have to let her think whatever she wanted.

She saved him from having to come up with something to say by holding out her hand and introducing herself. "I'm Emily Faraday."

"Ken Walker," he said as he took her hand. A notion struck him, a daring notion of the sort that he never had. "Would you like to, ah, go get a soda? There's a drugstore right down the street with a good fountain."

"That sounds lovely," Emily said, and she gave his hand a little extra squeeze before she let go of it. "It's been a long day, and I'd love to sit down for a while before I go on home." She dropped her voice. "My ma's not well, and I spend a lot of time taking care of her."

"I'm sorry," Ken said, his sympathy genuine. "You live around here?"

"Just a few blocks over."

"Me too."

They turned away from the newsstand but had gone only a few feet before the owner called after them, "Hey, are either of you love-birds plannin' on *payin'* for that magazine?"

Ken felt himself blushing as he turned around quickly. Emily started to open her purse, but he held up a hand to stop her. "Let me," he said.

"But I'm the one who wanted to read the serial."

"That's all right."

"I'll tell you what," Emily said. "We'll share it. I'll read the issue first, and then give it to you. Okay?"

In order to do that, they would have to see each other again, Ken thought. And that prospect was very pleasing to him. He grinned, took a quarter from his pocket, flipped it to the old man at the news-stand, and said, "Deal. Let's go get that soda."

Behind them, the newsstand owner dropped the coin in the till, shook his head, and muttered in disgust, "Lovebirds. Poor chumps don't know what they're in for."

# TWELVE

The scream of 75mm-shells filled the hot desert air, followed instants later by explosions as they landed. The thick hull of the General Grant tank muffled the sounds but couldn't shut them entirely.

The atmosphere inside the tank was stifling. The stink of oil and petrol mixed with the acrid reek of human sweat that was motivated as much by fear as by heat. Months spent commanding a tank in battle had taught Captain Neville Sharp that fear sweat had a different smell to it. No wonder animals, with their sensitive noses, could perceive fear so well in humans.

Another blast came from their right. Jeremy Royce called from the driver's seat, "I think they're gettin' the range, Captain!"

"Hard left," Sharp said from behind him.

"That'll just put us in range o' that other bastard," Royce muttered.

Sharp pretended he hadn't heard the comment from his driver. The middle of a battle was no place for dressing down a subordinate. That could be done later—if they survived. If they didn't, well, it wouldn't matter, Sharp thought.

With the hatch on top of the turret closed, Sharp couldn't sit in the commander's seat. Instead he stood behind Royce on the forward left side of the tank's crew compartment. The radio operator's seat, manned by Bert Crimmens, was on the right side of the compartment. Behind Sharp, Tom Hamilton sat on the fixed stool that served as the gunner's seat. From there, Hamilton could load and fire both the 75mm- and 37mm-guns. In tanks with a five-man crew, the fifth member functioned as a loader for both guns, but Sharp made do with a four-man crew. The extra man always made the already cramped quarters inside the tank seem too small for Sharp to get his breath, so he dispensed with the services of a loader. A touch of claustrophobia on his part, he supposed, but he'd had no idea he was so afflicted until he became a tank commander.

The inside of an M3 General Grant medium tank was no place for a man who couldn't stand small, enclosed spaces.

With its engine roaring and its treads clanking, the tank veered left as Royce pulled back on the rubber grip of the left-hand steering lever, slowing the track on that side. Sharp bent and peered over Royce's shoulder through the driver's vision port, resting his hand on the back of the driver's seat as he did so. He saw the German Panzer tank a couple of hundred yards ahead of them. There was another Panzer to the right, the one that had forced them into the turn.

"Ready, Tom?" Sharp called.

"Ready, Captain," the gunner replied as he squinted through the sighting periscope.

"Fire!"

Hamilton's thumb jabbed the firing button in the center of the wheel that controlled the big gun's limited transverse movement. The blast shook the men inside the tank. At the same time, Sharp saw smoke and flame belch from the muzzle of the German tank's cannon. Wouldn't it be bizarre, he thought, if the two shells impacted each other in midair and blew up?

That didn't happen. Instead the round from the Panzer landed about ten yards in front of the British tank, and the resulting explosion pelted the tank with shrapnel, gravel, and sand. Royce ducked as a couple of the little flying missiles came in through the vision port. Sharp felt a stinging in his left hand and looked down to see that a sliver of metal had pinned the web of skin between his thumb and forefinger to the back of the driver's seat. He reached over with his other hand, wrenched out the sliver, and dropped it to the floor of the crew compartment. Blood began to well from the minor wound. Sharp ignored it and asked, "What about our shot?"

"Can't see," Hamilton complained. "There's too much bloody dust! Wait a minute . . . Looks like a hit, Captain! We knocked some of the armor off the hull. The Panzer's not disabled, though. It's still coming at us."

"Can you put another in the same place?" Sharp asked. If the

Panzer's armor was damaged, a second shot stood a better chance of penetrating it.

"I can try," Hamilton said, but he didn't sound convinced of his ability to do so.

"Don't just try, Tom," Sharp said. "Do it."

"Captain!" Bert Crimmens called from his seat, where he was hunched over with the earphones of the Wireless Set No. 19 clamped to his ears. "Word from HQ, sir! We're to pull back immediately!"

"Nothing I'd like better," Sharp muttered as blood dripped from his wounded hand. "But I don't think the Jerries are in any mood to let us do that."

Hamilton had swiveled around on his stool and reached into one of the boxes of 75mm ammunition stored on the floor of the tank behind the cannon. Before he could pull out one of the shells, Sharp ordered, "Not the normal round, Tom. Use the M-forty-eight."

Hamilton glanced up and gave Sharp a nod. The High Explosive M48 Supercharge round was the most powerful ammunition the tank carried. It packed the most potent punch of any of the shells. Hamilton pulled the lever that opened the gun's breech and slid the M48 shell into it. When he had the breech dogged shut again, he put his eye to the periscope and began trying to aim for the next shot.

Another blast sounded close behind the tank. That round had come from the first Panzer, Sharp knew. He had been watching the one in front of them, and its gun had not fired. If his tank could dispose of that immediate threat, then he and his men could turn their attention to the other German tank.

For a second he thought about the news Bert had relayed from the wireless. He had an order to pull back. He could disengage from these Jerries, turn around, and run. The General Grants were faster than the German Mark IV Panzers. Sharp was confident that his tank could outdistance the heavier pursuers. But he doubted that it could get out of range of the German's cannon in time. At maximum elevation, the 75mm-gun could throw a shell a long way.

If he was going to die, Sharp decided, he wanted it to be with his face toward the enemy, not his back. He realized that he was making that decision for his men as well as for himself, but that was why he was in command of the tank. It was his job to make the difficult decisions that might cost men's lives.

The tank in front of them fired again, and the General Grant shuddered as a huge explosion rocked it. Bert Crimmens cried out in an involuntary reaction to the nearness of the blast. Royce filled the hot, foul air with curses. Hamilton picked himself up from where he had fallen on the floor.

Sharp was gripping the back of the driver's seat again. "How's our power?" he shouted at Royce.

Royce checked the gauges on the instrument panel and called over his shoulder, "Full power! The treads seem to be all right too. I think that shell glanced off the turret just before it exploded!"

They had been lucky, Sharp thought. The Panzer had almost scored a direct hit on them. "How about it, Tom?" Sharp asked the gunner. "Have you got your shot lined up?"

"Half a mo' . . . Got it!"

"Fire!"

The cannon recoiled against its shock absorbers as the thunder of its firing filled the crew compartment. With his eye glued to the periscope lens, Hamilton let out a jubilant whoop. "Got it! Dead on, skipper! The bugger's going up in flames!"

Most of the time, Hamilton was the stolid sort, not given to overexcitement. Right now, though, he was thrilled by the success of his shot, and so were the other members of the crew. Sharp tried to keep his own excitement under control. They still had the other Panzer to deal with.

"Hard right, Sergeant Royce!"

"Aye, sir," Royce grunted as he worked the steering levers and sent the tank into a right-hand turn. "Are we goin' straight at the other one?"

"It worked once," Sharp said as he bent over to peer out the vision port. His face was grim. "Let's see if it'll work again."

If it didn't, probably they would all wind up dead. But he didn't have to say that, because all four of them knew it.

Sharp straightened and stepped back, moving around Hamilton to enter the turret. He reached up, unfastened the hatch, and threw it open. Then he climbed onto the commander's seat and lifted his head through the open hatch. His goggles were pushed up on his leather helmet. He pulled them down and squinted through them. The German tank was no more than a hundred yards away now as the General Grant turned toward it. As Sharp wrapped his hands around the grips of the .30-caliber machine gun mounted just outside the hatch, he saw the Panzer's cannon fire. He knew he was just being stubborn, perhaps foolishly so, but he stayed where he was as the shell whistled toward his tank.

The round missed, exploding to the left as the tank continued to turn. The blast was near enough to pelt Sharp with gravel and sand. He squeezed the grips of the machine gun, activating its trigger. The weapon chattered loudly and its grips jumped in Sharp's hands as it poured lead toward the remaining Panzer.

It would be ever so nice if an airplane were to fly over right now on a bombing run and drop a few hundred pounds of high explosive down the throat of that bloody German, Sharp thought. But he knew that wasn't going to happen. If he and his men were going to be saved, they would have to see to their own salvation.

He kept firing the machine gun, hoping at least a few of the bullets would penetrate the openings on the Panzer and distract the Jerries while Hamilton finished loading and sighting. Through the Interphone, he asked, "How are you coming along, Tom?"

"All loaded and ready to go, Captain," Hamilton replied.

"I'll leave it up to you, then," Sharp said. "Fire when ready."

He thought he heard an audible gulp in his earphones, but it was difficult to be sure with so much noise going on. He knew he was putting a lot of faith in Hamilton, but the man was a fine gunner. He could do the job.

In the meantime, Sharp kept up the machine-gun fire until the belt of ammunition ran out.

No sooner had the machine gun fallen silent than the cannon roared. Sharp leaned forward, every muscle in his body tense. The shell flew too fast through the air to be followed with the eye, but a second later Sharp saw the result. An explosion sent dust and sand geysering high in the air next to the Panzer's left-hand tread, so close that the blast seemed almost to come from underneath the German tank. When the dust cleared, Sharp saw that the Panzer had lurched to a halt. Its left-hand tread was twisted and wrecked. The Panzer was paralyzed.

"Right!" Sharp shouted to Royce. "Hard right! Circle him!"

With the German tank immobilized, the General Grant could destroy it at leisure now. The British tank could circle, stop, fire a round into the Panzer, and start moving again before the German gunner could draw a bead on it. Sharp knew that—and if he knew it, so did the German commander. Sharp halfway expected to see the Panzer's crew come boiling out of it. None of the Germans showed themselves, though.

From inside the tank, Bert called, "Headquarters says to withdraw to the east!"

Sharp bent his head so that he was looking down through the turret at the wireless operator. "What?"

"Withdraw to the east!" Bert repeated. "We're to fall back to the Egyptian border!"

Sharp bit off a curse. "My God," he said under his breath, "they're abandoning Tobruk."

Ever since Rommel had begun his systematic destruction of the Gazala Line, the British and their Indian, Free French, and Australian allies had been falling back toward the port city of Tobruk. The year before, Tobruk had been besieged by the Germans, and it had not fallen. Now it was likely to be a different story, especially if the tanks that formed a defensive line in the desert south of the city were withdrawn.

But Sharp had his orders, and he had to follow them. General Auchinleck was conceding Tobruk so that he could save his tank corps. That made sense from a strategic standpoint.

Sharp just hoped that the poor bastards trapped in Tobruk would understand the strategy.

"Captain?" Bert asked. "What are we goin' to do?"

"We're going to follow orders and head for the Egyptian border," Sharp said. "But before we go, we're going to blow the hell out of that Jerry."

"I'm loaded again, skipper," Hamilton said over the Interphone. "Prepare to fire . . ."

Sharp's voice trailed off as he spotted something from the corner of his eye. He turned his head to look toward the south and saw several columns of dust rising into the hot desert air. The only thing that could kick up that much dust was a large group of tanks, and the only tanks down there now were German ones. More Panzers were on the way, a lot more.

"Blast it all!" Sharp said.

"Captain?" Bert asked. "What is it?"

Sharp ignored the question and said, "Bert, advise headquarters that we are complying with the order and will make all due speed east."

"We'll need a petrol lorry to meet us before we get to the border," Royce put in.

"Tell them about that too, Bert," Sharp instructed the wireless operator. "Tom, you'll have one more shot before we have to get out of here, so make it count."

"Yes, sir."

A moment later, Sharp ordered Royce to stop the tank. "Lock on quickly, Tom," he said. "And as soon as the round's on its way, get us out of here, Sergeant Royce."

"Yes, sir."

The General Grant lurched to a halt. Sharp gripped the edge of the turret to brace himself. In the distance, he could see the turret of the Panzer beginning to swivel toward the British tank. The 75mm-gun on the German tanks was mounted on the turret rather than the hull, so it was much more maneuverable. Still, it took time to move the gun, and time was something the Germans no longer had.

The round that Hamilton fired a second later smashed into the turning turret and lifted it off the hull of the Panzer. It was a perfect shot. Black smoke poured from the destroyed turret. They had crippled the Panzer, and then killed it.

As well as the men inside it, Sharp thought. None of them would escape the inferno that was now blazing inside the other tank.

He clenched a fist and struck it on the edge of the hatch. The gesture was partially one of triumph, but there was some frustration contained in it as well. As soon as the Panzer's tread had been blown off, its commander should have ordered his men to get out of there. There had been no way for them to save the tank, but they could have saved their own lives. Sharp would have given them time to get far enough away from the Panzer before he blew it to pieces.

But the members of the German crew had stayed where they were, and not only that, they still had been trying to fight back even as the shell that meant their deaths screamed toward them. They were either brave men or fools—or both—and Sharp didn't particularly relish killing them.

The General Grant was moving again, heading east toward the Egyptian border as ordered. It left the burning hulks of two Panzer tanks behind it, but the dust from the south was closing in rapidly on the twin pillars of smoke rising into the sky. They had almost waited too long, Sharp thought. Much more of a delay and the jaws of the German wolf—or rather the Desert Fox—would have closed on them.

But not today. This battle was over, and they would all live to fight again.

# THIRTEEN

"It's about time I met this girl of yours," Dale said as he knotted his tie in front of one of the mirrors in the barracks latrine. "What did you say her friend's name is?"

"Betty," Joe replied. He smoothed down his close-cropped dark hair as he looked in the mirror in front of him. "At least I think that's what Melinda said."

"She'd better be cute, that's all I've got to say. It's been a long time since I went on a blind date."

"Melinda says she's very nice."

Dale rolled his eyes. "Very nice? Hell, why would I want to go out with a very nice girl? Can't you find me one who's not nice?"

"You seem to be able to find that kind just fine on your own, judging by the amount of money you spend every time you go over to Giza."

"Hey, it's my money. I'll spend it however I want to."

"That's not what I'm saying. I just—" Joe shook his head, giving up. Arguing with Dale was a waste of time. It always had been and probably always would be. "Just be nice to her, okay, no matter what she looks like."

"All right. But she better not be too ugly."

They left a few minutes later, their overseas caps cocked at a jaunty angle. A cab took them into downtown Cairo. They were supposed to meet Melinda and Betty at the Continental Hotel for an evening of dancing in the hotel's roof garden.

On the way, the cab passed a knot of young Egyptian men who were shouting something and brandishing placards on which Arabic words had been written in bold black strokes. Dale looked out the rear window of the taxi at them, and several of the men shook their fists at him. Dale frowned and asked, "What the hell are they so upset about?"

Joe shot a glance at their driver, who didn't appear to be paying any attention to what was being said in the backseat of his vehicle. "They're supporters of the Germans," Joe said quietly.

"What? That's crazy!"

Joe shook his head. "I've learned a little bit of Arabic. I think those signs said something like *Welcome, General Rommel.*"

Dale snorted. "What a bunch of maroons. Rommel's still a long way from here."

"Not that far. Mersa Matruh's less than two hundred miles from here. El Alamein's only sixty miles from Alexandria, and that's where the Eighth Army is now."

"Yeah, yeah," Dale said with a frown. "But the Great Auk will stop them there."

Joe leaned back against the seat and crossed his arms. He wished he had as much confidence in General Auchinleck as Dale did. To tell the truth, though, after everything that had happened this summer, he wasn't sure the German advance would stop until Rommel's Panzers and the rest of the Deutsche Afrika Korps were rolling down the streets of Cairo.

Following Rommel's obliteration of the Gazala Line, the withdrawal of the Royal Tank Corps into Egypt, and the fall of Tobruk on 21 June after a short siege by the Germans, it looked inevitable that the Germans would smash any resistance before them and continue east. Rommel had, in fact, advanced to Mersa Matruh without much trouble. It looked bad for Alexandria and Cairo, so bad that orders came down to the British Embassy and Eighth Army headquarters that important papers, codebooks, etc., were all to be burned rather than allowing them to fall into German hands.

But then General Sir Claude Auchinleck had left Cairo and traveled by plane to Mersa Matruh himself, practically daring the German Stukas to shoot him down. Rommel was on the outskirts of the city. The Great Auk relieved General Neal Ritchie, field commander of the Eighth Army, and took command himself, ordering an immediate withdrawal to El Alamein, another Mediterranean port city some eighty miles farther east. It was another retreat before the inexorable German advance, another blow to the spirits of the British and their few American allies in Alexandria and Cairo. . . .

But El Alamein was as far as Auchinleck intended to go.

Cairo was nothing if not resilient. When word reached the city that the Eighth Army was digging in at El Alamein, the sense of crisis and impending doom that had gripped Cairo began to fade. Of course, not everyone considered the string of German victories and British retreats a bad thing. A sizable number of Egyptians such as the ones Joe and Dale had seen earlier believed that Cairo and indeed all of Egypt would be better off with the Nazis than they were with the British. Joe couldn't understand that sentiment, but he knew it existed. It seemed to him that all anyone had to do was look at what Hitler and his thugs had done in France and Poland and all the other countries that had been in their way to see that nobody was better off with the Nazis. Sure, the British looked down on the Egyptians, calling them wogs and regarding them as inferior, but at least they weren't killing people right and left.

"I hope you're right about El Alamein," Joe muttered.

Dale nodded. "I am. You'll see." He rubbed his hands together. "Right now, I'm more worried about these dames we're supposed to meet."

Joe started to tell his brother that Melinda wasn't a "dame," but then he decided not to bother. He'd been dating Melinda for several weeks now, and although he kept telling himself he wasn't in love with her, making it sound convincing was becoming more and more difficult. He thought about her all the time, even when he was supposed to have all his attention on the work he was doing with the British tankies. Not every date ended up with them in bed at Melinda's flat, but enough of them had so that Joe was firmly under her spell and knew it. She was a bold, inventive lover, and she inspired him to be bold and inventive too. And Dale thought he was such a goody two-shoes . . .

To tell the truth, he and Dale didn't know each other that well anymore. That bothered Joe, but there was nothing he could do about it. While they were still back home in Chicago, Joe had felt that he could keep an eye on his little brother and keep Dale from going too wild. That was why he had arranged things so that Dale could attend the University of Chicago with him. But now their fates were in the hands of other people. At any time, new orders might split them up, might even send them halfway around the world from each other, the way Adam Bergman had been sent to the Pacific. That uncertainty gnawed at Joe, as did the fact that Major Richardson had almost recruited him into intelligence work. Dale didn't know anything about that. At least Dale's adventures, like going off into the desert and getting into combat not once but twice, weren't secrets. Joe didn't like keeping secrets from his brother.

"There's the Continental," Dale said. "Ready to go?"

"I'm ready," Joe said. He tugged his overseas cap down a little tighter on his head as he followed Dale out of the cab.

They went into the lobby of the hotel, which was populated, like most places in Cairo, primarily by British servicemen and servicewomen. Joe spotted Melinda standing near the elevators with a tall, dark-haired woman who wore a khaki shirt, jodhpurs, and a cap similar to a U.S. Army overseas cap. He pointed out the two women and said to Dale, "There they are."

"Oh, hell," Dale said. "I hope mine is the one in the dress, because the other one looks like a man."

"No, Melinda's the one wearing the dress."

"Shit. I was afraid you were going to say that."

Joe gripped Dale's arm above the elbow. "Come on. And behave yourself. I don't want you being rude to the poor woman."

"Poor woman is right," Dale muttered. "Any gal who looks like that . . ."

Joe tightened his grip, and Dale shut up. They made their way across the crowded lobby toward the elevators. Melinda saw them coming and waved. So did the other woman, although her gesture was somewhat tentative.

As Joe and Dale came up, Melinda stepped forward to give Joe a quick kiss on the lips. "Hello, love," she said. She turned to Dale. "And this must be that handsome brother of yours I've heard so much about."

"This is Dale," Joe said, not commenting on the handsome part of Melinda's statement. "Dale, this is Miss Melinda Thorp-Davies."

Dale took the hand that Melinda held out to him. "Pleased to meet you. Joe's told me a lot about you."

"Not everything, I hope," Melinda said with a wicked grin and a laugh. The other woman laughed with her, sounding a little nervous. Still holding Dale's hand, Melinda turned him toward the other woman. "And this is Betty Rawlinson."

Dale took Betty's hand, and Joe was glad to see that his brother was making an effort to be at least a little polite. "Hello," Dale said. "Pleased to meet you."

"Likewise, I'm sure." From the looks of it, Joe thought Betty's grip was probably pretty strong. Dale seemed surprised by it, anyway.

Really, she wasn't that bad-looking, Joe thought. A little horse-faced, maybe, but hell, from what he'd seen, horsy British women weren't that uncommon. She didn't have much in the bosom department, either, but her hips curved nicely in the jodhpurs, her brown eyes were clear and intelligent, and her smile had a certain charm to it. Her attractiveness paled next to Melinda's, of course.

Melinda linked her arm with Joe's. "Let's go up to the roof garden, shall we? I hear the musicians there are excellent, and I'm ready to dance."

"Me too," Joe said.

Like a gentleman, Dale offered his arm to Betty, and she took it. Joe rang for the elevator, and the four of them stood there waiting for it.

Joe leaned forward to ask across Melinda and Dale, "What do you do, Betty?"

"I'm a clerk at Eighth Army HQ," she replied.

"I guess that's how you two girls met, since you work for Major Richardson, Melinda?"

"That's right. Betty works in the cartography section, don't you, love?"

Betty nodded, and Dale said, "Cartography . . . that's maps, right?"

"Indeed. My section is responsible for producing all the maps used at headquarters."

"Must be pretty interesting," Joe said. "You get to see everything that's going on."

"Not everything. Much of it is classified eyes only, and I'm lower than that."

"What's the scoop on El Alamein these days?" Dale asked.

Betty lowered her gaze to the floor. "I'm afraid I really can't discuss—"

She was saved from having to go on by the arrival of the elevator. An elderly, distinguished Egyptian operator slid the elevator door open and beckoned them inside.

"The roof garden," Joe said.

The operator gave him a grave nod and then closed the door after the four young people had gotten in. He moved the control lever and sent the elevator rising toward the roof in a smooth motion.

The strains of "Begin the Beguine" filled the air as the elevator door opened. The Egyptian bandleader was no Artie Shaw, but he had his boys doing a passable job on the song. The music reminded Joe of home, and he felt a sudden pang deep in his chest. It was moments like this that reminded him he was halfway around the world from Chicago, halfway around the world from the place where he had grown up and, except for Dale, from the people he loved. And he was very aware too that he was only twenty-three years old, with most of his life ahead of him—if the war allowed him to live it.

Melinda leaned her head closer to his as they left the elevator. "What's wrong?" she asked. "You turned rather pale there for a moment."

Joe shook his head. "It's nothing. I'm all right."

"You're sure?"

"Yeah."

"All right, then. You've no excuse for not dancing with me."

"I don't want an excuse," Joe told her. "I just want to hold you."

# FOURTEEN

Tables were scattered across one end of the roof garden. The bandstand was on the far side of an open area used for dancing. Dale tossed his cap on an empty table and motioned for a waiter to bring drinks. Then he took Betty's hand and led her onto the dance floor. Joe followed suit, leaving his cap on the table, along with Melinda's handbag.

He'd never been much of a dancer back home, but he found that it was easier when he had a partner as light on her feet and as beautiful as Melinda. They glided and swooped around the floor as the band segued into a hot Dorsey number. For a moment, it struck Joe as odd that he was hearing the same songs here in Cairo that he could have been listening to back home. He supposed that music really was universal. Then he forgot about such ironies and concentrated on the lovely young woman he was holding in his arms. That wasn't hard to do.

When they got back to the table after dancing through several songs, they found drinks waiting for them. The glasses contained rather weak highballs. Joe sipped his and was glad it wasn't stronger. He wanted to keep a clear head tonight. Any time he was out with Dale, odd things had a habit of happening.

The evening was a pleasant one. The four of them danced and drank and danced some more. Dale seemed to warm up to Betty. He listened as she talked about her work—what little she could discuss because of security regulations—and he laughed whenever she made a joke. He even held her hand for a while as they sat at the table, Joe noted.

When the ladies excused themselves to go to the powder room,

Joe leaned forward and said in a quiet voice, "See, Betty's not so bad, now is she?"

Dale shrugged. "She's an okay kid, I guess, for a British girl. You know what they say about them, though. They're pretty chilly in the sack."

Joe thought, *He doesn't know about Melinda.* He said, "You just met her tonight. You can't be thinking about taking her to bed already."

"Hey, there's a war on, pal," Dale said as he took out a cigarette and his lighter. "A guy can't afford to waste any time these days. There may not be any tomorrow."

Joe frowned. He didn't like that sort of thinking, but he had to admit that Dale had a point. Not about rushing into bed with every girl he met, necessarily, but there was no denying that as long as the world was at war, uncertainties would abound. Pleasure had to be taken where it could be found. Besides, considering the way he and Melinda had been carrying on, disapproving too much of what Dale had in mind would just make him a hypocrite. Betty Rawlinson was a grown woman, Joe reminded himself, perfectly capable of deciding what she did or didn't want to do.

"Just be careful," Joe said. "Betty's a nice girl. You don't want to hurt her."

"I don't plan on hurting anybody." Dale lit the Lucky Strike and tucked his lighter away, then glanced toward the alcove where the powder room was located. "Here come the girls."

Joe glanced in that direction and saw Melinda and Betty coming out of the alcove. At that moment, a man passing by and not watching where he was going bumped into Melinda. She stumbled ahead a step before righting herself. Joe felt a flash of anger at the clumsy man who had run into her.

Dale had been lounging sideways in his chair, but now he bolted upright. "Hey!" he exclaimed around the cigarette clenched between his lips. "Did you see that?"

"I saw a guy bump into Melinda—"

"He took something out of her handbag. He's a damned pickpocket!"

Joe shot to his feet and broke into a run across the room. Dale was right behind him. Just like they were back in one of the sandlots of their youth, pretending to be Jim Thorpe or Red Grange, they weaved through the crowded room like a couple of halfbacks avoiding tackles. Several British soldiers shouted questions at them, and one woman even screamed, but Joe and Dale ignored all the distractions. A man caught hold of Joe's arm. Joe shrugged him off. The commotion had alerted the sneak thief. The man dashed toward a door that opened onto the stairs.

If the pickpocket got onto the stairs, he stood a good chance of getting away. The elevator could lower itself to the ground floor faster than a man could run down all the flights of stairs, but there was nothing saying he had to try to get out of the hotel. He could lose himself on any of the floors between the street and the roof garden. It would take a room-by-room search to find him, and Joe knew the hotel staff wouldn't go to that much trouble over a simple pickpocket. The Cairo police wouldn't care, either. And there was the problem of identifying him, as well. Joe hadn't gotten that good a look at the man, and he suspected Melinda hadn't either.

He hoped Dale was right and hadn't just imagined seeing the man lift something from Melinda's bag.

The pickpocket jerked the stairwell door open. Before he had time to enter the stairwell, though, Joe and Dale burst from the crowd. Dale left his feet in a flying tackle. He hit the man from behind, and they both fell forward, through the door and onto the landing. "Dale!" Joe shouted, afraid that his brother was going to go tumbling down those stairs and maybe break his neck. Dale and the man he had tackled had fallen short of the stairs, Joe saw to his relief. They were wrestling around there now.

Joe moved up to stand over them. Dale was trying to pin the thief. The man gave a sudden lurch and roll that sent Dale toppling to the side. The pickpocket shoved loose from Dale's grip and tried to get up.

He ran right into Joe, who grabbed his arms and jerked him around so that the man was facing away from him. In a flash, Joe had the man's left arm bent behind his back. Joe's right arm went around the man's neck in a choke hold. "Hang on to him, Joe!" Dale yelled as he scrambled to his feet.

Joe backed away from the stairwell, hauling the thief with him. He was aware that the crowd in the roof garden had converged around him, forming quite an audience. Somewhere nearby, someone was blowing a whistle. Probably calling the cops, he thought.

Melinda pushed her way through the crowd, followed by Betty. "Joe!" she said. "Joe, are you all right?"

Joe didn't loosen his grip on the man he had caught. "Yeah, I'm fine," he said between clenched teeth. "I got him for you, Melinda. He didn't get away."

"Got who? I don't know this man!"

"He's a dip . . . a pickpocket," Dale said as Melinda looked confused by his original explanation. "I saw him take something out of your handbag."

"Oh!" Melinda put a hand to her mouth in surprise, and then started pawing through her purse.

"I did not steal anything!" the man insisted. "Let me go!"

"Fat chance, buddy," Joe said. "My brother saw you steal something from the lady."

"Maybe we should search him," Dale suggested.

"No!" Melinda said. She looked up from her bag. "I mean, there's nothing missing. He couldn't have stolen anything."

Betty asked, "Are you sure, dear?"

"I'm certain," Melinda said. "I don't carry that much with me when I go out. I know everything that was in my bag, and it's all still here."

Dale shook his head. "That's nuts. I'm sure I saw him take something."

"You must have made a mistake."

"You see?" Joe's prisoner said. "Now release me!"

With great reluctance, Joe let go of the man and took a step back. The man jerked on his coat to straighten it and turned to glare at Joe and Dale.

"You men are lunatics! But I see that you are Americans, so perhaps I should expect nothing less."

"Hey!" Dale said, clenching his fists. "What are you, some kind of wise guy—"

"Wiser than you will ever be," the man said.

Joe put up a hand as Dale stepped forward. "Hold on," he said. "This is bad enough already. We don't want it to turn into a brawl."

He wanted to believe his brother. Dale didn't have the greatest track record in the world when it came to honesty, but Joe didn't see any reason why Dale would lie about seeing this guy stealing something from Melinda's bag.

On second glance, though, the man didn't appear the type to be a sneak thief. He was in his forties, with dark blond hair dusted with gray. His suit was moderately expensive, as were his shoes and tie. He didn't have a British accent, and he sure as hell wasn't an Egyptian or some other sort of Arab.

In a cold voice, the man said, "Apologize immediately, or I shall file a formal protest with the American and British embassies."

"Yeah, and what makes you think we care about that, ace?" Dale said. "What are you, some kind of diplomatic muckety-muck?"

The man drew himself up and glowered at Dale. "I am a Swiss citizen."

"Hell," Joe said under his breath. "Take it easy, Dale. Switzerland's supposed to be a neutral country."

"Switzerland *is* neutral, you fool," the man said to Joe. "I work for one of my country's financial institutions, and I am here on business . . . though I certainly owe no explanations to you buffoons."

Melinda put a hand on Joe's arm. "Please, Joe, don't make any more of a scene. It's an honest mistake, that's all."

Joe looked at her. "You're sure nothing's missing?"

"Nothing."

Joe sighed, nodded, and looked at the Swiss banker again. "I'm sorry. It was just a misunderstanding."

The man crossed his arms and looked like he was waiting for something. He didn't seem any less angry. After a couple of seconds, Joe caught on and nudged Dale with his elbow.

"Sorry," Dale said with as much ill feeling as he could muster and still pretend to apologize.

Melinda said to the man, "Please accept my friends' apologies and forgive them. They were just trying to help me."

After a moment, the man nodded. "I suppose it would serve no purpose to bring the authorities in on this matter. I wish only to go on about my business with no further delays."

"Hold it a second," Dale said. "If you didn't heist anything from the lady's bag, why'd you run when you saw us coming after you?"

"Because you looked like madmen," the man answered without hesitation. "I was afraid you were going to attack me—and I was correct."

Joe couldn't argue with that. He might have been spooked too if the same thing had happened to him. "Look, we really are sorry," he said to the man. "If there's anything we can do to make it up to you . . ."

The man sniffed and brushed off his coat. "Nothing. Just leave me alone."

"Yeah, sure." Joe took hold of Dale's arm. "Come on. Let's go back and sit down."

"Yeah, yeah." Dale went reluctantly, still throwing angry glances over his shoulder at the man, who went to the elevator and waited for it. The man still looked huffy, as if the swelling in his injured dignity hadn't gone down yet.

When the four of them got back to their table and the music and dancing resumed, Melinda gave a little laugh and said, "Well, that was certainly a bit of excitement."

"I still think I saw him take something out of your purse," Dale said.

"I know you do, but it's impossible."

Joe said, "We all make mistakes, Dale. Even you."

"Yeah, well . . . You believed me."

"Don't remind me."

The waiter brought fresh drinks, and soon everything was back to normal. Dale started telling a story about his racing days on the dirt tracks of the Midwest, and Melinda and Betty both listened with expressions of rapt attention on their faces. They laughed when Dale reached the end of the story.

Joe just smiled. He knew what had happened; he had been there, after all. And despite everything he had said, he wasn't completely convinced that Dale had made a mistake. Dale had exceptionally good eyesight, and he'd had no reason to make up a story about the man being a pickpocket. Not even Dale raised a ruckus like that without something happening to set it off.

Melinda had insisted that nothing was missing from her bag, however. Joe had to believe her. She had no reason to lie, either. All he really knew was that he had a bad feeling and he couldn't quite shake it.

And for once that bad feeling didn't have anything to do with General Erwin Rommel and the rest of the *Deutsche Afrika Korps* barreling toward Cairo.

# FIFTEEN

The route taken by the convoy carrying the Marines of Combat Team 2 led far to the south, looping around Samoa. Once past Samoa, the ships turned toward the northwest and the Fiji Islands.

Though there still had been no official confirmation of their destination, Adam had seen enough maps of the South Pacific region to know what lay beyond Fiji: the Solomon Islands and New Guinea, all of which were in the hands of the Japanese. As long as the Japs were that close to Australia, they posed a threat. Adam had no doubt it would be the Marines who dealt with that threat.

Though the ships were crowded, the various companies took turns conducting drills wherever they could find a little open space on deck. Adam was watching his platoon go through one such drill on a morning several weeks after the ships had left San Diego. The hour was early, but the air already held a stifling heat. Dark sweat stains marked the green fatigues the men wore. There were irregular white blotches on the uniforms too where previous sweat stains had dried. For a while, the officers had tried to get the enlisted men to keep their greens clean, but most had given it up as futile. In this heat, even freshly laundered uniforms looked like hell after they had been worn for half an hour.

Adam looked around as he heard somebody yell, "Land ho!" just like they were in a pirate movie or something. Several Marines were lounging along the ship's railing, waiting for their company's turn to drill, and one of them was pointing ahead and to starboard. That would be north-northwest, Adam thought. At least, he believed that was right. For a landlubber like him, it was hard to keep track of the convoy's course.

After weeks of seeing nothing but ocean, the sighting of land was a big deal. Drilling was forgotten as men rushed to the railing to hang over it and stare across the water toward the dark smudge on the horizon. Adam thought about trying to get his men under control but then decided not to crack down on them. It had been an unpleasant voyage. He didn't know if they were going to be stopping at that island up ahead, but he couldn't blame the men for being interested in it.

That couldn't be one of the Fijis already. They hadn't come far enough for that, Adam told himself. The ships steamed on and gradually drew nearer the island. While the enlisted men watched and chattered about what this might mean, the officers were summoned to a meeting in one of the wardrooms. The commanding officer, Colonel John M. Arthur, explained the situation.

"We're going to be stopping for a liberty up here at Tonga," Colonel Arthur said. "The island is actually called Tonga Tabu. We'll be there the rest of today and tonight, but we'll be sailing again first thing tomorrow morning. Our destination will then be the Fiji Islands, which will serve as the staging area for further operations."

Adam, Ted Nash, Barney Gelhart, and the other junior officers exchanged glances. They all had a pretty good idea what those further operations would be. They would involve an invasion of one or more of the islands currently held by the Japanese.

"I want all our men to get ashore if possible," Colonel Arthur went on. "This will probably be their last liberty for quite some time."

For some of them, it would be their last liberty ever. Adam gave a little shake of his head as he tried to force that grim thought out of his mind.

"We'll take on a few stores while we're here, and any men who need medical attention will report to the U.S.S. *Solace*, one of our hospital ships that's docked here."

Adam stiffened on the folding chair, hardly able to believe what he was hearing. The *Solace*? That was Catherine's ship! Adam's hands had been resting on his knees as he listened to the colonel. Now they tightened as he had to force himself not to bolt to his feet and rush up on deck so that he could stare, as the enlisted men were doing at the approaching island. Catherine was there somewhere, and if he had liberty, that meant he could see her!

He had known the hospital ship where she served was somewhere in the South Pacific. There had been enough hints in her letters for him to figure out that much. But he hadn't known its exact location, and Catherine had never tried to tell him, knowing the military censors wouldn't let information like that go through. The possibility of a reunion with her was an unexpected gift that made his heart pound in his chest.

Barney Gelhart leaned over closer to him and whispered, "You okay, Bergman? You look like somebody just punched you in the gut."

"I'm fine," Adam whispered back. "I'm okay."

As a matter of fact, right now he was more okay than he had been for months.

*  *  *

Catherine watched Phil Lange walk along the deck of the *Solace* for his morning exercise, Missy close beside him, ready to reach out and steady him if he started to fall.

That wasn't going to happen, Catherine thought. Phil had made an excellent recovery from his wounds. His cracked ribs had knitted with no problem, his wrenched knee was a hundred percent again, and although he had a scar on his forehead from the gash that had been there, Dr. Johnston, the ship's chief medical officer, expected no complications from that injury. The most serious injury had been the bullet wound in Phil's arm, and that had healed as well. He had lost weight and was a little weak from being laid up for weeks, but other than that, Phil was fine.

The state of his health was so good, in fact, that within the next few days he was going to be released back to active duty.

Catherine knew that, but Missy didn't. The news was going to come as a blow. Missy had enjoyed having Phil on board so that she could look after him and make a fuss over him. Not to mention the other things they had been doing lately in odd, tucked-away corners of the ship. Missy was helping Phil's recuperation in her own way.

Soon that would be over. Catherine felt a little guilty for keeping that from Missy, but she rationalized her decision by telling herself that Missy and Phil deserved to enjoy the time they still had together. When the moment came for them to be separated, it would be difficult enough. No need for them to brood over it beforehand.

Catherine knew that from experience. She'd had to say good-bye to Adam so many times now. When he had passed through Pearl Harbor on his way to Wake Island the previous autumn, he hadn't even said good-bye to her, choosing instead to slip out of the bungalow while she was asleep. She had been furious with him for doing that, but she knew now it might have been the best thing. If he had died on Wake, her last memory of him would have been lying snuggled in his arms, warm and safe and loved.

"Be careful," Missy said to Phil.

"I am being careful," he said. "There's no need to be such a mother hen, Missy."

"Oh, I'm a mother hen, am I?"

"I didn't mean anything bad by it—"

"Why don't I try clucking at you? Maybe you'd actually listen to me then."

"I listen to you." Phil grinned as he turned to walk back the other direction along the deck. "What choice do I have?"

Catherine shook her head and smiled as she turned away from them and walked over to the ship's railing. Let them banter with each other. It was good for them. She rested her hands on the railing and looked off to the south, a hot breeze blowing in her face and tugging on the strands of short blond hair that strayed from under her white cap.

She frowned a little as she spotted something out on the ocean. At first it was only a cluster of small black dots, but as they came closer she realized they were ships. Her hands tightened on the railing as a touch of fear hit her. What if they were Japanese ships? The Japs weren't supposed to be anywhere around here, but they had pulled sneak attacks in the past, hadn't they?

She shook her head as reason overcame her fright. The Navy had patrol planes in the air all the time. If that were a Jap fleet out there, the word would have reached Tonga Tabu by now. They were probably American vessels.

That guess was confirmed a few minutes later when Dr. Johnston came on deck and said to the nurses gathered there, "Better get below, ladies, and take your patients with you. According to the radio message I just received, we've got a bunch of Marines on the way."

"Wounded?" Catherine asked.

Johnston shook his head. "No, they're troops from the States, stopping here for liberty on their way to Fiji. But it's possible some of them may need medical attention that they weren't able to get in their ships' infirmaries."

Catherine's eyes widened. Troops from the States? Adam's last letter had said that the Second Marines were leaving San Diego and sailing for some unknown destination in the Pacific. Could Adam be on one of those ships that were now approaching the island? It seemed entirely possible to Catherine. More than possible, really. It was even likely.

Her pulse raced as she went below with the other nurses and the ambulatory patients who came up on deck every morning to get some exercise. Her face felt even warmer than the usual heat justified. Missy must have noticed that, because she asked, "Are you all right, Catherine? You look like you might be coming down with a fever or something."

*Just a fever for my man,* Catherine told herself, then she laughed aloud at the corniness of the thought. "I'm fine," she said to Missy. "I think it's possible Adam may be on one of those ships that are coming in."

Missy's eyes widened. "Really? Golly, I hope so, for your sake, Catherine. I know you must miss the big lug." Her expression became more solemn. "But if he's with the Marines passing through here . . ."

"Don't say it. I know already. I'm not going to think about that. I'm just going to be glad I get to see him again—if I do."

Missy put her arms around Catherine and hugged her. "I hope you do, honey. If you need me to cover for you while he's here . . ."

Catherine just nodded, grateful for the offer.

The next hour dragged by. Catherine had to go on about her duties as if a potential reunion with her husband weren't imminent. When she finally heard that the transport ships were docking, she couldn't withstand the temptation any longer. She hurried up on deck to watch as they slipped into their berths along the docks. She could read the names on the big gray vessels, but they didn't mean anything to her. She didn't know which ship Adam was traveling on, if indeed this was even his outfit.

Then she leaned forward as she caught sight of a man standing at the railing of one of the ships. Of course, hundreds of Marines lined those railings, but there was something special about this one that caught her eye. He was tall and muscular—again, not that different from many of the other Marines—and he seemed to be gazing toward the *Solace* with special interest, as if he were looking for something—or someone—in particular.

Catherine's heart was in her throat. That was Adam. She knew it somehow. She was sure of it, even over a distance of a couple of hundred yards. What woman wouldn't know her husband when she saw him? She lifted her arm and began to wave. After a moment, the man spotted her and started waving in return.

Even if she was wrong and that wasn't Adam, some Marine was getting the thrill of having a pretty nurse wave at him, she told herself. But really, she had no doubt. That was Adam.

She kept her eye on him until the ship had docked and he started making his way along the crowded deck toward the gangplanks that were lowered. There were so many men in green fatigues . . . too many to keep track of one man. Catherine felt herself growing frightened. She couldn't see him anymore. Where had he gone?

Then she leaned forward and gasped as she saw him practically leap off the gangplank and start running along the piers toward the *Solace*. Oh, God, she thought, it was him, it was really him.

Without thinking about what she was doing, she hurried along the deck of the hospital ship until she reached the steep, narrow stairs that led down to the docking platform. She ran down them, knowing that she was moving faster than was safe on the ladder but unable to hold herself back. A moment later she reached the dock and turned to hurry toward him. She could see his face now under the dark green metal helmet. She knew every feature, the tiny lines around the corners of his eyes, the almost unnoticeable dimple in the middle of his chin, the strong jaw, the wide mouth . . .

"Adam!" she cried.

Then she was in his arms, reveling in their strength as they closed around her, tasting the heat of his mouth as he kissed her. Her feet left the dock for a second as he crushed her to his broad chest. Somewhere far off, men hooted and cheered and applauded, and she realized that she and Adam were putting on quite a show for the other Marines. She didn't care.

Her husband was holding her and kissing her with the same sort of desperate urgency she felt for him, and that was all that mattered. Let the Marines cheer. Let the whole world applaud. At times such as this, with war circling the entire globe and everything about life so uncertain, it was the little moments that counted, the small things that became so big nothing else was important. Like a husband and wife embracing after a long separation . . . what could matter more than that?

Catherine knew the answer. She had found it in Adam's arms.

# SIXTEEN

The fan attached to the ceiling of the hotel room rotated in lazy circles, stirring the hot air. The jalousies over the single window had been drawn almost closed, so that only tiny slivers of sunlight slanted between them, providing a dim illumination in the room. The blinds stirred as a gentle breeze wafted in through the open window, and the movement caused the bands of light and shadow in the room to shift and coalesce.

The bodies of the two people on the bed shifted as well, merging and drawing apart and then coming together again. Soft cries, gasps for breath, mingled with the sound of bedsprings and the murmur of the fan's motor, rising in intensity until they trailed off into a satiated silence.

Adam rolled to the side and sprawled on his back next to Catherine. His hand found hers. Their fingers laced together. Both of them were breathless from the heat, and from the passion they had just shared.

Adam said, "That was . . . that was great." He knew the words were inadequate, but he couldn't think of any other way to describe it.

"Yes, it was," Catherine agreed. "And you have Missy to thank for it."

Adam lifted his head from the pillow and frowned as he turned to look at her. "Missy? If she was here, I sure as hell missed it."

Catherine laughed, making her small, bare breasts move in a manner that Adam found delightful. "*I* wouldn't be here if she hadn't covered for me on the ship. And I don't think this would have been nearly as much fun alone."

"You got that right," Adam muttered.

Catherine rolled onto her side and snuggled against him. She kissed his shoulder and then moved her lips along his collarbone to the hollow of his throat. He closed his eyes and sighed as she slid down to his right nipple and started licking and sucking it.

"I'm supposed to be . . . doing that . . . to you," he said as delicious sensations washed through him.

She lifted her head. "You mean you don't like it?"

"I didn't say that!" he exclaimed, desperation in his voice at the thought she might stop.

"I won't stop, then."

"Please don't."

She went back to what she was doing. Adam lay back and let himself enjoy it.

After a while, when he was ready, she straddled his hips and lowered herself onto him, taking him into her body. Then she rested on his chest and he put his arms around her as they moved together in a slow, luxurious rhythm. This was even better than the first time, Adam decided.

Later, they both dozed off, even though Adam had been determined to stay awake. He didn't want to waste any of his precious time with Catherine by sleeping. But they couldn't make love *all* the time, he supposed, so as he slowly woke up in the late afternoon, he wasn't too upset about going to sleep.

He lay there for long minutes, silent and still, letting awareness seep back into him. Finally, his eyes opened, and he could tell by the light coming through the cracks in the blinds that it was late in the day. He shifted his body a little, expecting to feel Catherine's weight on the mattress beside him. But she wasn't there, and that fact made him roll over and sit up quickly.

She was sitting across the room in a wicker chair, watching him. Relief flooded through him when he realized that she was all right and still with him. "I thought you were gone," he said.

She shook her head. "No. I'm right here."

"What are you doing?" he asked, even though he already knew the answer.

"Watching you. I love to look at you."

"And I love to look at you."

But she wasn't telling the whole truth, he thought. Even in the shadowy room, he had been able to recognize the intensity with which she'd been looking at him. She was studying him, trying to memorize every detail about him, so that she could preserve the way he looked now in her mind.

Because she was afraid that when they parted this time, she might never see him again.

Adam looked down and scrubbed his hands over his face, partly out of weariness and partly to conceal the emotions he was feeling. He was a mess inside. *Big, strong Marine,* he thought, *and what you really want to do right now is break down and bawl like a baby.*

When he looked up he was more composed. "I guess we'd better start thinking about some supper," he said. "We missed lunch somehow."

"We were busy with more important things," Catherine said as she came to her feet. She wore a short robe that left most of her sleek, slender legs bare. When she stretched, the hem of the robe came up even higher, exposing more of her. Then she took it off and that didn't matter anymore, because she was naked.

"That's no way to get me out of here and into a restaurant," Adam said.

"You'll just have to be strong. Either that, or turn your back while I'm getting dressed."

"That would probably be a good idea." He swung his legs off the bed and stood up, keeping the bed between him and Catherine. Not that such a small obstacle would stop him or even slow him down if he wanted to bound across there and grab her. He had to rely on his own willpower to keep him from doing that. It was tough, but he managed to pull on the clean dress uniform he had brought with him to the hotel.

"We can eat downstairs in the dining room," Catherine said. "It's as good a place as any on the island."

Adam turned around and let out a wolf whistle. Catherine wore a white dress with red and blue flowers embroidered around the neckline and the sleeves. A red leather belt was cinched around her trim waist. She looked great, and Adam told her so. He knew from her smile that the compliment pleased her.

"A woman never gets tired of hearing that from her husband."

"Even after he's said it to her for fifty years?"

"Try it and find out."

"I intend to," Adam said. He took her arm, and they left the room.

Even though it was still a little early for supper, the dining room downstairs was fairly crowded. Not all the Marines on liberty had headed straight for the bars and dance halls and cribs as soon as they left the ships. Quite a few had gone in search of a good meal, and many of them had ended up here. Adam and Catherine had to wait a few minutes in the hotel bar before they got a table in the dining room.

While they were waiting, Catherine put her hand on Adam's arm and squeezed. At first he thought it was just a gesture of affection, but then she did it again. He looked at her and said, "What?"

She leaned her head close to his and said, "Look over there in the corner. Just don't be too obvious about it."

Adam turned his head, trying to appear as casual as possible, and saw the table Catherine indicated with a quick movement of her eyes. A man and a woman sat at the table. The woman looked familiar to Adam, but it took him a second to place her. "That's Missy, isn't it?" He hadn't seen her since his visit to Pearl Harbor the previous autumn.

"Yes, that's Missy."

"Who's the swabbie with her?" The guy was sort of handsome in a collegiate way, Adam supposed, but he sure was intense-looking. He didn't seem happy as he talked to Missy.

"That's Phil Lange. He's a naval aviator. He was hurt at the Battle of Midway and has been one of our patients on the ship ever since."

"He looks okay now."

"He is. He's recovered enough to be reassigned to active duty. From the looks of things, that's what he's just told Missy."

Adam looked at Catherine. "You knew about this, didn't you?"

"About Phil leaving?" She nodded. "Dr. Johnston gave me the heads-up a couple of days ago. He wanted me to break the news to Missy."

"Because she's in love with this guy Phil."

"That's right."

Adam shook his head. "Tough. But we know all about things like that, don't we?"

Catherine laid a hand on top of Adam's hand. "All too well," she said in a half-whisper.

After a moment or two of silence, Adam said, "I thought Missy was covering your shift on the ship."

"It's over now, I suppose. I'm not really sure what time it is. . . ."

"About sixteen-thirty, I think."

"Yes, the shift would have changed a half-hour ago. Phil must have gotten his orders today, and he brought Missy here to tell her about them."

Adam watched as Missy took a handkerchief from her bag and dabbed at her eyes. "Is she the type to make a scene?" he asked.

"Oh, I don't think so," Catherine said. "She's very strong."

But Missy was still crying a couple of minutes later when a waiter came and got Adam and Catherine, telling them their table was ready in the dining room. *Poor kid,* Adam thought as he left the bar. Saying good-bye to somebody you loved was damned hard, even when you were used to it.

Who was he kidding, he asked himself as he took Catherine's hand. Some things you never got used to, and saying good-bye was one of them.

*       *       *

"I don't believe this," Missy said. Even as the words left her mouth, she knew she must have said them a dozen times or more since she and Phil sat down at this tiny table tucked away in a corner of the hotel bar. But she couldn't stop the expression of disbelief. The news Phil had given her was just too much for her to accept.

"We knew this day was coming," Phil said. He glared across the table at her. "There's no point in getting upset about it."

He was being such a bastard about the whole thing, Missy thought. He told her he was leaving, told her that he was being assigned to the aircraft carrier *Enterprise*, and he expected her to just accept it and get on with her life. As if it weren't possible that he could be killed and never come back to her.

"Come on, Missy," he said. "It's just going to make things worse if you're mad."

"Mad?" she repeated. "You think I'm mad, Phil?"

He frowned. "Well, you look like you are. And you sound like it too."

"You idiot."

He leaned back in his chair. "Huh?"

"You damned idiot," Missy said. "I'm scared. I'm afraid I'll never see you again."

"Don't worry about that. I'll be fi—"

"Don't tell me you'll be fine!" Her voice rose on the last word, and she forced herself to control her reaction. She had never been one to care that much what people thought about her, but she didn't want to start screaming at him right here in the middle of the hotel bar. That would get the brass down on both of them. She took a deep breath and said, "I'm worried about you, Phil. You can't blame me for feeling that way. Ever since I've known you, you've been either injured or wounded."

"That broken ankle wasn't my fault. It was just a fluke—"

"What about the Japanese bullet through your shoulder? Was that just a fluke?" She made her voice harsh. "What about the bullet that killed Jerry? Just bad luck?"

He paled at the mention of his dead friend, but he said, "Yes."

Missy stared at him. "What?"

"Yes, it was just bad luck Jerry was killed. It's bad luck when anybody is killed. But that's part of war. Somebody has to die."

With a convulsive movement, she reached across the table and caught hold of his hand. "I don't want it to be you."

"I don't want it to be me, either. But that doesn't excuse me from doing my duty." He put his other hand on top of hers and rubbed the back of her hand with his thumb. "What if the *Solace* was sent somewhere else where she would be more in harm's way? Would you go?"

"Of course. I wouldn't have any choice."

"Neither do I."

"Damn you." Missy bit out the words. "You're being logical, and I want to be emotional right now."

"I'd say you're doing a pretty good job of it," Phil blurted, then winced as if he wished he could call the words back.

Missy stared at him for a long moment, not saying anything. Then, abruptly, she laughed. "I am, aren't I?"

"Missy, I didn't mean to hurt your feelings—"

She held up her other hand to stop him. "No, no, that's okay. You're right. I'm being emotional, and there's no place for that in the middle of a war. Everyone has to do their part, even if it puts them at risk. But let me ask you the same question: If the *Solace* had to sail in harm's way, how would you feel about me going with it?"

Phil swallowed hard. "I'd be scared for you. I'd be scared just about out of my mind."

"And that's just the way I feel about you."

Phil met her eyes and looked at her for another long, silent moment. Then he let go of her hand, picked up the almost forgotten drink on the table in front of him, and tossed it down his throat. He put the empty glass back on the table and said in a hoarse voice, "Let's see if they've got any rooms left in this dump."

Missy was on her feet in an instant, grabbing his hand. "Now you're talking, ace."

# SEVENTEEN

*Join the Marines and see the world.* Robert Gurnwall would have sworn he had read that on a poster. Or maybe the old, grizzled NCO in the recruiting office back in Tulsa had said it. Gurnwall didn't remember for sure. All he knew was that for him the world had shrunk to a rat-infested barracks and a barbed-wire–enclosed plot of muddy ground in the Woosung prison camp, a few miles outside Shanghai, China.

Gurnwall sat on the wooden steps below the door of the barracks and smoked a cigarette. It was the first one he'd had in over a month, and he wouldn't have it if Ishi hadn't felt sorry for him. Ishi wasn't a bad guy for a Jap, and he was definitely the friendliest of the guards who were assigned to the barracks where Gurnwall lived. But Gurnwall hated him anyway, and given the chance, he would have gladly shoved the muzzle of a rifle into Ishi's round, grinning face and pulled the trigger.

Most of the guys were asleep inside the barracks, exhausted from the day's labor. They worked all day, every day, from before dawn until after sundown, building roads, clearing brush, hauling rocks, anything their captors told them to do. They were slaves, after all. Major Devereaux tried to get them to believe they were still Marines, despite their captivity, but Gurnwall knew better. In reality they were no better than human cattle, nothing but beasts of burden. So naturally they were tired, and most of them stretched out on the thin straw mats that were the barracks' only furnishings and fell asleep as soon as they had eaten their meager supper.

Gurnwall usually had trouble falling asleep, though, so he had made a habit of coming out here to sit and think for a while each night. The compound was lit up by bare bulbs strung on wires and poles and run by a generator over at headquarters. The prisoners were not allowed to leave their barracks at night. Wandering around was a good way to get tortured or even shot. But the guards didn't seem to care that Gurnwall sat on the steps. They were used to him being out here by now. The Americans who had been captured when Wake Island was surrendered had been here at Woosung for more than six months.

Gurnwall smoked the butt down as far as he possibly could, then he pinched out the coal and slipped what was left into the pocket of his tattered uniform shirt. He would tear it apart later and add the few shreds of tobacco to the collection he was accumulating. Someday, maybe he would have enough to make an extra cigarette. Of course, the tobacco would be pretty dried out by then, but Jap tobacco was lousy to start with. Better than nothing, though, Gurnwall thought.

A footstep sounded on the step behind and above him. The man who had just come out of the barracks eased down the steps and sat beside Gurnwall. He clasped his hands together between his knees but didn't say anything.

"Can't sleep, either, huh?" Gurnwall said after a few moments of silence.

"Nah," Frank Conner replied.

Conner was a tall man who had once been one of the brawniest bruisers among the civilian construction crew on Wake Island. His broad shoulders gave some indication of how muscular he had been, but now he was scrawny like the rest of the prisoners. He had big hands with long, knobby-knuckled fingers, a rumpled thatch of red hair, and a short red beard.

Gurnwall remembered the brawl Conner had gotten into with Adam Bergman, back when the corp had still been on the island, before the brass sent Adam back to Pearl Harbor with Major Bayler, the last Americans off Wake before it fell. Conner and some of the other civilians had bulled their way into the Marines' slop chute one night looking for trouble, and they'd found it, all right. It had been a hell of a fight. Gurnwall had very fond memories of it. At the time, the leathernecks and the civilians hadn't gotten along well at all.

Now of course, those distinctions didn't mean much. The Japs treated everybody the same—like crap.

"How far you think it is to the fence, Gurney?" Conner asked.

"Too damned far."

"Those little bastards aren't very good shots. I bet I could get there and get over it before they winged me."

"They wouldn't just wing you," Gurnwall said. "They'd shoot you to pieces. Don't matter how good they can shoot, there's too fuckin' many of 'em, Frank. You'd never make it."

"Bet I would if there was some way to distract them."

Gurnwall shrugged. "Maybe. But say you get over the fence. Then what? You're still in the middle o' goddamn China. Nowhere to go, nobody to help you, nobody you can trust." Gurnwall took a deep breath and said something he hated to admit, even to himself. "You're better off right here where you are. We all are. One of these days, our guys will come get us and let us out of here."

"Yeah," Conner said, his voice thick with bitterness. "Just like they came and gave us a hand on Wake."

Gurnwall couldn't say anything in response to that, couldn't do anything except stare out into the dark night beyond the harsh glare of the lights. Conner was right. The guys on Wake Island, the Marines and the swabbies and the civilians who had all fought so hard and so valiantly to keep the Japanese from capturing the atoll . . . their reward had been to be abandoned and forgotten.

*   *   *

The surrender had taken place on 23 December 1941, two weeks and one day after the initial attack on Wake Island. Japanese troops came ashore early in the morning, and the fighting was fierce throughout the predawn hours all over Wake and Wilkes, two of the three islands that made up the atoll. The defenders were heavily outnumbered, however, and their only real hope lay in holding out until a relief force arrived. The island's commanders, Marine Major James Devereaux and Navy Commander Winfield Scott Cunningham, knew that such a relief force was supposed to be on the way from

Hawaii. But at seven o'clock on the morning of the 23d, during a grim conversation between the two men, Cunningham told Devereaux of the radio communication he had just received from Pearl Harbor stating that no American vessels were in the vicinity of Wake Island, nor would there be for at least twenty-four hours.

Devereaux and Cunningham agreed that was too long for their men to hold out. In order to prevent the defenders from being killed to the last man, the only option remaining to them was surrender.

Under a white flag, Devereaux and a small party approached some of the invaders, found a Japanese officer who spoke a little English, and indicated that they wanted to surrender. The word was passed, and Devereaux and another Marine were sent under heavy guard on a tour of the island so that the major could order the remaining defenders to lay down their weapons. This took most of the day. The American enlisted men and noncommissioned officers were rounded up, in many cases were stripped of their uniforms, and along with the civilian construction workers were herded into two concrete bunkers that had served as the island's hospital after Japanese bombers destroyed the actual hospitals. The hands of the men were wired together behind their backs, and the wounded received no medical attention. No one was given any food or water. As miserable as things had been during the long siege, captivity was worse.

The officers were interrogated but not tortured. Over the next couple of days, Devereaux was able to prevail upon his captors to improve conditions for the enlisted men and civilians. Lieutenant (j.g.) Gustave Kahn, the naval medical officer, and Dr. Lawton Shank, the civilian physician, were allowed to do what they could for the wounded men, which wasn't much because the Japanese had confiscated all the American medical supplies. They were given short rations—small bowls of rice and a scrap or two of fish twice a day—and water. And they were sent out on work details while guarded by Japanese troops. Bodies had to be buried, and the damage inflicted on the island over the past two weeks of battle had to be cleaned up. The Japanese wanted the island's defenses put back into shape too, and the American prisoners were assigned the task of cleaning the guns.

They did this, but in the process, they also sabotaged the

weapons right under the noses of their captors. Sand in the cannons' elevating gears, salt water down the barrels of rifles and machine guns to pit them and wreck the firing mechanisms, vital parts stolen and hidden in the brush . . . if they had been caught doing these things, torture and perhaps death probably would have awaited the saboteurs. But the Japanese, flushed with victory, were oblivious to what was going on.

This continued until 12 January 1942, when unexpected orders came. Except for a group of about a hundred of the civilian construction workers, all the prisoners were gathered up and marched at gunpoint down to the shore where small boats waited to take them out to the Japanese ships. They were forced to clamber into cargo nets that then lifted them onto the ships, dropping them on the decks with bone-jarring force. Then they were herded below into cargo holds. When the hatches were slammed shut, the holds were plunged into darkness. The prisoners sat there in the gloom, uncertain what their fate would be but knowing that it probably wouldn't be good.

A few days later, the ships carrying the prisoners docked at Yokohama. The officers were taken on deck so they could be questioned again. They were also put on display for the Japanese press. Word filtered down that the Americans were being taken to a prison camp in China. The Japanese promised that this would be a safer, better place for them.

Nobody believed a word of it.

The worst atrocity so far took place while the ships were sailing from Yokohama to Shanghai. Five of the prisoners—three sailors and two Marines—were chosen apparently at random and taken up on deck where over a hundred Japanese soldiers and sailors were waiting for them. With no idea what was going on but knowing that it couldn't be good, the five men were forced to kneel before an officer who read some sort of proclamation in his native tongue. Then five guards stepped forward, each man with a sword in his hand. . . .

The ritual beheadings were symbolic payment for all the Japanese who had been killed in the two weeks of attacks on Wake Island. When rumors of what had happened reached the rest of the prisoners, emotions ran high for several days. They wanted revenge for their murdered buddies. They wanted to rise up in force against their captors. But there was nothing they could do. They were outnumbered, unarmed, already weak from malnutrition and starvation, and many of them were still suffering from the effects of wounds they had received in battle. Eventually, the rage died down, but it was replaced by a simmering hatred that would never go away.

The prisoners' destination was Woosung. They were marched there through the streets of Shanghai. Japanese soldiers hooted and jeered at them as they passed, but the conquered Chinese citizens looked at the Americans with pity. They had lived under the heel of Japanese rule for several years, and they knew what awaited the prisoners. When the gates of the camp swung shut, it was as if the rest of the world ceased to exist.

The relief expedition that had been on its way to Wake Island, the task force that the men had counted upon to rescue them during those first twenty-four hours of captivity, had never come. Following orders from Vice Admiral William Pye, acting CINCPAC, who feared another disastrous defeat so soon after the attack on Pearl Harbor, Task Force 14 had turned back to Hawaii.

It was less than four hundred miles from Wake Island when it did so.

Gurnwall didn't know why nobody had come to help them. If he'd had to guess, he would have said that the brass decided Wake Island just wasn't worth it. And he supposed that meant the guys who had held out there weren't worth coming after, either. He knew he was bitter about it, but at least he wasn't scared anymore. He was cautious. He did what the Japs told him to do, because he didn't want to be tortured or shot or have his head lopped off with a sword. But the fright, the sheer terror that had once gripped him so strongly, that was gone. All they could do to him was kill him.

Sometimes, he dreamed about the first day the Japs had attacked the island. He had gone up on top of the water tower with the corporal of his squad, Adam Bergman. The corp said they were lookouts. The water tower had become Wake's observation post because it was the tallest thing on the island. Gurnwall hadn't liked being up there because he felt so exposed. Everybody else could hunker down, but there was no place for him and the corp to hunker. Then the Jap planes showed up, and one of the fighters strafed the water tower. Gurnwall still remembered the roar of its engine and the pounding chatter of its guns. Bullets had stitched a line right across the top of the tower, no more than a couple of feet from where he'd been stretched out on his belly.

Even when he dreamed about that day, he felt a little embarrassed now. He had been so scared he damned near wet his pants. He'd just lay there and shook from fear. Adam had seen that. Later, he'd seen Gurnwall's reactions swing to the other side of the pendulum. Gurnwall had grabbed a rifle and started blazing away at the Jap planes like he thought he could shoot down one of them, yelling curses all the while. That was almost as embarrassing as freezing up. The corp had never said much about any of it, though, and Gurnwall appreciated that. The corp was a good guy. He'd deserved his promotion, and he deserved to get off that godforsaken island before the Japs overran it. Rolofson was the new corp. He hadn't really had a chance to see how good he would have done at leading the squad. The surrender had come only three days after Adam flew off to Hawaii in that PBY. Rolofson had made it through the battle, as had Kennemer and Magruder, the other two surviving members of the squad. They were together here at Woosung, but there was no squad anymore, of course. They were all prisoners, all equal in the eyes of their captors. Except for Major Devereaux and the other high-ranking officers. The Japs still recognized their authority and counted on them to keep the enlisted men in line. Devereaux tried not to let discipline slip, even for a minute. They were Marines, and that was what was going to get them through this.

Conner put his hands on his knees and pushed himself to his feet. Gurnwall glanced up at him and said, "Goin' in?"

"Nope. Goin' out."

"What?" Gurnwall started to stand up.

Conner jumped from the bottom step and broke into a run toward the fence.

"Conner!" Gurnwall yelled. He was halfway up, and he

launched himself in a flying tackle from that position. He caught Conner around the knees. Conner was bigger and still stronger, but Gurnwall's tackle was perfect. Conner went down.

Gurnwall heard the guards shouting. Any second, they might start shooting if he didn't get Conner and himself back in the barracks. He clambered onto his hands and knees and grabbed the back of Conner's shirt, hauling the redhead toward the steps.

"Are you crazy?" Gurnwall said. "Come on, damn it!"

Conner struggled to break free, but Gurnwall hung on to him with the strength of desperation. Gurnwall lunged toward the steps. A machine gun ripped off a burst, the high-pitched burping sound typical of a Jap .25 caliber LMG. Dust flew in the air, kicked up by the bullets that struck the ground several yards from Gurnwall and Conner. Gurnwall got his arms around Conner's chest from behind and drove his feet against the ground, pushing them back out of the line of fire. He came upright, stumbling, and flopped back on the steps.

Guards ran through the harsh electric light toward them, carrying bamboo canes. Screaming curses in Japanese, the guards began slashing at Gurnwall and Conner while others stood back and covered them with rifles. Gurnwall put his arms up to protect his head and face from the blows. The canes smacked against his arms and torso and legs, and pain shot through him. He clenched his teeth and endured it. He knew the guards would get tired of beating him and Conner after a while. All the two of them had to do was live through it.

After all, what was the worst that could happen? The lousy Japs could beat them to death? Gurnwall laughed through the pain, and that made the Japs hit him harder.

Death . . . that was nothin'.

# EIGHTEEN

Sweat dripped into Ken Walker's eyes and made them sting, but he couldn't wipe it away. He couldn't let go of the handles of the manipulating arms he was using to mix the ingredients of two funnels in a platinum dish. The dish was on the other side of a thick lead barrier. Ken could see it through the heavy smoked glass of the barrier's single small window. He blinked the sweat out of his eyes and leaned closer to the glass, as if that would give him a better view of what he was doing.

A fleeting thought crossed his mind. He remembered watching the movie *Frankenstein* at one of the theaters in downtown Chicago when he was a kid. His uncle had taken him, after assuring Ken's mom that the movie wouldn't be scary.

And to tell the truth, Ken really hadn't found the show to be all that frightening. Sure, the monster was kind of creepy looking, and it had bothered Ken when the little girl drowned, but he was able to put all that out of his mind and concentrate on the scientific aspects of the film. He *loved* the laboratory scenes. All those machines with their dials and levers and gauges, the beakers with tendrils of smoke curling up from the chemicals they contained, the table that could be raised through the opening in the castle roof so that Victor Frankenstein could harness the power of the lightning . . .

It was all hokum, of course. Nobody could assemble a monster out of body parts taken from corpses and then animate it with an electrical shock. There was a nod toward realism with a mention of Luigi Galvani's experiments regarding the connection between muscle movement and electricity, but the whole thing was still bunk. Ken didn't care. He saw Frankenstein's laboratory, and he knew right then and there that he wanted to work in such a place, surrounded by the apparatus of science. Scientists couldn't create life, but they could do other things almost equally awe-inspiring that would improve the lives of people all over the world.

In a way, Ken thought, he had reached his goal. He was the mad scientist now. But instead of a hulking stone castle atop a rain-swept hill, he was working in a narrow room with walls made of poorly painted concrete blocks, underneath a football field. No fear-crazed villagers waving torches waited outside, only a bunch of scientists and graduate students in lab coats. No clouds of smoke rose from the platinum dish in which he mixed the chemicals. And he wasn't attempting to create life here, either.

If everything worked out, what he was helping to create ultimately would mean death for thousands, perhaps hundreds of thousands, of people.

Ken gave a shake of his head, trying to put that thought out of his mind. He was a scientist. There was no good or bad, only facts. Besides, even if what they were developing here was used for a weapon, in the end it would save lives by bringing the war to a quicker end. The sooner the fighting stopped, the fewer people would die.

The door behind him opened. He knew the footsteps of the person who came into the room. "Almost done, Jake," he said.

Jacob Ellinger moved up next to Ken and bent over to look through the glass at the dish. "What's your evaporation rate?"

"Point oh-oh-one-five-seven milliliters."

"Fluoride precipitation should be proceeding satisfactorily, then," Jake said.

"I think so. We'll be ready to concentrate the solution even more tomorrow."

"It's about time. Building a pile won't do us any good if we don't have pure elements for the rods."

Satisfied with his work, Ken let go of the manipulating arms and stepped back. Finally, he could wipe away the sweat on his forehead.

"It's not that hot down here," Jake said with a frown. "You're not afraid of that stuff, are you, Ken? It's not like it's going to blow up or anything, and it's not emitting enough radiation to hurt anything."

"I know. In fact, it should be harmless enough now that we can work on it without the shielding. That's good, because I'd hate to have to use those arms on the tiny amounts we'll be working with."

"So what's with the perspiration?" Jake pressed. "Not getting cold feet, are you?"

Ken felt a flash of anger. Jake was a graduate student, just like him. In fact, if anything Jake was lower down on the scientific totem pole. Ken knew that Dr. Fermi didn't rely on Jake as much as he relied on him. Jake didn't have any right to start questioning him.

"You're wrong," he said. "It is hot down here. At least it is to me."

Jake shrugged. "Sure, whatever you say, buddy boy." He pushed up his glasses. "I guess we're through down here until that stuff settles down. Got any plans for tonight?"

"Yeah, I do."

"Another date with the lovely Emily?"

Ken hesitated. He didn't like talking about his personal life. Especially to an annoying guy like Jake Ellinger. But then he shrugged and said, "Yeah. We're going out to dinner."

Jake shook his head. "There's no justice in the world. Here there's a shortage of available males because of the war, so that *finally* guys like me have a shot with the girls, and then somebody like you comes along to steal 'em all away."

"I'm not stealing anybody away."

"Hell, you probably have to beat the ladies off with a stick, big strong football-player-looking guy like you. Me, I look like what I am—a scientist. That's why I say it's not fair. Guys who look like you shouldn't be messing around with nuclear fission."

"Sorry," Ken said, his voice curt. "I'll try to be more stupid."

"Hey, don't take offense! I'm just talking about how the world works."

Ken took off his lab coat and draped it over the back of a chair next to the workbench. He turned toward the door.

"Some people just lead charmed lives, that's all," Jake went on. "They seem to just get what they want, no matter whether they work for it or not. That's all I'm saying."

Ken stopped and turned around. "Are you saying I'm like that? Because I *have* worked for what I've gotten. I've worked damned hard—"

Jake held up his hands, palms out. "Like I said, no offense meant. Take it easy, Ken. What are you so touchy about today?"

"Nothing," Ken said. "Everything's just peachy."

With that, he turned and walked out, leaving Jake to stare after him.

*   *   *

"Really, I don't mind not having meat, Ken," Emily Faraday said. "A salad is just fine. Actually, I've been thinking about giving up meat entirely, at least until this awful war is over."

From the other side of the table, Ken nodded. It was getting harder and harder to find a restaurant that had meat available all the time. Even though restaurants had more ration coupons than private individuals did, the supply wasn't what it had once been. Of course, that was true of just about everything. Gasoline, paper, metal, rubber . . . every resource that could be diverted to the war effort had been subject to shortages in recent months. Ken was as willing to make the necessary sacrifices as the next guy.

But there were times when he would have given almost anything for a nice, thick, juicy steak.

Well, he had Emily's company, he told himself. That was better than any cut of beef. When the waiter came, Ken ordered salads for both of them and two more glasses of wine. Emily laughed when the waiter was gone. "Are you trying to get me giddy, Kenneth Walker?"

"Not at all."

Emily drank what was left in her first glass and smiled at him over the rim. "Well, maybe you should."

Ken looked down at the white linen tablecloth. He didn't know what to make of that comment. It almost sounded like she was inviting him to be a little more forward with her. Maybe it was time, he told himself. They had been dating for a while, and he hadn't done anything but kiss her. Maybe they were both ready for a little more.

Emily changed the subject by saying, "I read in the paper that the British are replacing the commander of their army in Egypt. Some man named Montgomery is going to take over."

Ken wasn't sure whether to be disappointed or relieved that she didn't want to talk about them right now. He said, "I hope he can do some good. From what I hear, they're really bottled up over there. That German general Rommel has driven them back almost to Cairo." He thought about Joe and Dale Parker and wondered if they were still in Egypt.

"I think they should just stop fighting."

Ken frowned. He and Emily had talked about the war before—the subject was never very far from the minds of most people—and he had gotten the feeling that she didn't really approve of it. Her comment now was the most blatant indication of that so far, however.

"What do you mean, stop fighting? If they do that, the Nazis will take Egypt."

"Would that be so bad? I've heard that a lot of the Egyptians would prefer it that way."

"But then the Germans would control the Suez Canal. We couldn't get any oil or any other cargoes through there."

Emily looked across the table at him. "So?"

Ken wasn't sure what to say. He knew Emily wasn't stupid. She wasn't saying these things because she didn't comprehend what the war was about. But he was having trouble understanding how any reasonable person could hold such an opinion.

When he didn't say anything, she went on, "It seems to me that the only way countries can really settle their differences is by talking, and they can't talk to each other if they're fighting all the time, now can they?"

"That's what Neville Chamberlain thought. Peace in our time, remember? And then Hitler took Poland."

Emily's face flushed, and Ken realized she was irritated. "I didn't say we should appease Hitler. I just said we should talk to him. Everyone should sit down and work out their differences. There's no need for all the . . . the killing."

Ken shook his head, knowing he shouldn't say what he was about to say but unable to stop himself. "Sometimes there's no other way."

"So in order to solve things, people have to die?" It was Emily's turn to shake her head. "I don't accept that. I can't accept that."

"What about Pearl Harbor?"

"You've just proven my point," she answered without even a second's hesitation. "If Japan feels like they have legitimate grievances against us, they should have addressed those grievances through negotiations, not a sneak attack."

"They were negotiating," Ken said. "They kept on negotiating even after the planes had taken off from their carriers, and their diplomats knew it."

"Then you're saying that we should be just as bad as they are?"

*What the hell happened here?* Ken asked himself. They had been having a nice evening, they'd been on the verge of eating a nice—albeit meatless—meal, and all of a sudden, without him even knowing how they'd gotten to this point, they were about to start arguing. No, he corrected himself, they were already arguing. Emily looked mad, and he supposed that he did too.

"All I'm saying is that there are times when there's no other way to deal with a situation except by force."

"By killing, you mean."

"If that's what it takes." He thought about the work he was doing at the MetLab. If he and the other scientists were successful, they would have the basis for the most destructive explosive device in the history of man. The most efficient killing machine . . .

Emily took her napkin out of her lap and put it on the table. "I think I want to go home."

"Look, there's no need—"

"I'm beginning to think I don't know you as well as I thought. Please, Kenneth, take me home."

Miserably, he said, "What about our salads?"

"I'm not hungry anymore."

He still had a little wine. The service was slow and the waiter hadn't refilled their glasses yet. Ken lifted his glass and drank the rest of the wine. He set down the empty a little harder than he intended to. "Fine. I'll take you home."

He stood up and started around the table to help her with her chair, but she was on her feet before he got there. Since it was a warm night, she hadn't worn any sort of wrap, so he didn't have to help her with that, either. She turned and walked toward the front of the restaurant, and all Ken could do was drop a bill on the table to pay for what he'd ordered and then hurry after her. He passed the waiter on the way. The man lifted a hand and said, "Sir . . . ?"

"Sorry," Ken said. "The lady and I have to go. We'll come back another time."

Assuming, of course, he thought bitterly, that Emily would agree to ever see him again after tonight.

# NINETEEN

Mike Chastain stood in the doorway leading to the restaurant kitchen and watched the good-looking brunette dame stalk out of the place, followed by her blond boyfriend wearing a confused, hangdog look. Obviously, the kid didn't know what he'd done to get his ass in a sling with his girl. If Mike could have talked to the kid, he would have recommended a nice bunch of flowers to get him back in his girl's good graces. Chocolate would work too, but that was harder to get these days.

*Yeah, you're a fine one to be giving anybody any advice about romance,* he thought. *You can't even keep your own girl happy.*

Mike's mouth tightened into a grim line as he remembered the last time he had talked to Karen. It had been several days earlier, and once again, she had told him that he ought to get out of this business with Roger Hale. Hell, she had practically begged him to get out of it. And then she had stomped out of the penthouse, mad as a hornet. Just like the girl who had left the restaurant here tonight.

Dames didn't understand, Mike told himself. They just didn't get how a guy had to do certain things in his life. He had to keep his word, especially to a partner. Maybe you didn't even like the guy—Hale was a slimy son of a bitch, no question about that—but once you said you'd do business with him, you didn't have any choice. You had to hold up your end of the bargain.

It was getting more and more difficult to say no to Karen, though.

A hand fell on Mike's shoulder. He tensed, and his hand made an involuntary move toward his coat and the little pistol snugged into a shoulder holster under his left arm. The guy who had come up behind him jerked back as Mike turned his head.

"Geez, I'm sorry, Mr. Chastain," the guy said in a hurry. He held up his hands, palms out. "I didn't mean to startle you."

Mike forced himself to relax. "That's all right," he said. He pasted a smile on his face. "How you doin', Guiseppe?"

"I'm fine, Mr. Chastain. I was just a little surprised when my maître d' told me you wanted to see me. What can I do for you?"

Now it was Mike's turn to put his hand on the restaurant owner's shoulder. "It's not what you can do for me but what I can do for you," he said. "Why don't we go back to your office and talk about it?"

Guiseppe swallowed hard and looked nervous. "I already got a partner, Mr. Chastain. Several of 'em, in fact."

"Hell, I know that." Mike lowered his voice so that no one would have been able to hear him over the clatter of pots and pans and dishes from the kitchen and the murmur of voices from the tables. "I know all about your arrangement with the boys. It's out of respect for them and for you that I'm here to see if you want to do a little business."

Guiseppe was still nervous, but now he was confused too. "I didn't know you had anything to do with the boys anymore, Mr. Chastain."

"My partner and I are what you could call independent contractors these days. But I assure you, Guiseppe, it's all right for you to be talking to me."

"Well, okay." Guiseppe still didn't sound completely convinced. "Come on back with me."

Mike followed the man down a hallway behind the kitchen and into an office that was paneled in dark wood and dominated by a large, glass-topped desk. A comfortable leather chair stood in front of the desk. Mike sat down in it without being invited. Guiseppe moved behind the desk and started to stand there, his knuckles resting on the glass, but the stare that Mike fastened on his midsection made him uncomfortable. Mike Chastain didn't look up to anybody, especially somebody he was doing business with. After a moment of silence, Guiseppe sank down into the chair behind the desk and said, "Now, what's this all about?"

"Can I get a good steak tonight, Guiseppe?"

The restaurant owner looked surprised again. "You want to eat, Mr. Chastain?"

Mike shook his head. "No, it's just, what do you call it, a hypothetical question. If I walked in here tonight as a customer, could I order a nice thick steak?"

"Well, no, I'm afraid not. We're not offering any cuts of beef tonight. Only got a certain amount in the freezer, you know, and we got to make it last until the end of the month."

"I'll bet people don't like that much, they come in with their mouths all set for a steak and your waiters tell them they can't have it."

Guiseppe shrugged. "Probably not, but the customers understand. There's a war on. We all got to do our part."

"But they'd be happier, and you'd do better business, if you had all the meat you could use."

"Yeah, sure, but with the rationing . . ." Guiseppe spread his hands. "We'll make do."

"You don't have to," Mike said.

In a cautious tone, Guiseppe asked, "What are you talking about, Mr. Chastain?"

"I can put you on to a deal where you can get all the meat you want. Steaks, roasts, chops, even those little chickens."

"Cornish hens?" Guiseppe shook his head in disbelief. "I ain't seen one of them in months. Not that I get much call for them."

"You want 'em, you got 'em," Mike said.

"But I don't have coupons—"

Again Mike waved a hand. "Forget about coupons. This deal isn't between you and the government. It's between you and me."

"You're talking about the black market." The words came out in a whisper.

Ice crept into Mike's voice as he said, "It's a business arrangement, that's all."

"Yeah, sure, Mr. Chastain, I didn't mean any offense." Guiseppe scrubbed a hand over his paunchy face. "I got to think about this."

"Don't think too long. The offer's good only for a limited time."

Guiseppe looked across the desk. "You're sure the boys are okay with this?"

"Don't worry about the boys. They get a cut of this action too. As long as they get theirs, they'll be happy."

"How come nobody ever said anything to me before?"

"They let me handle things the way I see fit. Like I said, my partner and I are independent contractors."

"Who's your partner?"

Mike shook his head. "You don't have to know that."

"No," Guiseppe said quickly. "I guess I don't."

Mike sat there, calm and unworried, while the restaurant owner thought about the deal. He didn't want to bring Hale's name into the discussion as long as he could avoid it. Those two cops—what were their names? Bowden and Corey, that was it—were always trying to tie him up some way with Hale, but so far Mike had avoided leaving any evidence that Hale was anything more than a casual acquaintance from the occasional card game. That was the way Mike wanted it to stay.

"It sounds like too good a deal to pass up," Guiseppe said at last.

"That's because it is."

"You'll give me a good price?"

"You got my word on that. It'll be higher than what you're paying now, of course, but your supply will be unlimited."

Greed shone in Guiseppe's eyes. "What about the competition?"

Mike trotted out the usual assurances. "Our distribution is limited to only certain establishments, and we make sure none of them are too close together." He didn't like this part of the job. It was too much like being a salesman, too much like real work. But it had to be done. Hale was better at it, but Hale hadn't done much since he'd gotten shot.

Guiseppe rubbed his hands together. "Okay, Mr. Chastain, it sounds like we got a deal. When can I get delivery on the first shipment?"

"Whenever you want it," Mike said.

"Your guys will be discreet?"

"Nobody will know they've been here."

"As soon as possible, then. Tonight, even."

"I can't set things up quite that fast. But how about tomorrow night, say three o'clock?"

"I'll be here. I guess you want cash?"

Mike just gave him a look.

"Yeah, that was a dumb question," Guiseppe said with a little laugh.

Mike came to his feet, and the restaurant owner followed suit. They shook hands over the desk. "Pleasure doing business with you," Mike said.

"Likewise." Guiseppe hesitated and then said, "I got to admit, though, I'm surprised."

"About it being a pleasure?"

"Oh, no, not that. You're a good guy, Mr. Chastain, everybody knows that. It's just that I didn't know you were in the rackets anymore. The word was that you'd given that up and were retired. I heard you spent most of your time playing cards at the Dells and hanging around with your girlfriend, that pretty redheaded torch singer . . . what was her name?"

"Karen," Mike said, his insides tightening up again. "Karen Wells."

"Yeah, that's her. One of the prettiest girls I've ever seen. Great set of pipes too."

Mike felt like reaching across the desk and smacking the oily little bastard. Only when he looked at Guiseppe, he saw that the restaurant owner wasn't giving him the needle. Guiseppe was just talking, probably so relieved to have made the deal that he didn't even know what he was saying. Besides, everything he'd said was true. Mike *had* gotten out of the rackets, and until Hale came along, he'd spent most of his time at the Dells. Cards and Karen had been plenty to keep him occupied.

So why the hell hadn't he told Hale to take a long walk off a short pier the first time the guy approached him about coming in the black market meat deal? Mike couldn't answer that. Maybe he'd been bored. Maybe it was just that old habits were hard to break, and when he'd seen a chance for a good payoff, he had to take it. Mike wasn't certain about that, but he knew he wasn't all that happy with the way things had worked out. Sure, he was making good money, but he didn't really need the dough. What he had should have been enough. . . .

"You ever see her anymore?" Guiseppe went on.

"Yeah. Yeah, I see her," Mike said.

"Tell her for me I think she's swell."

"I'll do that."

But he knew he wouldn't. He hadn't talked to Karen for three days, and he didn't know when he'd see her again. He could go to the Dells, of course, but if she spotted him in the audience, she'd head for her dressing room after the show and not come out until the place was closed and everybody was gone. She hadn't come right out and said it, but Mike knew the only way he could fix things was to get out of the deal with Hale.

And that wasn't going to happen. He couldn't walk away. No matter how much it hurt to have this barrier between him and Karen, he didn't have any choice in the matter.

He got his hat from the girl at the check stand and walked out into the night, his thoughts full of the choices he had made—and those he hadn't.

★　　★　　★

The two men in the front seat of the Dodge sedan watched Chastain leave the restaurant. Pete Corey expected him to hail a cab, but Chastain didn't do that. He walked off down the street, alone.

"We could grab him easy," Pete said.

"You always say that, and I always ask what good it would do." Bowden picked a fleck of tobacco off his bottom lip, a leftover from the cigar he had smoked earlier. "We need a new act, Pete."

Pete sighed. "Yeah, I guess so. You think he went in there to sell the greaseball that owns the place some meat?"

"That would be my guess."

Pete drummed his fingers on the steering wheel. "So if we stake out the restaurant, maybe we'll catch Chastain's guys making a delivery. We scoop them up, they spill what they know, and we've got the goods on Chastain."

Bowden gave a dry chuckle and said, "I wouldn't expect it to be quite that easy."

"Maybe not, but we can't afford not to give it a try."

"No," Bowden agreed, "we can't."

156

# TWENTY

Joe walked down the Cairo street toward the building where Melinda's flat was located. Evening was settling down over the great city. A warm breeze blew from the west, carrying the smell of the Nile. It wasn't a particularly pleasant smell, but anybody who stayed here very long got used to it.

It was August now; Joe and Dale had been in Egypt for over seven months. In a way the time seemed longer, as if they had been here for years. That was how this country worked, with its heat and its seductive pleasures. It was easy to forget the passage of time, to just sit back and let the ancient land work its magic. That was why the atmosphere in Cairo was so casual, so languid, even in the face of danger. Less than 150 miles away, the Eighth Army was still bottled up at El Alamein, with the German forces concentrating more and more as Rommel prepared to deal a deathblow to the British. Ever since Rommel's arrival in North Africa the year before, the war had been a seesaw affair—the Germans advanced, and then the British pushed them back—but following the destruction of the Gazala Line, Rommel had pushed ahead steadily. Joe knew that his friends in the Royal Tank Corps, Captain Neville Sharp and Corporal Bert Crimmens, were still alive. His contacts in the Eighth Army GHQ had told him their names had not appeared on any casualty lists. But that could change at any time. They were still out there fighting, as tank patrols ranged along the front lines and protected the supply routes from Alexandria to El Alamein.

Joe and Dale had wondered what would happen if El Alamein fell and the British army was routed. Joe was convinced the Desert Fox would head for Cairo with all possible speed. When he had discussed the matter with Colin Richardson, the major hadn't disagreed

157

with him. Richardson believed that Cairo was Rommel's ultimate target too, though one school of thought within the British intelligence apparatus held that the Germans might swing around Cairo and try to capture Port Said first. Cairo would be well and truly surrounded then.

If either of those scenarios unfolded, what would happen to the Americans in Cairo? Would they be pulled out before the city could fall, or would they stay to fight side-by-side with their British allies? If that were the case, they would be the first American GIs to strike a blow against the Germans. That was an honor he could probably live without, Joe had decided. He wanted to do his part, but not in a doomed effort.

On the other hand, he thought as he paused in front of Melinda's building, could he leave her here, just abandon her to whatever fate awaited her when the Germans came? Would the British try to get their civilian employees out of the city before it fell? Joe knew there was no way he'd be able to take her with him if the Army ordered him and Joe and all the other American instructors and advisors out of Egypt.

Maybe it wouldn't come to that. The British were about to get a new commander. Lieutenant General Bernard Law Montgomery was going to replace the Great Auk. Joe didn't think Auchinleck had done such a bad job under the circumstances, but he had to admit that the Eighth Army wasn't in very good shape right now. Could Montgomery turn everything around? Joe had no idea. It seemed like a hopeless job.

With those thoughts running through his head, he wasn't paying much attention as he entered Melinda's building. They were going to dinner at Shepheard's, and then they would come back here and make love. At least Joe assumed they would. His thoughts were full of that possibility too. He went through the building lobby to the lift and got there just as its door opened.

The man who stepped out seemed to be equally distracted. His shoulder bumped Joe and made him stumble. Joe caught himself and said, "Watch it, buddy." The man brushed past him and headed for the street door without apologizing or even looking back. Muttering,

Joe stepped into the lift and gave the elderly Egyptian operator the number of Melinda's floor.

Then, suddenly, Joe's hand shot out and gripped the edge of the closing door, stopping it. He stared at the street door of the building. The man who had run into him had reached the sidewalk now and turned to the left, his profile visible for a second before he went out of sight.

"Open the door," Joe snapped at the lift operator. The man slid the door back, and Joe rushed out into the lobby. He ran to the street door.

The way the man had bumped him so rudely had brought to mind the confrontation with the Swiss banker on the roof of the Continental Hotel several weeks earlier. Then, when Joe had caught a glimpse of the man's face, he'd recognized him. It was the same man.

As Joe stepped out onto the street, he couldn't have said why he had decided on a whim to follow the guy. After all, just because somebody made a habit of being rude, that didn't mean he was up to no good. But Joe didn't like the idea that the man was hanging around Melinda's building. Maybe he held a grudge against her because of what had happened at the Continental. Joe knew that was pretty far-fetched, but he couldn't think of any other reason for the man to show up here.

Unless, of course, he knew somebody else in the building or had some equally innocent reason for being there.

Joe pushed that thought to the back of his head as he started following the Swiss. He had some time to kill, since he was early for his date with Melinda. What the hell, maybe he was just being silly, but he didn't think it would hurt anything to see where the guy was going, maybe even figure out what he was up to.

As always, the streets of Cairo were crowded, and the light wasn't always good. But the Swiss banker was wearing a tan suit and a cream-colored fedora, so he wasn't hard to follow against the dark background. Joe kept an eye on him, hanging back about a block as he did so. After he had followed the man for several blocks, he glanced at his watch. He didn't want to waste too much time on this. He didn't want to go from being early for his date to being late.

When he looked up again, the guy was gone.

"Son of a bitch," Joe said as he came to a stop and stared up the street toward the next block. All he could think of was that Jimmy Christopher, hero of the *Operator 5* pulp magazine, wouldn't have let somebody he was tailing slip away that easily.

As that thought went through his head, he realized that he might as well admit it. He had seized the opportunity to play secret agent, just like he was Operator 5 or some other pulp hero. He'd been a childish fool. He knew good and well there was no reason to suspect somebody of being a spy just because he didn't like the guy. He might as well go back to Melinda's flat, because the man from Switzerland had disappeared.

Still, it wouldn't do any harm to take one last look around, a little voice in the back of his head urged. He checked his watch again. He could spare another few minutes. Making up his mind, he strode forward into the next block, not trying to be discreet about it now as he looked around.

Like most Cairo streets, this one was narrow and dirty. The right side of the block was lined with booths that formed a bazaar where merchants and vendors of all kinds could sell their wares. There were rugs, pottery, cheap souvenirs, jewelry, books, and all sorts of other things for sale. Brightly colored flags and banners, many of them with Arabic writing or symbols on them, overhung the booths. On the other side of the street, to Joe's left, were run-down apartments and a few office buildings populated during the day by doctors and lawyers and accountants. Now, in the early evening, most of those offices were dark. Pushcart vendors had moved in to fill the sidewalk, calling out and hawking various food items. The air was full of spicy smells and shouts from the pushcart men and the merchants in the bazaar across the way.

The guy Joe was following had been on the left-hand sidewalk, weaving his way around the pushcarts. Joe was sure of that. It seemed unlikely that during the second or two Joe's eyes had been on his wristwatch, the guy could have crossed the street to the bazaar. It made more sense that he had ducked into one of the buildings on the left. Joe walked along the block, ignoring the entreaties of the pushcart men, and looked at the doors, thinking that he might find one standing open. He started rattling the knobs as he came to them, but all the ones he tried were locked, the buildings closed for the day.

One of the entrances was set back from the sidewalk in a shadowy alcove. Joe stepped into it, thinking as he did so that this probably wasn't a very good idea. It was the sort of foolhardy thing Dale would do. Anything could be waiting there in the darkness, or anybody—with a gun or a knife.

He stopped short and reached inside one of the pockets of his uniform trousers. His fingers closed around his Ronson lighter. He didn't smoke except on rare occasions, but he carried a lighter anyway because it sometimes came in handy. Like now. He pulled it from his pocket, flipped up the top, and spun the wheel with his thumb. Sparks flew as the lighter lit. The little flame cast its flickering glow over the alcove. Joe jumped and jerked back as something shot past his legs. He looked down and caught a glimpse of a furry tail. Only a cat.

With his heart pounding, he took a deep breath and looked around the alcove. Nothing but dust and a grimy shop window with some cobwebs in one corner. He stepped closer to the door and tried the knob. It was locked. His quarry couldn't have gone this way unless he'd locked the door behind him. And the dust on the concrete floor of the alcove looked like it hadn't been disturbed for a while.

Joe turned back toward the street and closed the lighter, snuffing out the flame. At that moment a figure loomed in front of him, silhouetted against the uncertain light from the bazaar. The figure's arms were up, holding something above its head. Joe's eyes widened in alarm. He couldn't see very well. The glare from the lighter had caused his pupils to contract.

He flung himself to the side as the figure threw whatever it was holding at him. A large pot sailed past Joe's head to smash against the floor of the alcove. Hot liquid splashed on Joe's legs. The aromas of spices and meat were sharp in the air. He realized the man had just thrown a pot of boiling stew at him.

The man bored in, throwing punches. Joe got his arms up and blocked them as best he could. He hooked a left of his own at the man's midsection and connected. The man hesitated in his attack.

That gave Joe a chance to jab a right into his face. The man's head rocked back, his cream-colored fedora falling off.

Joe's eyes had adjusted well enough now so that he had no doubt whom he was fighting. The man must have hidden somewhere among the throng of pushcarts and waited until Joe was in the alcove before striking. That meant the guy must have spotted Joe tailing him. Again, that was something Operator 5 wouldn't let happen. But Operator 5 was a fictional character, and this was real life.

Joe stood there and traded punches with the man, the two of them slugging back and forth for a long moment. Joe's only advantage was that he had his back against the wall of the alcove and his opponent had to come to him. But the guy was bigger and probably stronger, and he fought with a quiet intensity that showed how seriously he took this battle. Panic nibbled at the edges of Joe's brain. If he lost this fight, he thought, the guy might actually kill him.

A fist caught him in the solar plexus, knocking the wind out of him. Desperation made Joe lash out with his foot, and luck guided the kick. The toe of Joe's boot slammed into the man's groin. The guy let out a strangled cry of pain and hunched over. He growled something that sounded like *"Verdammt Amerikaner!"*

The words were in German, Joe thought wildly. The guy wasn't Swiss at all. He was a Kraut!

That realization was so shocking Joe paused for a second and didn't capitalize on his momentary advantage. The man swung a backhand that staggered Joe and then chopped at his neck with the side of a hand. The blow numbed Joe's shoulder and arm and made him cry out. He went to a knee. The man moved in on him, doubled over in pain from the kick in the balls but still plenty dangerous.

The pounding of feet nearby made the man hesitate. He twisted his neck so that he could look over his shoulder, and what he saw down the street made him stagger out of the alcove and break into an awkward, weaving run. Joe's hands scrabbled against the wall as he pulled himself upright and stumbled out onto the sidewalk. He caught a glimpse of a light-colored suit vanishing around one of the pushcarts. The vendor yelled Arabic curses after the fleeing man.

Joe looked the other direction and saw several British soldiers hurrying toward him. As they came up, one of them caught hold of Joe's arm to steady him. "Hullo, Yank!" the Tommie said. "Are you all right?"

"Yeah, I guess." The numbness in Joe's neck and shoulder was starting to wear off now, and pain was taking its place.

One of the other Englishmen said, "Somebody told us there was a fight goin' on down here between two Yanks, so we thought we'd come take a gander."

Joe shook his head. "That guy was no American."

"No? A bloody wog, was it? Fella try to nick you, did he?"

"No, just . . . a disagreement."

How could he explain what had just happened? If he told these Tommies that he'd been playing secret agent and tailing the guy, they would want to know why. The whole thing was too complicated and confusing—especially the fact that the man had cursed him in German.

Or had it been Swiss? Did the two languages sound enough alike so that he had confused them? Was there even a Swiss language? Joe didn't know anything about Switzerland except what he had learned in geography class back in elementary school. Maybe they spoke German. The more he thought about it, the more right that sounded. He was crazy to have followed the guy in the first place.

"You're sure you're all right?"

"Yeah." Joe worked his shoulder back and forth, trying to loosen the assaulted muscles.

"Where're you headed? We'll go with you, just to make certain no one else bothers you."

"Back down the street about four blocks. My girl lives there."

The three soldiers grinned. The one holding Joe's arm said, "We'll just see you there safely, then. I'm sure we'll be leaving you in good hands."

"Thanks. I appreciate it."

Joe started away from the alcove but stopped as his foot hit something. He looked down and saw it was the man's fedora. He stooped and picked it up. He wasn't sure why.

"Combat souvenir, eh?" one of the soldiers said.

"I guess you could say that."

But was it a souvenir of a victory or a defeat? Joe couldn't answer that question.

# TWENTY-ONE

The three British soldiers were pleasantly drunk, but their presence was still reassuring to Joe. Nobody would bother him while he was in the company of three battle-hardened Desert Rats on temporary leave from El Alamein. While they were walking down the street with him, they told him that the standoff with the Germans would soon be over.

"Rommel and his bloody Afrika Corps don't know it yet, but we're gettin' ready to run them back to where they came from," one of the Tommies said as he slapped Joe on the back. "Only a matter of time before Monty sends 'em packin'."

Joe knew the man was referring to General Montgomery. "I've heard he hasn't really done much in the past."

"Hasn't done much?" Joe felt a twinge of guilt at the outraged tone in the British soldier's voice. After all, this man and his comrades had quite possibly saved Joe from being killed. "It's true, this is his first major command, but he served with distinction in the Great War. He's a first-rate soldier, or so we're told."

"Well, I wish him luck."

"Rommel's the one going to need the luck," one of the other men said.

When they reached the building where Melinda lived, Joe said, "This is it. Thanks for your help. I'm sure glad you boys came along when you did."

"You never did tell us why that bloke attacked you."

Joe had to shake his head. "I don't really know. He came at me without any warning."

"Daft from the heat, probably. It's enough to make any sane man go off his pot. That's why it doesn't bother these wogs. They're all balmy to start with."

Joe doubted that, but he didn't argue the point. He waved and said his farewells, and one of the Tommies called to him as he went into the building, "Better get some kip, Yank. You look done in."

Joe could have used some rest, all right. He had put in a full day working with the British at the armor depot on the outskirts of town, and then he'd had to fight for his life when all he really wanted to do was go out to dinner with his girl. He looked down at the fedora, which he still held in his hand, and thought about throwing it in the gutter. But the moment of anger passed, and he still carried the hat as he rode the lift up to Melinda's floor.

As he walked down the corridor toward her flat, he checked his watch. Even after everything that had happened, he was right on time. That was a stroke of luck. He paused before her door, adjusted his overseas cap, and brushed off his clothes, making sure they were straight after the tussle in the alcove. Then he knocked on the door.

Melinda opened it almost immediately, wearing a neat blue frock and looking lovely. She must have been waiting for him, he thought. Maybe she was just as anxious to see him as he was to see her. He liked that idea.

"Hullo, dearest," she said as she put her arms around his neck and gave him a quick kiss. As she stepped back, she looked down at the fedora in his hand and said, "Good heavens, what do you have there?"

"It's a hat," Joe said.

"I can see that. Where did you get it? You're not thinking of wearing it, are you?"

Joe glanced down at the hat with distaste. "Good grief, no. The guy who was wearing it probably has cooties."

"Cooties? Oh, you must mean he was lousy."

"In more ways than one."

Melinda took his arm and drew him on into the flat. "Really, love, your American slang is quite confusing."

"And the way you British talk isn't?"

Melinda plucked the hat from his hand and tossed it onto a table.

"Here, let's put the smelly old thing away. As for the way we talk, well, I prefer the universal language, myself."

"And that would be . . . ?"

"The language of love, of course." She moved closer to him and put her hands on his chest. She reached up with her head and found his lips with hers again.

Joe kissed her for a long moment and enjoyed every second of it. His arms went around her and urged her against him, and he felt the warm curves of her body molding to him. As he reacted to the closeness of their embrace, he thought that they had better be careful, or they'd get occupied with something else and miss their dinner at Shepheard's.

He put his hands on her shoulders and stepped back. "We'd better go," he said. His voice sounded breathless even to his own ears.

"We've got a few minutes," Melinda insisted. "How about a drink first?"

"Well . . . I don't suppose that would hurt anything."

Melinda moved over to a sideboard where a bottle of brandy and a pair of glasses sat on a silver tray. She had been ready for his arrival, Joe thought. She poured the drinks and gave him one of the glasses, then clinked her glass against his. "To better times ahead," she said.

"To better times," Joe echoed. He drank. The brandy was smooth and warmed him as it went down.

"You didn't say where you got that hat."

"I thought you wanted to forget about it."

"Well, I'm curious," she said. "Can't blame a girl for that. Her beau shows up with a strange fedora, she begins to wonder."

Joe had to laugh at the absurdity of her statement, but then he grew more serious. "Actually, it does have something to do with you," he said.

She looked surprised. "What in the world do you mean by that?"

"Remember a few weeks ago when we went dancing at the Continental's roof garden? The night you introduced your friend Betty to Dale?"

"Of course I remember. There was such a row, how could one forget?"

Joe went over to the table, set down his drink, and picked up the hat. "Well, this fedora belongs to the man who bumped into you that night, the one Dale was convinced stole something from your purse."

"What? Are you sure?"

"I'm the one he bumped into tonight," Joe said. "I saw him downstairs, leaving your building, and . . . well, I went after him. I followed him to see where he was going."

"Why in the world would you do that?"

Joe grimaced, feeling embarrassed by what he was about to say. "I thought the guy might be up to no good. I mean, first he steals something from you—"

"But I told you that night, nothing was missing from my bag."

"Yeah, but I'm still suspicious of the guy. Especially since he's lurking around here now. Something's not right about him."

Melinda looked worried. "Love, it sounds to me like you're letting these wild ideas run away with you. You should just forget about this man. I'm sure he's harmless and had a perfectly good reason for being here. If it was actually him you saw."

Now she thought he was seeing things. He sprang the last bit of information on her. "If he was harmless, why did he try to kill me?"

Melinda gasped, her hand going to her mouth. "He what?"

"I thought I'd lost him, so I closed in on where he'd been and started looking for him. But then he jumped me."

"He attacked you?"

"That's right. First he threw a pot of boiling stew at me that he'd grabbed from one of those street vendors, and then he tore into me with his fists."

"That's terrible! But perhaps he was afraid of you. If he'd seen you following him, he might have thought that you planned to rob him."

Joe hadn't thought about that, but after considering the idea for a second, he discarded it. "If that was the case, why didn't he just yell for a cop? No, he wanted to get me out of the way. He was trying to kill me."

Melinda stepped over to him. "Listen to me, Joseph Parker," she said. "I want you to stop playing detective. You're not Sexton bloody Blake! You could get hurt."

Joe looked into her soft brown eyes and saw the concern there. The world was at war, and here they were in a city being menaced by a steadily advancing army, and she was worried about one man posing a threat to him. That was touching, and Joe wanted to reassure her, but he knew he couldn't.

"It's not that easy," he said. "This guy could really be dangerous, not just to me but to other people as well. While we were fighting, he cursed me in German. I'm thinking he could be a Nazi spy."

"He said he worked for a Swiss bank! They speak German in Switzerland. It's one of the country's official languages, along with French and Italian."

"I wondered about that. Still, I think we have to take this seriously, Melinda. After all, you work for Major Richardson, and he's in intelligence. That guy could be planning to kidnap you and try to torture information out of you!"

Melinda shook her head. "That sounds like something out of one of your American pulp magazines."

"Maybe. But we can't afford to ignore this." Joe had made up his mind. "I'm going to talk to the major. Maybe he can find out who that bozo really is."

Melinda stared at him, a stricken expression on her face. He wondered why she was so upset about this. If that mysterious so-called Swiss banker was really after her, she ought to welcome some help from British Intelligence.

Joe's thoughts were in such a whirl that he was barely aware of the click of the knob as the door to the flat's bathroom opened behind him. But he heard the voice that spoke, loud and clear.

"Do not move, Sergeant Parker."

Joe had seen enough movies to know what that tone of voice meant. The guy had a gun pointed at him. He recognized the voice too. It belonged to the man who had tried to kill him a little while earlier.

Joe started to turn, thinking that he would keep himself between Melinda and the gun. He was too stunned to think about how the man had gotten into her flat. If he'd been forced to guess, he would have said that he must have come up the fire escape and climbed in through the bathroom window. Was there a fire escape? Joe didn't know. All he knew was that he was in the middle of something from a pulp story or a B movie, and he reacted accordingly.

"Joe, no!" Melinda said.

Joe didn't listen. He whipped around and threw the hat he was still holding. The fedora sailed through the air in a perfect throw, straight at the face of the man holding the gun. Joe tensed, waiting for the guy to duck. Then Joe would jump him, take the gun away, and—

The man batted the hat aside with his free hand. The pistol in his other hand didn't budge as it pointed at Joe.

"Oh, shit," Joe said.

From behind him now, Melinda said in a cold voice, "Well, you've gone and mucked it all up."

Joe twisted his neck to look in amazement over his shoulder. "Melinda?"

She stepped over to the sideboard, opened a drawer, and took out a small pistol. As she pointed it at Joe, she said, "Do you have to kill him?"

It took Joe a second to realize she was talking to the other man. The guy said, "Of course *we* have to kill him. He knows now of the connection between us."

"He wouldn't if you'd had a bit of bloody patience! But no! You have to come out and start waving a gun around like some sort of American gangster!"

"Shut up! I am in charge of this operation, not you."

Joe felt like the world had suddenly started spinning the wrong way. He was dizzy, disoriented. Yet he heard the exchange clearly enough and knew what it meant. The man really was a Nazi spy, and Melinda was in on it with him.

"You heard him yourself," the German agent went on. "He would not let it be. He was going to keep pressing until he caused trouble for us. We cannot have Richardson suspecting you!"

Joe stood there between the two guns and tried not to give in to the fear that was making his insides jump around wildly. He said, "Wait a minute. That night on the roof of the Continental . . . this guy really did take something out of your bag, didn't he, Melinda?"

She didn't answer, but the German agent did. "Of course I did. It was vital information your Miss Thorp-Davies got from that Rawl-inson woman."

Joe's eyes jerked to Melinda. "Betty's part of this too?"

"No," she said. "She has no idea I've been using my friendship with her to pick up intelligence from the cartography section." Melinda gave Joe a sad smile. "I know what you're doing, Joe. I really did read your stories, and a lot of others in those magazines. You're stalling for time and trying to get us to explain everything to you, so that when you turn the tables on us, you'll have the evidence you need to bring us to what you consider justice. But it's not going to happen that way, love."

"No," the German agent agreed, "what's going to happen is that I'm going to knock you unconscious, drag you out, and cut your throat in an alley somewhere blocks away from here, so that your death will seem to have no connection with Melinda."

"My brother knows I came here tonight," Joe said. He was close to panicking.

Melinda shook her head. "Dale knows this was your destination. He doesn't know that you arrived. He'll think that you were murdered by a thief on your way here."

How could she speak so coldly of his death? Hadn't anything that happened between them meant anything?

"Why?" he asked, his voice breaking. "Why did you go out with me? I don't know anything that would interest a Nazi spy!"

"I couldn't very well make Major Richardson suspicious when he decided to play Cupid, so I agreed to that first date." Again Melinda smiled that sad smile. "After that . . . well, I really did like you, Joe. One thing had nothing to do with the other."

"You liked me," he repeated. "But you'll let this bastard kill me!"

"I have no choice. You know too much now."

Joe looked back and forth between them. He was going to die. Not in combat, but with his throat slashed in some filthy Cairo back alley. He wanted to cry or beg for his life, but he wouldn't give that cold-eyed German son of a bitch the satisfaction.

"Just tell me why you'd betray your country like this."

She shook her head. "You don't want to know."

"Enough," the man said. "Hold your gun on him while I . . ."

Joe heard the man moving up quick behind him. He knew the guy was going to clout him over the head with the heavy pistol in his hand. That would be the end of it. Joe would go out, and he would never wake up.

The hell with that, he thought as he turned. If they were going to kill him, they were going to have to shoot him. He ducked his head and threw himself at the German like a football lineman throwing a block.

The man chopped down at him with the butt of the pistol. It cracked against Joe's shoulder. Pain shot through him. But Joe rammed into the man's thighs and knocked him backward. The guy went down with Joe lying half on top of him. Joe grabbed for the wrist of the man's gun hand.

"Shoot him!" the man hissed at Melinda as he tried to squirm out of Joe's grip.

"But the noise—"

"Press the muzzle into his body!" The German tried to throw Joe off of him. "It will muffle the shot!"

Melinda hesitated. Joe kicked back at her and felt his foot connect with her shin. She cried out in pain and fell. Joe threw an awkward punch at the man's face but missed. The German's knee came up into his stomach. The vicious blow made him feel sick, but he managed to hang on to the man's wrist.

Then somebody kicked open the door of the flat and several men rushed into the room. A gun went off, its report loud and painful to the ears in the close quarters. He saw a booted foot smash into the side of the German's head, just above the ear. The guy quit fighting and went limp. A hand plucked the pistol away, and then another hand fastened around Joe's arm and hauled him to his feet.

He found himself staring in confusion into the bland face of Major Colin Richardson. "Good work, my boy," Richardson said as he tugged Joe toward the door. Joe saw three or four other British officers in the room. They closed in around the unconscious German agent and also around Melinda, who lay slumped on the floor in front of the sideboard. Joe looked around as Richardson was hustling him out of the flat and caught a glimpse of bright red blood in a pool around Melinda's head.

"Don't look, Sergeant," Richardson said in a quiet voice as he led Joe into the corridor. "It won't do anyone any good now."

"You . . . you shot her!" Joe managed to say.

Richardson shook his head. "She shot herself, Joe. All of us saw it, but there was nothing we could do. I suspect she couldn't stand the thought of being arrested, taken back to England, and put on trial as a traitor." He pulled the door of the flat shut, leaving the other officers inside to clean up the mess.

"She . . . she really was working for the Nazis?"

Richardson nodded and said, "She was. We'd suspected her for a while, but she was very good, never a slipup. So I decided to sic you on her."

Joe stared at the major. "I thought you were just trying to fix us up! So did Melinda!"

"That's what both of you were supposed to think. She had a genuine love for those magazine stories. You wrote them." Richardson sighed. "It was too good an opportunity to pass up. I knew you were a bright young man. Our hope was that if something were indeed awry with Melinda, you would spot it, just as you did. I didn't expect that you'd be in any real danger, though. I . . . regret that."

Joe's voice shook with emotion as he said, "What about Melinda? Do you regret that she's dead?"

"Of course I do. I should have liked to have had the chance to interrogate her. We'll just have to make do with her partner."

Joe's hands were trembling. He lifted them and looked at them for a second and then said, "You son of a bitch. You used me."

"I told you all along I thought you'd be good at intelligence work. Seems that I was right, doesn't it?"

Joe didn't think about what he was doing. He just reached out and bunched the collar of Richardson's khaki shirt in his fists. He jerked Richardson toward him and said, "Don't you ever do that to me again!"

The major's face was impassive. He said, "Manhandling a superior officer is a serious offense, but since there are no witnesses, I shan't make an issue of it."

Joe let go of him and stepped back, struggling to maintain control.

Richardson straightened his shirt and went on, "As for making such use of you in the future, unfortunately, that won't be possible. You see, you and your brother will be leaving Cairo shortly."

"You're getting rid of us?"

"*I'm* not doing anything. It's your own army behind your departure."

Joe stared at him. "What?"

"I probably should allow this news to proceed through the regular channels, but under the circumstances I deem it best to inform you, Sergeant Parker, that within the week, you and your brother and the rest of the American force on temporary detached duty to the Eighth Army will be receiving new orders. You're being reassigned back to your own forces, Sergeant."

"But . . . but why?"

"I expect your superiors have something else for you to do that they consider more important."

This was it, Joe thought. Finally, the United States was going to do something to get into this war on more than a limited basis.

"You know, don't you?" he said as he saw the faint smile on Richardson's face. "You know what's going to happen."

"Let's just say that soon, the torch will be lit."

# TWENTY-TWO

Their time together was too short. It always was. If he spent eternity with Catherine, that still wouldn't be long enough, Adam thought as he stood at the railing of the *Jackson* and waited for the word to scramble over the rail, onto the net, and down into the waiting Higgins boat. Even at this moment, when all of his attention should have been focused on the job at hand, she was in his thoughts. She would never be far from them.

They had slept as little as possible during the one night he had spent on Tonga Tabu. They made love again and again, and in the intervals between they had lain there caressing and exploring each other's bodies and talking in quiet tones of all they felt for each other and meant to each other. And when the dawn began to creep grayly into the room, they made love again and held each other as if they would never let go.

But let go they had. There was no choice. Adam had to get back to the ship, back to the men he would lead into battle. And Catherine had to return to the *Solace*, where she would continue to help healing the men who had been wounded in earlier battles. Their love was so great it should have filled the whole world, Adam thought, but it had to make room for the war. . . .

"Go! Go! Go!"

"Over the side! Now!"

"Move! Move! Move!"

Shouted orders filled the air. With helmet, weapons, and full pack Adam went over the railing, clinging to the net. He turned so that his back was to the water and he was facing the side of the ship. Then he started climbing down, moving as quickly as he could without falling. Back in the States, when they had practiced this maneu-

ver in the warm waters off La Jolla, many of the Marines had gotten in too much of a hurry and fallen. The lucky ones went into the water. The less fortunate hit the Higgins boat or got a foot tangled in the net and hung up in it. Broken bones were common, especially broken ankles.

Moving one hand and one foot at a time, Adam went down the net. He looked over his shoulder and saw that he was close enough to the landing craft to let go. He dropped onto the wooden floor of the Higgins boat. The steel sides of the rectangular, ungainly-looking vessel were about the same height as Adam's head. He could see over them, and far in the distance to the southeast, he picked out the dark smudge low on the horizon that marked the location of Fiji.

"Look out below!" somebody yelled.

Adam glanced up to see one of the Marines plummeting toward him, arms flailing as he fell. Adam jumped out of the way. The guy smashed feet first into the deck and cried out in pain as he crumpled into a heap. That was another broken ankle, Adam thought. He and another of the Marines already in the boat bent to help the injured man to his feet. The man cursed and whimpered as he tried to stand up and put weight on his right leg.

Adam looked along the high, curving gray wall of the ship's hull. Dozens of nets hung down with the waiting Higgins boats below them, and Marines were hung up all over the nets. Others fell into the water and had to be hauled out by sailors in small boats before the weight of their weapons and packs pulled them down. This practice was going badly. But for all that, it was still better than the disaster that the previous day's practice landing had produced. In that drill, less than half the men who had swarmed over the sides of the transport ships had reached the landing craft safely and on the first try.

The little improvement Adam could see today wasn't much, but it would have to be enough. There wouldn't be time for any more practice landings.

Following the brief liberty at Tonga Tabu, the ships carrying the Second Regiment of the Second Marine Division had sailed on to Fiji for a rendezvous with the First Marine Division. During that part of the voyage, official word of their ultimate destination had been given to the officers, from which it filtered down the chain of command to the rest of the men. As nearly everyone had suspected, they were on their way to the Japanese-occupied Solomon Islands. The First Division's goal was Guadalcanal, the largest island in the chain. Intelligence gathered from agents who were familiar with the situation, most of them Australian, indicated that the Japanese were building an airfield on Guadalcanal. Most of their troops were there as well. CINCPAC and the other brass in the high command had decided that the Japs must not be allowed to finish that airfield. Planes based there would pose too great a threat to Australia. Also, if the Marines could recapture the island from the Japanese troops stationed there, it would be a great morale booster. The naval victories in the Battle of the Coral Sea and at Midway had exposed weaknesses in the Japanese juggernaut that had looked so unstoppable only six months earlier. Now an equally meaningful triumph on land was needed.

It appeared unlikely, though, that the Second Regiment would have much to do with such a triumph. It was being held in reserve while the First Division went ashore on Guadalcanal. Only the 1st Battalion of the Second Regiment would see action. It was scheduled to land on the smaller islands of Florida and Tulagi, across the strait to the northeast of Guadalcanal.

Adam's platoon was part of the 1st Battalion, as was that commanded by Ted Nash. So Adam, Ed Collins, and Leo Sikorsky would all get their chance to go ashore with the first wave of troops. A year earlier, while they were all together at Parris Island, crawling through the sand of the obstacle course and swatting at fleas, they had trained for the day that would soon be upon them. They had gone from being little better than sand fleas themselves to being Marines. Adam had already put his training to use, fighting the Japs on Wake Island. Now it was time for Ed and Leo and all the other leathernecks on these ships to do their part. As the second day of landing practice concluded and the men climbed wearily out of the Higgins boats and up the nets, an atmosphere of mingled fear and eagerness hung over the ships. The Marines knew that practice, even though it hadn't gone all that well, was over. There was no time for more. The ships would sail from Fiji even before the sun rose again.

The next stop would be the Solomons.

\*　　\*　　\*

Several days passed as the convoy steamed northwestward. The men sweated in the hot compartments belowdecks as they waited to arrive at their destination. Some of them chattered nervously and played cards; others sat and wrote letters or read. The brass weren't expecting too much resistance on Florida and Tulagi, but taking the islands wouldn't be a walk in the park and everybody knew it. All it took was one Jap, one bullet with a guy's name on it. Men thought about what was coming, and some felt a sense of fatalism, like their number had already come up. Others experienced a feeling of invincibility, a knowledge that, sure, some guys would die, but it would always be the other fella, not them. Some men wrestled with both emotions, confident one minute that nothing would happen to them, plunging into despair the next as if they were being measured for a coffin.

It was one hell of a way to be, Adam thought as he watched his men and wished there was something he could do to make it easier for them. But he was struggling with his own feelings at the same time and thinking of Catherine. Always Catherine.

On the evening of 6 August 1942, Adam got the word from the company CO. The landing would be the next morning. The men were to prepare for it and then get some sleep.

Not much chance of that. They would prepare . . . they would be ready to go when the time came . . . but there wouldn't be much sleeping going on tonight.

The first thing to do was check on the packs the men would carry. Each Marine had a small shoulder pack containing underwear, socks, and a shaving kit. The larger double pack carried on the back was where the men stowed their mess kits, rations, extra uniforms, and whatever personal belongings—books, Bibles, photographs of their families or girlfriends—they might have. Their blanket, shelter half—a piece of canvas that could be joined with another Marine's to form a tent—and poncho formed a bedroll that was draped around the pack and strapped into place. They carried clips of extra ammunition in the large snap pockets on their uniform blouses, and they had grenades fastened to their belts.

Each squad's sergeant was responsible for inspecting his men's gear. When he was satisfied, he reported to the platoon leader that everything was ready. When the last of Adam's sergeants had given him the thumbs-up, he gathered them around and said, "Everybody gets a shower, then some sack time."

One of the sergeants, an old China hand named Lederer, laughed and said, "What, we gotta be clean to fight those yellow heathens?"

"That's right, Sergeant," Adam said. "It's been a long, sticky, grimy trip. We might as well take advantage of the opportunity to spiff up a little."

There was another good reason for the showers, but Adam didn't explain it. When a bullet tore into flesh, it took whatever was on the skin with it. Dirt would cause a wound to become infected more easily.

The noncoms filed out of Adam's quarters and went to carry out his orders. Once they were gone, he looked to his own gear, putting everything in order. When he was done, he cleaned his Springfield and the Colt .45 1911A1. Satisfied that the weapons were in good working order, he took out a small whetstone and sharpened the combat knife he would wear in a sheath on his left hip. The blade shone in the dim light from a bare bulb in a wire cage on the ceiling of his compartment. He held it up, studied it, ran his thumb along the edge of the blade. If he had to, could he plunge that cold steel into the body of another human being?

If it was to save his own life, or the life of one of his men, he knew that he could. He would pray for the souls of the men he was forced to kill, but he hoped he would not hesitate to kill them if he needed to.

It was late before he got his own shower. The tepid water trickled from the showerhead, the supply of fresh water running low by now. He scrubbed up, rinsed as best he could, dried off, and went back to his compartment to put on fresh skivvies and stretch out on the hard, narrow bunk. As an officer, he had some privacy and didn't have another bunk a mere two feet above him. Right now, though, he wouldn't have minded some company. Back on Wake Island, he could always count on Private Gurnwall to break up any tense moments. Gurney hardly ever shut up, and he usually had something funny to say.

Adam stared at the darkened ceiling and wondered where Gurnwall was now, wondered if the young man from Oklahoma was even still alive. When Wake fell, all the Americans on the atoll had been either killed or taken prisoner by the Japanese. Adam didn't know what to hope for. After a while, he decided that he hoped Gurnwall and Rolofson and all the other guys he had known there were still alive. Being locked up in a Jap prison camp might be hellish, but if they could hold out, sooner or later the war would be over and they would be freed.

So in a way, Adam told himself, he would be fighting tomorrow for Gurnwall and the others, as well as for the tens of thousands of troops who would come after him in the campaign to push the Japanese out of their Pacific strongholds. The sooner that was done, the fewer people who would die in the long run.

Somebody had to be first, though, and that duty . . . that honor . . . had fallen to Adam and his companions.

That thought was going through his brain, along with memories of Catherine, when he surprised himself by going to sleep.

*　　*　　*

The call to quarters sounded at 0300. Adam sat up and rolled out of his bunk, his movements automatic because he wasn't fully awake yet. He turned on the light and then reached for the clean set of greens he had put out the night before. Actually, that had been only a few hours ago, he thought. He pulled on the clean uniform and sat down on the bunk to put on his socks and boots. As he did so, he paused and looked at his hands. The fingers trembled just a little, but as he watched them, the shaking stopped. He went back to what he was doing, the moment of fear having passed. It was time for action now.

The sergeants had the men up and moving through the chow lines. There wasn't much talking going on. The loudspeakers were silent. Until now, music had played over the speakers much of the time, usually big band tunes with plenty of swing to keep the men in a good mood. Nobody wanted to listen to sad ballads when they were sailing off into the unknown, leaving wives and sweethearts behind, maybe forever. Now the quiet was a little unnerving, Adam thought as he moved through the line in the officers' mess and got his food. It was simple fare this morning: beans and cornbread, milk and orange juice and coffee. The servers put plenty of food on each man's plate. There was no way of knowing when they would have a chance to eat again, and when they did, it was likely to be the unappetizing rations in their packs.

And for some, this meal would be their last.

Adam put that thought out of his head as he ate. Someone sat down beside him at the steel table. He looked over and saw Ted Nash, dressed in the same sort of green uniform Adam wore. Nash gave him a curt nod and started eating, but after a minute or so, Nash paused and said, "Bergman."

Adam was sipping his coffee. He put the cup down and said, "Yeah?"

"Look, I'm sorry about the hard feelings between us since we left the States. We started out as friends. Do you think we could end up that way?"

"I was never not your friend, Ted," Adam said. "And I didn't mean to cause trouble between us."

"Yeah, well, I'd rather not start hashing out who was to blame and who wasn't." Nash put out his hand. "I'd rather shake and wish you the best of luck."

Without hesitation, Adam took Nash's hand. "Good luck, Ted. You're a good officer. You and your platoon will do fine."

"They're good men. Even Collins and Sikorsky. Just don't ever tell them I said that."

Adam smiled. "It'll be between you and me."

They went back to their breakfast and were almost done when orders began to come over the loudspeakers instructing each company in turn to move to its debarkation station. Adam gulped down the last of his coffee, followed it with a final swig of orange juice, and then went up on deck to the area where his company was gathering.

A warm, humid wind was blowing. Adam felt beads of sweat on

his face. He wanted to wipe them off with his sleeve but didn't do it, thinking that to do so might make him appear nervous. Of course, he *was* nervous. Only a fool wouldn't be under these circumstances.

The decks were blacked out, and it was a cloudy night with only a few stars peeking through the overcast. Adam tried to check on his men, but he couldn't see much. Sergeants Lederer, McDade, Vardeman, and Richards moved among their squads, and Adam knew they would report to him any problems they couldn't handle themselves. Considering how competent all four of them were, Adam didn't expect much if any trouble.

For the men already on deck, time dragged as the other companies climbed the ladders and emerged from the hatches to line up at their appointed spots. Adam checked his own gear again, well aware that he had everything and it was all where it was supposed to be, but it was something to do. When he was finished, he stared out into the darkness, trying to orient himself. Was he looking south toward Guadalcanal or north toward Florida? He wasn't sure, but after a few minutes he decided he was facing toward Florida. His company was on the starboard side of the ship, so that had to be correct. Unless he had gotten really turned around . . .

A huge roar split the night, so loud that the deck seemed to shake under Adam's feet. At the same instant, great gouts of yellow and orange flame tore apart the darkness. Adam knew what was happening because the CO had advised all the junior officers of the battle plan. The Navy had begun its bombardment of the targets. All the battleships and cruisers and destroyers accompanying the convoy of transport ships were opening up on Guadalcanal, Florida, and the smaller islands—Tulagi, Gavutu, and Tanambogo—clustered along the southern shore of Florida. This barrage was intended to soften up the Japanese defenders. It also served to announce that the Marines were there, as if the Japanese didn't already know that from the flights of their reconnaissance planes. This was no sneak attack like what the Japs had pulled at Pearl Harbor.

The bombardment was awesome, a symphony of noise and flame that filled the vast theater of sky and water and land. During one of the few lulls in the firing, Adam heard a man in one of the other platoons exclaim loudly, "Son of a fuckin' *bitch!*" and recognized Ed Collins's voice. For once, though, Ed's casually coarse comment sounded more like a prayer than a curse.

The flashes from the big guns revealed the true nature of the convoy. More ships than Adam had imagined had joined them during the night as they moved into position in the strait. This was the biggest armada he had ever seen. To his inexperienced eyes, it looked like the entire United States Navy was gathered here. He knew that couldn't be the case, but seeing that stretch of black water covered with American ships was still an awe-inspiring sight.

Dawn was approaching now, and as the gray light grew stronger, Adam could make out more details on board the ship. He saw the men of his platoon standing stiff and ready, their faces grim. The sergeants, all of them veterans of combat in China and Nicaragua, looked almost bored. They had made fighting, and preparing to fight, their life's work, and this was their time.

Adam took a deep breath and turned his head to look out across the water. Dark shapes began to form where the islands lay, phantoms that became more solid only as the light grew stronger. He had studied the maps and knew where they all lay: Florida, the largest, most rugged shape; Tulagi, long and narrow with a ridge of mountains running down its spine, just off the thick peninsula that jutted out to the southwest from Florida; Gavutu and Tanambogo to the right across a bay, the smallest of the bunch. Until this moment, they had just been names. Now, as Adam stared at them, they became real at last, the places where battles would be won and lost, where men would live and die.

Captain Hughes bellowed orders through a bullhorn so that he could be heard over the thunder of the bombardment. "C Company, prepare to move out!" A moment later, "C Company, move out! C Company, move out! Go! Go! Go!"

Adam started toward the railing, echoing the captain's orders. "Over the side! Move! Move!" The sergeants took up the chant, and with a roar of anticipation, the Marines surged forward to go over the rail, down the nets, and into the Higgins boats that would serve as landing craft.

The American invasion of the Solomon Islands had begun. It was not quite 0600, 7 August 1942.

# TWENTY-THREE

Adam took his time going down the net. No point in hurrying now, he told himself. The Japs weren't going anywhere. When he was low enough he dropped into the Higgins boat. A glance up at the net above him revealed the men of his platoon climbing down in the same unhurried but efficient manner. He looked along the side of the ship and saw the same thing happening as the other platoons in the company descended the nets. For some reason, now that it was the real thing, the debarkation was proceeding in smoother fashion than it ever had in practice.

Within ten minutes, all the men of Adam's platoon were in the landing craft. He checked with the sergeants and made sure no injuries had been sustained. They assured him that everyone was in the boat safe and sound. Adam looked to the Navy coxswain at the controls of the boat, expecting the man to start edging the craft away from the hull of the transport ship. Instead, the coxswain stood there stolidly, his hand on the wheel of the Higgins boat.

"Aren't we going in?" Adam asked.

The sailor shook his head. "Not yet, Lieutenant. I got my orders."

Adam pushed his helmet back a little on his head and nodded. There was no point in arguing with the coxswain. He would get underway when he was supposed to, and not before.

Looking through the gray dawn light and the morning mist, Adam saw that several of the landing craft had pulled away from the transport ships and were on their way toward Florida. He couldn't hear their motors, but he knew the diesels were rumbling powerfully as they carried the craft through the bay between Tulagi and the matched pair of Gavutu and Tanambogo. The naval bombardment

185

was still going on, though the pace of the firing had slackened somewhat since the men of the 1st Battalion had started ashore.

Standing not far away from Adam, Sergeant McDade muttered, "What the hell are we waitin' for? An engraved invitation?"

Adam had expected them to go on in too, but he supposed the brass had good reasons for holding them back. He stared toward Florida, looking for the flashes that would indicate the Japanese were firing on the American landing forces. The only shots were the ones coming from the naval vessels, however.

What was going on here? Adam wondered. Could their intelligence have been wrong? Maybe there weren't any Japanese troops here in the Solomons. That seemed impossible considering all the reconnaissance that had been done, but there had to be some reason the boats going ashore weren't encountering the resistance they had expected.

The possibility of a trap leaped into Adam's mind. Perhaps the Japanese gunners were just waiting for the landing to take place, and then they would drop a rain of death on the beaches. Considering the treacherous nature of the attack on Pearl Harbor, springing such a deadly trap didn't seem beyond them.

As the light grew stronger, Adam dug his binoculars out of his pack and focused them on Florida. He saw the Higgins boats bobbing on the waves that washed ashore. As he watched, the first landing craft reached the beaches and dropped their ramps. Still, no fire came from the thick jungle on the far side of the sand. Adam couldn't make out the details, but he could tell that the Marines of B Company were going ashore now, the first American troops to set foot on Japanese-held ground. He felt a pang of inexplicable jealousy. It didn't matter who was first, he told himself. What was important was who won the battle for these islands.

Adam was sure that before the day was over, he and his men would be doing their part to win that battle.

But to Adam's great frustration, that proved not to be the case. For long hours, as their impatience grew, the men of Third Platoon, C

Company, waited in the Higgins boat. The landing craft rose and fell in the water more than the big transport ship did, and some of the Marines began to get seasick. That didn't bother Adam nearly as much as did the fact that they were being held back, out of the action.

That wasn't true of all the landing parties. Though it was still quiet on Florida, firing erupted from Tulagi and Gavutu. According to intelligence reports, only a few Japanese troops were posted on those smaller islands, but as the roar of artillery and the clatter of machine gun and small arms fire drifted over the water, it became obvious to the men waiting to get into combat that Tulagi and Gavutu were the real hot spots this morning.

Noon came and went while Adam and his men sweated and waited in the landing craft. The men were hungry, but no one wanted to break into his pack and make lunch on the rations carried there. They might need those rations even more once they went ashore—assuming they ever did. Some of the men groused that all the fighting was going to be over before they ever got their chance.

Adam doubted that, but he shared the same impatience his men were feeling. He wanted land under his feet again, even if it meant that somebody might be shooting at him.

In mid-afternoon, C Company was ordered back up the nets and onto the ship. Reluctantly, and with a lot of cursing, they complied. Once they were back on the ship, they wasted no time in trying to get the latest scuttlebutt from the sailors. Everyone wanted to know what was going on ashore.

While the enlisted men had to be content with rumors, Adam and the other officers attended a briefing where the day's action was explained to them. On the other side of Sealark Channel, the First Marine Division had gone ashore on Guadalcanal, expecting strong resistance. Instead they had encountered no enemy fire on landing and had moved inland to find deserted camps that the Japanese soldiers had abandoned. Judging by the evidence, the Japs had left recently and in a hurry, probably when the naval bombardment started. American patrols had run into a few snipers as they pushed into the jungle, but by and large the landing had been free from danger. By late afternoon, the Marines of the First Division found themselves in control of a large strip of land along the northern coast of

Guadalcanal, including the partially finished airfield the Japanese had been building.

On Florida, the Second Division Marines had had much the same experience. They took no fire upon landing, and as they moved inland they found only deserted villages and camps. No one believed that the Japanese were gone; the best guess was that they had moved inland into the hills. But for now they weren't putting up a fight.

That wasn't the case on Gavutu and Tulagi. Led by Colonel Merritt Edson's Marine Raiders, the landing force had gone ashore and run into stiff resistance from the Japanese on both islands. They would need reinforcements, and when Adam heard that, he assumed that he and his men would be among those fresh troops going to the assistance of the Raiders. His spirits fell when the briefing officer explained that some of the men on Florida would be pulled off that island and sent to Tulagi and Gavutu. Adam's face was taut with disappointment as the briefing concluded and he went to break the news to his platoon that they wouldn't be going anywhere today.

The men were still up on deck. As Adam emerged from the hatch, he heard excited shouts and the high-pitched roar of aircraft engines. A second later, an explosion sounded, then another and another. Adam rushed to the railing where his platoon was gathered. "What's going on?" he demanded.

Sergeant Vardeman, a tall, lean man from New Mexico, pointed into the sky and said, "Jap dive-bombers!"

Adam looked up and saw the enemy planes streaking through the air above the channel. Antiaircraft fire burst out from the American ships, puffs of black-and-white smoke spreading through the sky as the AA shells exploded. The Japanese bombers roared through the screen of fire, somehow untouched by it as they launched into their steep, screaming dives toward their targets. Adam watched, powerless to do anything, as bombs rained down around the American vessels. Luckily, the direct hits were few. Most of the bombs fell into the channel, throwing columns of water high into the air as they exploded. Everything was chaos, though.

Barney Gelhart crowded to the rail next to Adam and gripped his arm. Adam looked over at his fellow lieutenant. Gelhart pointed and said, "What's that son of a bitch doing?"

Adam's eyes followed Gelhart's finger and found a Japanese plane that was flying straight at one of the other ships. Adam thought it was the *Crescent City,* but he couldn't be sure. He saw that the plane had already released its bomb, but even though its deadly cargo was gone, the Japanese pilot must have intended to make a weapon out of the aircraft itself. That had to be why he had aimed it directly at the bridge of the American ship.

"He's going to crash right into it!" Adam exclaimed. His stunned mind could barely comprehend such a thing. The pilot would die, but the explosion that would take place when his plane hit the ship could do horrible damage.

Adam saw the ship's gunners bailing out from their gun tubs as the Japanese plane shrieked through the air toward them. Suddenly, one of the forward machine guns began to erupt in flame and smoke once more. The green uniform of the man firing the gun told Adam that he was a Marine who had jumped in to man the abandoned gun. Wrestling the AA machine gun around to keep his aim centered on the suicide plane, the Marine hosed a steady stream of lead into the sky. Adam's hands tightened on the railing as he saw the plane's propeller smashed by the Marine's bullets. The plane's nose dropped as fire billowed from its engine. With a huge splash, the bomber hit the water only yards from the bow of the ship.

Wild cheers rose from the hundreds of Marines and sailors gathered along the railings of the other ships. As fighters from the carriers swarmed into the air, the Japanese dive-bombers climbed to a higher altitude and turned to run back to the field where they had taken off, probably at Rabaul on the island of New Ireland. The Wildcats downed several of the bombers and made sure none of the others doubled back to continue the attack.

The naval bombardment resumed at full strength as reinforcements from Florida were dispatched to Tulagi, Gavutu, and Tanambogo. C Company remained on board ship with orders to secure their packs and weapons and remain ready for movement on short notice. It had been a frustrating day for Adam and his fellow Marines. They had been ready for action, but instead, they had only stood and watched. And as night fell over the Solomons, hardly a one of them would have put much stock in the old saying about how "they also serve who only stand and wait" . . .

*   *   *

Just like riding a bicycle, Phil Lange thought as he pulled back on the stick and sent the Douglas SBD Dauntless into a screaming climb toward the heavens. Once you knew how to fly one of these babies, you never forgot.

A couple of heartbeats earlier, Phil had thumbed the bomb release button on top of the stick and sent the pair of 800-pound bombs attached to the bottom of the Dauntless plummeting toward the rudimentary airfield below. As soon as the bombs were away, he pulled out of the dive and headed back up into the sky. The Japs weren't even trying to fight back; Phil hadn't seen even a single burst of antiaircraft fire during the several flights he had made today from the *Enterprise*. He wasn't sure why they weren't trying to defend Guadalcanal, but these milk runs were all right with him. He didn't mind not being shot at.

The bombs he had dropped exploded somewhere below. Phil didn't look back to check the damage. He'd aimed at what appeared to be a storage building off to the edge of the runway the Japanese had been constructing. The American pilots were trying to avoid dropping their bombs on the runway itself. Once the Marines on the ground had control of the area, the Pioneer Battalions would move in and finish the runway so that American planes could use it. The less it was torn up, the easier that job would be.

"Good shot!" Ensign Roy Kirkland called over the Dauntless's cabin radio. "You blew that building into a million pieces, Lieutenant!"

Phil just grunted. He didn't want to engage in long conversations with Kirkland. The kid was fresh-faced and eager and obviously looked up to him, but Phil didn't care. He had lost one friend already when Jerry Bennett died somewhere over the Pacific west of Midway. If anything happened to Kirkland, Phil would be losing a crew member, that was all. He would regret it, but he would be able to go on.

"What the hell's that?" Kirkland exclaimed. "Look over there at, uh, nine o'clock, Lieutenant."

Kid was so green he had to think about it before he indicated the direction, Phil thought. And that was who they had given him to serve as rear gunner and observer in the two-man SBD.

Phil put that thought out of his mind and turned his head to peer through his goggles at the planes Kirkland was talking about. They were large, twin-engined jobs flying in a V-formation. Phil recognized the type right away: they were Mitsubishi G4M bombers, better known to the Americans as Bettys. Phil looked higher and saw the accompanying fighters. Zeros, the same kind that had shot down his first Dauntless and killed Jerry.

They had been expecting trouble all day, and now here it was. The Japs had a lot of planes based at Rabaul, and they would have been in the air as soon as word was received of the American invasion of the Solomon Islands. The Japanese soldiers on the ground might not be putting up a fight, but their air forces were ready to enter the fray. The Bettys angled down sharply and headed for the U.S. ships that clogged the strait between Guadalcanal and Florida.

Phil climbed, getting the Dauntless out of the way so that the American fighters already in the air and those that were scrambling to take off from the carriers would have a free hand in attacking the Japanese planes. In a pinch, the Dauntless could serve as a fighter; it had sufficient armament and speed to put up a good fight even matched against a Zero. But the Wildcats were better suited to aerial combat. The Thach Weave, a zigzag maneuver named after its originator, American combat aviator Jimmy Thach, was particularly effective against the Zeros when the Wildcats carried it out.

Phil circled, well above the puffs of antiaircraft fire from the ships, and watched as the Japanese bombers carried out their mission. They performed well when it came to avoiding the AA bursts, but their bombing itself left something to be desired. Phil watched stick after stick go into the drink, exploding without doing any harm. He didn't see any major fires on any of the ships.

The most dramatic moment came when one of the Bettys tried to ram a ship. Phil had never seen such a thing before. The Jap pilot was using his plane like it was a bomb itself. From the rear cockpit,

Kirkland exclaimed, "Holy crap, he's going to crash right into that ship!"

Phil thought the same thing, but somebody on the ship shot down the plane just before it reached its target. Heaving a sigh of relief, Phil said, "That guy had to be crazy."

He knew he wouldn't have the guts to fly right into a ship like that. To an observer, it might appear that a Dauntless was plummeting straight down at its target during a bombing run, but the pilots always left themselves room to pull up after releasing their bombs. Oh, sure, from time to time something might happen—the pilot could get hit, or the plane could suffer some sort of mechanical failure—that would cause a dive-bomber to crash, but it was never intentional.

After that suicidal Betty crashed, the rest of the Jap flight turned and ran. The Wildcats went after them, harrying them and shooting down a couple more. Phil banked toward the *Enterprise*. Now that the excitement was over, he could land.

"Look out, Lieutenant!" Kirkland screamed. "Above us!"

Phil jerked his head back and saw the Zero diving toward them. Flames were already licking out from the muzzles of the Japanese plane's machine guns. Phil kicked the Dauntless into such a sharp turn that for a moment he thought he was going to lose control. He wrestled the stick back into position before the plane could go into a roll and then looked around for the Zero. It was below them now, having shot past while Phil was making the desperate maneuver to get the Dauntless out of the line of fire. He thought about going after the Jap but decided not to. Where the hell were all the Wildcats? Hadn't any of them stuck around to make sure something like this didn't happen?

He didn't see any of the F4F-4s, only the lone Zero now banking and climbing into position to make another pass at him. From the rear cockpit, Kirkland called, "You can get him, Lieutenant! You can get him!"

How in blazes did the kid know that? The rear gunner in a Dauntless sat facing backward so that he could see where the bombs landed after they were dropped and protect the plane from being attacked from behind. Kirkland must have unbuckled his safety belt and turned almost completely around in the seat.

"Man your gun, Ensign!" Phil snapped over the intercom. He had to fight to keep his voice from shaking.

He had been fine during the first part of the action, calm and cool, no nerves at all as far as he could tell. But when that Zero had dived at them, guns blazing, fear had come rushing back into Phil's mind. He had reacted on pure instinct, without thought, because if he had stopped to think, he would have been so frightened that he and Kirkland wouldn't have stood a chance.

It was too much like that other day, the day Jerry had died and Phil had been wounded. High in the sky, attacked by a lone Zero. Pounded by bullets. The crash landing, the water closing in, Jerry dead in the rear cockpit, Phil losing blood until he was almost too weak to move. Then the waves coming up, closing over his head in an embrace that would pull him down to his doom, while he struggled to find the cord that would inflate his life jacket. . . .

The memories were too strong. In the back of his mind, he had expected to have trouble the first time he got back in a cockpit after reporting to the *Enterprise,* but to his surprise, that hadn't bothered him at all. Neither had carrying out today's bombing runs. Everything had been fine, and he attributed that in part to the strength that loving Missy had given him.

But now the terror was back, and with it the thought that if he died up here, he would never see Missy again, would never again hold her and feel the warmth of her body, never again taste the sweetness of her mouth, never again be complete the way she completed him. It was too much. He had to get out of here, had to run and hope that one of the Wildcats would come along and get the Zero off his tail.

He pressed his foot against the rudder, hauled the stick over, and sent the plane into another screaming turn. The Zero was still banking toward him but wasn't in position yet to fire. Phil dropped the Dauntless's nose, almost like he was about to dive on a bombing run.

The rear machine gun opened up, sounding like nothing else so much as giant hammers pounding the sheet metal of the heavens.

Ensign Kirkland kept firing for so long Phil began to worry that the gun's barrel would melt. But then a huge explosion sounded behind them, and Kirkland let out an excited whoop.

"I got him!" the ensign yelled. "I got the bastard!"

Phil pulled up a little and looked over his shoulder. Sure enough, a cloud of smoke and a lot of falling, burning debris marked the place where the Zero had been a couple of seconds earlier. Kirkland's bullets must have found the fuel tank of the Japanese plane. The Zero was no threat to anybody now. It had been blown to bits.

Phil swallowed hard and said, "Good job, kid." His voice sounded hoarse and strained in his ears.

"Thanks, Lieutenant. Thanks for doing what you did."

"What do you mean?"

"I know you could've shot down that Jap yourself. I appreciate you setting it up so that I could be the one to get him."

Phil's right hand was on the stick. He lifted his left and rubbed it over the lower half of his face, feeling the sweat that made his skin slick. After a moment, he gave a hollow chuckle and said, "You're welcome, Ensign. Now let's go home."

With Kirkland chattering happily behind him, Phil pointed the Dauntless toward the *Enterprise*.

# TWENTY-FOUR

The routine of the night before was repeated on the evening of 7 August 1942, aboard the transport ships of the American convoy in Sealark Channel. If anything, though, the men were even more nervous now than they had been the previous night. After steeling themselves mentally to the prospect of dying when they went ashore, only to have to stand around and wait all day, they didn't have much left in the way of emotional reserves. Adam knew the men of his platoon were in bad shape. They weren't all that scared, just shaken by the unexpected turn of events.

Action would take care of that, he told himself. Once they were under fire, their jitters would go away. He hoped that was true, for himself as well as for the men under his command.

Once again, the call to quarters sounded well before dawn on the morning of 8 August. The procedure was the same: a last check of gear, a solid breakfast, and then the order to report to debarkation stations on the deck.

"Think we'll actually go anywhere today?" Adam overheard one of the Marines asking as they climbed the ladders to the hatches that opened onto the deck.

"It's Saturday, ain't it?" another Marine responded.

"Yeah, I think so."

"Then we'll go somewhere. I always go out on Saturday."

Adam grinned to himself as he followed the men up the ladder. He had a feeling they would be going somewhere today too.

The debarkation process was a little more ragged, but only a couple of men got hung up in the nets and injured themselves to the point that they had to return to the ship, cursing bitterly all the way because they were going to miss out on the action. Adam and his pla-

195

toon dropped into a Higgins boat and crouched there waiting, but not for long. With a roar of engines, the landing craft pulled away from the transport ship and headed shoreward.

This was it, Adam told himself as his hands tightened on his Springfield. This was the real thing. He and his men were going into battle. He forced himself to relax his grip on the rifle.

As the flat-bottomed boat bounced through the waves, he wondered briefly how Ed and Leo were doing. They were in one of the other landing craft with Ted Nash's platoon. Adam hadn't seen them the night before, but he knew that Nash's men hadn't gone ashore yesterday with the first wave of Marines. They would do fine, he told himself. Ed was a hell of a Marine, and he would look out for Leo as much as he could. Besides, Leo had a habit of rising to the occasion. Probably he would acquit himself well too, Adam thought.

The gray light that was spreading slowly across the water revealed the landing craft's destination. They were on their way to Tulagi, an island of steep bluffs surrounded by jungle and a narrow strip of beach. Adam remembered what he'd read about Tulagi, how it had been the seat of government in the Solomons when the British were still running things around here. Tulagi Harbor was a fine natural anchorage and had a small settlement at its head. Adam could understand why the Japanese would want to hang on to it, but he was less certain why the Japs were putting up such a fight on Tulagi, Gavutu, and Tanambogo when they weren't on Guadalcanal and Florida. Probably because on those smaller islands, there were fewer places to run, he told himself. The enemy could withdraw and fortify themselves in the hills of the larger islands and maybe hold out there for a long time. On Tulagi, Gavutu, and Tanambogo, the issue was more immediate.

As the dark bulk of Tulagi drew nearer, Adam prayed, not only for himself but also for his men and for all the other Marines who were going ashore today, as well as the ones who were already in combat. He prayed too for his mother and for Catherine. He had written short letters to both of them two nights earlier, when he'd thought he would be landing on 7 August. He hadn't added anything to the letters but decided to let them stand as they were. The day's delay really didn't change anything when it came to how he felt about his wife and his mother. He had told them both how much he loved them and asked them not to worry about him. Of course, he knew that they would, but that was all right. He worried about them too. He wished he could be with Catherine on the *Solace,* and he wished he could be back in Chicago with his mother. It would be nice to be able to see Joe and Dale Parker too. They were good guys, especially Joe.

The Higgins boat was almost at the beach now. Only about fifty yards to go. Adam was peering toward the shadowy jungle beyond the strip of sand when he saw a flash. Something hit the top of the boat's ramp and whined off into the dawn. "Get down! Get down!" Adam shouted as he crouched. That was a muzzle flash he had seen. They were under fire.

More bullets hit the steel walls of the landing craft, some of them ricocheting, others impacting with a dull thud. The coxswain crouched a little lower behind his shield. Adam caught a glimpse of something arching through the air above them, sunlight catching it for an instant even though the sun was not yet up from his perspective. Then something splashed into the water behind the craft and exploded. The Japs had a mortar out there in the jungle.

Adam felt like sticking the barrel of his rifle over the wall of the boat and blazing away at the jungle. There was nothing at which to aim, though. The jungle seemed to be an impenetrable gray-green barrier. But it was hardly impenetrable, because steady rifle and machine-gun fire raked out of it.

Where were Colonel Edson's Raiders? C Company was supposed to go to Edson's support, but how could they if they didn't know where he was? Adam got out his binoculars and risked a quick look along the beach, searching for any sign of the American forces that had landed the day before. He didn't see anything except sand and palm trees and brush, and beyond that the rugged bluffs that rose at a steep angle.

With a lurching jolt that threw several men off their feet, the Higgins boat grounded against the beach. Adam stood at the raised ramp, Sergeant Lederer beside him and Lederer's squad right behind them. Bullets were still spanging off the walls of the boat and whipping through the air around it. Adam's heart was pounding louder than the surf as the waves crashed to the shore. It had been different on Wake Island. There he had been one of the defenders. The enemy had had to come to him, into the face of his guns. Here it was just the opposite. When that ramp went down, he would be the one charging out directly into hostile fire. But there was nothing else that could be done, and he knew it. He gave the coxswain a curt nod.

"Go!" the man shouted as he threw the lever that dropped the ramp. "Go!"

Adam hesitated for just a second as the ramp fell. Charging out while the ramp was still going down could throw a man off balance. He waited until the top of the ramp hit the wet sand and dug into it, then he charged down the angled steel wall. His boots pounded against the ramp and threw up a spray of water around his legs. "Follow me!" he shouted, and he didn't look back to see if his men were there. He knew they would be.

Firing the Springfield from the hip, churning his knees high, Adam advanced through the edge of the water and onto the beach. He knew he wasn't likely to hit anything firing as he was, but he kept it up anyway, hoping the bullets he sent into the jungle would be at least a distraction for the Japanese. He spotted a fallen tree at the edge of the jungle with a shallow depression on the beach side of it. Aiming toward that tree, he ran full-tilt ahead and stopped shooting long enough to wave his right arm to the right and then to the left. "Spread out!" Lederer bellowed to his squad, seeing Adam's signal. The other sergeants repeated the command. "Spread out! Spread out!"

Down the beach more landing craft were coming ashore. Marines charged out of them and dashed across the beach toward the jungle. Men were hit and tumbled forward off their feet or went backwards as if they had smashed into a brick wall, depending on how solidly they were hit. At the spot where Third Platoon had come ashore, Adam heard a bullet whine past his head, and then he reached the depression beside the fallen tree and threw himself forward into it. In midair, the horrifying thought crossed his mind that this was just the sort of place the Japs might have mined. If they had, he was doomed, because there was no way to stop his lunge.

He smacked down in the wet, muddy sand. Some of it splashed

up into his face. He tasted the grit in his mouth, and as he spit it out, he thought it was the best mud he had ever tasted. It meant he was still alive, that the Japs hadn't mined the hollow.

Sprawled on his belly, he raised himself on his elbows and looked up and down the beach. Most of the landing craft had come ashore, and the ones that had already discharged their load of Marines were backing away from the beach to turn and head back to the transport ships. The beach was covered now with green-uniformed Marines. Some were wounded, writhing on the sand as their life's blood pumped out. Others were already dead, lying face-down in the sand as the water swirled around them and tugged on their bodies. But most of the men were up and moving, heading for the jungle. They wouldn't be safe there, but at least it was better than being out in the open.

As he reloaded his rifle, Adam looked for his sergeants, finding them one by one. Each of the noncoms gave him a thumbs-up signal as they crouched at the edge of the jungle behind whatever cover they could find. When Adam checked the beach behind their current positions, he saw that none of his men were down. All of them had made it to shelter.

The walkie-talkie slung on a strap behind Adam's left shoulder crackled. He pulled it around and heard, "Third Platoon, report!"

"Third Platoon here," Adam said as he pressed the switch to send. "We're all safe at the edge of the jungle!"

"Advance inland one hundred yards and hold position."

Adam keyed the mike. "Aye, aye!"

He slung the walkie-talkie on his back again and used hand signals to relay the orders to the sergeants. The noncoms passed along the orders the old-fashioned way, shouting at the tops of their lungs. "Into the jungle!" McDade bellowed as he lurched to his feet. "Come on, you feather merchants!"

Adam stood up and threw a leg over the fallen tree. As he did, a bullet hit the trunk about two feet away from him, chewing splinters from it. Adam saw movement in the brush ahead of him. He brought the Springfield to his shoulder, sighted and fired in one smooth motion. Then he worked the bolt and fired again before starting forward.

The brush clung and clawed at him. He moved in a crouch, sometimes using the barrel of his rifle to push branches out of his way. Bullets began to rip through the jungle just to his left. He heard a high-pitched rattling sound and knew it was a light machine gun, the .25 caliber that the Japanese favored. One of Adam's men cried out as he was hit. Leaves and branches and splinters flew through the air as the bullets swept toward Adam. He dropped to hands and knees and sensed as much as heard the fire from the LMG burning through the air only inches from his helmet. The path of the bullets moved on, chewing through the jungle to Adam's right as the Japanese gunners swept their weapon from one side to the other. They would be starting back in his direction in a matter of seconds, Adam knew.

He thought he had the machine-gun nest spotted, about thirty yards away behind a pair of palm trees that had grown at angles so that their trunks crossed about ten feet off the ground, forming an X. The brush was particularly dense between the bases of the two trees, and Adam thought he saw movement and gun flashes from that thicket. But there was a small, open triangle of space above the brush and between the trunks of the two palms.

Adam reared up on his knees, jerked a grenade loose from his belt, and pulled the pin. His arm went back. He didn't have much of a target at which to aim, but hell, it was only ninety feet, he thought. From center field, he had thrown out more than one runner at the plate during his playing days.

Of course, he had been able to one-hop some of those throws to the catcher.

His arm flashed forward and the grenade's spoon flew through the air as it was released. The grenade traveled in a beautiful arc toward the leaning palm trees. Adam hit the dirt again as machine-gun bullets chewed the brush around him. He couldn't see the explosion, but he felt it as the grenade went off. The ground jumped a little underneath him.

He looked up and saw that the thicket between the palm trees had been torn apart by the blast. The Jap LMG was silent now. Adam scrambled to his feet and yelled, "Move up! Move up!"

The line of men advanced through the jungle, their sweat-soaked green uniforms hard to see against the foliage. Adam came to the trees and saw that his guess had been right. Two Japanese soldiers lay there, sprawled in unmistakable attitudes of death, next to an overturned machine gun. The explosion had blown off the Japs' helmets. Adam saw them lying a few feet away, covered with twigs that had been tied onto them for camouflage. The bodies were torn up pretty badly, the brown uniforms sodden with blood. Both of the soldiers wore canvas shoes, sandal-like affairs that had split toes. For some reason, that struck Adam as odd. The footgear looked more like something a person would wear for an outing at the beach, not into combat. He swallowed and moved on.

With a roaring of engines, several airplanes flew overhead. Adam looked up and caught a glimpse through the trees of the silvery fuselages, but he didn't get a good enough look to identify the planes. A few moments later, however, large explosions began to sound inland. Bombers from the carriers out in the channel were striking at the Japanese positions, Adam realized. The blasts made the ground shake under his feet. It was a good feeling. It meant the Japs were being pounded from the air as well as from the ground. The more of the enemy that were taken out by those bombs, the easier it would be to gain control of the island.

When Adam estimated the platoon had pushed about a hundred yards into the jungle, he called out the order to halt and dig in. The command went along the line, and one by one the Marines found themselves the best cover they could and hunkered behind it, ready to hold their position. Adam still wondered where Colonel Edson was, but he supposed he would find out sooner or later—if he lived long enough. For now, he had done what he was supposed to do. His men would hold this strip of ground until they were ordered otherwise. Even though casualties had been light so far, there *had* been casualties. The beach and the narrow bit of jungle had been bought and paid for with Marine blood. It would not be given up.

Adam crouched behind a tree, leaning his shoulder against the trunk, and tilted his head back to look up and search for the sun. When he found it, its light filtering through the trees and taking on a greenish tint, he saw that it was still fairly low in the sky. Adam looked at his watch: 0900. Nine o'clock on a Saturday morning in the South Pacific. It sounded almost peaceful.

# TWENTY-FIVE

In combat, everything else went away. Adam had learned that on Wake Island, and now on Tulagi, the knowledge was reinforced. While he had been under fire, he hadn't thought about Catherine or his mother Ruth or anything else except what was happening right that second. Clearing the mind like that gave a man his best chance to live through what was happening. Survival was the triumph of the uncluttered mind.

But when the shooting stopped and a man had the chance to take a deep breath, that was when reaction set in. And with it came the thoughts of loved ones and the realization of how close he had come to never seeing them again. All it would have taken was a single bullet aimed a few inches one way or the other. . . .

Adam felt the shakes go through him as he leaned against the tree. His knees were so weak he didn't think he could have stood up at that moment if he had to. He took a few minutes to try to put that feeling behind him. Dragging deep breaths into his lungs, he smelled rich damp earth, rotting vegetation, and the fragrance of wild flowers that grew in clumps here and there. The jungle was quiet. There seemed to be no birds singing in the trees, no small animals moving around in the brush. All the usual occupants of what should have been an idyllic paradise had fled, leaving the jungle to the human animals who were trying to kill each other.

Adam felt his nerves settling down. When he trusted himself to speak, he pulled the walkie-talkie around and checked in with the company command post. He wasn't sure where the CP was; somewhere along the line of men that had penetrated into the jungle, he supposed. He talked to Lieutenant Butala, one of Captain Hughes's staff, and reported that his men were in position. Butala told him to hold fast, that someone would be along to tell him what to do next.

That someone turned out to be the captain himself. Hughes approached from the beach about half an hour later. The beach was secured now, all the Jap snipers and machine gunners cleared away from the vicinity. Hughes, along with a couple of men from his staff, called Adam back for a quick conference in a thick clump of trees.

The captain knelt and spread a map of Tulagi on the ground as Adam and the other men gathered around. Tulagi was narrow and oriented on a northwest-southeast axis. Hughes pointed toward the eastern end of the island. "This is where Colonel Edson's Raiders came ashore yesterday. They didn't encounter much opposition until they came to these bluffs several hundred yards inland. Then the Japs started putting up a fight. They even tried a few counterattacks, but Red Mike's boys kept on pushing them back."

Adam nodded in understanding, knowing that Red Mike was Colonel Merritt Edson's nickname.

Hughes's finger jabbed a point on the map along the southwest shore of Tulagi, about in the middle of the island. "This is our position. We're going to advance into the hills so that we'll be pressuring the enemy's right flank. Our intelligence indicates that the Japs have hollowed out quite a few caves in those hills, so we'll probably have to smoke 'em out."

Adam didn't know if the captain meant that literally or not, but he nodded. He said, "Intelligence indicated that this island was lightly defended too."

Hughes frowned at him for a second, then chuckled. "I'd be careful about taking that tone around some officers, Lieutenant. However, I'm inclined to agree with your point. I think our intelligence is more likely to be right about those caves, though."

Adam tended to agree. The rugged heights that made up the interior of Tulagi looked like just the sort of place to be full of caves.

"So your platoon's orders are to advance toward the center of the island, Lieutenant," Hughes went on. "The rest of the company will be doing the same. Deal with the Japs as you come to them, but don't let them stop you. By the time we meet up with Colonel Edson's forces, we should have pinched out all the opposition between us."

"Aye, aye, sir," Adam responded. In theory, at least, the operation was going to be a simple one.

Hughes folded up his map and moved on to brief the commanders of the other platoons. Adam went back to his tree, hurrying in a bent-over run to make himself a smaller target. He heard the popping of scattered rifle fire. Probably Jap snipers, he thought. From time to time a burst of heavier fire sounded. That would be the Marines responding to the threat of the Japanese riflemen.

Adam caught the eye of the nearest sergeant, who happened to be Richards, a burly, broad-shouldered man from Arkansas. Pointing inland, Adam indicated that they were to advance. Richards passed along the order. Within minutes, the men of Third Platoon were on their feet, slipping forward through the jungle, darting from tree to tree and bush to bush.

A rifle cracked up ahead. Adam heard one of his men curse and then groan, probably wounded by the sniper. He searched for the source of the shot but couldn't see anything except the jungle. Adam bit back a curse of his own. Why didn't the Japs come out and fight in the open?

Because they stood a better chance of winning this way, he told himself. Only a fool used tactics that didn't work.

Again the sniper's rifle cracked as the line of men moved forward. This time Adam was ready, and when he heard the shot he looked toward the sound. He thought he saw a frond shift high up in one of the palm trees. Bringing the Springfield to his shoulder, he snapped off a shot. Other men followed his example, concentrating their fire on the top of the same tree. A moment later, with a great thrashing, a Japanese soldier fell out of the tree, plunging to the ground some forty feet below. His body landed with a soggy thud, and a second later it was sieved by rifle fire as the Marines made sure the sniper was dead.

Adam passed a good distance to the left of the corpse as the platoon advanced again. He was just as glad he didn't have to get a close-up look at the Japanese soldier. The body had been riddled to the point where it must have appeared only vaguely human.

For the next hour, the platoon moved in a slow but steady manner toward the bluffs. They killed four more snipers and blew up a

Japanese machine-gun nest behind some fallen trees. Adam could see the steep, thickly wooded slopes of the hills rising in front of them. He thought they would reach them by the middle of the day.

He had just moved in a crouch from the shelter of some brush when something slammed into his helmet. The impact was tremendous, knocking him back and to the left. He felt himself falling, felt the rifle slipping from his hands. He crashed to the ground, his head spinning and darkness pouring into his vision from the sides like rising floodwaters. As he fought to stay conscious, he heard someone yell, "The lieutenant's hit!"

This was it. His last thoughts before he passed out were of Catherine.

*　　*　　*

Ed Collins knelt at the bottom of the bluff. It rose almost perpendicular above him. A monkey would have trouble climbing that mother, he thought, and he was no monkey.

A Jap machine gun at the top of the bluff yammered and spat lead at the Marines below, pinning them down. Ed had raced forward, hoping to find some way up there, but now that he had reached the bluff, he saw how hopeless it was. Lieutenant Nash would have to figure out how to get past the machine gun.

Ed grimaced as that thought crossed his mind. If Nash's brains were pigshit, he couldn't fertilize a thimbleful of dirt. The guy wasn't a coward; he just didn't know what he was doing. That Ivy League education of his qualified him to be an officer, but it hadn't taught him how to think like one.

"Yow, yow, yow, yow!"

Ed turned his head and saw Leo Sikorsky sprinting toward him from the edge of the jungle. Machine-gun bullets tore up the ground around Chopper's feet, but he kept going somehow, yelling as he came. He threw himself forward, landing in an ungainly heap at the base of the bluff next to Ed. The MG couldn't reach them here because its barrel couldn't be depressed far enough. They were safer than the guys still in the jungle but just as trapped.

"Damn it, Chopper, you gone nuts or somethin'?" Ed demanded. "Why didn't you stay where you were?"

Chopper was breathing hard. He squirmed around so that he was sitting with his back against the bluff. He drew his knees up and clasped his arms around them. "What?" he said. "And let you have all the fun?"

"Crazy bastard," Ed muttered. He twisted his neck to look up at the machine-gun nest. "How high you reckon this cliff is, Chopper?"

"Hell, I dunno. Forty, fifty feet, something like that?"

"Maybe we could throw grenades up there and blow up them Japs."

"I don't know. We'd have to throw them almost straight up, and if we missed, they'd fall back down on top of us."

"Yeah, there's that to consider," Ed said. "Got any other ideas?"

"What if we . . . or maybe . . . no, that wouldn't . . ." Chopper threw his hands in the air. "I'm stuck. I don't have any idea what to do."

The rest of the platoon fired toward the machine-gun nest from the jungle, but the Japs must have hollowed out a place for themselves up there, because nothing was visible except the very tip of the MG's muzzle. Plinking away at it with rifle fire wasn't going to do much good, Ed thought. They needed a bazooka or something like that. But they didn't have one, so they might as well wish that hogs had wings.

"We gotta chance it with the grenades," Ed said. "We're the only ones close enough to do it."

"I tell ya, we'll wind up blowin' our own asses off."

"Nah, we can do it. You'll see."

"The only thing I'll see is pieces of me flying through the air after that grenade falls back in my lap and goes off."

Ed grinned. "Look at it this way. If it does, that'll be the only thing goin' off in your lap here lately."

Chopper muttered curses, but he pulled one of the grenades from his belt. "If we gotta, we gotta."

Ed gripped one of his own grenades in his right hand and pulled the pin with the left. "Here goes nothin'."

He took a step out from the bottom of the bluff, cocked his arm, and threw. At the same time, Chopper pulled the pin on his grenade and let fly with it. Both grenades soared into the air, going almost straight up, curving only a little toward the face of the bluff. Ed and Chopper watched them, and Ed muttered, "Come on, babies, come on . . ."

One of the grenades arched in far enough to fall on top of the bluff. The other one hit on the lip as it fell, then started to bounce back down. Ed never knew which one was which. He let out a yell and threw himself sideways. Chopper went the other way. Both Marines hit the dirt, facedown.

The grenade exploded in mid-bounce. At the same time, the one that had dropped into the MG nest went off. The members of the platoon still in the jungle let out a cheer as the blast toppled the machine gun off the bluff. The gun went end over end and crashed to the ground not far from where Ed and Chopper lay huddled against the base of the bluff.

Ed rolled over and sat up. He didn't think he'd been hit by any of the shrapnel thrown out by the exploding grenade, but he did a quick inventory to make sure. No blood anywhere he could see on his uniform, and all his muscles seemed to work all right. He looked around and spotted his friend lying on the ground a few yards away. Chopper wasn't moving, and there was blood on the leg of his uniform.

"Chopper!" Ed cried out as he scrambled over to the other Marine. He grabbed Chopper's shoulder and rolled him onto his back.

Chopper blinked his eyes open. He looked dazed. "Am I dead?" he asked in a croaking voice.

"Hell, no, you ain't dead! Do I look like St. Peter to you?" Ed reached for Chopper's bloodstained leg. "Don't move. You been hit."

Chopper jerked upright. "I'm wounded? I'm wounded? Where?" He moved his leg and let out a howl of pain. He clutched at Ed's arm and said, "I'm hit! I'm hit!"

"That's what I just told you, you knucklehead." Ed got thick fingers in the rip in Chopper's trouser leg and tore it even more, laying bare the calf. "Looks like you just got nicked."

Chopper leaned forward. "Where? Where? Look at all that blood!"

"It's bleedin' pretty good, but it don't look all that deep," Ed assured him.

The rest of the platoon rushed forward out of the jungle, able to move again now that the Japanese machine gun was out of action. Lieutenant Nash came up to Ed and Chopper and said, "Good work, men. Are you wounded, Sikorsky?"

Chopper looked up at him and said, "I'm hit!" Then he swayed back and forth and fell over backward in a dead faint.

"It's just a scratch, Lieutenant," Ed said. "I reckon ol' Chopper ain't too fond of the sight o' blood, especially his own."

"Does he need a medical corpsman?"

Ed shook his head. "Naw, I'll just clean it up, dust a little sulfa powder on it, and slap a dressing on there. He'll be good as new in no time."

"All right, then." Nash turned away and called to the rest of the men, "Let's find a way up this bluff!"

Ed tended to Chopper's wound as he had promised the lieutenant. Chopper came to while Ed was wrapping a bandage around the gashed calf. "Ooh," he said as he sat up and held his head. "What the hell happened?"

"You passed out," Ed said. "Fainted just like a girl."

"Hey, I passed out from loss of blood! It's lucky I didn't go into shock or something."

"Yeah, or something."

"What? What did you say?"

Ed waved a big hand. "Nothing. Come on. Looks like the boys've found a path over yonder that'll get to the top of the hill."

He pointed to where the rest of the platoon was snaking along a zigzag trail cut into the face of the bluff. He came to his feet and reached down to help Chopper. When Chopper stood up and put weight on his wounded leg, he winced.

"Damn, that smarts. Are you sure it's not too bad?"

"You won't even need stitches."

Chopper frowned in thought as Ed put an arm around his waist to help him along the base of the bluff. Ed had his rifle slung over his shoulder with his own. "No matter how bad it is," Chopper said, "it's a wound suffered at the hands of the enemy, ain't it?"

"Seems to me like it. You got it tryin' to blow up that Jap machine-gun nest."

"That means I just won a Purple Heart. I beat you, pig farmer." Chopper cackled. "Everybody thought I wouldn't even make it through basic training, and I'm the first one to win a medal!"

"Yeah, yeah," Ed muttered. "I reckon that's right."

Together, they struggled up the trail to the top of the bluff. They found that Nash had halted the platoon there for a few minutes of rest. "Take me over to the lieutenant," Chopper said. "I wanna make sure he puts my name in for a Purple Heart."

"You don't want to be botherin' the loot right now—"

"Help me over there, damn it, or I'll just have to hobble along by myself!"

Ed thought about it, then sighed and nodded. "Okay." He let Chopper lean on him as they walked over to the rock where Lieutenant Nash was sitting.

"Lieutenant, I gotta talk to you," Chopper began.

Nash looked up. "Yes, Sikorsky, what is it?"

"I just want to make sure you're gonna put in for my Purple Heart."

"What are you talking about?" Nash asked with a frown.

"My Purple Heart!" Chopper waved a hand at his wounded leg. "On account of how I got hit while fighting the Japs."

"Oh." Nash shook his head. "I don't think that really qualifies you for the Purple Heart, Sikorsky. You weren't wounded by enemy fire."

Chopper let out an outraged yelp. "What? What are you talking about, Lieutenant? Can't you see the bandage on my leg?"

"That wound came from your own grenade. The Corps doesn't pass out medals to men who injure themselves, Sikorsky."

Ed had to look down at the ground and bite his lip to keep from laughing. If there had been any doubt that the law was Nash's proper calling, it had just been disposed of.

"You're kiddin' me, right?" Chopper asked in disbelief. "You gotta be kiddin' me!"

210

"Like I told you, you and Collins did good work back there. I'll make sure your names go in my after-action report. But that wound . . . it's just not Purple Heart material, in my opinion."

Chopper was getting ready to start foaming at the mouth, Ed thought. He started trying to urge his friend gently away from the lieutenant.

"Not Purple Heart material?" Chopper repeated in amazement. "Whatta those Japs have to do, blow me into a million fuckin' pieces before I get a medal?"

Nash frowned, and Ed got a little more forceful with Chopper. "Thanks, Lieutenant," he said. "Me an' Chopper will get back to the squad now—"

"Wait just a damned minute!" Chopper burst out, but Ed ignored him and hauled his friend away. Chopper was quite a bit taller, but Ed outweighed him and was stronger. "Let me go, blast it!" Chopper protested as he tried without success to struggle out of Ed's grip. "I gotta talk to that . . . that . . ."

"Better hush up now," Ed said. "You're just goin' to make things worse, Chopper." He lowered his voice so that Nash couldn't over hear. "Yeah, that was a pretty chickenshit thing the loot just did, but don't let it get you down. There'll be other medals. Hell, before this war's over, I reckon both of us will win a whole chestful o' medals and ribbons. The brass'll run out o' places to pin 'em on us."

Chopper stopped fighting. "You really think so?"

"I sure do. You and me, we're just natural born heroes, old son."

"Yeah, I always thought I had heroic tendencies." Chopper hooked his thumbs in his belt and tried not to limp as he swaggered. "Come on. I saw the rest of the squad over there, heading farther inland. Let's go catch up to them."

"Sure, Chopper," Ed said. He was still carrying Chopper's rifle, but he supposed that was all right. If the squad ran into any trouble, he'd just give the rifle back. War was sure simple, especially when you compared it to farming. You didn't have to keep track of when the best times were to plant or to butcher hogs or anything like that.

All you had to do was kill folks, and that was pretty easy when they were trying to kill you first.

# TWENTY-SIX

Adam was amazed that he was still alive. That was his first thought when he regained consciousness. His second thought was that his head hurt terribly.

He forced his eyes open. A man loomed over him, wearing a look of concern on his face. "Are you all right, Lieutenant?" the man asked.

Adam became aware of the markings on the man's uniform and helmet and realized that he was from the Medical Battalion. "I . . . I'm okay, corpsman," he managed to say. But as soon as the words were out of his mouth, he remembered what had happened and knew that he wasn't all right. "I was shot in the head!" he exclaimed.

A faint smile touched the corpsman's face. "Nope, not really, sir. A Jap bullet hit your helmet and glanced off. It knocked you down and knocked you out, but that steel pot did its job."

"I'm not wounded?"

"No, sir. You just lost consciousness for a couple of minutes. Far as I can tell, you're fine."

*A couple of minutes.* To Adam, it seemed as if he had been unconscious for a lot longer than that. But he heard scattered gunfire nearby and knew that it came from his platoon and from the Japanese snipers who were trying to slow down their advance. He had to get up, had to lead his men.

As he pushed himself into a sitting position, the world seemed to stop with a jolt and then start spinning the wrong direction on its axis. Adam was so dizzy he would have fallen over if not for the strong hand of the corpsman on his shoulder, steadying him. After a few seconds, the insane rotation slowed and the earth righted itself.

Adam took a deep breath. His head hurt, but his thoughts were clearing. He knew where he was and what he had to do.

"Thanks, corpsman. I'll be all right now. I've got to get back to my men. If you'll just help me up. . . ."

When Adam was on his feet, the medical corpsman said, "You'd better not push yourself too hard, Lieutenant. That bullet gave you a hell of a lick on the head, even if it didn't penetrate your helmet. You'll probably be hearing bells for a while, and you may have some double vision or blurred vision. You may even have a concussion." The man hesitated for a second, then went on, "It might be a good idea if you went back to the aid station we've established on the beach. . . ."

"No!" Adam caught himself. The corpsman didn't deserve to be yelled at. He was just trying to do his job. More calmly, Adam went on, "I mean, I'm all right, and I want to get back to my platoon. Thanks for your help, corpsman."

"You're welcome, Lieutenant. That's what we're here for." He gave a small, hollow laugh. "Hell, compared to some of what I've seen today . . ."

He left the rest unspoken, but Adam knew what he meant. Adam's injury, such as it was, was insignificant when it was stacked up against what many of the other Marines who had come ashore on Tulagi had suffered.

Moving forward through the jungle, Adam kept his pace slow and careful. His brain wasn't completely clear of cobwebs. He didn't want to come busting up behind some of his men, either, and spook them into shooting him.

He figured the platoon was all right. All four of his sergeants were good men, seasoned veterans who weren't going to panic or do anything stupid. They had in common the quality that makes the best noncoms: they made sure the job got done but tried to take care of their men at the same time.

Adam heard a pair of grenades explode in the distance to the west, probably a half mile or more away. More platoons were advancing through the jungle and into the hills over there. All along the island, the Marines were closing in on the Japanese defenders.

Adam caught up with the platoon just as Vardeman's squad

started up the first bluff they had come to. The slope was fairly steep but was dotted with bushes and could be climbed without too much trouble. The men couldn't climb and fight at the same time, though, so the other three squads had taken cover at the edge of the jungle and were covering the rim with their weapons just in case any Japs showed up. Adam took in the situation at a glance and nodded in approval. Once the leathernecks had their orders, they didn't really need any officers most of the time, just their sergeants. While Adam was lying unconscious behind them, they had gone ahead with the task at hand and were doing a good job of it.

Adam came up next to Sergeant McDade and knelt beside him. "How's it look, Sergeant?"

"All right if there's not a few hundred Japs on top of that hill," McDade answered with a grin. Then he asked, "Are you okay, Lieutenant? I heard you got hit."

Adam touched his helmet, feeling the small dent in the steel. "I'm fine, just had a bullet glance off my helmet and knock me out for a little while."

McDade grunted. "Lucky."

"Yes, I was."

Neither of them had taken their eyes off the slope while they were talking. The first men in Vardeman's squad reached the top and scrambled over, rifles ready to fire if need be. Vardeman was right behind them, and after a moment, the sergeant reappeared at the crest and waved to the men below, signaling that the way was clear. Adam nodded to McDade, who stood up and shouted, "Come on! Come on! Follow me!"

The squads hurried up the slope, with Lederer and a couple of men forming a rear guard just in case any Japs came out of the jungle behind them. Nothing happened, though. Adam didn't think there were any Japanese soldiers left in the jungle except perhaps for a few snipers who had been bypassed by the Marine advance. The main part of the Japanese force was up there in the hills, digging in and getting ready to hold those caves Captain Hughes had talked about.

When he reached the top of the bluff, Adam saw that there was another hill rising behind it, perhaps a quarter of a mile away. It would be like that all the way to the center of the island, he thought, the hills forming dangerous stepping-stones. He hefted his rifle and said, "Let's go." His head didn't hurt as much now, and there was more spring in his step.

For the next hour the platoon advanced, climbing several hills along the way. When Adam paused and looked back to the south, he could see across the top of the coastal jungle to the waters of Sealark Channel, dotted with American ships. There was no bombardment going on now, and the planes were back on their carriers. The Navy had done what it could. It was up to the Marines now to root out the last vestiges of Japanese resistance.

A runner came back from McDade's squad, which had the point now. The private was panting, and his uniform was soaked with sweat. Now that the hour was approaching midday, the heat had grown to be almost unbearable. The air was sticky, like a steam bath, and thick with bugs. Adam brushed a hand in front of his face, shooing away a cloud of mosquitoes, as he said to the runner, "What's the word, Private?" The mosquitoes came back as soon as he lowered his hand.

"We've found a cave, sir," the private said. "Sarge is pretty sure there are Japs in it. He wants to know what we should do now."

"We have to advance on it. Our orders are to meet and overcome any enemy resistance."

"Yes, sir." The runner saluted. "I'll tell Sergeant McDade."

McDade already knew that, Adam thought. The sergeants were every bit as aware of the platoon's orders as he was. But Marines were liable to get killed taking that cave, and McDade wasn't going to commit his men to that task until he was ordered to do so. Of course, if Adam had been killed by that sniper or had gone back to the aid station, McDade and the other noncoms would have taken on themselves the responsibility for continuing the mission. McDade had deferred to him now only because he was back in the chain of command.

The runner took off for the point, staggering a little from the heat as he ran. Adam followed, picking up his own pace. He wanted to be on hand when the assault on the cave began.

He reached the edge of some trees and saw McDade's squad advancing across a strip of open ground toward a hill. The slope rose at a steep but negotiable angle for thirty or forty feet and then jutted skyward in a rocky bluff that went almost straight up and down. At the point where the angle changed, a dark, irregular opening marked the mouth of a cave. Adam estimated that it was eight feet in height and at least a dozen feet wide.

Something poked out of the cave and started firing. It was another of those lightweight machine guns. Adam could tell by the sound of the shots. How many of those things did the Japs have? It had to be their favorite weapon.

The bullets scythed through the grass where McDade's men were walking. As the MG opened up, McDade yelled, "Spread out! Get down!" The squad obeyed without hesitation, and that saved some lives. The bullets tore a path between several of the men, but no one was hit as far as Adam could see. They were still in a dangerous spot, though, halfway across the strip of relatively open ground. The men hit the dirt and were shielded somewhat by the grass, but the machine gun could still seek them out.

Adam brought his rifle to his shoulder and shouted, "Give them some covering fire!" He began to squeeze off shots, emptying all five rounds from the Springfield's magazine as fast as he could work the bolt between shots. The butt of the rifle jolted against his shoulder in a regular rhythm as he concentrated his fire on the mouth of the cave. All along the edge of the tree line, the members of the other three squads followed suit. After a few moments, the Japanese machine gun was pulled back out of sight.

"Go! Go!" McDade shouted as he lunged to his feet. He had seen the muzzle of the MG disappear from the mouth of the cave too. He sprinted forward, covering the rest of the open area in several bounds, and then threw himself back to the ground when he reached the bottom of the slope. The members of his squad were with him.

From this angle, it was impossible to tell how deep the cave was. All Adam could see was the opening of it. All the rounds that he and his men were throwing in there might be ricocheting around harmlessly while the Japanese soldiers withdrew deep into the hill. They had to get something inside the cave, maybe a grenade. . . .

McDade must have had the same thought. The sergeant motioned to two of his men, and as the rest of the platoon continued their covering fire, the pair of Marines jumped to their feet and ran toward the cave, pulling the pins on grenades as they did so. They had gone about ten feet and were drawing back their arms to heave the grenades when shots crackled from the mouth of the cave and they were thrown back. The grenades tumbled back with them, and as McDade saw what was happening, he bellowed, "Grenade! Eat dirt!"

The squad tried to burrow into the ground like so many gophers. Both grenades went off, throwing dirt and grass and rocks into the air. The men who had been shot by the Japanese lay motionless a few yards away, their uniforms shredded by the blasts. If they hadn't been dead when they fell, they were now, Adam thought, horror filling his mind. He had just seen two of his men die.

Rage welled up inside him, and he wanted to charge the cave himself. He knew that would be nothing more than a quick way of getting killed, so he forced himself to control the emotion. His thoughts had to remain calm and clear, so that he could come up with a way of getting to those Japs.

The Pioneer Battalions had what they called satchel charges, literally bags of explosives that could be placed on the end of a long pole and extended to wherever they needed it before they triggered the explosion. Something like that might work here, Adam decided . . . but they didn't have any Pioneers with them and sure as hell didn't have any satchel charges.

But they had grenades, and some sturdy twine, and in the jungle there were saplings that could be cut down and lashed together to form a pole. . . .

As soon as the idea came to him, he began putting it into action. He called Vardeman over to him and said, "Keep them pinned down in that cave." Then he drew his knife and withdrew a short distance into the woods, motioning for a couple of men to follow him as he went. "Cut down some of these skinny little trees," he told them as he began to hack at a slender trunk with his own blade. "We'll need five or six of them, at least."

The men didn't ask why he wanted the saplings cut down; they just got to work doing it. The wood was tough and hard to cut, but the Marines kept their knives honed to razor keenness. In less than half an hour, Adam and the two men with him had several of the trees cut down and the trunks trimmed of branches. While the other two continued cutting down saplings, Adam began tying together the ones they already had. He made the bonds as secure as he could. The makeshift pole didn't look like much, but as long as it worked for what they needed, that didn't matter.

Six of the saplings lashed together formed a crude pole between 35 and 40 feet long. Adam thought it would reach from the bottom of the hill to the cave mouth. He lifted it in the middle. The pole wasn't terribly heavy, but it was awkward and unwieldy. "Each of you get one end," he told the men with him. "We have to take this up to Sergeant McDade."

Again, they didn't question his orders. They just picked up the ends of the pole and weaved through the trees with it.

"Heavy covering fire!" Adam called to the rest of the platoon as he and his companions reached the edge of the open ground. They started forward at a shuffling run as the firing behind them increased.

The Japs must have seen them coming and figured out what they were doing, because bullets began to fly through the air around Adam. They whispered in the grass and made whipcrack sounds in the air. He tried to ignore them as he trotted forward.

When he and the other two men reached the bottom of the hill, they dropped the pole and threw themselves forward on the slope. McDade was already crawling over to join them, and he had several grenades in a knapsack, as well as the ones clipped to his belt. With a big grin on his rugged face, he said to Adam, "Here you go, Lieutenant. Instant satchel charge."

Adam took the bag of grenades. "We'll have to rig a line to their pins so that we can pull all of them at once. It won't be easy to do over a distance of forty feet."

"Nah, but it can be done. I've got a roll of wire in my pack. We can use that."

"Why do you have a roll of wire in your pack, Sergeant?"

"Hey, it's goin' to come in handy, ain't it? A good noncom anticipates problems. Besides, it's good for riggin' booby traps. I picked up that trick in Nicaragua."

Adam nodded, grateful for the man's combat experience. For the next several minutes, he and McDade worked together rigging the impromptu bomb at one end of the pole. McDade used a pair of wire cutters to snip off short lengths of wire, which he then wound around the pins in the grenades. When that was done, he twisted together the other ends of the wires and attached them to the end of the roll.

"Somebody can play out the roll as the bomb goes up the hill," he said to Adam. "A couple of men are going to have to take the pole up, though. It's too heavy to just push it up the slope, especially with those grenades on the end."

Adam was lashing the grenades to the pole with twine. "I'll go up," he said.

McDade shook his head. "Not a good idea, Lieutenant. You're the CO."

"I don't believe in staying out of the line of fire just because of that, Sergeant."

McDade looked uncomfortable. As a noncom, he didn't want to argue with an officer, but he had definite ideas about how this business should be carried out. Adam realized that, and he realized as well that McDade had a point.

"But you're probably right," Adam went on. "I'll stay down here and unroll the wire."

"That's a good idea, sir," McDade agreed, gratitude in his voice.

The charge was ready. McDade signaled for one of his squad to join him as he wrapped his hands around one of the tree trunks that formed the pole. "Come on, Terry. Let's deliver this present to the Japs."

McDade and Terry turned the pole until it lay longwise up and down the slope. Then with McDade on one side and Terry on the other, they began sliding it over the rough ground toward the mouth of the cave. The rest of the squad fired up the hill, and the rest of the platoon continued their barrage from the jungle. Adam held the roll of wire, turning it to play out more as McDade and Terry ascended.

Despite the amount of lead the Marines were pouring into the cave, the Japanese defenders were still putting up a fight. Adam saw bullets strike the ground around McDade and Terry, kicking up rocks and dust. Terry let out an involuntary yell as one of the slugs creased his shoulder, but he shouted right away, "I'm all right, I'm all right!" He and the sergeant kept going, thrusting the pole up the hill with them. Adam could tell now that the cave mouth was higher than he had first estimated. The deadly bundle of grenades was only a few feet away from the opening, though.

The grenades rose higher and higher, and at last McDade and Terry thrust them just below the rim of the cave mouth. Adam didn't hesitate. He pulled on the wire, a nice steady tug that wouldn't jerk any of the grenades loose. He felt the tension on the wire go slack as the pins came out of the grenades. The safety levers flew off. McDade and Terry waited, and Adam knew they were counting off the seconds just like he was. When he reached four, they gave one final heave on the pole that lifted the grenades into the mouth of the cave. Adam watched as a screaming Japanese soldier dashed out of the darkness and reached for the pole in an attempt to shove it away. He was too late. The grenades detonated, and the Jap vanished in the blast.

Adam and the members of McDade's squad surged to their feet and charged up the hill. The other squads followed suit. Smoke and dust billowed out of the cave mouth. Anyone still alive in there had to be blind and deaf right now from the explosion. Yelling at the tops of their lungs, the Marines went up the slope and began shooting as they reached the cave. The sound of gunfire was tremendous, overwhelming. Nothing in the cave could have lived through that storm of lead.

Adam hung back and stopped when he reached McDade and Terry. The sergeant had pulled back Terry's uniform blouse and was examining the bullet wound. "You'll be all right," he said as he slapped Terry on the good arm. Then McDade looked down the slope at the bodies of the two men who had been killed in the initial attack. "We lost a couple of guys."

"I know, Sergeant," Adam said. "But that cave's cleaned out now, and we can move on to the next one."

McDade grunted. "Yeah. Come on, Terry. You can't sit around loafin' all day."

# TWENTY-SEVEN

Adam's platoon, along with the rest of C Company, moved steadily inland during the afternoon, cleaning out the caves that honeycombed the bluffs and hills of Tulagi. Across the bay on Gavutu and Tanambogo, the Marines who had gone ashore on those islands were engaged in the same sort of mopping-up operation. By late afternoon, when C Company joined up with Colonel Edson's Raiders, the job was pretty much complete. A few snipers were left here and there, so the men couldn't relax completely, but all the organized Japanese resistance had been overcome. Tulagi, Gavutu, and Tanambogo were under the control of the United States Marine Corps.

To the south, on the other side of Sealark Channel, the First Marine Division under the command of General Archer A. Vandegrift had a firm foothold on Guadalcanal, occupying the half-finished airfield and a strip of northern coastline from Lunga Point to Kukum. The Marines had gained this territory without much of a fight from the Japanese. Only a few snipers had opposed the landing and advance, and they had been located and killed or captured in short order.

So as night fell on 8 August 1942, the battle for the Solomon Islands was going well. More resistance had been encountered on the smaller islands than was expected, but it had been overcome. And the hard, dangerous job of landing men on Guadalcanal had never materialized. The Marines felt pretty good about themselves as they settled down for the night in hastily pitched camps.

Second and Third Platoons, C Company, were back near the beach on Tulagi, having received orders to withdraw from the hills and make their camps there. Several men in Adam's platoon had been wounded, but the only deaths were the two that had been suf-

223

fered during the initial attempt to take the cave in the hillside. A burial detail from HQ Company had taken charge of the bodies, and Captain Hughes would write letters to the families of the dead men to follow the formal notification by telegram from the Secretary of War's office. Adam thought that he ought to write to the families too, since he had been in command of the platoon when the men were killed and had been on the scene. He didn't know if his words would mean anything to the grieving relatives, but it seemed like the right thing to do.

Since Second Platoon was camped right next door, so to speak, Adam walked over there during the evening to check on Ed and Leo. He ran into Ted Nash before he found his two friends.

Nash was sitting under a shelter half he had propped up on some sticks, smoking a cigarette and eating from a packet of rations. "Hello, Bergman," he said. "Pull up a patch of sand and sit down."

Adam sat, waving away some mosquitoes as he did so. He knew the gesture was futile; the bugs would be back in a second or two. He already had bites all over the exposed skin of his hands and face. It took a lot of willpower not to claw at the itchy spots. He figured he had better get used to it, though.

"How did your platoon come through?" Adam asked.

"Good. Light casualties, no one killed in action. Your boys?"

"We lost two men."

Nash drew deep on his cigarette and blew out the smoke. "That's tough. Your friend Sikorsky was hit, by the way."

Adam's head jerked toward Nash. "Leo? Was he hurt bad?"

"No, just a shrapnel cut on his leg. It looked messy, but Collins said it wasn't deep. He treated it. Sikorsky didn't even need a corpsman."

"I'll go say hello to him, if it's all right with you."

"Sure." Nash laughed and shook his head. "You know what that feather merchant wanted me to do? He thought I ought to put his name in for a Purple Heart."

Adam frowned. "Why not, if he was wounded in action?"

"Because it was shrapnel from his own grenade that gashed him. He tried to throw it up into a Jap machine-gun nest on top of a bluff, and it fell right back down on him. What a goofball."

Adam felt anger welling up inside him and made an effort to force it down. "What happened to the machine-gun nest?"

"Oh, Collins blew it up with his grenade. At least, I think it was his. I suppose it could have been the other way around. But either way, Sikorsky wasn't wounded by enemy fire, so he doesn't get a Purple Heart."

Adam's jaw tightened even more at Nash's smug tone, and he didn't trust himself to speak for a few seconds. He supposed that Nash's interpretation of the matter was correct, at least as far as the regulations went. Maybe Leo didn't deserve a medal. But Nash didn't have to find it so damned amusing, especially considering the fact that Ed and Leo might have saved Nash's whole platoon by their actions.

"I'll have a word with them before I go back to my platoon," Adam finally said.

"Sure, go ahead. Just don't be surprised when they tell you I'm a chickenshit bastard."

Adam wasn't going to be surprised if that happened. He had just been thinking the same thing himself.

He found Ed and Leo sitting on a fallen log at the edge of the jungle, finishing off their supper. They looked up and greeted him with grins. "Hey, Lieutenant," Ed said, then added, "That's pretty good, ain't it? I remembered not to call you Adam."

"Yeah, but neither one of you saluted," Adam said, and his tone was only half-joking. Ed and Leo must have sensed that, because they stood up, set their rations aside, and snapped crisp salutes, which Adam returned with an "At ease. Go back to what you were doing."

He sat down on the log next to Leo, who thrust out his bandaged leg and said with pride, "I got hit."

"I heard about that. Sounds like the two of you did good work today."

"Yeah, but Lieutenant Nash says I ain't gettin' a Purple Heart," Leo said with a frown. "It don't seem right to me."

"It's the lieutenant's call to make. Anyway, even if he put your name in, Captain Hughes might disallow it when he reads the after-action reports. Or the recommendation might get thrown out somewhere else along the line."

Ed said, "Yeah, but the platoon leader ought to stick up for his men, even if the brass don't agree with the recommendation. Don't you think so, Adam? I mean, Lieutenant."

Adam held up both hands. "Don't get me in the middle of this. I'm not going to interfere with another officer's decisions. It's bad enough I'm even here talking to you."

Ed shook his head and said, "I wish we were in your platoon."

"Don't be so sure about that. We're friends, but we're Marines first. If you stop and think about it, you wouldn't have it any other way."

Ed and Leo were silent. The atmosphere had grown a little tense. Adam didn't like it, but that was the way things had to be. He was going to do what he could to preserve his friendship with Ed and Leo, but in the end, they all had to be Marines first. Maybe it would be a good idea, he thought with regret, if he didn't come around to see them anymore, at least for a while.

Gunfire popped somewhere in the distance. Adam lifted his head and looked toward the center of the island. "There are still a few snipers on the loose," he said. "Even as small as Tulagi is, we couldn't clean out all of them in one day."

"We did a pretty good job, though," Ed said. "I reckon it ain't goin' to be as hard as we thought it would be, takin' back all these islands from the Japs."

"We'll see," Adam said. "We'll see."

*　　*　　*

A short time later, thunder rolled over the channel to the northwest of Tulagi, but it was no storm. Instead it was a battle at sea, as a task force of Japanese cruisers slipped around Savo Island under cover of darkness and opened fire on American, Australian, and British cruisers and destroyers in the area of the channel known as the Slot. Earlier in the day, Japanese bombers had struck and set fire to one of the transport ships, the *George F. Elliott.* The blaze was still out of control that night, giving the enemy cruisers plenty of light by which to aim their big guns. In fifteen minutes of heavy fire, the Japanese inflicted so much damage that three U.S. cruisers—the *Astoria,*

*Quincy,* and *Vincennes*—and an Australian ship, the HMAS *Canberra*, all sank. The cruiser *Chicago* also suffered heavy damage. The only good thing to come out of the engagement was that the Japanese task force, once it had thrown its first, deadly punches, turned and steamed north again, rather than pressing its advantage.

Adam didn't know what had happened until the next day, and even then there was more scuttlebutt about the naval battle than hard facts available to the Marines on the islands. Sunday dawned muddy and miserable, because around the middle of the night before, after the battle in the Slot, the heavens had opened up and a drenching rain had sluiced down, heralded by real thunder. The shelter halves offered a little protection from the downpour, but not much. And somehow the clouds of mosquitoes still managed to fly, even in the rain.

Adam's sleep was restless. He woke up seemingly as tired as he had been when he dozed off, and wetter besides. He ran a hand over his beard-stubbled cheeks and thought about shaving, then decided it would be too much trouble. Not to mention it would probably make the insect bites on his face itch that much worse.

He halfway expected at least some of the Marines to be taken off of Tulagi and returned to the transport ships in the channel. Not all of their force was needed to hold the islands and finish the job of rooting out the last of the Japanese holdouts. That was Adam's opinion, anyway. Of course, the brass seldom asked for advice from the junior officers.

But Sunday, 9 August 1942, dragged by with no sign of the Higgins boats coming ashore to take men back to the ships. Adam and the other Marines spent the day patrolling along the beaches and through the jungles, on the lookout for any sort of Japanese counterattack, as unlikely as that possibility sounded to them.

Early Monday morning, Sergeant Richards shook Adam awake as he dozed fitfully under a tree. "Y'all better come look at this, Lieutenant," Richards said. He sounded upset, so Adam rolled out of his soggy blanket and stood up.

"Is it the Japs?"

Richards shook his head. "No, sir. It's them damned swabbies."

*The Navy?* Adam thought. What was wrong with the Navy?

227

As he came onto the beach and looked out over Sealark Channel in the gray dawn light, he saw right away what was wrong with the Navy. It wasn't there anymore.

The channel was empty. The cruisers, the destroyers, the aircraft carriers, the transport ships . . . all gone. Sometime during the night, the convoy had sailed, leaving behind the Marines who had landed on the Solomon Islands.

Singly and in small groups, the men came out on the beaches as the news spread on Tulagi. Adam knew the same thing would be happening on Gavutu, Tanambogo, and across the channel on Guadalcanal. Men who had depended on those ships for artillery support, for bombing runs from the carriers, for food and ammunition and medical supplies, for a way off the islands in case of disaster, those who could came out of the jungle and stared at the empty waves and realized they had been abandoned for some reason unknown to them.

One of the corporals from Adam's platoon even took a couple of steps out in the surf and said in a half-angry, half-scared voice, "My God, they've hauled ass."

Adam felt an impulse to defend the Navy's decision to withdraw, but after a moment he decided to hell with it. He couldn't defend what the convoy's commanders had done. The Navy had indeed, for whatever reason, hauled ass.

And until the ships came back, Adam and all the men with him were stuck here on Tulagi.

# TWENTY-EIGHT

The call came over the radio at ten minutes until two o'clock: armed robbery in progress, shots fired, an officer possibly wounded. Pete Corey and Carl Bowden looked at each other in the darkened interior of their car parked a couple of blocks down the alley from the back door of the restaurant. The location of the shooting was only half a mile away. They could be there in a matter of minutes. That would mean abandoning their stakeout. But if a fellow cop had been hit . . .

Corey did the only thing he could. He hit the starter, fed the motor some gas, and backed up the car until he could turn down another alley and head for the street. The vehicle was a dark, unmarked coupe with no flashers, but in the middle of the night like this, Corey figured it would be safe enough to run the red lights as they sped toward the scene of the shooting.

Mike Chastain stepped out of a doorway farther along the alley and chuckled as he watched the two cops drive away. "Like I've always said, you guys are knuckleheads."

Decoying the police away from the restaurant had been easy. All it had taken was one anonymous phone call from a guy jabbering about a robbery and gunshots and some cop getting hit. Once they'd heard that over the radio, Bowden and Corey had taken off in a hurry, leaving the back door of the restaurant unwatched. Now, Chastain strolled down the alley and made a come-along motion with his hand. A motor ground to life somewhere nearby, and a minute later a large truck pulled up in the alley, stopping behind Guiseppe's place. The restaurant door opened. A couple of men hopped out of the cab, went to the back, rolled up the door of the truck, and began unloading the crates of black market beef.

229

Guiseppe stood to one side, wringing his hands nervously as he watched the meat being carried in.

Chastain came up to him and said, "Take it easy. There's nobody around."

"No offense, Mr. Chastain, but how do you know the cops aren't watching the place?"

"They were until a few minutes ago."

"What?"

"Relax, I tell you. I sent 'em off on a wild goose chase."

Guiseppe rubbed a hand over his face. "I don't like the cops watching my place."

"They were only here because they've got a burr up their asses about me. This is a big shipment. We won't be doing business again for a while. They'll forget all about you."

"I hope so. Not that I want them bothering you, Mr. Chastain," Guiseppe added.

"They don't bother me. They're not smart enough for that."

Mike hadn't known for sure the cops would be here tonight. It seemed like a possibility, though, considering the way they were always bird-dogging him. He'd had the phony call made to check out his hunch as much as anything else. Now he knew he'd been right.

"You got the money?" he went on to Guiseppe.

"Oh. Yeah. Here you go, Mr. Chastain." The restaurateur reached inside his coat and brought out a thick envelope. Mike took it and put it away inside his own coat. Guiseppe frowned and asked, "Ain't you going to count it?"

"I trust you, pal. Gotta trust the people you do business with."

"Yeah, I guess so. Anyway, you know I'd never short you or the boys, Mr. Chastain."

Mike smiled and nodded, but the smile didn't reach his eyes. He said, "Good night, Guiseppe," and turned to walk down the alley. He didn't need to stand around and supervise the rest of the unloading. The guys he and Hale had working for them would take care of that part of the deal. They were trustworthy and plenty tough.

"You come back for dinner any time you want, Mr. Chastain," Guiseppe called after him. "On the house!"

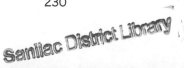

Mike just lifted a hand in an acknowledging wave without turning around.

*   *   *

He had two visitors when he got back to the penthouse. One was expected, the other wasn't. Karen Wells and Roger Hale sat there on opposite sides of the sunken living room, drinks in their hands. Mike felt the tension in the air like a physical thing.

"Hello, baby," he said as he tossed his hat on the table and went straight toward Karen. He held his hands out to her. "I didn't expect to see you tonight."

"I'm sorry if I'm intruding," she murmured. She set her drink aside and reached up to take his hands. He pulled her up out of the overstuffed armchair and put his arms around her, bending his head to kiss her. She returned the kiss with a little enthusiasm, but not the way it had once been between them.

"You could never intrude on my life," he told her. "You've always got a place in it."

"How touching," Hale said from the other side of the room. He threw back the rest of his drink.

He was older than Chastain, medium height, and had been stocky and muscular until taking the bullet in the guts that had almost killed him. Now he was thin, almost fragile. He had more gray in his brown hair and in the neatly trimmed mustache too. But even in his recuperation, he gave off an aura of menace. Mike didn't like him, didn't really trust him all that much, but he had to admit that their partnership had been lucrative. That was all that mattered, he told himself whenever he started thinking too much about Hale.

Partnership or not, he didn't like anybody cracking wise about him and Karen like that. He turned half away from her, reached into his coat, and brought out the envelope that Guiseppe had given him. As he sailed it across the room to Hale, he said, "There's the payoff."

Hale caught the envelope, took out the wad of bills inside, and riffled through it. "Looks like it's all there."

"What did you expect? Guiseppe wouldn't double-cross us."

231

"It never hurts to check these things." Hale crossed his legs. "I thought you didn't like talking business in front of the lady."

Mike glanced at Karen. Her face was taut, her eyes shadowed and unreadable. She knew what he did for a living. She had known that when she first took up with him. Sure, he'd gotten out of the rackets for a while, but he'd never made any promises, never said that anything was permanent.

"Don't mind me," she said, her voice cool.

Hale started to sit up. "Maybe I should go . . ."

"Wait," Mike said, holding out a hand toward Hale. He thought Karen was a swell kid, but Hale was his partner. It was time the two of them learned how to get along. He didn't intend to dump either of them for the sake of the other. Swinging back to Karen, he went on, "I thought you intended to go to your place after the show tonight."

She nodded. "I did, but . . . I started thinking, Mike. We have to settle this." She looked past him at Hale. "Things can't go on like they are. So I came here to see you . . . and Mr. Hale let me in. It seems he was waiting to see you too."

"Except that Mike was expecting me," Hale put in, his voice smooth and mocking.

Mike felt a sudden urge to throw both of them out. Either that, or lock them in a room together and see if they killed each other. Of course, he would never do that. He knew Hale too well.

"Mike, I'd really like to talk to you," Karen continued in low, intense tones. "Can't we be alone?"

"I need to discuss a few things with Roger first. Why don't you go in the bedroom and wait for me? It won't take long."

He knew as soon as he spoke that he'd made a mistake. Anger flared in Karen's eyes. "Wait in the bedroom," she repeated. "Is that the only place I'm worth anything to you, Mike?"

"I never said that—"

"No, but that's how you feel. You do your business with *him*—" She practically spat the word at Hale. "—out here, and you do your business with me in the bedroom."

"Everything in its proper place," Hale said with a smirk.

Mike turned, his hand starting under his coat again, but this time he wasn't reaching for an envelope full of cash. The reaction was instinctive, automatic. Hale saw it too, and tensed in the chair where he sat. His own hand wasn't far from his pocket.

"Stop it!" Karen cried.

Mike froze in that expectant attitude, his fingers not quite brushing the butt of the small pistol holstered under his left arm. A little tremble ran through him, not from fear but from the effort it cost him to stop the gesture before it reached its deadly conclusion.

"Forget it!" Karen said as she reached for the light shawl thrown over the arm of the chair where she had been sitting. She jerked it around her shoulders and stalked toward the door. "Both of you can go to hell! Go ahead and shoot each other if you want, but not over me! Your blood's not worth getting on my fingers."

Chastain didn't move as she opened the door and went out into the little hall. She slammed the door behind her. He still didn't move until he heard the door of the elevator slide open and then closed.

"Well, that was a near thing, wasn't it?"

Mike looked at Hale and for a second thought about going ahead and shooting him. It would certainly simplify things. But Hale was good. There was no guarantee they wouldn't both wind up dead. Even worse, Hale might kill him and not die himself. That was no good. Mike decided not to risk it.

He took his empty hand out from under his coat and squared his shoulders. "No need for anybody to get worked up."

"Tell that to your girlfriend."

"Karen will come around."

Hale shook his head. "You're fooling yourself, Mike. But that's your own decision to make."

"Yeah, it is. You'd do well to remember that."

Hale picked up his empty glass and said, "Why don't you pour me another drink? And pour one for yourself too. We have business to discuss."

"You saw the money. Everything went all right at the restaurant."

Hale shook his head again. "That's not what I'm talking about. I think it's time we branched out."

"What do you mean?"

"We're doing all right with the meat, but there are things in short supply that people will pay even more for."

"You're talking about tires, gasoline, things like that?"

"Drugs," Hale said.

Mike frowned. "I'm not getting mixed up with hopheads."

"Not dope. I'm talking about medicine, drugs like the doctor gives you when you're sick."

Mike rubbed his chin as he thought about what Hale had just said. With so much of everything going to the military these days, everything was hard to get, including medical supplies. And any time there was a shortage of something, there was a black market to supply it—for a price.

But medicine? The sort of stuff that kids and old people needed to help them when they were sick? Getting mixed up in that racket was a lot different than supplying beef to a restaurant so that some rich guy could dig into a steak any time he wanted one. Mike Chastain had never been the sort to worry too much about right and wrong when there was a buck to be made, but some things rubbed even him the wrong way.

Still, Hale was right. People would pay more for medicine than they would for meat.

"I can see you're thinking about it," Hale said. He held out his empty glass again. "Here, pour me a drink. Talking about how rich we're going to be is thirsty work."

# TWENTY-NINE

"All right, open your mouth wide . . . wider . . . now say *Ahhhh* . . ."

Dr. Gerald Tancred found himself saying "Ah" right along with the little boy whose throat he was examining. Just as he expected, the tissues of the throat were inflamed. The boy had the grippe, that was all. Tancred turned off the light he was using and took the tongue depressor out of the boy's mouth.

"Will he be all right, Doctor?" the boy's mother asked. Her voice contained a considerable amount of anxiety.

"It's nothing to worry about," Tancred told her as he threw the tongue depressor in the wastebasket in the corner of the tiny examining room. "Just a simple case of the grippe. Keep him warm, see that he rests, and give him plenty of fluids. Orange juice, if you have it."

"What do we look like, the Rockefellers?" The woman gasped and put her hand to her mouth, as if unable to believe she had actually spoken those words. "Oh, I'm sorry, Doctor! I had no right—"

Tancred raised a hand and shook his head. "It's fine, Mrs. Malone. I understand. It's quite all right."

"No, it ain't. I mean, it isn't. Here you are, a big fancy doctor from the North Side, and you're running this clinic so poor people like us can come to you when we're sick. It's just the finest thing anybody could ever do."

Tancred kept shaking his head, but the woman babbled on in her gratitude and embarrassment. Couldn't they see that he didn't want their thanks? That would mean that he was doing something for them, and that wasn't the case at all. The time he had spent here during the weeks since the clinic opened was for Elenore. That was the only reason he came down here to this squalid neighborhood and did what he could to assist its miserable occupants, such as the ragged urchin who sat on the examining table.

"Yeah, Doc," the boy said, his voice hoarse from the inflammation. "Thanks."

"You're welcome," Tancred said. Treating his patients in a civil manner was the quickest, easiest way to get rid of them. He went on, "You be sure and mind your mother now, Tommy—"

"My name's Timmy!"

Tancred gritted his teeth for a second before he trusted himself to continue. "You be a good boy and rest, Timmy, and you'll be well before you know it."

"Okay." The boy hopped down off the table and buttoned up his shirt.

When the boy and his mother were gone, Tancred washed his hands in the small sink, then closed his eyes and rubbed his temples for a moment. He had a wonderful bedside manner; all his regular patients told him so. But that manner was easier to produce when the patient was some wealthy middle-aged society matron who enjoyed being petted and pampered by a suave, handsome doctor with just a hint of Europe in his voice.

He thought about all the women and about how easy it would have been for him to be more than a physician to many of them. Time after time, certain of his patients had dropped hints. A few had even made blatant attempts to seduce him. But not once had he strayed. To be truthful, only seldom had he even been tempted. He loved his wife. He knew there had been times when Elenore doubted that love because he had spent so much time on his practice and not as much on her and the children, but what he felt for her was true and abiding and perhaps the only constant in his life. The children had been such disappointments, Catherine with that Jew she had married in secret and Spencer with his wild antics that had gotten him expelled from school after school . . .

Tancred felt a chill go through him. Spencer would never be expelled from another school. Spencer was dead.

And that was why he was sitting here in the Spencer Tancred Memorial Clinic, doing good works in the name of his son.

Doing penance.

Tancred shook off the dark thoughts as the door of the examining room opened and the nurse, a woman named Mrs. Walsh, stuck her head in and asked, "Ready for the next one, Doctor?"

He took a deep breath. "Yes, I suppose."

Mrs. Walsh dropped her voice to a stage whisper. "I think it's chicken pox."

Tancred felt a flush of annoyance. He started to snap at the woman that he would make the diagnoses, not her, but he suppressed the impulse. She was a competent nurse, and she worked for low wages. Not only that, but she lived down here on the South Side and knew the denizens of these neighborhoods. He hadn't wanted to ask any of his regular nurses to come down here to work even one day a week, so finding Mrs. Walsh had been a stroke of good fortune.

She was correct about the case of chicken pox, of course. She had an irritating habit of being right.

When the afternoon was over and the last patient had been seen, Tancred went into his office to write up his notes and bring the files up to date. With his regular practice, he usually did this work at home, in his study, but he wanted to keep the clinic's business here at the clinic. When he drove away from here, he liked to leave the place completely behind him, so that he didn't even have to think about it until the next week.

He had been busy with the paperwork for only a few minutes when a tentative knock sounded on the door. He looked up and said, "Yes, what is it?"

Mrs. Walsh opened the door, an uncertain expression on her face. "There's someone else out here to see you, Doctor."

Tancred shook his head. "The clinic's hours are over—"

"The lady says she's not here as a patient."

*Lady?* Tancred didn't know anyone down here who would answer to such a description.

Again, he shook his head. "I'm sorry, it's impossible. Tell her to come back next week." He looked down at the desk again and went back to writing on one of the charts in front of him.

Mrs. Walsh hesitated, then said, "She told me to tell you that she knew your son."

Tancred's head snapped up, and he felt the muscles in his neck tighten. He thought about the type of woman with whom Spencer had associated. The visitor was doubtless some trollop with a mewling brat in her arms, and she would insist that Spencer was the child's father. Tancred was surprised no such creatures had come out of the woodwork before now to try to finagle money out of him.

He set his pen aside and said, "Send her in." He would deal harshly with this woman, and she would regret coming here. She would see that Gerald Tancred was no one to be made a fool of.

Mrs. Walsh backed out of the office doorway, and Tancred heard her tell someone, "The doctor says you can go right in, ma'am."

"Thank you." The voice was low, controlled, the slightest bit husky in timbre but with a touch of culture to it. Tancred was taken somewhat by surprise by it.

He was really surprised a second later when she stepped into the doorway.

She was almost heart-stoppingly beautiful. Oh, she had flaws, certainly. The mouth was just a bit too wide, the jaw a little too strong, and the fair skin of her face was dusted with tiny freckles across her cheeks and nose. But none of that mattered, not when she looked at a person with those luminous green eyes and smiled with those full red lips. . . .

Her hair was red too, a mass of auburn curls that tumbled from under her hat and fell around her shoulders. Her hat was tan, as was the lightweight camel's-hair coat she wore over a dark green dress. And those were sheer silk stockings on her firm calves too, or Tancred was no judge of the finer things in life. This woman, indeed, was one of the finer things he had seen recently.

If she noticed the appreciation with which he gazed at her, she didn't say anything about it. Instead, as she came into the room she asked, "Dr. Tancred?"

"Yes?"

She held out her hand, the fingers long and slender and smooth. "My name is Karen Wells," she said. "I was a friend of your son Spencer."

Tancred forced himself to stand and reach across the desk and take her hand. Her skin was as cool as he had thought it would be.

"I was so sorry to hear about Spencer," she went on. "You have my deepest sympathy. I should have called on you and your wife before now. . . ."

"That's all right," he said. "Thank you. Spencer's death was quite a blow, of course."

"At least he died defending his country."

"Yes," Tancred murmured. He became aware that he was still holding her hand. He let go of it and said, "Please, Miss Wells, have a seat."

When they were both sitting down, he behind the desk and she in front of it, he went on, "Now, Miss Wells, what can I do for you? Or were you calling just to pay your respects . . . ?"

"Not entirely," Karen Wells said. "Perhaps I should explain how I came to know your son, Doctor. I'm a singer. I work at a nightclub called the Dells."

Tancred stiffened in his chair. The woman must have seen his reaction, because she went on, "I know how you felt about Spencer going to such places and associating with the people who frequent them, Doctor."

Tancred toyed with his pen and tried to control his anger. At first glance, this woman had seemed to possess the sort of class that he was accustomed to in his practice and in his circle of friends. Now he knew that despite her appearance she was nothing more than a saloon singer, probably a common slut.

"He stole from me," Tancred said with a slight tremor in his voice. "My own son stole from me because of a woman from that . . . that nightclub of yours."

Karen Wells nodded. "I know all about that."

"I'm certain you do."

Now it was her turn to stiffen, and he saw those green eyes flash with anger. "I'm the one who put Spencer wise to what Jocelyn was trying to pull, Doctor. I wanted to help him. She told him she was pregnant, but it was all a lie."

Tancred forced himself to remain calm as he took a deep breath. He said, "I would really prefer not to discuss these matters, Miss Wells. They are in the past. My son is gone, and dwelling on his . . .

youthful indiscretions . . . does no one any good. If you will simply tell me what you want. . . ." He spread his hands. "I'm certain we can reach an arrangement."

Karen Wells sat back in the chair and stared at him, eyes wide with disbelief and still more anger. "My God!" she said after a moment. "You think I'm here to shake you down, don't you?"

"Why else—"

"Why else would somebody like me come here? Maybe to tell you how sorry I am about Spencer, because I know he was a good kid. I'm starting to think maybe I know that better than his own father."

Tancred slapped his palms on the desk and came to his feet. "I think you had better leave now, Miss Wells."

She stood up as well and looked across the desk at him. The icy stare he was giving her had quailed dozens of servants over the years, but she met it squarely and without flinching. "I'm not going anywhere until I've done what I came here to do." She reached into her purse. Tancred took a sharp breath, startled by the gesture. She noticed and said, "Oh, for God's sake, take it easy. I don't have a tommy gun in here." She pulled out a roll of money and threw it on the desk. "There! That's why I came here, to give you that."

Tancred looked down at the money in confusion and then raised his eyes to hers again. "I don't understand."

"Of course you don't. You don't think anybody's capable of doing something good unless they're high society muck-a-mucks like you." She pointed to the bills. "That's a donation for your clinic. I heard about it, and I wanted to come down here and do something to help."

"Why?"

"Because I knew Spencer, and I liked him. This place has got his name on it, so I want it to succeed." She shook her head. "I thought I might do even more than give you some money, but now . . ."

She started to turn toward the doorway. Tancred stopped her by saying sharply, "Wait!"

She looked back over her shoulder at him. "Why? Going to accuse me of stealing something?"

"Miss Wells . . ." Tancred's mind was whirling, and he didn't quite know what to say. So he tried, "I'm sorry."

She looked taken aback. "What?"

The feelings going through him now were unexpected. He didn't know what to make of them. He said, "I meant no offense—"

"Sure you did. I know offense when I hear it."

He turned a hand in acknowledgment of her statement. "My apologies. I should not have spoken to you in the manner that I did. Even after all this time, I am still upset by the way my son behaved."

"You ought to be proud of him," Karen Wells said. "He had really straightened up, joined the Navy and everything. The last letter I got from him, he said he was going to be a pilot. . . ." Her eyes shone with moisture and her voice choked off. She looked down for a few seconds to regain control of herself and then raised her eyes to Tancred again. "I thought you must be proud of him, or you never would have started this clinic to honor him."

"It was . . . my wife's idea. Spencer's mother."

"Oh. I see. Well, then, you wouldn't want me around."

Tancred shook his head. "I don't understand."

"I told you I wanted to do more than just make a donation. I thought I'd volunteer too. My days are pretty much free. I'm not a nurse, but I can type and file and answer the phone. Whatever help you need that I can do . . ."

"You want to work—" Tancred waved a hand around at the dingy office. "Here?" The disbelief was plain in his voice.

"That's right. That's what I had in mind, anyway. I can see now it wouldn't be a good idea. You wouldn't want to be reminded of all your son's unsavory acquaintances."

The words had a sting to them, and some truth as well, Tancred thought. It *would* be difficult to be reminded constantly of the things Spencer had done. But what right did he have to take away the opportunity for someone else to honor his son's memory?

Why would a woman such as Karen Wells want to do such a thing, though? She had money and fine clothes and seemed to be accustomed to a lifestyle that was much different than what went on down here on the South Side. Surely she and Spencer had not been such good friends that she was motivated by that alone.

"I appreciate the gesture, Miss Wells, but I have Mrs. Walsh to act as my nurse, and I keep my own reports and files. Nor do I need your money. My regular practice funds this clinic."

"So you won't take my help?" Her voice now held a hollow note.

"I'm sorry." He spread his hands. "There's simply no need—"

"So you can make amends for what you've done in your life, but I can't."

The charge shocked him. "I don't understand. Make amends for what?"

"For being such a coldhearted bastard that your son should have hated you. He didn't, though. Spencer loved you, Doctor. Even when you shipped him off to boarding schools and then practically threw him out of the house."

He felt his anger building again. "These are private matters, family matters."

"And I'm not family, I know that. I was just Spencer's friend. But I saw how much he really wanted to please you, and he just couldn't, no matter what he did." She shook her head and then said quietly, "I know all about how that feels."

From somewhere in the recesses of his memory, an old saying popped into Tancred's head. He had no idea where he had heard it. It was the sort of crude homily he despised. But it seemed to have some application to this moment.

*Never sleep with a dame who has more problems than you do.*

Not that he would ever entertain thoughts of sleeping with this woman. But the saying could be adapted to apply to working with such a woman too. And clearly, Karen Wells was a woman with problems. She was conflicted about something, he sensed, and the conflict was so deep that it was troubling her greatly. However, he was no psychiatrist. He couldn't help her, and having her around the clinic might well make the situation worse not only for her but for him as well. Elenore might object to such a beautiful woman volunteering here, working side-by-side with him. She had never exhibited such jealousy before, but it was certainly possible.

"Look, Doctor," Karen Wells said, "we're getting nowhere fast.

Why don't you just take the money, and I'll tell you again how sorry I am about Spencer, and we'll leave it at that, okay? This was a bad idea and I'm sorry I came."

"Miss Wells," he said, stopping her yet again as she tried to leave. "If you wish to volunteer here at the clinic . . ."

*Leiber Gott,* what was he doing? He had to control himself before the unexpected impulse made him say too much.

"I have no objection."

She looked at him with suspicion in her eyes. "You're sure about that?"

"What harm will it do to . . . see how things work out, so to speak?"

"Well, if you're sure . . . Spencer was a great guy. I'd like to think I'm doing some good in the world and that his friendship inspired me to do it."

"Next Thursday, then. That is the next day the clinic is open."

"I'll be here," Karen promised. "I really appreciate this."

"Of course." He held out a hand toward the door. "Now, we must go tell Mrs. Walsh that you will be working here and assure her that she is not being replaced. She should have left for the day already, but I'm certain she has not."

"How can you be so sure?" Karen asked.

"Because she is listening at the door." Tancred found himself smiling, to his great surprise, as he raised his voice and went on, "Aren't you, Mrs. Walsh?"

They both heard her scurrying away from the other side of the door. Karen laughed. It was a pleasant sound, Tancred thought. Quite pleasant indeed.

# THIRTY

Adam lurched up out of his bedroll as his guts spasmed. Weak and dizzy, he stumbled into the jungle and barely made it behind a bush before he had to drop his trousers and void his bowels. He hunkered there, groaning as he struggled to keep from toppling backward into his own shit. He'd had the runs for the past two days, and he was so dehydrated that he couldn't think straight. One of the doctors from the 2d Medical Battalion, which had set up a field hospital on the beach at the edge of the jungle, had given Adam doses of bismuth and paregoric, but so far the treatment hadn't helped. This had to stop soon, he thought. He had nothing left inside him. He was all emptied out, or at least he should have been by now.

Flies buzzed around his head and crawled on his face. He was too tired to shoo them away. The flies were to blame for the dysentery that was sweeping through the Marines of the Second Regiment on Tulagi. They spread the contamination and made sure that sooner or later nearly everyone got sick with vomiting and diarrhea and fever.

This was one hell of a way to fight a war, Adam thought.

Well over a thousand Japanese troops had been killed here on Tulagi, and most of them hadn't been buried yet even though more than a week had passed since the Marines had come ashore and captured the island. Sad to say, not even all the American casualties had been laid to rest yet, although burial details augmented by some of the Melanesian natives were working on it. The heat and the sun took a terrible toll on the bodies. Corpses swelled and burst, and putrefaction ran rampant. Not only that, but cases of canned fish left behind by the Japanese had been broken open in the fighting, and those were rotting too. There were no latrines; the Marines had not had time to dig them. So with thick clouds of flies covering the island, conditions were perfect for the spread of disease.

"Hey! Hey, gimme that, you son of a bitch! Come back here with those butts!"

The angry shout came from somewhere nearby. A moment later, Adam heard more shouts and the sound of fists thudding against flesh. Wearily, he dug a few sheets of precious toilet paper out of his pocket, wiped his ass as best he could, pulled up his trousers, and staggered out of the jungle to see what was going on.

Not far away, surrounded by jeering onlookers, two Marines were going at each other, swinging wild punches, grabbing each other in clumsy wrestling holds, falling down, and getting up to start the battle all over again. Adam recognized them as two men from his platoon, one from Vardeman's squad and one from McDade's. The two sergeants didn't seem to be around, though, so it was up to him to put a stop to this.

"Atten-*hut!*" he shouted, putting most of his remaining strength into it. "Break it up, you two! Now, damn it!"

The men didn't snap to attention as they once had; being stuck here on this Godforsaken island, sick and on short rations for over a week, had sapped their normal discipline. But the men surrounding the two brawlers moved back, getting out of Adam's way. He strode closer and shouted again, "Break it up, I said!"

This time the two men stopped throwing punches. Instead they stood there panting, their arms hanging loose at their sides, alternating between glaring at each other and glaring at Adam.

"What the hell's this all about?" Adam asked, even though he knew the answer.

One of the men pointed at the other. "He stole my smokes! I only got two left!"

An outraged howl went up from the bystanders, and the man who had just spoken flinched. Most of the Marines had run out of cigarettes a couple of days earlier. A man with two of them to his name was rich, a man to be envied—and hated.

"I only stole 'em because that bastard pinched 'em from me first!" the second man protested. That didn't surprise Adam, either.

Petty larceny, especially of cigarettes, was as widespread in the camp as the dysentery was.

"Where are the cigarettes now?" he asked.

The first man pointed again. "He's got 'em. Give 'em back, asshole!"

"Oh, shit!" the second man exclaimed, his eyes going wide with horror. He started digging in the pocket of his shirt. "I had 'em in here, and then we fell down—"

More groans went up as the man pulled out the pair of cigarettes. Both of them were torn and crumpled beyond repair.

"My butts!" the first man screamed. "Look what you did to 'em, you big ape!"

"They weren't yours, they were mine," the second man insisted. Tears ran down his sunburned, beard-stubbled cheeks as he stared at the shreds of tobacco and paper. "All mine . . ."

He clenched his fists on the remains of the cigarettes and turned to run. Adam knew what he was thinking. The guy might be able to wrap the debris in something else and still smoke it.

The first man started after him, but Adam reached out and grabbed his arm. "Hold it," Adam said. "That's enough."

"But Lieutenant—"

Adam shook his head. "I'll deal with him later. Right now, get back to wherever you're supposed to be, Marine."

The man didn't like it, but he went along with Adam's order. Grumbling under his breath, he went to his bedroll, picked up his helmet and rifle, and moved off down the beach. The Marines were still patrolling day and night. It was thought that some of the Japs had escaped by swimming over to Florida, and if that were the case, they might try to come back and infiltrate the American positions.

Adam went back to his bedroll and picked up his canteen. He took a long drink, replenishing a little of the moisture his body had lost to illness. At least the water here was safe. Patrols had found springs up in the hills that seemed clean, and just to make sure, the Marines boiled the water and added purification tablets to it. Adam lowered the canteen, dug out a couple of salt tablets, and swallowed them with another swig from the canteen. He knew the stuff would go right through him like . . . well, like water, but he had to at least try to get some of his strength back, and he couldn't do that while he was dehydrated.

What the hell was wrong with the Navy, anyway? When the ships had sailed off, they had taken with them several companies of fresh Marines who had never made it ashore during the initial landing. If the convoy hadn't left, those troops could have been sent to Tulagi and the other islands to relieve the men who had done the dirty work of securing the beachheads. Under normal circumstances, that was what would have happened. Adam and his platoon would have had the chance to return to the transport ship, clean up, rest, and eat some decent food. They had carried only seventy-two hours' worth of rations with them when they went ashore, and those seventy-two hours were long since up. They had existed since then by breaking into the undamaged supplies left behind by the fleeing Japanese. Some of those supplies had belonged to the British and Australians who had occupied Tulagi before the Japs captured it.

So food was in short supply, cigarettes were even scarcer, and nearly all the men had been sick at one time or another. Yeah, this was one smooth-running operation. That bitter thought went through Adam's head as he sat down cross-legged on his blanket and waved a hand at the flies and mosquitoes swarming around him. He'd heard rumors that there was malaria in some of the other platoons, spread by the ever-prevalent mosquitoes, but so far his men had been lucky—if you could call anything about this fouled-up mission lucky—and avoided that disease.

He dozed off with his back against a tree and slept for a couple of hours. When he woke up, he expected to have to trot for the bushes again, but his belly seemed to be fairly calm for a change. Maybe he had turned the corner on the dysentery. The bugs that had been wreaking havoc with his system had to die out sooner or later, either that or kill him first, and he was too strong to be knocked out by a bunch of filthy, microscopic creatures like that. He told himself he was going to be fine.

Lieutenant Butala came wandering along the beach a little later. Butala was a little guy with glasses, hardly the stereotypical Marine, but he was smart as a whip and a valuable member of Captain Hughes's staff. He greeted Adam with a wave and said, "Better get ready to hunt a hole. The Japs'll be along soon."

Adam grunted, unimpressed. Nearly every day, Japanese bombers flew over the islands and dropped some bombs. Some of them went in the water and exploded harmlessly, while others fell in the deep jungle where there wasn't anything. Only occasionally did one of the bombs do any actual damage. The Marines had trenches and dugouts in which they could take shelter, but after the first couple of bombing runs, they stopped going to that much trouble.

"What do you hear from the 'Canal?" Adam asked.

"The Japs have tried several counterattacks, but we've turned them back every time," Butala said. "We keep hearing rumors that they have reinforcements on the way, but there's no telling if that's true or not. Our troops still control Henderson Field and all the territory around it."

Adam nodded. The half-finished airfield the Japanese had been building was being completed by engineer battalions and already had been dubbed Henderson Field after Major Lofton Henderson, a Marine aviator who had been killed in the Battle of Midway. As soon as it was ready, Marine pilots in Grumman Wildcats would begin flying patrols from the field. That would be a good day, because it would give the Marines on the islands some protection from the Japanese bombing runs.

In the meantime, Colonel Merritt Edson's Raiders had been ferried over to Guadalcanal from Tulagi in the few landing craft left in the area. Red Mike's men were reinforcing General Vandegrift's troops and helping to hold off the Japanese forces still on the 'Canal, which were becoming more daring as each day went by. The Marines had expected trouble on Guadalcanal but had gone ashore with ease. Now it was becoming obvious that although they had gained their beachhead, they were going to have to fight for the rest of the island. Not only that, it would be a struggle just to keep the Japs from pushing them back into the sea.

As long as he was stuck on Tulagi, though, there was nothing Adam could do to help the men on the other side of the channel. All he could do was wait.

"I'm collecting medical reports," Butala went on. "How many sick do you have in your platoon, Bergman?"

"It might be easier to count up the men who aren't sick," Adam said. "Let me think . . ."

Before he could come up with a figure, he heard airplane engines droning in the distance. Looking up at Butala with a grin, he said, "You were right. Unless I miss my guess, that's a flight of Bettys."

Butala's eyes widened. "You're not going to get under cover?"

"What's the point?" To Adam, the sentiment sounded practical rather than defeatist. "Sit down under a tree. You'll be just as well off. You're not in any danger unless one of the bombs lands right on top of you, and the odds of that are slim."

Butala didn't look convinced, but he took Adam's advice and hunkered down next to the thick trunk of a palm tree. The sound of the airplanes grew louder, and then the bombs began to fall. The earth trembled a little from the explosions, but as Adam had predicted, none of them came close to the spot where he and Butala waited out the attack.

When it was over and the Japanese Bettys had hummed off up the Slot toward Rabaul, Butala took a handkerchief from his pocket and wiped the sweat off his face. He said, "You're a brave man, Bergman, to just sit there like that while bombs are falling."

Adam just grunted. Butala didn't understand. Bravery had nothing to do with it. He was just too sick and bored to give a damn about much of anything anymore.

A couple of nights later, Adam wasn't feeling quite so casual about what was going on. Under cover of darkness, Japanese ships had slipped into the channel, and with no warning, their guns opened up on Tulagi, Gavutu, and Tanambogo. All the Marines on shore could do was hunt a hole in which to hide.

Adam found himself in one of the trenches that had been dug along the edge of the jungle. As the rounds crashed in from the heavy naval guns, he burrowed down as best he could, digging the front edge of his helmet into the dirt on the bottom of the trench.

The ground jumped and heaved underneath him from nearby explosions.

The wry thought crossed his mind that at least his dysentery had gone away. If he crapped his pants now, it would be from fear instead of illness.

Some of the big guns that the Japanese had abandoned when the Marines came ashore were still in working order. Over the past week and a half, those guns had been dragged down to the beach and mounted there in makeshift emplacements, just in case the Japs attempted an amphibious landing of their own. Marine gunners now fought back with these artillery pieces, but the weapons were too light to do much damage to the Japanese cruisers.

The bombardment went on nearly all night, insuring that no one on Tulagi got any sleep. By the time the gray light of dawn began creeping over the eastern horizon, Adam was exhausted. But he was unhurt, and he believed that most of the men in his platoon were all right too. As the firing from the channel died away, he lunged up out of his trench and began running along the beach, checking on his troops. The sergeants reported that all four squads were intact. One man in Lederer's squad had a broken arm, suffered when he threw himself to the ground when the first blast went off. That was the extent of their casualties.

Adam walked to the edge of the water and raised his binoculars to his eyes. It took a few minutes of searching in the uncertain light, but then he spotted the Japanese ships. They were steaming northward, out of the channel. The attack was over.

Adam didn't know why the Japs weren't pressing their momentary advantage. Perhaps they were low on supplies too. Whatever the reason, the worst appeared to be over—for now.

He had no doubt they would be back.

The United States Navy returned first, however. Two days after the bombardment from the sea, a flotilla of cruisers and supply ships showed up in Sealark Channel. The Marines greeted the sight with raucous cheers. The ships meant reinforcements, better food, cigarettes, and a break from the horrible, sweltering monotony that filled most days here in the South Pacific.

The ships brought new scuttlebutt as well. Word was that the First Division leathernecks on Guadalcanal still had their hands full holding the ground they had gained on the largest island in the Solomons. That evening, as several of the junior officers sat around eating and drinking coffee—glorious *coffee,* fresh off one of the supply ships—Barney Gelhart said, "I suppose it's only a matter of time before the brass sends us over there to Guadal' to clean up First Div's mess."

Ted Nash took a drag on his cigarette and blew out the smoke. "I'm ready to get off this stinkin' island, that's for sure."

"Even if it's just to go to another stinking island?" Adam asked.

"Damn right, if it means some action. Those feather merchants in my platoon would rather just sit here on their keisters where it's safe, but not me."

Adam and Gelhart exchanged a glance. Both of them knew that Nash was a blowhard. Not necessarily a bad officer, mind you, but pompous and full of talk. Still, he was a Marine, and no matter how much a Marine mouthed off, he could usually back it up. If the Second of the Second did get sent to Guadalcanal, Nash would have his chance to prove he meant what he said, that was for sure.

After a minute, Nash went on, "You haven't been around to see those two friends of yours lately, Bergman. Not so pally with the enlisted men now?"

Adam felt a surge of annoyance. "Why are you being such a jackass tonight, Nash? Hell, you ought to be happy that we've got fresh supplies. Everybody else is."

Nash glared at him and said, "What makes you think I'm not happy? You got a problem with me, mister?"

Adam shook his head. "No problem. As for Collins and Sikorsky, they're in your platoon, not mine. They're your responsibility."

"That didn't stop you from bailing them out of the brig the night before we left the States."

Adam set his tin of C rations aside. "Are you still holding a grudge about that?"

"No grudge," Nash said with a shrug. "I just don't like to see an officer buddying around with enlisted men. It's bad for discipline."

"Adam hasn't done anything to undermine discipline," Gelhart put in. "He's right, Nash. You *are* being a jackass tonight."

Nash laughed. "Take it easy, you guys. I'm just kidding you. I guess I'm a little antsy because I want to kill some Japs again."

"You'll get your chance," Gelhart said, echoing what Adam had thought a few moments earlier. "But you know what that means, don't you?"

"What?" Nash asked.

*"They'll* have a chance to kill *you* too."

Nash didn't say much after that.

# THIRTY-ONE

It was still an hour before dawn in Egypt. The sky would soon begin to lighten, but for now, the night was at its darkest point. The blackness was broken from time to time by distant flashes that were followed seconds later by the faint sounds of the explosions that caused them. Those were mines going off, Captain Neville Sharp knew as he stood next to his tank, a cold pipe clenched between his teeth. He wouldn't light it until the sun rose, just in case there were any watchers out there who might see the flare of a match and report back to Rommel that someone was waiting on the ridge known as the Alam el Halfa.

All through the night, Monty—General Montgomery, of course, but every man jack in the Eighth Army referred to him fondly by the nickname—had moved his tanks onto the ridge that overlooked the desert to the east of the Qattara Depression. The previous evening, 30 August 1942, General Rommel had launched an attack that was designed to blast the British out of El Alamein and open wide the door to Alexandria, Cairo, and the Suez Canal beyond. The Desert Fox had sent four armored divisions around the southern end of the Qattara Depression. From there they were supposed to charge northward toward the Mediterranean, skirting El Alamein to the east and cutting off the British forces there so that they could be destroyed at Rommel's leisure.

The plan might have worked if the British had not gotten wind of it in time to lay down heavy minefields right in Rommel's path. The anticipated lightning advance of the Deutsche Afrika Korps had slowed to a crawl. There would be no blitzkrieg over the sands of the Egyptian desert, at least not on this night.

A grim smile tugged at the corners of Sharp's mouth as he

thought about how the German tanks and trucks and armored cars had been forced to slow down after the first few mines went off. All they could do now was inch along behind the minesweeping troops who went out in front of them. It was those poor blighters who ran the risk of being blown up now, Sharp thought. Still, though he knew that many members of the German army were not members of the Nazi Party, he wasn't going to lose any sleep over the risks they ran.

Bert Crimmens popped his head out through the open hatch of the tank and said, "Message on the wireless from GHQ, Captain. They say the Jerries ought to get here just about the time the sun rises."

" 'One generation passeth away,' " Sharp murmured, " 'and another generation cometh: but the earth abideth forever. The sun also ariseth.' "

"What was that, Captain?" Bert sounded confused.

"Just a verse from Proverbs. Did you know that back home, my father was a minister?"

"No, sir, I don't believe you ever mentioned that."

"Well, it doesn't matter now," Sharp said. "When the sun comes up, we'll be ready for them."

Indeed, as dawn approached and the light grew stronger, Sharp could look along the ridge and see the tanks lined up there, their guns all pointed out into the desert where the Germans crept closer and closer. Sharp could hear the grinding of the engines now as they approached. The noise rose steadily. Monty had ordered that all his available General Grants be positioned here along the Alam el Halfa, but still the forces of the Royal Tank Corps were outnumbered. They had the high ground and, with luck, the element of surprise. That would have to be enough.

More minutes dragged by. Bert leaned out of the hatch, resting his crossed forearms on its edge. After a while, he said, "I think I can see 'em out there, Captain. Quite a lot of them, ain't there?"

"Quite a lot indeed," Sharp replied. "I'm sure they've lost some of their tanks to the minefield, but we'll still have our work cut out for us."

"Had we better button up, sir?"

"In a moment." Sharp glanced to the east. The sun was about to peek over the edge of the earth. The sky was rosy in a vast arc above it, and the world was taking on a golden glow. Sharp took out a match, flicked it into life with his thumbnail, and held the flame to the tobacco packed into the bowl of his pipe. He drew in, relishing the bite of the smoke as it curled through the mouthpiece. When the pipe was burning properly, he dropped the match to the sand and ground it out under his boot.

"Captain?"

"There's time, Bert, there's time." Sharp puffed on the pipe in great content for several minutes before knocking the dottle out against his heel. He tucked it away in his pocket and turned toward the tank.

*And it goeth down in the evening,* he thought as he climbed to the hatch and lowered himself inside.

Bert had the headphones of the wireless clamped to his ears as he huddled next to the set. Tom Hamilton was checking his ammunition supply for at least the fiftieth time since the tank had moved into position in the middle of the night. Jeremy Royce was perched on a small seat behind Hamilton, where he would function as the gunner's loader. The tank wouldn't be going anywhere when the battle started, so Royce's skill as a driver wouldn't be needed. For a change, the General Grant would fight from a stationary position. If movement was required, Royce could get in the driver's seat quick enough.

The glow of dawn slanted in through the observation port, as well as through the open hatch. Hamilton said, "The Jerries are nearly here, are they?"

"That's right," Sharp said. "I've no doubt they'll notice us up here soon, if they haven't already."

"They'll turn and run when they do," Royce said.

Sharp shook his head. "Not the Afrika Corps. They'll go where Rommel has sent them."

"I still say old Tom here will be puttin' his rounds right up their arses."

Hamilton looked over his shoulder at Royce. "I don't care much for the way that sounded, Jeremy."

"Damn it, you know what I mean!"

Bert chuckled, and Sharp hid a quick grin. His crew wasn't overly nervous. That was good. They were ready for this fight, and so was he.

"Are you loaded, Tom?" Sharp asked.

"Loaded and ready to fire, Captain."

"Shouldn't be long now . . ."

It wasn't. Mere moments later, Bert's head lifted as he listened to the orders coming over the wireless. "GHQ says fire at our own discretion, Captain!" he reported.

Sharp nodded. "You heard the man, Tom," he said to Hamilton. "Whenever you're ready."

Hamilton's eye was pressed to the sighting periscope. "I'm ready *now!*" he said as he thumbed the firing button on the 75mm-cannon.

The big gun roared, and its recoil sent a jolt through the entire tank. Sharp heard other blasts from the tanks lined up along the ridge. Shells whistled through the air and arched down toward the desert and the front line of the German advance. Sharp leaned over to peer through the port and saw the explosions among the scattered Panzers and armored cars leading the attack. At the same moment, the roar of aircraft overhead added to the growing tumult as a flight of RAF bombers swept past and targeted the Germans. Powerful bombs plummeted down and set off even larger explosions than the rounds from the cannons of the M3s. It was chaos down there, utter chaos. Many of the vehicles in the front ranks were crippled by the blasts and blocked the path of the tanks and armored cars behind them. The ones that could still move raced forward in an attempt to get in some licks of their own, but the screen of fire was too dense to penetrate. One by one they were set on fire or had their treads blown off. It had to be pure hell for the crews, Sharp thought as he watched the destruction. What had promised to be a glorious golden morning was now shrouded with thick clouds of black smoke and tinted by the flames of brightly blazing tanks.

The sun had arisen, Sharp told himself as the tank's cannon belched another round, and today it would go down on death.

*   *   *

Dale nudged Joe in the side with an elbow. "Hey! There's Churchill."

Joe looked where Dale was indicating. After a moment, he said, "No, it's not. That's just some fat, bald guy. He looks more like Oliver Hardy than Churchill."

"Are you sure?" Dale didn't sound convinced.

"Look at it this way: Would the prime minister of England be going into a pawnshop in the middle of the day by himself?"

Dale frowned. "He might if he wanted to pawn something." His shoulders rose and fell in a shrug. "But yeah, I guess you're right. That's not him. Probably."

The two of them moved on down Dean Street in London's Soho district. Dale wanted to go to a pub, but Joe was more interested in finding a place to eat. He looked around, enjoying the hustle and bustle of the crowded streets. They reminded him a little of Chicago, and that made him feel homesick, but it was also nice to be back in a city. They had been stuck on an isolated base in the countryside for weeks after returning to England from Egypt.

The detachment from the Army Service Force had sailed from Alexandria on a British cargo vessel heading back to Liverpool after delivering its load. Upon arrival, the men had found new orders waiting for them. They were being transferred to the First Armored Division of the U.S. Army. Their experience with the General Grant tanks would be put to use, but no longer merely as instructors. Rumor had it that the Allies were planning some sort of invasion, and for the first time, the Americans would be active participants. It wasn't known exactly where the invasion would take place. North Africa was a possibility, but so was the Channel coast of France. The U.S. was under a lot of pressure from Russia to open a second front somewhere in Europe. To Stalin's way of thinking, a second front would force Hitler to divert some of his war machine from Eastern Europe, where the Soviets were fighting tooth and nail to stop the Nazi advance. Joe tried to keep up with what was going on in the war by listening to the BBC and reading *Stars and Stripes* and the English papers, though most of the time Dale couldn't be bothered to do so. He was content to go where he was told to go and do what he was told to do. He hadn't minded when they were pulled out of Egypt and sent back to England. The voyage had been nerve-racking, as sea voyages always were when German U-boats were lurking around, looking for some nice fat ship to sink, but luck had been with Joe and Dale once again. This time the convoy hadn't even sighted any of the Nazi wolf pack.

Joe had his own reasons for being glad to get out of Egypt. The whole affair with Melinda Thorp-Davies had left a bitter taste in his mouth. She had played him for a fool—but so had Major Colin Richardson. Richardson hadn't trusted him with the truth but had put him together with Melinda in hopes that he would stumble into trouble, which was exactly what had happened. So Richardson had gotten what he wanted, but Joe had nearly gotten killed for it. It would be all right with him if he never crossed paths with another intelligence officer. They seemed to fight their wars by different rules than everyday soldiers, and that was all Joe had aspired to be when he joined the Army.

"It's changed some since we were here last, hasn't it?"

Dale's question broke into Joe's thoughts. He looked around and said, "You mean London?"

"Yeah. They've cleaned it up a lot."

That was true. When they had traveled to London a year earlier to pay a visit to Joe's friend Arthur Yates, the pounding that the city had taken during the blitz was still obvious. Piles of rubble littered streets lined with bombed-out buildings. Hardly a whole, unbroken pane of glass could be found anywhere. Much of that destruction had been cleared away, and quite a bit of construction was going on as new buildings went up. The Londoners were getting on with their lives.

"I hope we can get up to Kensington and see Arthur while we're here," Joe said.

Dale shook his head. "You can go if you want, but we've only got a two-day pass, and I don't want to spend any of it listening to him complain."

Anger welled up in Joe. "He's got every right to complain. He lost his fiancée, remember, and was blinded to boot."

"Yeah, and I'm sorry about both of those things. I really am. But they weren't my fault and Arthur was your friend back at the university, not mine. He's a good egg and all, but—"

"But you don't have the time for him," Joe said. "You'd rather spend it getting drunk and whoring around."

"You said it, big brother, not me," Dale replied with a grin. "Besides, as GIs we have a tradition to uphold. What is it the Limeys say about us? We're overpaid, oversexed, and over here?"

Joe had to chuckle despite his irritation. "That's what they say, all right."

"So you see, I can't let our hosts down." Dale pointed. "As a matter of fact, I see a good place to start right there. With a name like that, I'll bet the champagne flows like water."

"The French House," Joe read off the sign above the front door of the building. A French flag hung next to the sign, and quite a few people went in and out the door, including several attractive young women. Joe noted that several men in what seemed to be French army uniforms were going in as well, including one tall, distinguished-looking man with a prominent nose. With a shock, Joe recognized him as General Charles de Gaulle, the leader of the Free French movement now headquartered in London. Earlier, Dale had been convinced he'd seen Prime Minister Winston Churchill. Now, Joe actually had spotted someone famous. In a whisper, he said to Dale, "Hey, that guy who just went in was General de Gaulle."

Dale rubbed his palms together. "Unless he's buying the drinks, I don't give a damn. Let's go. I want to get started. There's less than forty hours left before we have to catch that train back to the base, and I intend to make the most of all of them."

Joe was sure that would be the case. He just hoped he wouldn't have to come up with money to get Dale out of jail before the weekend was over.

And he wondered if they still locked people up in the Tower of London.

# THIRTY-TWO

The last time Joe had visited the Yates house in Kensington, fire damage had still been visible on the upper stories, a result of the bomb that had landed there. The explosion and ensuing blaze had blinded Arthur Yates, who had been one of Joe's best friends at the University of Chicago. Arthur was the son of a British diplomat and an American woman he had met while posted to the British Embassy in Washington. He had come to his mother's native country to go to college, but when war had broken out in Europe and the Nazis had begun bombing London, Arthur had returned home. The blitz had taken from him not only his eyesight but also the woman he loved and planned to marry, and that double loss had left him a bitter young man. When Joe and Dale had come to visit him before, Arthur had thrown them out of his room.

So Joe felt a little nervous as he knocked on the door of the Yates house. With the fire damage repaired, it was once again a beautiful, elegant residence, on a narrow street lined with nice houses not far from Kensington Park.

A white-haired woman in maid's uniform opened the door and looked surprised to see an American serviceman standing there on the stoop. "Good morning, sir," she said, her natural politeness overcoming her surprise. "Are you perhaps lost?"

"No, ma'am," Joe replied with a shake of his head. "I'm here to see Arthur Yates. I'm a friend of his from America. My name is Joseph Parker." He didn't remember the maid from his previous visit. Either she hadn't been on duty that day or had gone to work for the Yates family since then.

"I'm afraid Master Arthur isn't here right now," the maid said.

That came as a surprise to Joe. Not only was it Sunday morning, but when he and Dale were here before, Arthur had been spending all his time cooped up in his room, sitting and brooding in the dark. Of course, the darkness didn't really mean anything, since Arthur was blind, but the withdrawing from life did. After seeing Arthur, Joe had been pretty pessimistic about his friend's prospect for the future. He didn't want to be too judgmental, though. He had no idea how he would react if he lost his eyesight, but he would have been willing to wager that it wouldn't be good.

"I expect him back shortly," the maid went on. "Would you care to come in and wait?"

Joe thought about it. Dale was in their room in a small hotel not far from Piccadilly Circus, sleeping off a day and a night of debauchery. He probably wouldn't even wake up until noon, and when he did he would be fighting a massive hangover. Joe would have to force coffee and food on him and try to get him in shape for the train ride back to the First Armored's camp that evening. They were to report in by 2200 hours, when their pass expired.

But that problem could be dealt with later. Joe had a little time to spare, which was why he'd caught a taxi outside the hotel and had it bring him up here to Kensington. That was another difference in London: Taxis were plentiful again now. In the days during and following the blitz, most of them had been pressed into service as ambulances.

Those thoughts went through his head in a matter of seconds. After the brief hesitation, he nodded to the maid and said, "Thank you, that would be fine." Maybe Arthur's mother was here. She was American, and although she had adopted some of her husband's British reserve, she had been quite friendly to Joe and Dale when they came here. He would enjoy talking to her again. "Is Mrs. Yates here?"

The maid moved back a step to let him into the house. "No, sir, her and the mister have gone to church."

"Oh, of course. Is Arthur with them?" In the States, Arthur had never been the religious sort, but maybe after everything he had endured, he had turned to God to help him get through it.

"No, sir, he's gone to his office. Something important, most likely."

Once again Joe was taken aback. He paused just inside the threshold of the doorway and repeated, "His office?"

"Yes, sir, at the ministry—" The sound of a vehicle pulling up outside made her pause. She looked past Joe and said, "Ah, there's Master Arthur now. I'm sure he'll be quite pleased to see you, sir."

"To see me?" Joe leaned closer to the maid and lowered his voice. "Can he see again?"

"Oh, no, that's not what I meant. He's still blind, the poor boy." The woman's voice became fierce. "But don't you tell him I called him that, mind."

Joe shook his head to indicate that he wouldn't and then turned to look at the vehicle that had come to a stop at the narrow curb.

Yet again, he was surprised. It was a jeep, the standard model, what the army in its backwards nomenclature called a truck, quarter-ton, four by four. But it had British markings on it, indicating that it was one of the vehicles that had been sent over in the Lend-Lease program. It also flew a small flag that Joe guessed had some military or diplomatic significance, or both.

Arthur sat on the left side, since the jeep had right-hand drive. The driver, a young woman in uniform, got out and went around the jeep to help him get out. He had already opened the jeep's door on that side by himself. He wore a dark suit and hat and smoked glasses. A white cane was in his right hand. As he stepped onto the sidewalk, the cane came down and its tip searched out his surroundings. Arthur's movements with the cane were quick and sure. He started up the walk to the house even before his female companion shut the door and came after him. She looked at the house, saw Joe standing in the doorway, and put a hand on Arthur's arm. Leaning close to his ear, she spoke in a low voice. Joe couldn't hear any of the words.

Arthur's head lifted. If Joe hadn't known better, he would have sworn that his old friend was looking at him through those smoked glasses. In a loud voice, Arthur said, "What's that? There's one of those Yank dogfaces in the house? Better call a constable before he steals the silver and a kiss from Mrs. Maudsley!"

Joe heard the maid give an involuntary giggle and knew she must be Mrs. Maudsley. He looked at her, feeling his face start to heat up with embarrassment, and said, "I would never—"

"Oh, that's all right, sir," she said with a laugh and a wave of her hand. "Master Arthur's just havin' a spot of fun with you."

He realized that she was right. Arthur came toward him, hand extended, and said, "Joe? Is it Joe Parker? I can't think of any other American soldier who would come to see me, unless it was General Eisenhower."

"Ike?" Joe burst out. "You know Ike?"

"Ah, it is Joe. I thought it must be."

Joe stepped forward and clasped Arthur's outstretched hand. Arthur's fingers closed strongly over his.

"God, it's good to see you again, Arthur," he said. "I mean—"

"It's perfectly all right for you to see me, Joe. No need to apologize. As you may be able to tell, I'm not quite as sensitive on the subject as I was the last time you were here."

"That's great. To tell you the truth, Dale and I were pretty worried about you."

"You were, perhaps. I don't doubt that. But I don't imagine your brother really cared all that much."

Arthur could still be blunt in expressing his opinions. That quality went all the way back to their days at the university. Joe felt compelled to defend Dale, but he knew there was some truth to what Arthur said. Dale wasn't a bad guy, but he and Arthur had never been close. The fact that Dale was holed up in a hotel sleeping off a binge instead of being here in Kensington was proof enough of that.

"Dale couldn't be here, but he said to tell you hello and that he hoped you were feeling better," Joe said. That was stretching the truth, but Dale might have said something like that, if he had thought of it.

"Well, be sure to convey my good wishes to him too." Arthur reached out and took hold of Joe's arm, fumbling only a little as he did so. "Let's go inside and sit down, shall we? Perhaps we can talk Mrs. Maudsley into fixing us a spot of brunch."

"I'd be glad to, Master Arthur," Mrs. Maudsley said. "You know that."

She hurried off to the kitchen while Arthur and Joe went into the parlor, followed by the young woman in uniform. "Mrs. Maudsley's an old dear," Arthur said in a quiet voice. "Don't you love the way she calls me Master Arthur, as if I were eight years old?"

Joe looked at the young woman. She was slender and very trim in the dark blue uniform. A cap of the same shade was perched on her short blond hair. She returned Joe's look with a small, civil smile that didn't quite reach her blue eyes.

As if Arthur had sensed the glance that was exchanged between his two companions, he said, "Oh, Lord, I'm being rude again. I've come to depend so much on poor Gretchen that sometimes I tend to forget she's there."

She spoke for the first time. "If I were a woman, sir, instead of a naval yeoman, such a comment might prove quite offensive."

"I shall have to remember that," Arthur said with a chuckle. "Joe, this is Yeoman Gretchen Ames of the Royal Navy. Yeoman Ames, my good friend from the United States, Sergeant Joseph Parker."

Joe nodded to her. "I'm pleased to meet you, Yeoman."

"Sergeant." Her nod in return was just a bit sharper than his.

"Gretchen is my driver and assistant," Arthur went on. "She's very competent, and though she steadfastly refuses to admit it, I suspect that she's very beautiful as well."

"I'm sure she is," Joe said.

"What, competent . . . or beautiful?"

Yeoman Ames glared at him, but he ignored the warning look and said, "Both, actually."

"You see, Gretchen, it's been confirmed by the United States Army. Can't go against our friends and allies."

She paid no attention to the banter. Instead, she said, "If you'll give me your hat, sir . . ."

"Of course." Arthur handed over his hat and then used his cane to find an armchair. "Have a seat," he told Joe as he sank down into the chair. "We have some catching up to do."

"I'll say." Joe sat down in another armchair and clasped his hands between his knees as he leaned forward. "What's this I hear about you working at some sort of office?"

"I'm an assistant minister in the Ministry of War," Arthur said with pride in his voice. "I analyze and summarize intelligence reports."

Yeoman Ames came back from putting Arthur's hat on a small side table. "Sir, you really shouldn't be discussing your work with someone not in the ministry."

"Oh, don't worry about Joe here," Arthur said. "I'd sooner believe that John Wayne is a Nazi spy, rather than Joe."

"I appreciate the vote of confidence, but Yeoman Ames is right. You know what they say about loose lips."

"And how would you describe Yeoman Ames's lips, Joe?"

Although he tried to control the reaction, Arthur's question made Joe look at the yeoman's lips. At the moment, they were pressed together in a rather firm line of disapproval. Under other circumstances, though—with a little lipstick on them, in a room with soft light and some music playing, say—Joe suspected they might be very nice lips indeed. But he wasn't completely convinced that Yeoman Ames wouldn't throw something at him if he said that, so instead of answering Arthur's question, he said, "Why don't you tell me about how you came to be working for the Ministry of War?"

"Oh, all right, if you insist on spoiling a poor blind man's fun. . . . My father is to blame, actually. He insisted that I come with him to the Foreign Office one day. He had thoughts of putting me to work for him. I resisted, of course. I was . . . not in the best of moods during that time of my life."

Arthur's jovial attitude vanished for a moment, and Joe knew he was thinking about his fiancée. Joe didn't say anything. He had expressed his sympathy during his last visit, and he didn't know what else to say. Arthur sighed and shook his head. A faint smile appeared on his face.

"No point in dwelling on the bad old days," he said. "I was saying about my father . . . He insisted I accompany him, and when I dragged my feet, my mother, the dear, put her own foot down. I could go with my father or I could go to hell, she told me, but one way or another, I *was* leaving this house. So I went to the Foreign Office, and while I was there I heard my father and one of the other men discussing a report that the Ministry of War had sent over. It was frightfully written, you understand. I mean, you could look at it and see that the words were in English, but it didn't seem to *mean* anything. At least, that was the sense I got from listening to the discussion. I piped up and told them what I thought the fellow who had written the report meant to say, and there was silence in the office. Then the other fellow said, 'You know, I believe the lad's right.' So my father read some of the other reports to me and asked me what the bloody hell I thought they were talking about." Arthur steepled his hands together in front of his face and then leaned his chin on the fingertips. "I think it has something to do with the way the words look on the page. I can't see them, so that has no effect on me. All I can do is listen as they're read to me. You see, even when someone reads aloud, they still see the words on paper. That has an effect on how the words are perceived, whether the reader is aware of it or not. That's my theory, anyway, and I haven't found anyone who can refute it to my satisfaction. When I listen to a report being read, it's as if I can see through all the gibberish to the information that the person who wrote it meant to convey. It's quite simple, really."

"Maybe so, but it doesn't sound all that simple," Joe said. "Anyway, they put you to work, right?"

"Exactly. I didn't want to do it, of course. I just wanted to come home and go upstairs to my dark little hole and be left alone. But once they assigned the lovely Yeoman Ames to look after me and chauffeur me around and do all the reading and typing, how could I refuse?"

Yeoman Ames added, "I'm sure the fact that you're helping your country had nothing to do with your decision, sir."

"Well, I don't want to sound too noble...." Arthur said. "Remember, Joe knew me during my college days, when I was young and wild."

"You always studied more than anybody I ever knew—except maybe me."

"Hush! You'll ruin the dashing image that I'm trying to cultivate."

Joe could only grin and shake his head. Arthur had made such a dramatic turnaround in the past year that it was hard for Joe to accept. Joe suspected that at times his friend was still gripped by the same melancholia that had led him to withdraw to a dark room for weeks on end. But having a job to do, and valuable work at that, had been good for Arthur Yates. That much was obvious. Arthur seemed to enjoy teasing Gretchen Ames too. Joe wondered if there might be something more between them than just a professional relationship. Probably not. Yeoman Ames looked like she would bite the head off of anybody who made a pass at her. She must spend a lot of time around Arthur, though, Joe mused. There was no telling what might happen in unguarded moments. . . .

Best not to speculate about that, he decided. He was just glad to see that Arthur was doing so much better.

"You must tell me about everything you've done since you were here last," Arthur went on. "I seem to recall that you had come over here to instruct our lads in the proper care and feeding of those new tanks you Yanks sent us."

"You could say that," Joe agreed. "Dale and I wound up going to Egypt with the tanks. We helped the Royal Tank Corps learn how to use them."

"And a good job you must have done, from all accounts. I heard just the other day that Monty put all his tanks up on a ridge south of El Alamein and turned back Rommel's attempt to get around and cut off the Eighth Army."

The battle at Alam el Halfa wasn't classified information, Joe thought. He had read about it in the *London Times*. He had wondered when he read the stories if his friends from the 3RTC had taken part in it. He suspected that they had, if they were still alive. As long as he was breathing, it would be difficult to keep Captain Neville "Hell on Treads" Sharp out of the action. And if Sharp was there, so too would be Bert Crimmens, as well as Jeremy Royce and Tom Hamilton. Joe didn't know Royce and Hamilton as well as he knew Bert and Captain Sharp. Dale was really the one who was close to them; he had shared the dangers of battle with them.

Over the next half hour, while Yeoman Ames went off to do something elsewhere in the house, Joe told Arthur about what he and Dale had been doing in Egypt. He left out any mention of the fiasco involving Major Richardson and Melinda Thorp-Davies, but he expounded at length about Dale's adventures in the desert west of Cairo. Arthur was duly impressed, although he said, "Quite a few people high up in the government would not be happy to learn that an American sergeant commanded one of our tanks as well or better than the captain whose job it was to do so."

Joe shook his head. "Don't give Dale too much credit. Some of what he did was just pure dumb luck. And nobody can blame Captain Sharp for being wounded."

"No, I suppose not. The chaps who really fell down on the job were the rest of the crew."

"You won't say anything, will you, Arthur? I thought this was just between you and me."

Arthur waved a hand and said, "Of course not. We're just two old friends talking. Nothing leaves this room. That's why I feel safe telling you that I'll be glad when you Americans start giving us a hand in Africa."

Joe felt his pulse quicken. "We're going to Africa?"

"Now, don't say anything more," Arthur said, holding his hand up. "I shouldn't have mentioned that. I'm not the stickler for regulations that some of the chaps in the ministry are, but there are some things I really can't discuss."

"That's all right," Joe said, nodding. "There are already rumors that we're going to be landing in North Africa sometime soon. I'll just regard this as one more rumor."

Arthur nodded. "Yes, that's exactly what you should do."

Mrs. Maudsley called them to brunch not long after that. Joe enjoyed the meal and was glad that Yeoman Ames joined them. She was still rather taciturn, but she loosened up a little, he thought, before they were finished. She even smiled as she said, "I suspect I was assigned to assist Mr. Yates because I'm the oldest of eight children."

"So you're accustomed to dealing with brats, is that it?" Arthur asked with a smile of his own.

"You made that comment, sir, not I."

Arthur laughed and shook his head. "You see what I have to deal with, Joe."

"Yes," Joe said, nodding and thinking that Gretchen Ames was even lovelier when she smiled. "I certainly do."

# THIRTY-THREE

The Solomon Islands were not far south of the equator. In the tropics, the weather was hot year-round but being south of the equator meant that the seasons were reversed from what Adam and the other Marines were used to. As August turned into September and September dragged toward October, what was early autumn in the States became the beginning of spring in the South Pacific. The sultry heat that gripped the islands grew worse, with the promise of even greater heat to come. Uniforms were soaked with sweat—when the men wore them. Much of the time, they wore only skivvies, and bare chests were common. Torn uniforms went unpatched, and beards grew long. Even though the Navy had returned with fresh supplies, the Marines were still on short rations because no one knew how long they were going to have to stay here. Bellies shrunk, and faces became lean under the ragged beards. Adam looked at his men and thought they resembled a gang of pirates more than anything else. He supposed he looked the same way. Since he seldom bothered to shave, he didn't see himself in the mirror very often.

Heat and boredom drained the men of all their energy. Left to their own devices, they would have crawled in their tents and slept twenty hours a day, like cats. The officers and noncoms kept them busy patrolling and shoring up the island's defenses, but only so much of that could be done. All the Japs had been cleaned off of Tulagi, and the Second Division, under General William H. Rupertus, established its headquarters there. What it amounted to was that the Marines of the Second were back to serving garrison duty, and an extended amount of garrison duty always made the men lackadaisical, no matter what the officers did to combat that attitude.

Across the channel on Guadalcanal, the situation was much different. One night in the middle of September, all hell broke loose over there, and Adam and the other men on Tulagi could see the flashes in the sky and hear the rumble of artillery. Airplanes appeared in the sky, releasing flares so that bombers could swoop in and drop their deadly loads on the American positions around Henderson Field. The Japanese on Guadalcanal had tried several times to take back the territory they had abandoned when the Marines came ashore, but they had been unsuccessful on every occasion. Now they were pouring everything they had into a fresh assault.

As they watched from the beaches of Tulagi, Ed Collins and Leo Sikorsky, rifles canted over their shoulders, speculated on what was happening over there.

"I bet the Japs brought in reinforcements," Leo said. "That's all they been waitin' for."

"We oughta be over there," Ed said. "Hell, we ain't doin' a damned thing here on Tulagi. We might as well be over on Guadal' so we could relieve some o' them boys who've been there all along."

"The way I hear it, MacArthur and the Army are coming to relieve all of us."

Ed snorted in contempt. "A bunch o' damned dogfaces? I don't think so, Chopper. I ain't gettin' my hopes up based on anything the Army might do, 'specially ol' Dugout Doug."

The battle raged all night on Guadalcanal. From Adam's vantage point near General Rupertus's HQ, he saw the flares and heard the bombs going off, and a sense of guilt gnawed at him. He should be over there helping his fellow Marines, he thought. But his orders, the orders that applied to all of the men of the Second Division, were to hold Tulagi now that it was secured.

By the next day, things were quieter on Guadalcanal. A couple of days after that, several war correspondents who had been there came over to Tulagi on one of the small landing craft that served as ferries across Sealark Channel. Adam was able to talk for a while with one of them, a tall, slender man with a neatly trimmed mustache.

"Yes, the Japs tried to come over the ridge that overlooks the Tenaru and the Ilu Rivers," the journalist said as he sat on a log next to Adam. "That's east of Henderson Field. The Raiders met them right there at the ridge, though, and threw them back. Red Mike's boys are some fighters, let me tell you. That ridge was covered with blood when they were through, and most of it belonged to the Japs. They're already calling it the Battle of Bloody Ridge."

Adam shook his head. "Part of me wishes I could have been there."

The journalist lit a cigarette and grinned around it. "And the sensible part of you is glad that you weren't."

"All of us on Tulagi want to do our part," Adam protested. "We had a couple of days of fighting when we came ashore, and that's been it so far."

"All the Japs are gone?"

"There may be one left here and there, hiding out in a cave," Adam said, "but they're not a threat now."

"What about the air raids?"

Adam smiled. "What about 'em? Nobody pays much attention to them anymore."

"It's been the same on Guadalcanal," the journalist said with a nod. "At first the boys went hunting for a hole every time we heard planes coming, but lately the poker games don't even break up."

"I suppose there's a sense of fatalism at work," Adam said. "A feeling that if a bomb or a bullet is meant to get you, it will, and if it's not, what's the use in worrying?"

The journalist chuckled. "Exactly. Fatalism is a good description. You sound like a college man, Lieutenant."

"University of Chicago," Adam said. "I was in law school there when I enlisted."

"The day after Pearl Harbor, eh?"

Adam shook his head. "Actually, no. Some friends and I decided to go into the service back in February of last year. They joined the Army, but I decided to enlist in the Marines."

"Let me get this straight—you left law school to join up months before the war started?"

"Months before it started for us in the United States," Adam said. "It had been going on in Europe for a while."

"Yeah, yeah, I know. What made you leave school, you and your buddies?"

Adam thought about Joe and Dale Parker and the mess Dale

had gotten in with that banker's wife. "My friends had reasons of their own, and you'd have to ask them about that. As for me, my name is Bergman."

"Oh," the journalist said. "You wanted to get a crack at Hitler and his bully boys because of what they've done to your people."

Adam nodded. "That's what I had in mind. My grandparents . . . my mother's parents . . . live in the Ukraine. After the Nazis went through there . . . well, as far as I know, my mother hasn't heard from them since."

"I'm sorry, Lieutenant. You didn't wind up going to Europe, though."

Adam gave a hollow laugh. "I figured the Marines would be the first to fight, just like it says in the hymn, and I was right. Only it was out here in the Pacific against the Japs, not in Europe against the Nazis."

"I suppose it's all one enemy, when you get right down to it," the correspondent said. "Us against them, good versus evil, the light of day battling to hold off the fall of eternal night."

"I guess you could put it like that. One of my friends who's in the Army would like the way you talk. He's a writer."

"You mean a war correspondent?"

"No, he writes stories for the pulp magazines. Joe Parker is his name."

The journalist shook his head. "Sorry, haven't heard of him."

Adam smiled faintly. He wouldn't tell Joe that his fame as a writer hadn't penetrated to this corner of the South Pacific.

"Well, Lieutenant, I've enjoyed talking to you," the correspondent said as he stood up. "What do you intend to do now?"

Adam got to his feet as well. "Whatever I'm ordered to do, of course. But I hope that sooner or later we'll get to go over to Guadalcanal and help with the mopping up there. Maybe if that ever happens, I'll run into you again, sir."

"Not me," the war correspondent said with a shake of his head. "I'm being relieved pretty soon. I'll probably be on my way to the States while you're just getting your first taste of the scenic beauties of the 'Canal."

"I can't wait," Adam said. And the funny thing about it was that he meant it.

*   *   *

On 20 August 1942, the first American planes had landed at Henderson Field on Guadalcanal. There were thirty-one planes in the group, twelve Douglass SBD Dauntless dive bombers and nineteen Grumman Wildcat fighters. Their presence in the Solomons meant that the planes based on the aircraft carriers no longer had to be solely responsible for providing air cover for the Marines on the islands.

This was a good thing, because four days later the American carriers had problems of their own. Using the carrier *Ryujo* as bait, the Japanese navy set a trap for the Americans. When patrol planes spotted the *Ryujo* less than three hundred miles to the northwest of the *Enterprise* and the *Saratoga*, Admiral Frank Jack Fletcher ordered a strike on the Japanese ship. A large flight of Dauntless dive bombers and Avenger torpedo bombers took off from the American flat tops and headed northwest.

Not long after that, bad news arrived in the form of numerous blips on the radar screens of the *Enterprise* and *Saratoga*. Japanese bombers, accompanied by numerous Zero fighters, were headed straight for the American carriers. The Wildcats were able to get in the air before the Vals arrived, but the screen of Zeros was too thick for them to penetrate. The bombers ignored the *Saratoga*, concentrating on the *Enterprise* instead. Several bombs struck the flight deck, penetrating into the interior of the ship before exploding. Soon, thick clouds of black smoke billowed up from the *Enterprise*, and the carrier appeared to be on the verge of sinking.

That appearance was deceptive. The fires were brought under control before too much damage could be done. The flight deck had holes in it where the bombs had torn through, but large squares of sheet metal soon were riveted in place over the holes to serve as temporary patches. Not only was the *Enterprise* not dead in the water, as the Japs had intended, but its flight deck was still functional. As the planes that had attacked—and sunk—the *Ryujo* began to return, the Japanese navy withdrew. They had set the trap, but the Americans had stolen the bait in the Battle of the Eastern Solomons.

A few days later, Phil Lange was stretched out in his bunk reading a magazine when Roy Kirkland hurried into the compartment that was shared by four of the aviators. He seemed to be excited about something, but then, Ensign Kirkland was always excited about something or other.

"Have you heard the news, Phil?" Kirkland asked. Without waiting for an answer, he announced, "We're going back to Pearl!"

Phil sat up, but not too sharply so that he didn't crack his skull on the bottom of the bunk above his. He set aside the magazine—a Western pulp with a story in it by that friend of Catherine's, Joe Parker—and said, "What?"

"We're going to Pearl Harbor," Kirkland repeated. "I mean, the ship is, and of course, we're going too. The admiral's decided that patch job on the flight deck isn't going to hold up well enough for us to stay out here. So we have to put in at Pearl for repairs."

Phil's eyes narrowed. It was true that the sheet metal fastened over the holes in the desk was just a stopgap measure, but he hadn't thought that permanent repairs would require going all the way back to Pearl Harbor. He swung his legs out of the bunk. "When are we leaving?"

"Later today. At least, that's the poop that I heard."

Phil stood up. "I'm going to talk to Captain Ramsey." He was wearing skivvy shorts and shirt. He reached for his uniform trousers. If he was going to talk to the captain of his flight group and ask a favor, it would help to be properly attired.

"What are you going to do, Phil?" Kirkland asked as Phil pulled on his uniform.

"Ask to be transferred to the *Saratoga*."

Kirkland stared at him in disbelief. "You don't *want* to go back to Hawaii?"

"Not particularly."

"But . . . how could you leave the *Enterprise*?"

Phil wasn't sure how to explain it. The *Enterprise* was the only carrier Roy Kirkland had flown off of. Phil, on the other hand, had been stationed on the *Lexington* and the *Yorktown* as well. The only ship he'd really felt any sentimental attachment to had been the *Lady Lex*, and she had gone to the bottom of the Coral Sea. He supposed it must be the same for Kirkland: The first ship was always the best.

But since he didn't feel that way, he wanted to stay out here in the Solomons where he could do some good. He owed that to Jerry and to all the other pilots and gunners and navigators who had gone down at the hands of the Japanese.

Besides, out here he was closer to Tonga than he would be in Hawaii, which meant he was closer to Missy. He might not be able to be with her, but he didn't want to increase the distance between them any more than he had to.

As Phil buttoned his shirt, Kirkland shook his head and said, "The old man's not going to like it when he hears you want to transfer out."

The old man—Captain Ramsey—was twenty-four, which was only a year older than Phil himself. Ramsey might not like the request Phil was going to make, but Phil didn't care. He had to do what he thought was right.

"Anyway, we make a good team," Kirkland went on. "I hate to break that up. Hell, you saw the way we put a bomb right down the smokestack of that Jap carrier."

"You could ask for a transfer too," Phil pointed out.

Kirkland looked alarmed. "I couldn't do that!"

Phil shrugged. "Suit yourself." He headed out of the cabin, leaving Kirkland sitting disconsolate on one of the bunks.

Ramsey wasn't in his cabin. Phil found him in the wardroom, drinking a cup of coffee. Several other officers were in the room, so Phil said, "Could I have a minute of your time, Captain? In private?"

"Sure, Phil." Ramsey carried his coffee cup into the companionway, following Phil for several yards until they were out of easy earshot of the wardroom hatch. The easygoing look on Ramsey's face disappeared and was replaced by a solemn expression. "What can I do for you, Phil? You look like you've had some bad news."

"I have, sir. Ensign Kirkland tells me that we're headed back to Pearl Harbor."

"And that's *bad* news to you?"

"I'd like to stay out here, sir. In the Solomons. I could fly off the *Saratoga*, or the *Wasp*, when it gets back." The *Wasp* had sailed off to the north the previous week to rendezvous with a convoy of fleet oilers and refuel.

Ramsey was shaking his head almost before the words were out of Phil's mouth. "There's no need for noble gestures," he said. "You've flown plenty of missions in the past couple of months. You could do with some rest, Phil. We all could. Pilots can't keep going indefinitely any more than planes and ships can."

"I'd just like the chance—"

"To stick your finger in Tojo's eye again? Hell, we all would. It did my heart good to see that Jap carrier going to the bottom the other day. But there'll be other carriers to sink. The war's not going to be over while we're in Hawaii getting this ship patched up."

"What about the Marines on the islands? We're already run off and left them once, right after they got here. How are they going to feel when they hear we're leaving again?"

Ramsey's face hardened, and anger flashed in his eyes. "Listen, Lieutenant, the decision to withdraw after the initial landings was made by the men whose job it is to make those decisions. The way I see it, we've done what we can to support the Marines. Besides, the whole task force isn't pulling out, just the *Enterprise*. And the Marines have planes of their own now, flying patrols out of Henderson Field."

"Maybe I should have been a Marine pilot," Phil said, though he didn't really believe that. He had been a reservist when the war started, but he was Navy through and through.

"Maybe you should have," Ramsey shot back, "if you don't have the confidence to believe in the decisions of your superior officers." He shook his head. "Request denied, Lieutenant. I won't put in for a transfer for you. You're going to have to enjoy the palm trees and the beaches in Hawaii with the rest of us poor bastards." Ramsey grinned and slapped Phil on the arm. "Relax, Lieutenant. It won't be that bad."

"No, sir," Phil said, his voice sounding hollow in his ears. To everybody else on the *Enterprise,* maybe going back to Pearl Harbor wouldn't be so bad, but for him it meant he would be farther away from the woman he loved.

And in a case like that, every mile made it hurt that much worse.

# THIRTY-FOUR

The Battle of Bloody Ridge on Guadalcanal had almost immediate repercussions. The 3d Battalion of the Second Regiment of the Second Marine Division was pulled off Tulagi and ferried across the channel to reinforce the First Division Marines on Guadalcanal. It was thought that the Japanese might try to follow up on their push that had been turned back at Bloody Ridge, and if that happened, the First Division might not be strong enough on its own to stop them again. Added to the casualties suffered in combat, disease and malnutrition were taking quite a toll on the American troops too. But that was just as true on the other islands as it was on Guadalcanal.

The 1st and 2d Battalions were left on Tulagi to continue guarding that island against seemingly nonexistent threats. Adam knew the situation could change quickly and with little or no warning, so he did his best to keep his men alert, even while he was wishing that he had been part of the force to head over to Guadalcanal.

The Matanikau River lay west of Henderson Field, and rumor had it that the Japs were building up their forces in that area. They had tried coming in from the east only to be stopped by the Raiders at Bloody Ridge. Now the Marines expected that the next attack would come from the other direction. The reinforcements were moved to the defensive lines facing the Matanikau, but even with the extra men, the perimeter was stretched thin, almost to the breaking point.

Not all was peace and quiet. Snipers still lurked in the jungle around Henderson Field. The Marines never knew when bullets would come zipping out of the trees to wound or kill. Japanese planes still bombed the American positions almost every night, although the aim of the bombardiers never did improve much. At night, enemy destroyers loaded down with reinforcements and supplies slipped down the Slot and put their cargoes ashore. This happened with such regularity that it became known as the Tokyo Express. Even though the U.S. Navy was aware of what was going on, it seemed unable to put a stop to it, so the Japanese forces on Guadalcanal continued to grow in strength. Another showdown seemed inevitable.

In early October, the Raiders tried to carry the fight to the Japs by way of an expedition west of the Matanikau. They met with heavy opposition and were forced to fall back. The only successful tactic for the Marines seemed to be to hold the territory they already had. But in the long run, they couldn't win that way. Sooner or later, the Japanese would be strong enough to push them off the island. The Marines had to go on the offensive first, and they had to do so with better results than the first foray beyond the Matanikau had generated.

Even though he knew that things could change at any moment, the orders still caught Adam a little by surprise. His platoon, indeed all of C Company and the 1st Battalion, was to be ready to move by the afternoon of 9 October 1942. The orders came that morning along with a briefing conducted by Lieutenant Colonel Hill.

An air of mingled fear and excitement gripped the platoon as they readied their gear and moved down to the beaches. They found a flotilla of eight Higgins boats waiting for them. Instead of the usual formation, however, the Higgins boats were connected to each other by cables, in two groups of four. Each group was also connected by a cable running to one of the faster, more powerful craft known as YP boats.

"What the hell's all that for?" one of the men asked.

"They want to get us across the channel faster," Adam said. He had grasped the significance of the unusual arrangement as soon as he saw it. "The Japs still have quite a few ships and subs out there, not to mention the Zeros flying over. The Navy's going to help out the landing craft with the YP boats."

As the men loaded into the Higgins boats, it became obvious that

Adam's guess was correct. The YP boats led off, the cables growing taut as the engines growled to life.

Adam looked around at the men packed into the landing craft. Some of them had shaved when the word came that they were moving out. If they were going into battle, they didn't want to look quite so disreputable. Overall, though, they were still a far cry from the men who had gone ashore on Tulagi a couple of months earlier. Gaunt, hollow-eyed, they were veterans now. Back home they had been farmers, accountants, store clerks, salesmen, and a host of other occupations. Now they were all Marines, and one of the mottoes of the Marines was "Every man a rifleman." As he looked at them, Adam knew they wouldn't let him down.

He raised his voice over the grumbling of the boat's engine. "Here are our orders," he told the men. "We're bound for a place on Guadalcanal called Aola Bay. It's a good long way east of Henderson Field, where the First Division and our boys from the Third Regiment are concentrated. According to the briefing the other officers and I were given this morning, there's going to be a major offensive across the Matanikau River today. That's on the other end of the island from where we're going."

"If our guys are attacking the Japs on the other end of the island, what are we doin' goin' to this Aola Bay?" Sergeant McDade asked.

"Our intelligence indicates that there are quite a few Japs clustered in a couple of villages on the bay. They're the leftovers from the bunch that tried to get across the Tenaru River a while back. The brass thinks that unless somebody else takes care of them, they're liable to hit our forces from the rear during the movement across the Matanikau."

One of the Marines shook his head. "I'm gettin' lost, skipper," he said. "Why don't you boil it down for us?"

"All right," Adam said. "We're going into those two villages on Aola Bay and kill or capture all the Japs we can find. Is that simple enough for you, Private?"

The man grinned up at Adam from where he knelt next to the wall of the Higgins boat. "Now you're talkin' my language, Lieutenant," he said. "I can handle that job."

Adam returned the grin and gave the Marine a thumbs-up. He

could feel the sense of anticipation inside the landing craft growing even stronger. After two months of being cooped up on Tulagi, sweating out the days and nights, the men were ready for action.

Adam turned his head to look to the south, toward Guadalcanal. This crossing of the channel was not without its own dangers. Although the Higgins boats were moving faster than usual because of the YP boats attached to them, they would still be easy prey for any Japanese submarine or cruiser that came along. U.S. Navy vessels patrolled the channel too, but none were in sight at the moment, and they were dispersed so widely that the Japs could slip between them without much trouble.

Even with the extra speed provided by the YP boats, the crossing took quite a while. It was late afternoon, and Adam figured it would be dusk by the time they reached Guadalcanal. They would make camp for the night and then move out in the morning, their objectives being those two villages where Japanese troops were gathered. Adam rested a hand on the side of the boat and looked out across the water. A wind sprang up, and the waves began to get higher.

"Shit, look at that!" The startled exclamation came from one of the Marines in Adam's boat, and he turned to see the man pointing across the water at the other group of landing craft, a few hundred yards off to starboard. The extra speed provided by the YP boats had caused the shallow Higgins boats to ride lower in the water than usual, and one of the vessels was floundering. A wave must have broken over the bow and filled the boat, at the same time sweeping some of the Marines overboard. Adam felt horror surge through him as he saw the men struggling to stay afloat. At this distance, he couldn't make out all the details, but he could tell that some of the thrashing figures in the water were sinking and not coming up again.

The members of his platoon crowded against the side of the Higgins boat, and Adam saw the look of concern on the face of the bo'sun's mate at the helm. The boat was beginning to list, and if it angled much more, the same fate might await it that had overtaken the boat in the other group.

"Back in your places!" Adam bellowed. "Everybody down on the deck!"

The men moved away from the side of the boat, and it began to right itself. Adam heaved a sigh of relief. He felt sorry for the men who had gone into the water from that other boat; the weight of all the gear they were carrying must have dragged down many of them and drowned them. But he couldn't do anything about that. What happened here in *his* boat was a different story. He was responsible for the safety of these men.

The little convoy continued on and landed on Guadalcanal as night was falling. Of the men who had been swept out of the swamped boat, eighteen had drowned. The tragic accident wiped out most of the sense of eager anticipation that had caught up the 1st Battalion earlier, and it was a grieving, subdued bunch of Marines who made camp that night on the shores of Aola Bay. It didn't help matters that no fires were permitted. The men huddled in the darkness, ate cold rations, and tried to get a little sleep under miserable conditions. When morning came, they would move on to the two villages that were their targets.

Captain Hughes had given Adam a map showing the locations of the two villages, Koilotumaria and Garabusa. Garabusa was the farthest away from the landing point, some five miles around the bay, and it was also the target picked out for C Company to attack. There was no road; the Marines would have to make their way around the bay through the jungle as best they could. In camp that night, Adam gathered his squad leaders and explained the operation to them. The four sergeants listened in silence. No questions were needed. They grasped the objectives and knew what would be necessary to achieve them. Adam knew he was lucky to have these men as his noncoms. When the briefing was over, he leaned his back against the trunk of a tree, stretched his legs in front of him, and dozed off.

By morning, the tragedy of the day before hadn't been forgotten, but it had faded a little from the thoughts of the Marines as they prepared to move out. If they had the chance later, they would mourn their lost buddies and lift a beer in their memory, but right now there was a job to do. After a quick breakfast, they headed into the jungle, C Company bound for Garabusa, the rest of the battalion for Koilotumaria.

The going was slow. Even early in the morning like this, the air was hot, stifling. Sunlight slanted through gaps in the tree cover so that shafts of brilliant light were interspersed with areas of gloomy green shadow. The sickly sweet scent of flowers and rotting vegetation filled the air, growing stronger as the Marines' boots crushed leaves and petals underneath them. Despite the heat, Adam felt a clammy chill enveloping him as he walked through the jungle. He looked at the dense growth surrounding them and knew that anything could be hiding out there. Anything.

Adam was near the point, with his platoon strung out behind him. About twenty yards in front of him and ten yards to the right, Captain Hughes and Lieutenant Butala moved along, Butala using a large knife to cut away some of the creepers that clutched at them. Sometimes Adam could see Hughes and Butala, and other times he couldn't because the growth was too thick. Ted Nash's platoon, including Ed Collins and Leo Sikorsky, was off to the left, and another platoon was to the right. All the men moved as quietly as they could, but some thrashing around in the brush was inevitable. Tarzan might be able to move through terrain like this without making much noise, Adam thought with a wry grin, but there were no lords of the jungle in C Company.

A rifle shot cracked through the air, making Adam jerk to a halt. Birds that had been dozing in the trees a second earlier bolted from their branches with a lot of fluttering and squawking. Adam heard Butala yell, "Captain! Captain Hughes!"

Adam looked that direction and saw that Hughes was down, a victim of the sniper's bullet. He started toward the captain but had taken only a couple of steps when more shots rang out. Bullets whipped through the leaves not far from his head. "Down!" he shouted to his men. "Everybody down!"

He hit the dirt, feeling splinters sting his cheek as a slug smacked into the trunk of a tree beside him. The *crack-crack-crack* of sniper fire was loud. More rifles began to blast as the pinned-down Marines tried to return the fire, but they were shooting blind, Adam knew. There was no way of knowing where the Japanese were concealed.

He lifted his head and found his field of view blocked by some brush. Knowing that he risked drawing even more shots, he crawled forward until he could see better. A lane of sorts opened in front of the Marines' position, a long open area bordered by the trees of the jungle. The area was brightly illuminated by the sun, which was almost straight overhead now.

Adam caught his breath as he saw a figure step out into that lane and start forward. He recognized the shape of the Marine. It was Ed Collins. Ed carried his Springfield rifle slanted across his chest, and his head swiveled on his thick neck as he peered around him.

"Ed!" Adam hissed, not knowing if he was close enough for his friend to hear him or not. "Ed, get back under cover, damn it!"

Ed wasn't stopping, though. Adam knew what he was doing. Ed was trying to draw all the sniper fire to him, so that the other men of the company could locate the Japanese riflemen and deal with them. It was a brave, foolhardy thing to do—and it might be the only chance the rest of the company had.

Adam saw the sleeve of Ed's shirt jerk as a bullet tore through it. In the blink of an eye, Ed brought his rifle to his shoulder and snapped off a shot. Adam's eyes widened as he saw a brown-uniformed Japanese sniper tumble out of a treetop some fifty yards past Ed, falling to the jungle floor in a lifeless sprawl. Another shot cracked, and this time Ed stumbled a little as the bullet burned across his upper right thigh. But that didn't stop him from firing a second shot of his own, and to Adam's amazement, another sniper toppled out of a tree and crashed to the ground in front of Ed.

Another figure bolted into the sunlight as more shots tore through the air around Ed. Leo Sikorsky was backing up his friend. Leo fired up into the treetops as he hurried after Ed. Why didn't Nash order the rest of the platoon into action as well? Adam knew he couldn't wait any longer. Ed and Leo had the Japs looking and shooting at them. It was time to take advantage of the opportunity.

"Third Platoon, follow me!" Adam shouted as he surged to his feet. He saw movement in the top of a palm tree and fired at it, worked the Springfield's bolt and fired again. More shots sounded behind him. A third and then a fourth Japanese sniper fell to the ground, shot out of their treetop nests by the other Marines while they were trying to zero in on Ed and Leo.

Adam's trot became an all-out run. Ed and Leo were still ahead of him, but he was catching up. Ed let out an excited whoop as he fired on the run. He had never been one to fight in silence.

A screen of brush blocked the end of the lane. Ed burst through it, followed by Leo, and Adam wasn't far behind with the rest of his platoon. Adam came out into a clearing and saw huts and tents clustered in the open area. They had reached Garabusa, and the Japs were here just like the intelligence reports had said they would be. Machine-gun fire crackled from several of the huts. Adam jerked a grenade from his belt and ducked to the left as bullets kicked up dirt around his feet. He pulled the pin and heaved the grenade through the open window of the nearby hut where one of the machine guns was set up. He went down, rolling over a couple of times as the grenade went off and blew the flimsy hut apart.

Coming to rest on his stomach, Adam looked up and saw the Marines pouring into the village, raking the huts and tents with bullets and tossing grenades at the machine-gun nests. The noise was tremendous. Clouds of choking black smoke rolled through the village as several huts caught on fire and burned intensely.

Adam scrambled to his feet as he saw a Japanese soldier burst out of one of the tents and start running straight at him. The Jap hadn't seemed to notice him yet. He was an officer of some sort, wearing a peaked cap, and he had a sheathed sword in one hand. A leather dispatch case was slung over his shoulder and flapped against his hip.

Adam worked the Springfield's bolt and realized that the rifle was empty. At the same moment, the Japanese officer finally spotted him and yelled something, probably a startled curse. The man had a pistol in a flap holster at his hip, but instead of reaching for it he jerked the sword from its sheath and came at Adam, slashing back and forth with the weapon. Sunlight sparked reflections off the blade.

Adam reached for his own pistol and pulled the Colt .45 1911A1 from its holster. He dropped the Springfield and worked the Colt's slide to chamber a round, then raised the pistol as the Japanese officer let out an ear-splitting screech. The blast of the Colt cut it off in midscream. The Jap went hurtling backward as the .45 caliber slug smacked into his chest. He landed on his back after flying a good five feet through the air. The Colt had one hell of a lot of stopping power, and at this moment, Adam was damned grateful for that.

The Japanese soldier was dead, but Adam stepped forward and kicked the sword out of his hand anyway. Then he holstered the pistol, drew his knife, and cut the strap of the dispatch case. He thought the man he had just killed was a colonel, but he wasn't sure of the Japanese insignia. Regardless of that, there was a good chance whatever was in the leather case would be of interest to the Marine G-2 (Intelligence) officers.

As Adam turned away from the corpse, he became aware that the firing was dying down in the village. Now only isolated shots sounded as the last holdouts were overcome. Smoke still climbed into the air from the burning huts. There had been a time when the Melanesian natives of Guadalcanal had lived in those modest dwellings. Then the Japanese had come to the island, and the natives who hadn't been killed when the Japs occupied the village had been forced to flee into the mountains. Adam felt sorry for the people who once had lived in those burning huts, but they could build new homes for themselves when the invaders were gone for good.

He moved around the perimeter of the village, looking for the men of his platoon. Within minutes, he had found all four sergeants and listened to them tell him with pride that their squads had come through with no casualties, not even any wounded. That was the case with all three platoons. Ed Collins had a couple of bullet burns where the snipers had creased him, but those wounds weren't serious. His escape from serious harm was near miraculous, but Adam had learned that such things sometimes happened in combat.

Adam ran across Lieutenant Butala, who despite his small stature had carried Captain Hughes all the way to the edge of the clearing where the village of Garabusa was located. When Adam asked how the captain was, Butala shook his head and said, "He didn't make it."

"I guess that means you're in command now."

Butala's eyes widened. "I'm a staff officer, Bergman. I can't take charge of the whole company, especially not here in the middle of this damn jungle!"

Ted Nash and Barney Gelhart walked up in time to hear Butala's protest. Gelhart slung his Springfield over his shoulder and said, "If it's up to me, I'd just as soon see you take command, Adam."

"Wait a minute," Nash said. "I'm longer in grade than Bergman. I'm the ranking officer here."

Adam nodded. "That's right. So what do we do now, Nash?"

"Well . . ." An uncomfortable look settled over Nash's face as he realized what his pride had let him in for. "I guess we head back to the beach. We weren't supposed to stay over here on Guadalcanal. Our orders were to subdue any enemy opposition in the two villages and then return to Tulagi."

"Hadn't we better search the place first and see if we can find anything valuable?" Adam suggested. He held up the dispatch case. "I got this off a dead Jap officer. I don't know what's in it, but I'll bet our intelligence boys would like to have a look through it."

"Yeah, that's a good idea," Nash said, seizing on the suggestion. "We'll secure the village and then give it a thorough search." He hurried off to issue the necessary orders.

When Nash was gone, Barney Gelhart looked at Adam and said, "Are you going to hold his hand and tell him what to do next until we get back, or just do the smart thing and take over yourself?"

"He's right. He's longer in grade, so he outranks me," Adam said. "But we've been lucky, only one man killed so far, and I'd like to keep it that way."

Gelhart grunted. "Me too. I guess if that means baby-sitting Nash, I can put up with it." He grinned. "Funny how things work out sometimes, ain't it?"

"Stinkin' hilarious," Adam said.

# THIRTY-FIVE

The search of Garabusa turned up several more dispatch cases containing maps and documents. The Marines also found an undamaged antiaircraft gun and one lone survivor from the Japanese force that had been garrisoned there. The prisoner was a lieutenant who seemed eager to talk, although there wasn't anyone in the outfit who could understand what he was saying. Once they got him back to Tulagi and interrogated him through a translator, he might prove to be a fount of information concerning the disposition of Japanese troops on Guadalcanal. Adam hoped that would be the case, anyway.

As he had told Gelhart, he was prepared to guide Nash through the rest of the mission with suggestions and timely nudges, if necessary, but that proved not to be the case. That afternoon, before C Company could leave the village, a party of officers arrived including Lieutenant Colonel Hill, the commander of the 1st Battalion. They brought with them the news that the rest of the battalion had encountered no resistance at Koilotumaria. In fact, there had been only one Japanese soldier in the village, an officer who had surrendered without a fight. The brass had expected Koilotumaria to be a tougher nut to crack than Garabusa, but as happened quite often, just the opposite had turned out to be true.

Nash greeted the officers and turned over the captured papers to Hill's G-2. "Good work, Lieutenant," Hill said. "What happened to Captain Hughes?"

"He was killed in action, sir." Now that he was dealing with a superior officer, Nash was smooth and confident again. "As the officer longest in grade, I assumed command of the company upon Captain Hughes's unfortunate death."

"Casualties?"

"Only Captain Hughes, sir."

Hill nodded. "All right, Lieutenant. Prepare your men to move back to the drop-off point on Aola Bay. You'll remain there tonight, then be taken back to Tulagi tomorrow."

"Aye, aye, sir."

"There's just one more thing," Hill went on. "I need some volunteers for a special mission."

Adam was standing off to one side, listening to the conversation between Nash and Hill. His interest perked up at Hill's mention of a special mission. Nash looked a little leery again as he asked, "What sort of mission, sir?"

"It's eighty miles from here to our original beachhead at Lunga Point, north of Henderson Field. With our attention turning west and our operations taking place around the Matanikau, we need to have a better picture of what's over here on this side of the island. The brass wants to know how many Japs are left and how well supplied they are. So I need a patrol to travel overland from here to Henderson and take a look around. Think you're up to it, Lieutenant?"

Adam suppressed a grin as he saw the color leave Nash's face. He knew Nash wouldn't refuse if he was ordered to lead the patrol, but that didn't mean he wanted to strike out across eighty miles of enemy-held jungle. On the other hand, the alternative was to go back and sit on Tulagi and wait to be relieved by the Army.

Without thinking too much about what he was doing, Adam stepped forward and said to Colonel Hill, "Excuse me, sir, but I believe you said you wanted volunteers for this mission?"

Hill turned to look at him. "That's right, Lieutenant . . . ?"

"Bergman, sir. And I'd like to volunteer." He nodded toward Nash. "You need Lieutenant Nash to get the rest of the company back safely to Tulagi."

Hill glanced at Nash, and Adam thought he saw a flicker of awareness in the colonel's eyes. Hill had an idea of what was going on. He had to possess at least some ability in judging men in order to have advanced to his present rank.

"All right, Lieutenant Bergman," Hill said. "I think your suggestion is a reasonable one, and I appreciate your willingness to take on this job. Who would you like to take with you?"

"Anybody who wants to go, sir."

"I'm goin'."

The flat declaration came from Ed Collins, who stepped out of the group of Marines standing nearby at the edge of the village. The bullet crease on his leg had bled a little, and he had a crude bandage tied around it.

"You're injured, Marine," Hill said.

"Naw, it ain't nothin' but a scratch," Ed said. "Back on the farm, we had an ol' banty rooster who hurt me worse'n this ever' time he got his feathers in an uproar. I'm fine, Colonel. And I'm up for a hike through this stinkin' jungle."

Adam could tell that Hill was trying not to grin. "All right. Are you in Lieutenant Bergman's platoon?"

"No, sir."

"Well, you are now."

Leo stepped forward. "Me too, Colonel, sir. Even though I think it's crazy."

Hill frowned and said, "What was that?"

"I mean, goin' through eighty miles of Japs? It's nuts, sir. No offense."

"But you're willing to volunteer anyway?"

Leo jerked a thumb toward Ed. "The farm boy and me, we're pals. If I don't go along, he's liable to get in all sorts of trouble."

"All right," Hill said. "But a word of advice, Private—it's usually not too smart to tell an officer that his plan is nuts."

"Yes, sir, I'll remember that."

Hill turned to Adam. "I'll leave it up to you to round up the rest of your volunteers, Lieutenant. You'll need about ninety men."

"Yes, sir."

"General Vandegrift knows you're coming. Report to him when you get there."

That was being pretty optimistic, Adam thought. Under the circumstances, there was no guarantee the patrol would ever reach Henderson Field. It was more likely they would vanish forever in the jungle. He wasn't going to think too much about that, though.

When the colonel was gone, Barney Gelhart came up to Adam and said, "Damn it, I wish I was going with you."

Adam shook his head. "You've got to look after Nash and the rest of the company."

"I know. That's why I didn't try to volunteer. You know what Sikorsky said was right, don't you? Going on this patrol is nuts."

"It's just a little nature walk," Adam said with a grin. "We're just going to look at the birds and the trees and the flowers."

"Yeah, and maybe a few hundred Japs," Gelhart said.

*   *   *

Lieutenant Butala had been carrying one of the Thompson submachine guns. While Adam was getting the rest of the volunteers together, Butala came up to him, held out the weapon, and asked, "You know how to use one of these, Bergman?"

Adam's Springfield was slung over his shoulder. He reached out and took the submachine gun. "I fired a tommy gun like this during training back at Camp Kearney," he said.

"You any good with it?"

Adam shrugged. "Fair, I guess. One of these babies throws so much lead you don't have to be the best shot in the world. You just have to be strong enough to control the recoil and point it where it's supposed to go."

"And I'm not. Strong enough, that is. I don't know why they issued me the damned thing in the first place. I've never been any good with it. I'll trade it for your Springfield."

Adam ran his fingers over the wooden stock of the deadly-looking weapon with its long clip under the breech. "Are you sure about this, Butala?"

"Yeah, I'm sure. A gun like that might come in pretty handy in the jungle, where you can't always see what you're shooting at."

"True enough." Adam unslung the Springfield and gave it to Butala. "We may get in trouble if the Quartermaster Corps ever hears about this. We're supposed to use the weapons we've been issued."

Butala smiled. "I won't tell them if you won't." He took a canvas pouch from his shoulder and handed it to Adam. "Here's my extra clips and ammo."

"Thanks."

"You're welcome. I'm just glad it's you and not me who's going on this patrol."

A short time later, Adam had his men lined up at the edge of the jungle. Colonel Hill had told him to take ninety men, and he had eighty-eight. He figured that was close enough. They were all volunteers and had come from all three platoons in the company. Adam knew quite a few of the men from the other platoons, and the ones he didn't, he thought he probably would know pretty well by the time they reached Henderson Field. There was nothing like an eighty-mile trek through enemy territory to bring guys closer together, he told himself with a wry smile.

Then a pang of guilt struck him as the image of Catherine entered his mind. Since he had volunteered for this mission, it had to be considered an unnecessary risk. A part of him felt that he had no right to be doing such things. He owed it to Catherine to take care of himself, not to risk his life needlessly.

But this was war, and in war there were risks. There was no avoiding that. If he weren't leading this mission, somebody else would have to. And that guy would have a wife too—and a mother and a father, maybe brothers and sisters, maybe even kids. Everybody had somebody who loved them. Everybody had somebody who wanted them to come home safely and not take unnecessary chances. It wasn't fair to shirk a duty that could get somebody else killed, not if it was something he was capable of doing.

Adam took a deep breath and tightened his grip on the tommy gun Butala had given him. He could stand around and think about the mission all day, and that wouldn't get a damned thing done. He raised his voice and said, "All right, let's move out!"

Walking two and three abreast, the members of the patrol headed into the jungle west of Garabusa. The other Marines who were still in the village lined up to watch them go, waving and shouting both encouragement and insults. Adam was up front, one of the first to disappear into the thick vegetation. He had Ed and Leo close behind him. Ed had wanted to take the point, but Adam thought he had done enough of that for the day, considering his actions back there where the snipers had had them pinned down. Instead, Adam put a slender young Marine named Hamm on the point, knowing that he had good eyes and ears and wasn't likely to miss much.

Progress was slow during that first day. Adam tried to keep the patrol headed due west, but sometimes that was impossible owing to jungle that was too thick to penetrate. This coastal plain along the northern shore of Guadalcanal offered no real physical barriers except the jungle. A few creeks flowed from the mountains down to the channel, but they were all shallow enough to wade across with ease. If not for the jungle, the patrol could have done the eighty-mile march in a couple of days without much problem. But as it was, their progress was slowed to a matter of yards, feet, sometimes even inches in an hour's time.

Late in the afternoon, they came across a trail of sorts, and their pace picked up. The narrow, twisting path made Adam worry a little, though. He studied the vegetation along the sides of the trail and saw that it wasn't trying to reclaim the opening. That meant the path had seen recent heavy use. For months now, the only people on this part of the island had been Japanese troops. They had to be responsible for beating down the trail, and it hadn't been long since they were using it, either. At any moment, Adam and the rest of the patrol could stumble right into trouble. The Japs might even spot them and set up some sort of trap.

Now that the going was easier, Hamm had gotten farther ahead of the rest of the patrol. In fact, Adam couldn't even see him anymore. He was about to send someone ahead to find Hamm and tell him to close up the gap between them, when several shots blasted somewhere up ahead.

Adam recognized the sound of a Springfield '03 like the one Hamm was carrying, but there were a couple of sharper cracks that probably came from a pistol. Adam threw up a hand and called, "Hold it!" as the Marines surged forward, eager to go to the aid of their friend. Adam couldn't let them go charging into an ambush. He turned to Ed and said, "Keep the men here. Leo, you're with me."

"Damn it, Adam—" Ed began, and Adam knew what he was going to say next. He was going to complain about being left behind.

"That's an order, Private!" Adam snapped. He hefted the submachine gun and started along the trail at a fast trot. Leo was close behind him.

They hadn't gone even fifty yards when Hamm showed up in front of them, coming around a bend in the trail, his long legs carrying him toward them at a fast run. As he came to a halt, he said breathlessly, "There's a creek up there, Lieutenant . . . with a Jap boat on it! They came around a bend . . . while I was wading across . . . opened fire on me."

"What sort of boat?"

Hamm shook his head. "Little one, with an outboard motor on the back." He was catching his breath now. "But it was piled up with crates. I don't know if they had ammo or some other kind of supplies in them, but the Japs were mighty excited to see me, like they were ferrying something important."

"How many Japs?"

"Four. But I heard some rustling in the brush on the other side of the creek. The boat might have an infantry escort with it."

That was possible, Adam supposed, though men on foot, moving through the jungle, would have a hard time keeping up with a boat. Either way, the patrol had to find out. It was their job to discover as much information as possible about the Japanese forces on this part of the island, as well as to inflict any damage they could.

"How far is this creek?"

"Maybe two hundred yards."

Adam's thoughts raced. If he and the patrol went along the trail to the spot where it crossed the creek, the Japanese boat would be long gone.

"Which way was the boat going?"

There was no hesitation in Hamm's answer. "South."

"We've got to get ahead of it." That would mean leaving the path and plunging back into the thick jungle. But there was no other way. Adam turned and waved to the patrol. "Come on! Follow me!"

He headed into the brush, angling to the south. Right away, creepers clutched at his ankles and legs and thorns clawed at his hands and face. He shifted the tommy gun to his left hand and drew his knife with his right. What he really needed was a machete to chop his way through this mass of vegetation, but he didn't have one. He had to make do with the knife he had. It was better than nothing. At least the blade was sharp.

Hacking and slashing, Adam worked his way through the jungle. Ed moved on his left, Leo on his right. Both of them attacked the jungle with their knives too. Slowly, the three Marines cleared a path for the eighty-six men following them.

Over the panting of his breath and the grunts of effort from his companions, Adam became aware that he could hear something else. It took him a moment to identify the sound. Then he realized it was the *putt-putt-putt* of an outboard motor, sounding for all the world like a fisherman's boat making its way across a placid lake early in the morning.

That peaceful image was about as far from the reality of the situation as it could get, Adam thought. He hacked harder at the clinging brush, knowing that he had to be getting close to the creek. It was difficult to pinpoint the location of sounds in the jungle. He couldn't tell from listening to the boat's motor if it had already gone past the point where the patrol would reach the creek. If it had, catching up to it would be next to impossible.

Suddenly, the ground sloped sharply under his feet and he had to grab the slender trunk of a sapling to keep from falling. Five feet below him, he saw the smooth green surface of the creek. The stream was about twenty feet wide. Trees grew right up to the edge of the bank and overhung it, their branches reaching out and joining to form a tunnel of sorts. And coming down that tunnel toward him with all the speed it could muster was the Japanese boat.

Just as Hamm had described it, the craft was loaded down with crates so that it rode low in the water. The stern was lower than the bow. One soldier sat in the stern, holding the tiller in one hand and a pistol in the other. Three more men were up front, one of them with a pistol and the other two struggling to set up a light machine gun. They had the mount attached to the side of the boat and were trying to lift the gun into place and fasten it down.

Adam brought the Thompson to his shoulder and braced it firmly. He squeezed the trigger and the submachine gun began to chatter. The recoil tried to force the barrel up, but he held it down and directed a stream of lead across the bow of the boat. Beside him, Ed and Leo were firing their rifles, and more rifle fire began to come from the jungle as the rest of the patrol reached the creek.

One of the Japs in the front of the boat fell into the water, his arms flung wide and blood spraying from his chest as bullets tore into his body. Another crumpled where he was. The third man, however, still knelt by the machine gun, and he had it ready to fire at last. Flames spouted from its muzzle as he raked the creek bank with slugs.

The gun's elevation was too low, and before the gunner had a chance to correct it, his head jerked back as a bullet blew away half his skull. As he collapsed next to the machine gun, the fourth man stood up in the stern, dropping his pistol and yelling something in Japanese. Adam figured the man was trying to surrender, and he was about to shout for the patrol members to hold their fire, when a huge explosion erupted in the middle of the creek, right where the boat was. The boat vanished, along with the men on it, consumed by the fury of the blast. Heat and concussion from the explosion slapped Adam in the face, knocking him down along with the other Marines who were the closest to the creek. The noise was so tremendous that he found himself deafened as he lay there on the muddy ground, his helmet lying beside him where it had been blown right off his head.

Adam pushed himself up on his hands and knees. He was disoriented, but as a ringing began in his ears, the cobwebs inside his skull began to clear. He knew where he was and what had happened. He came to his feet and rested a hand on a tree trunk to steady himself. Around him, the other members of the patrol were picking themselves up as well. Ed stumbled over to Adam and said something. Adam heard only muffled, incoherent noises. He shook his head and pointed to his ear. Ed pointed to his own ear and nodded. He was deaf too. So was Leo, who clapped his hands over his ears. His mouth worked, and Adam knew he had to be complaining a mile a minute.

Ed kept talking too and pointing to where the boat had been, and after a few moments, Adam heard, "... ah ... appen ..." He knew Ed was asking what had happened to the boat.

"Ammo," Adam said, not knowing if Ed could understand him or not. "Those crates had to be full of ammunition. One of our bullets set it off."

Ed nodded, telling Adam that he'd understood enough to know what Adam was saying.

That infantry escort Hamm had mentioned must not have existed after all, because now that the echoes of the explosion had died away, everything was peaceful again along the creek. Over the next half hour, as the patrol checked up and down both banks for several hundred yards without finding any Japanese troops, Adam's hearing returned. His ears ached a little, but he knew they would be okay. None of his men had been hurt in the encounter. He was thankful for that, thankful as well that they had destroyed a boatload of ammunition that otherwise might have been used against them or their fellow Marines.

As day faded, they made their way back to the trail they had been following earlier. They would have to find a place to make camp and wait to see if anything would develop from the fight with the Japs on the boat. That explosion had been large enough to be heard a long distance away. It might draw a lot of enemy attention. One thing was certain, Adam told himself: That boatload of ammunition, which probably had been unloaded from one of the Japanese destroyers that ran the Tokyo Express, wouldn't have been headed inland if there weren't soldiers waiting for it at the end of its journey.

# THIRTY-SIX

Before the patrol had left Garabusa, the men who were returning to Tulagi donated part of their rations to the others. The volunteers had no idea how long it would take them to cross the eighty miles of jungle to Henderson Field, but they had to plan on being out at least three or four days. With the extra rations, they might have enough to last them, but they would have to eat sparingly. They knew there were wild pigs in the jungle. If need be, they might be able to kill and roast one of the animals. Of course, Adam reflected as he thought about the situation that evening, such a meal would hardly be kosher. He tried to follow the tenets of his religion as much as he could, but that might not be possible here in this South Pacific wilderness. Maybe it wouldn't come to that, he told himself as he peeled back the cover on a tin of C rations.

Adam had decided that it might not be a good idea to make camp right on the trail. Ed had agreed with him, saying, "When you're out in the woods on a huntin' and campin' trip, you want to watch the game trails, but you sure don't want to pitch your tent in the middle of one. That way the varmints you're after are bound to see you before you see them, and that ain't good."

Adam had never been camping in his life, nor had he done any hunting in the woods. But common sense told him not to camp on the trail, and since Ed agreed with him, that was good enough. Instead, the patrol found a thick grove of trees and bedded down for the night there, eating cold rations. The men didn't mind that nearly as much as they did the order not to smoke. The smell of tobacco would be a dead giveaway that somebody was in the jungle.

After posting a pair of sentries on each side of the camp and arranging the guard duty for the rest of the night, Adam curled up under one of the trees. He felt bugs crawling on him, but he was so accustomed to the sensation by now that he hardly noticed it. He kept his helmet on, even though sleeping in it wasn't very comfortable. If a guy took his helmet off at night while he was asleep, he often found a snake coiled in it in the morning. Grabbing a helmet and putting it on in a hurry, say in case of an unexpected attack in the middle of the night, could have disastrous consequences.

It had been a long day. First the battle at Garabusa, then the explosive encounter with the Japanese boat and its cargo of ammunition. Adam dozed off and slept about as soundly as anyone could in the jungle, possibly surrounded by the enemy. He was taking one of the last shifts on guard duty, and his mental alarm woke him at the proper time. Standing up, he stretched to ease aching muscles that hadn't been relieved much by sleeping on the ground.

He moved to his position and found that the other guard on this side of the camp had already been relieved. The new sentry who would stand this duty with Adam was a Marine from New Jersey named Warren Bloch.

"Hey, Lieutenant," Bloch greeted him. "Everything's quiet."

"Just the way I like it," Adam said, his voice little more than a whisper. "Let's spread out a little, but stay in earshot."

"Aye, aye, sir."

Adam moved to his left, being careful not to make too much noise in the brush. He stopped when he estimated that he was about twenty yards from Bloch. He heard a faint rustling that soon stopped, indicating that Bloch had found a good place too. Adam hunkered on his heels and leaned his back against the trunk of a tree. He held the Thompson across his knees. It had a full clip attached to it. All he had to do was pull back the arming lever on the side of the breech, and the weapon would be ready to fire.

He gave a jaw-cracking yawn and shook his head. He didn't think he would have any trouble staying awake until dawn, but just to be sure, he thought about Catherine, remembering the way her hair smelled and the sleek, smooth warmth of her skin and the hot, inviting taste of her mouth. It didn't take long for him to realize that calling up such memories was a mistake. They just made him ache with loneliness and longing for her. On the other hand, maybe it hadn't been such a bad idea, he told himself. He might be a little frustrated and uncomfortable, but he was convinced that he wouldn't be going to sleep any time soon. Blue balls had a way of keeping a guy awake.

But thinking about Catherine was comforting in a way too, because it reminded him of why he was out here in the first place. He had a wife and a promising future once the war was over. That was more than a lot of people in Germany, Italy, France, Poland, Czechoslovakia, Russia, and a bunch of other places could say. The Nazis had gone through Europe like a terrible storm, destroying everything in their way. Blitzkrieg—lightning war—was a pretty good description of the havoc Hitler and his goons had wreaked. Not to mention the atrocities the Japanese had committed in China and the Philippines, Burma, and Malaysia. And on Wake Island, Adam recalled. His mouth tightened into a grim line at those memories. Politicians liked to make a lot of fancy, high-flown pronouncements. Probably back home they were spouting off about how the Allies weren't fighting just for democracy this time, but to save the freedom of the entire world. And regardless of the rhetoric, that was true, Adam thought. If the Nazis and their Italian and Nipponese buddies won, that would be the end of life as most of the globe had known it.

Yeah, there were plenty of good reasons to be out here. Catherine was just the first of them.

Adam was so caught up in his thoughts he almost didn't hear the odd noise that came from the jungle to his right. It was a gurgling sound, almost like a fountain. Bloch was over in that direction; maybe he knew what it was. Adam edged toward Bloch's position. When he got close enough so that Bloch should have challenged him, he called softly, "Bloch? You okay?"

A whisper came back to his ears. "Okay."

"Did you hear that noise a minute ago?"

"No."

Adam peered toward the clump of brush where Bloch was. In the stygian jungle night, the brush was nothing more than a slightly darker patch of shadow. Adam's nerves crawled. He whispered, "You didn't hear anything?"

"No, Sarge."

Adam's hand was already on the arming lever of the Thompson. He ripped it back and pressed the trigger. The tommy gun jumped in his hands as he sprayed the brush with bullets. A rifle cracked, orange flashes stabbing back at him. A few yards away in camp, guys came thrashing and yelling out of sleep. Adam hoped they didn't get too trigger-happy and shoot him by mistake.

With a crash of branches and leaves, a figure toppled out of the brush. Adam hosed it with another stream of lead from the submachine gun, just to make sure the Jap was dead. Some instinct warned him and made him swing around to his left just as another figure lunged out of the darkness at him. He thrust the Thompson in front of him and felt it collide with the barrel of a rifle, turning aside the bayonet thrust that would have disemboweled him if he'd been a second slower. In a continuation of the same movement, he drove the butt of the tommy gun into the face of the Japanese soldier who was charging him. Bone and cartilage crunched under the powerful blow.

Adam shoved the second man aside and fired another burst from the Thompson, swinging the submachine gun from side to side as he peppered the jungle with bullets. He didn't know how many more Japanese soldiers were out there, if any, but they weren't going to get into the camp without a fight.

Several members of the patrol ran up alongside Adam and started firing into the jungle as well. He let the fusillade go on for a couple of minutes, then shouted, "Cease fire! Cease fire!" As the shooting died away, he added, "Everybody down! Hunt some cover!"

He went to his belly as the men around him followed suit. He wanted all of them to present the smallest targets possible if there were any more Japanese troops out there in the darkness. His ears were ringing again, this time from the fearsome barrage he and his men had just laid down. When the ringing stopped, he listened intently, honed for any sound from the jungle that might represent a continuing threat.

Adam didn't hear anything except an occasional rasp of breath from one of his men. An eerie quiet hung over the area. He had a hunch that his friends were somewhere close by, so he whispered, "Ed? Leo?"

"Right here, Lieutenant," Ed replied, using Adam's rank for a change. "Chopper's with me."

"Let's spread out and work our way ahead. Take it slow and easy. The rest of you men stay alert."

That last order wasn't really necessary, he thought. The odds of anybody goofing off or goldbricking right now were pretty slim. He came up on his knees and then lifted himself into a crouch. Carefully, he started forward into the brush, the tommy gun held ready in his right hand while he used his left to move some of the branches aside.

For the next half hour, Adam, Ed, and Leo checked out the perimeter of the camp. They found no more Japanese. If more of the enemy had been here, they had withdrawn when the first attempt to slip into the camp failed.

When the three of them returned to the camp, they found that some of the men had already brought in Bloch's body from where it had been found in the brush. The soldier's throat was cut, a deep slash that went almost from ear to ear. That strange noise Adam had heard had been Bloch dying. He had thought as much. The Jap who'd killed Bloch had tried to fool Adam with a few words of English. But using the word "Sarge" had given him away. Bloch had known that Adam was a lieutenant and would never have made that mistake.

So they were left with one dead comrade and the bodies of two Japanese infiltrators. Adam's blow to the face with the butt of his machine gun had fractured the skull of the second Jap, and he'd died sometime during the shooting. Adam wasn't going to lose any sleep over the two Japanese soldiers, but he hated to lose one of his own men. Even though he knew the odds were against it, he had hoped to bring the patrol through without any casualties.

Again he reminded himself that they would be lucky if any of them reached Henderson Field alive. He had to take the inevitable losses in stride, he told himself as he said aloud, "All right, we've got a grave to dig as soon as it gets light."

*　　*　　*

The two dead Japanese were left where they had fallen. As soon as Bloch had been buried and a short prayer said over the grave, the members of the patrol ate a hurried, tasteless breakfast and pushed on. They returned to the trail and headed west. The morning passed without any more signs of the enemy. At midday, though, as the Marines rounded a bend in the path, they saw huts ahead of them. Adam's hand jerked in a gesture that ordered them to spread out. Everyone found some cover and trained their weapons on the little cluster of crude dwellings. As Adam knelt beside a tree, he sniffed the air. No smoke. No food. That meant there weren't any cooking fires burning in the village. He dug his map out of his pack and studied it for a moment. The village wasn't marked on the map. According to the best intelligence the Marines had, the place didn't exist. But it was right there in front of Adam. He saw it with his own eyes, and so did everybody else in the patrol.

As minutes dragged by, though, he had to admit that the village looked deserted. He motioned for a couple of the men to check it out. They stole forward, darting from tree to tree, until they were close enough to lunge up to one of the huts and thrust the barrels of their rifles through a window. After a moment, one of the men looked back at Adam and shook his head. He waved for them to check out the rest of the village.

The settlement wasn't very big. It took only about ten minutes to make certain that all the huts were empty of human habitation. The Japanese army had been here, though. Several huts were full of crates of canned food. Another hut had a stack of gasoline cans in it, and all of them seemed to be full. The searchers also found several crates full of brand-new engine parts.

"This is a supply and repair depot," Adam said as the members of the patrol gathered around him after searching the village. "It hasn't been long since the Japs were here, and they're probably planning on coming back."

One of the men asked, "We're not goin' to just leave it for them, are we, Lieutenant?"

Adam shook his head. "No. We'll take as much of the food as we can carry without weighing ourselves down too much, and then we'll use the gas to blow up the rest of it. Let's get busy. I don't want to hang around here any longer than we have to."

The next hour was busy as Adam and the other men broke open the cases of food and picked out what they wanted to put in their packs. Adam chose cans of oranges and peaches. When everyone had all they could carry—Ed's pack was really stuffed full—the rest of the food crates were stacked in a big pile in the center of the village, along with the crates of engine parts. Then the cans of gasoline were arranged around and on top of the other supplies. Adam unscrewed the cap from one of the cans and poured out the gas on top of the pile. More gas was splashed all around it. The smell was strong, almost overpowering. Finally, a trail of gasoline was laid to the edge of the jungle, where the members of the patrol gathered. The trail they had been following seemed to end here at the Japanese supply depot, so they would have to push on west through the jungle again.

Leo pulled out his lighter and held it up, raising his eyebrows as he looked at Adam. "Go ahead," Adam said. "Light it up, Chopper."

Leo knelt beside the end of the gasoline trail and spun the wheel on the Ronson. It sparked and caught, and he lowered the flame to the ground. The gas caught with a *whoosh!*, going up so violently that Leo let out an involuntary yelp and went over backward, sitting down hard. Ed grabbed his arm and hauled him to his feet as flames shot across the clearing toward the inferno that was waiting to happen.

"Let's go, let's go!" Adam said. "Everybody out of here!"

"Damn stuff singed my eyebrows off!" Leo complained as Ed tugged him along. He pawed at his forehead. "I can't feel my eyebrows!"

"Your eyebrows are fine, damn it," Ed said. "Come on, Chopper!"

Adam hustled them along as behind them, the flames reached the pile of gas cans and supplies in the center of the village. Fire shot high into the air as the gas that had been poured out ignited, and then the cans exploded, sending a ball of flame straight up fifty feet or more. Adam glanced back and thought that the sight was spectacular, even viewed through a screen of brush. Heat from the blast washed over him. Burning debris, what was left of the pile of supplies, came raining back down to earth as a pall of black smoke hung over the jungle.

Somebody was bound to notice that fire and smoke, Adam told himself. The blaze would be visible for miles around, and any watchers up in the hills would see it easily. If the Japanese hadn't known already that something was going on over here, they would know now.

And Adam was going to be very surprised if they didn't try to find out what the hell it was.

# THIRTY-SEVEN

Even though Adam was expecting trouble at any moment, the rest of the afternoon passed peacefully except for the continuing struggle against the jungle as the patrol made its way toward Henderson Field. Adam was grateful that he had a compass, otherwise he would have gotten lost in this trackless wilderness. The jungle looked all the same to him, and it would have been very easy to start going around in circles.

When night fell, the men made camp again in the thickest brush they could find. Adam posted even more sentries than he had the night before, not wanting a repeat of the tragedy that had happened with Bloch. He made sure enough teams were assigned to guard duty so that no man would have to stand watch alone. Already he had been plagued by guilt over Bloch's death. If he'd been with him, maybe that Jap wouldn't have been able to sneak up on both of them.

But there was no way to change what had happened, and Adam didn't brood over it so much that it became a distraction. He took one of the guard shifts again, standing watch with an eighteen-year-old private from Wisconsin.

The night passed quietly, and after breakfast the patrol set out again, hacking its way through the jungle. Adam rotated the men up front, because cutting through the thick, clinging vegetation was exhausting work. At mid-morning they came to another stream and refilled their canteens, adding purification tablets to the water. It still had a green, mossy taste to it, but at least with any luck it wouldn't make them sick.

A break at midday and then the Marines pushed on. Adam wasn't sure how many miles they had covered since leaving Garabusa, but he estimated they had come at least half the way to

Henderson Field, maybe more. If they could find another trail, they might be able to reach the American airfield in another day or so.

The heat was even worse today than it had been before. Men took off their shirts and tied the sleeves around their waists. Undershirts were soaked through with sweat. The worst part about it was that the heat dulled the senses. The men shuffled along, heads down for the most part. Adam tried to keep them alert, but it wasn't easy. He had a difficult enough time preventing himself from getting groggy.

In the middle of the afternoon, he heard something that snapped him back from the sodden reverie into which he had fallen. His head lifted as the sound of a truck engine came to his ears. He held up a hand, motioning for the men to stop. Some of them had heard the truck too, and excited whispers ran through the group. Adam pointed to a couple of the men and motioned for them to follow him as he started forward.

The growling of the engine got louder. Adam went to hands and knees and crawled forward through a screen of brush. When he got to the edge of it, he saw an open space in front of him. It was a road, he saw to his amazement, a road where there weren't supposed to be any roads. True, it was narrow, just a pair of ruts that wound through the jungle, but it was still a road. And from the sound of the engine, the truck was coming down it toward him.

Adam looked over his shoulder. The two men were with him, but the rest of the patrol was about a hundred feet behind them. He hoped they would have the sense to keep their heads down. "Don't move," he whispered to his two companions. They waited, hands taut on their weapons, as the truck approached.

It came into view, lumbering along the crude road, wheels bouncing and jolting in the ruts. The truck was big, probably a deuce-and-a-half, Adam judged. At one time, the back of the truck had been covered with canvas; the framework of thin metal rods that had supported it was still in place. The canvas had been torn away, though. Tattered shreds of it still clung to the framework. A machine gun was mounted in the back of the truck. A Japanese soldier stood next to the gun, swaying back and forth and holding on to the mount to brace himself against the jouncing movement. There were several more soldiers in the back of the truck, sitting cross-legged on the wooden slats that formed the floor. Another man rode beside the driver.

For a moment, Adam considered trying to capture the truck. He discarded the idea almost immediately. The truck wasn't big enough to hold more than a couple dozen men, and besides, the road ran north and south, or from the coast to the interior. Like the creek where they had encountered the boat, it probably served as a supply route for the troops up in the hills.

Adam ducked his head lower as the truck rumbled past. He plucked a grenade from his belt and motioned for the two men with him to do likewise. When the truck had gone about twenty feet beyond him, Adam leaped to his feet and lobbed the grenade after it. The other two men threw their grenades as the Japs in the back of the truck spotted the Marines and yelled in alarm. The one next to the machine gun tried to swivel it around.

The shouting made the driver jam on the brakes, which played right into the hands of Adam and his men. The grenade Adam had thrown landed in the back of the truck and bounced a couple of times. One of the soldiers, gibbering in terror, tried to grab it and toss it back out, but he fumbled it away like a halfback unable to get a handle on the ball. One of the other grenades sailed into the back of the truck as well, while the third one hit the ground and rolled underneath the vehicle.

The three grenades went off so close together that the blasts sounded like a single huge explosion. The truck's gas tank blew up as well, adding to the conflagration. Adam saw the machine gun fly into the air along with a grisly shower of body parts. As the gruesome debris pattered down, flames roared around what was left of the truck.

"Damn, Lieutenant," one of the Marines said over the crackling of the fire, "we blow up stuff real good."

Adam sniffed the air, and along with the acrid stench of gasoline and rubber burning, he smelled another odor that threatened to turn his stomach. As the rest of the patrol came up, he said, "That burned-out truck will block the road for a while. Let's fell some trees and build a barricade too, so that the next time the Japs try to use this road, it won't be easy."

While some of the men stood guard, others set to work with hatchets from their packs, chopping down trees and piling them in the road. Adam pitched in too, and he didn't order the men to stop until they had a barrier a good eight feet tall.

With sweat running down his face in rivers, Adam regarded the pile of trees and brush with satisfaction. That would slow down the Japs the next time they tried to bring supplies through here.

But it wouldn't stop them, he reminded himself. The Japanese buildup would continue until they were ready to take back the island. Everything that Adam and his men had accomplished amounted to little more than an insect bite as far as the overall enemy plans were concerned.

However, their reconnaissance had proven that there weren't large numbers of Japanese troops in this area of Guadalcanal. At least, they hadn't encountered any so far. If that remained the case and he and his men could deliver that intelligence to Henderson Field, the brass could continue with their plans to push westward beyond the Matanikau River, knowing that they didn't face an imminent threat from the other direction.

With the barricade across the road finished, Ed asked, "What now, Lieutenant?"

Adam picked up the submachine gun from where he had leaned it against a tree. "What do you think?" he said. "We move on."

\* \* \*

That night, the sounds of a huge bombardment filled the air. Even the thick jungle foliage could not muffle the massive explosions off to the west. The fact that the ground trembled underneath Adam and the other Marines in the patrol told them that somewhere, all hell was breaking loose. And unless Adam missed his guess, "somewhere" was Henderson Field and the Marine beachhead around it.

"Sounds like the Japs are throwin' everything they have at our boys," Ed said in a hushed voice. No one in camp was trying to sleep tonight. The racket was too great for that, and so was the knowledge that other Marines were being pounded.

"I'll bet the bombers will be next," Leo said. "Wait and see."

They didn't have to wait long. The roar of airplane engines was added to the thunder of artillery, and then the high-pitched whine of falling bombs joined in. The cacophony was enough to make the men in the patrol want to jump up and run screaming through the jungle. Either that, or start digging a hole. Adam could only imagine what it must be like to be in the middle of the attack.

The barrage finally stopped with the dawn. The grim silence was reflected in the members of the patrol as they ate breakfast and got ready to move out. Adam knew they had to be wondering what they would find when and if they reached Henderson Field. Would it be back in the hands of the Japs? Adam was asking himself the same question.

They pushed on through the jungle. By noon, Adam knew they couldn't be too far from their goal. A short time later, they heard planes again, and then the earth shook once more as bombs pounded down from the heavens. It sounded as if the explosions were no more than a few hundred yards away, but when that distance had been covered, the bomb blasts were still up ahead somewhere. The Marines plodded on, hacking with their knives at the vegetation and wading across a good-sized stream. Adam wondered if it was the Tenaru River. If so, they really were close to the airfield now.

When it finally happened, the transition was abrupt. One moment the men were still fighting their way through the jungle, the next they were stumbling out into the open. And this was no mere trail they had come across. Hundreds of yards of cleared ground stretched in front of them.

"Hold it! Don't move, damn it!"

The shouted orders came from Adam's right. He looked in that direction and saw a field artillery battery with the guns set up so that they pointed into the jungle. The gunnery crews on duty had grabbed up their rifles and were pointing them at the haggard, bearded men who were stumbling out of the trees.

"Take it easy, Marines," Adam called to them. "We're on your side."

313

"Who the hell are you?" one of the men demanded.

"A patrol from C Company, First Battalion, Second Regiment, Second Division," Adam replied. "I'm Lieutenant Bergman, the CO. Where's General Vandegrift?"

The gunner pointed toward the airstrip and the cluster of buildings around it. "The CP's over there," he said. He lowered his rifle and motioned for the other members of the gun crew to do likewise. "Where the hell did you guys come from?"

"Aola Bay."

"Aola Bay! That's eighty miles from here!"

A weary grin stretched across Adam's face. "Yeah. We know."

He tucked the Thompson under his arm and walked on toward the command post, the other members of the patrol straggling along behind him. He heard Ed call out to the gunners, "Sounded like you boys had a party over here last night."

"Yeah, and we invited the whole fuckin' Jap navy and air force too."

Adam looked past the airstrip, which slanted crossways in front of him, toward Lunga Point, and was surprised to see several transport ships heaved to off shore. Landing craft were making their way in from the transports, and a lot of men in uniform were already ashore, milling around in the way soldiers always do if they haven't been landed under fire. Officers trotted here and there, yelling orders.

Adam and his men skirted the airstrip, not wanting to be in the way if any of the Wildcats needed to land. Beyond the strip was a building with prefabricated walls, so that it could be assembled in a hurry. An American flag flew from a pole in front of the building. Adam's pulse picked up when he saw it. Corny though it might be to some people, the flag fluttering in the wind was a beautiful sight.

A sentry challenged Adam as he approached. Adam identified himself and said that he needed to see General Vandegrift. The guard relaxed a little and said, "He's over yonder with the Army, Lieutenant."

"The Army?" Adam repeated.

"Yes, sir. Those boys coming in from the transports are doggies, sir."

So after months of rumors, the United States Army had arrived in the Solomons at last. Adam reminded himself that they were all on the same side and tried not to think that it was damned well about time the dogfaces had gotten here.

"Take five," he said to the members of the patrol, then he started over toward the spot where Vandegrift was conferring with an Army officer who was probably the newcomers' CO. Before he could get there, he noticed that the transport ships were pulling away from Guadalcanal. He got the impression they were hurrying.

Farther out in the channel, more ships were gliding toward the island. Adam was no expert on naval matters, but he suddenly knew somehow that they were Japanese destroyers.

General A. A. Vandegrift was a stocky, balding man with a stern but friendly face. He said to the Army officer, "Better get your men under cover, General."

"I agree, General," the doggie brass hat replied, then he turned to bellow orders at his subordinates. The soldiers who had just disembarked from the landing craft ran farther inland, surging forward like a green wave.

Vandegrift was turning away when he spotted Adam and stopped. He seemed to know instantly that Adam was not one of the lieutenants under his command. "Who are you, son?"

With a naval attack imminent, there wasn't much time for formality, but Adam saluted anyway. "Lieutenant Bergman, sir. In command of a patrol from C Company, First Battalion, Second Regiment."

Vandegrift returned the salute and frowned. "The bunch that hit those villages up by Aola Bay a few days ago?"

"That's right, sir. Colonel Hill wanted us to check the situation between here and there."

"So you came overland through the jungle?" Vandegrift's eyes widened. "I'd heard some talk about that, but I didn't know any of Colonel Hill's boys were actually going through with it." Out in the channel, a gun on one of the Japanese destroyers boomed. The general took hold of Adam's arm. "Come on, Lieutenant, let's get inside. It won't help much, but those prefab walls are better than nothing, I suppose. Tell your men to find whatever cover they can."

"You heard the man!" Adam shouted to the members of the patrol. "Find a place to hunker down until the shelling's over!"

Moving at a fast trot, Adam and Vandegrift went to the command post as more shells from the boats began to crash on the shore and around the airstrip. They went inside, and Vandegrift shut the door behind them. He went to a desk and sat down, then said, "All right, Lieutenant, tell me what happened and what you found between here and Aola Bay," as if an enemy bombardment weren't going on right outside.

Adam struggled to keep his nerves under control. Explosions marched around the command post, and he knew that at any second, a shell could land right on the building and blow it—along with him and General Vandegrift—to smithereens. But Vandegrift had taken off his helmet and was looking at him with an expectant expression on his face, so Adam launched into an impromptu report, telling the general about their encounters with the Japanese and the indications they'd found that the Japs were using the eastern part of the island to supply their troops in the interior.

"I'm not surprised," Vandegrift said. "The Navy's trying, but they haven't been able to do anything to stop the Tokyo Express from getting up and down the Slot. What about casualties, Lieutenant?"

"We lost one man, sir. He was killed by a Jap trying to infiltrate our camp."

"And how many casualties did you inflict on the enemy?"

Adam had to stop and think. "I'm not sure exactly, sir," he said after a moment. "I think we killed around a dozen of them."

"And destroyed a boatload of ammunition and an entire supply and repair depot." Vandegrift leaned back in his chair and smiled. "All while losing only one man."

"Yes, sir." When it was boiled down like that, the patrol's accomplishments sounded pretty impressive, Adam decided. He hadn't thought about it that way while everything was going on. He had just been trying to stay alive and keep his men alive.

"We'll have to see about a commendation for you, Lieutenant, perhaps even a medal. Right now, though . . ." Vandegrift leaned his head toward the wall as another explosion sounded outside. "We have our hands full with other matters."

"I understand, sir."

"I'm curious about one more thing, though—are you anxious to get back to Tulagi with the rest of your regiment?"

Adam didn't have to think about the question. Even though life hadn't been as dangerous on Tulagi, he didn't feel any compulsion to go back there. "Not particularly, sir."

"Good," Vandegrift said, "because I think I'd like to keep you here on Guadalcanal."

# THIRTY-EIGHT

It didn't take long for Adam to catch up on everything that had happened on Guadalcanal in recent days. That night, after the Japanese ships had ceased their barrage and withdrawn back up the Slot, and while work crews were busy repairing the damage done to the airfield by the bombs and artillery shells, Adam sat and talked with some of the junior officers who had been on Guadalcanal for weeks.

"You boys over on Tulagi had it easy," one of the men said, and Adam couldn't argue with him. "A couple of days of fighting and then nothing to do but sit around and fan yourselves."

"And nearly starve to death the first couple of weeks, after the Navy pulled out," Adam said.

"We went through the same thing here. My belly was so empty it thought my throat had been cut."

That joking comment made Adam wince as he remembered what had happened to Warren Bloch, but he didn't say anything. The guy who had made the comment didn't know any better.

"Anyway, they kept telling us we were going to get reinforcements, but they never got here—until today. That's the Hundred-and-sixty-fourth Infantry Regiment that came ashore. They're dogfaces, of course, not Marines, but they don't look like bad guys for Army. And they brought a bunch of pogey bait with them and don't mind trading for Jap souvenirs. If nothing else they'll give the Japs somebody else to shoot at for a while. They're moving up beyond the Matanikau."

During the days that Adam and his patrol had been making their way through the jungle, the Marine offensive to the west had been carried out successfully. In a couple of days of fierce fighting, the front lines had been pushed well past the river. That meant more

319

territory for the U.S. forces to protect, but with the Army on hand now, maybe the task could be accomplished.

"The Navy whipped the Japs a few nights ago up at Cape Esperance, on the northwest end of the island," another lieutenant told Adam. He lit a Lucky Strike, blew out the smoke, and went on, "That's about all they've been good for lately, though. The Japs might as well have engraved invitations to cruise up and down the channel all they want. Our flyboys go after their ships, especially the dive bombers, but there's only so much they can do. It's almost like the Navy doesn't want us to win here in the Solomons."

Adam knew that couldn't be the case. But he was familiar enough with the rivalry between the various services so that he wasn't surprised to hear the comment. The Marines were under the jurisdiction of the Secretary of the Navy, but that didn't mean they had any great fondness for the swabbies.

"The Japs pound us day and night," a third lieutenant put in. "If they're not shelling us from their ships, they're dropping bombs on us. Or both at the same time. Seems like I've spent most of the last week in a foxhole, hoping a few hundred pounds of explosive won't land on my head."

"They're bringing in more supplies all the time," Adam said. "At least, that's what it looked like from what we found between here and Aola Bay."

"I don't doubt it. We're in the shit, buddy, make no mistake about that. If I was you, I'd be on my way back to Tulagi."

Adam shook his head. "General Vandegrift suggested that my men and I should stay here. He said he doesn't want to risk a landing craft to take us across the channel, not with so many Japs prowling around."

"The old man can say that if he wants to, but I imagine he just wants all the men and guns he can get. And I don't blame him. When the Japs finally come, we're going to need all that extra help. What do you say, Bergman? Gonna squat here on the 'Canal with the rest of us poor bastards?"

Adam grinned. "Just let 'em try to get me off."

"Oh, the Japs'll try. You can count on that. They won't be satisfied until all the Marines are off Guadalcanal . . . one way or the other."

\*   \*   \*

Adam wasn't sure what was in the message General Vandegrift sent to the Second Division brass over on Tulagi, but if there was any problem about him and his volunteers staying here on Guadalcanal, he never heard anything about it. The Third Regiment of the Second Division was already over here, along with the entire First Division and the U.S. Army's 164th Infantry Regiment. That added up to a good-sized force. Adam didn't know how many troops the Japanese had on the island, but he didn't see how they could outnumber the Americans by all that much. When the big fight came, the two sides would be pretty evenly matched, he thought. Unless the nearly constant bombardments from air and sea whittled down the number of defenders, which was clearly what the Japs were trying to do.

An Australian in ragged shorts, sandals, and no shirt brought more bad news to Henderson Field. He was one of the coast watchers, mostly Australian and a few British, who had lived here in the Solomons before the outbreak of the war. These men had stayed behind, living in the jungle, usually with the natives, and functioning as an unofficial intelligence service for the Allies. This man told General Vandegrift that while the shelling was going on at the American beachhead, the Japanese had managed to land an entire division of troops at Tassafaronga Point, several miles west of the Matanikau. It was obvious what they intended to do with those troops. A counterattack was coming, and soon.

For more than a week, the shelling went on, with a new element added. The Japanese forces on the island now had long-range howitzers firing at the Marine camp. The 150mm-rounds tore up the western end of the airstrip. The Marines called the new weapons "Pistol Pete," and whenever the shells began to scream in from beyond the Matanikau, somebody was bound to comment, "There's old Pistol Pete again."

The command post was moved into a large dugout, but even so, a bomb that fell near it killed forty-one men and caused considerable damage. General Vandegrift himself only narrowly avoided death.

Another casualty of the continuing bombardment was the supply of aviation fuel. Several dumps of avgas had gone up in flames, ignited by bombs and artillery rounds falling on them. Only a daring run up the channel by the seaplane tender *McFarland* to deliver forty thousand gallons of fuel enabled the Marine fliers to keep their Wildcats and Dauntlesses in the air. The Marine fighter squadron, which had been nicknamed the Cactus Air Force, did its best under abysmal conditions.

Adam and his group of volunteers, which was nearly company strength, moved right in with the other defenders, taking their turns on the front line, guarding positions along the Matanikau. As days dragged past, nerves grew more taut under the vicious bombardment and the knowledge that sooner or later, the Japanese ground troops would be coming.

On Saturday, 24 October 1942, Adam was sitting in a foxhole about five hundred yards east of the Matanikau in the middle of the afternoon when it began to rain. Ed Collins and Leo Sikorsky were with him, and as drops of rain pattered on their helmets, Leo complained, "Damn it! This hole's gonna fill up with water. What else can go wrong?"

"I sure wish you hadn't said that, Chopper," Ed said. "That's what you call temptin' fate."

The rain began to fall harder. "My fate is to be wet and miserable," Leo said. "Wherever the damn Japs are, I hope they're gettin' wet too."

Leo's prediction proved to be right. Water began to puddle in the bottom of the foxhole. Adam, Ed, and Leo tried to stay out of it, but the situation was hopeless. By nightfall, which came early because of the thick overcast, all three of them were soaked to the skin. All along the front line it was the same for the American troops.

As it grew dark, Pistol Pete started his nightly serenade. The howitzer shells screamed through the rain and crashed into the area around Henderson Field. On the western front, several miles away, Adam and the other men felt the muddy ground quaking beneath them as the blasts shook the earth.

The water in the foxhole had risen so that Adam's boots were almost completely submerged. His feet were wet and cold. The toe rot, which was already prevalent among the Marines, was going to be even worse after the soaking their feet were taking tonight. More guys were laid up from the creeping fungus, and from dysentery and malaria, than the Japs had managed to injure with all their shelling. They weren't just fighting the Japanese here on Guadalcanal, Adam thought as he raised himself a little to get one foot out of the water. They were fighting bugs and disease, heat and cold and bad food. It was enough to get a guy down, to break his spirit. He lifted his head a little more. Maybe it had been a mistake after all when he had decided not to go back to Tulagi. . . .

At first the shape was just a darker shadow moving in the darkness. Then, suddenly, it became the figure of a man lurching out of the jungle a few yards away from the line of foxholes. Adam stiffened and started to lift his tommy gun as the figure screamed in heavily accented English, "Marine, you die!"

Adam opened up with the Thompson, firing a burst that threw the charging Japanese soldier back onto the ground. He kept firing as more shadowy figures loomed out of the black jungle. Flanking him, Ed and Leo began to shoot as fast as they could work the bolts on their Springfields. It was too dark to aim. All they could do was fire blindly into the jungle.

But there were so many Japanese troops pouring out of the trees that it didn't really matter. Chances were that any bullet fired in their direction would hit one of them. Adam sure hoped so, anyway, because he and the other men along the front line had just minutes, perhaps only seconds, to blunt this attack or they were going to be overrun.

Like lightning, the flashes from the muzzle of the Thompson lit the night in front of him. He had a crazy, kaleidoscopic view of the Japs coming at him. They jittered and jerked, moving like people in an old silent movie. No stirring organ music accompanied this scene, however, only the ear-pounding roar of the guns and the screams of dying men. Adam's vision blurred as rainwater ran into his eyes. He realized the machine gun's clip was empty. He ejected it and rammed home a full clip from the pouch at his waist. The move took only a second and then he was firing again, but that second's delay had allowed the line of the Japanese attack to surge toward him. One of the brown-uniformed soldiers flopped and died only five feet from the edge of the foxhole, his head blown off his shoulders by a burst from the Tommy gun.

From a foxhole down the line, a BAR opened up. In the hands of a man who knew how to use one, the Browning Automatic Rifle was a fearsome weapon, especially at close quarters like this. The stream of fire chopped almost a dozen of the Japanese in half, slicing through the front ranks of the attack with devastating effect.

Ed began lobbing grenades into the jungle. The blasts cut a swath through the Japanese ranks. Men fell over their dead comrades, piling up and slowing the advance. Those who were already up front were mowed down by the close-range fire from the Marines in the foxholes. Adam emptied the second clip of bullets and started on a third. The recoil of the Thompson had the muscles in his arms jerking and jumping so that he wondered if they would ever settle down once the fight was over.

Of course, he might not have to worry about that, he thought. He had to live through the battle before being concerned with its aftereffects.

Time had no meaning under these circumstances. After a while—Adam had no idea how long—the Japanese pulled back, but only to regroup. It seemed to Adam that he and his companions had barely had time to catch their breath before they were fighting again. He had asked Ed and Leo if they were all right and gotten affirmative answers from both, and then it was time to start killing again.

Elsewhere along the line, the Marines and the dogfaces of the 164th were facing wave after wave of Japanese soldiers. The attack was spread out all around the American beachhead as the Japs struck in several places at once. All the way back at Henderson Field, Japanese troops attacked from the south, trying to drive along a ridge that ran between the airstrip and the Lunga River. The defenders threw everything they had right back at the Japs and somehow held them off. For most of the soldiers from the 164th, this was the first time they had been in combat. They acquitted themselves well, wielding their new M1 Garands with deadly accuracy despite the horrible weather conditions and the darkness.

Adam didn't know what was going on elsewhere, didn't know if the other Marines and the doggies were managing to hold on. He concentrated on what was right in front of him and didn't worry about anything else. That was the only thing he could do. He lost track of how many clips of ammunition he fired, but he began to worry that he would run out before dawn. The break of day seemed to be a long way off. . . .

But at last morning came, though the sky was so cloudy it was hard to tell at first that the sun was rising. With the dawn, the Japanese began to pull back, leaving their dead behind. Those corpses were stacked up three or four or even more deep in front of the American lines. The attack was over—for now. There had been no breakthroughs. The front lines were intact.

Adam slumped in the muddy foxhole and grimaced as the Japanese howitzers resumed their shelling. "The ground troops may have pulled back, but Pistol Pete is still in business," he said.

"Yeah," Ed agreed. "Stinkin' cannon."

Leo didn't say anything. He sat with his back against the side of the foxhole, his head drooped forward on his chest. Adam couldn't see his face, only the top of his helmet. It was unusual for Leo not to be griping during every spare moment, and for a second Adam felt a surge of fear that his friend had been hit. He reached over and took hold of Leo's shoulder, gave it a shake.

"Chopper! Chopper, you okay?"

Leo's head popped up, eyes wide. "What? What?" He looked around. "What the hell!"

Adam leaned his head against the side of the foxhole and laughed. "You were asleep, weren't you?"

"Ah, hell, can't a guy catch forty winks without gettin' in trouble with some goddamn officer? Cripes, I'm tired! It was a long night."

"Yeah, it was," Adam agreed with a weary smile. "It sure as hell was."

Afterward, they called that day Dugout Sunday, because everybody spent it hunkered down in dugouts and foxholes while the Japanese pounded the area with bombs and artillery yet again. The only ones who ventured out of their shelters were the men who had to deliver fresh ammunition to the front lines, and several of them were killed by howitzer rounds or exploding bombs. The airstrip was in a shambles, too muddy and shell-pocked for the fighters to take off, so the Japanese bombers had clear sailing as they flew over and dropped their sticks.

The rain stopped and the sky cleared, and the heat came down on the men like a mallet. The air was so humid it was like being in a steam bath, and the heat had an effect on the corpses that had been left behind by the Japanese too. Before the day was over, the stench coming from them was awful, but there was nothing that could be done about it. Snipers still lurked in the trees, and it was worth a man's life to venture out of his hiding place. Besides, there were just too many bodies. Thousands of Japanese soldiers had lost their lives in the nighttime attack, many of them cut down at almost point-blank range.

Even under these circumstances, rumors managed to circulate. Not even combat could stop the scuttlebutt. One rumor had it that reinforcements were on their way from Tulagi, that all the remaining men from the SECMARDIV were coming to Guadalcanal. Knowing what a strong presence the Japanese navy had in the channel these days, Adam doubted if that was true. It was nice to think about, though. On the other hand, even if he and the other men on the line were relieved, where could they go? They couldn't get away from the fighting. In some ways, it was better to be up here where you held at least some of your destiny in your own hands, rather than being stuck back at Henderson Field where the only thing you could do was put your hands over your head and pray that you didn't get blown to hell.

"Hey, watch it, you're pissin' on me!" Leo squawked, breaking into Adam's thoughts.

"If a man's gotta go, a man's gotta go," Ed said as he buttoned up his trousers. "What the hell you want me to do, step outta the foxhole to take a leak? One o' them Jap snipers'd be liable to shoot it off!"

"Yeah, and then all the heifers back in the cornfield would go into mourning, wouldn't they?"

"Damn it, that ain't funny!"

"Oh, I don't know, I found it rather amusing," Leo said.

Adam started to tell them to can the chatter but then thought better of it. Let them rag on each other all they wanted, he told himself. It gave them something to do while the bombs were exploding and the Japanese were girding themselves up for another attack, probably as soon as night fell.

It was too much to hope that they had given up, Adam thought. They wanted this island too badly for that. They would be back. He was sure of it.

\* \* \*

Reinforcements did come, but not from Tulagi. The 3d Battalion of the Second Regiment, which was already on Guadalcanal, had not taken part in the previous night's battle. But they moved up to the front lines late in the day on Dugout Sunday. The Japanese had suffered tremendous losses during their first attack, but they were not likely to deviate from a plan of action once it had been set forth. Their leaders had said they would attack the Americans and drive them from the island, and so that was what they would do. Or they would die trying.

As darkness fell, men were still gasping from the heat and from the terrible odor in the air. No one had eaten much during the day. Rations were short, and besides, they were too sickened by the smell of rotting corpses to have much appetite. Tonight had to be the end of it, at least for a while, Adam thought as he waited in the foxhole with Ed and Leo. They just couldn't take much more.

Even though the sky wasn't overcast, the night seemed every bit as dark as the one before. Somewhere above them were stars, but the overhanging canopy of the jungle rendered them invisible. Adam looked up and wished he could see them. They were only tiny pinpricks of light against a sable backdrop, but right now it would have been comforting to be able to see them and wonder if Catherine was looking up at the same stars. He liked to think that she was.

Muzzle flashes suddenly split the darkness. Howling like madmen, the Japanese troops charged out of the trees, and the fight was on again.

Adam fired the Thompson until his shoulder was numb from the pounding it was taking from the butt of the submachine gun. Now the corpses that had stunk so much all day served a purpose. They were piled so high in front of the American lines that they slowed down the attack. The Japs had to clamber over the bodies of their fallen comrades before they could reach the defenders. It was like a wall of rotting flesh, Adam thought grimly as he added to it by mowing down more of the charging, brown-clad soldiers.

Ed let out a yell and fell backward in the foxhole. "Ed!" Leo cried. "Ed, you hit?"

Adam threw a glance over his shoulder as he kept firing at the oncoming Japanese. Ed was struggling to get up again. "I'm all right," he said. "It's just a scratch!" But then he fell again, collapsing against the wall of the foxhole.

Leo knelt beside him and felt desperately around his torso. "Oh, shit, Adam! There's blood all over him!"

"It's just a hole in my shoulder," Ed said, his voice weak. Adam could barely hear him over the shooting.

Leo screamed, "Corpsman! Corpsman!" and started to stick his head up out of the hole. Adam lowered the Tommy gun, reached back, grabbed Leo's shoulder, and shoved him down.

"There aren't any corpsmen out here, Chopper," he snapped. "Keep your head down and get that rifle going again. The sooner we get rid of those Japs, the sooner we can get some help for Ed."

Leo wiped the back of a hand across his nose and then pushed himself up to the edge of the foxhole. He thrust the barrel of his rifle over the lip and started firing. "You lousy yellow bastards!" he screamed over and over as he pulled the trigger and worked the Springfield's bolt.

Adam knew just how he felt. It might be too late for Ed already.

Sometime during the night, Adam emptied a clip, reached for another, and realized that he was out of ammunition for the Thompson. He let it slip out of his hands and fall to the bottom of the foxhole. He tugged the Colt from the holster on his hip, racked the slide, and started firing the handgun toward the Japanese troops. How could there be so many of them? Was the whole Imperial army here on Guadalcanal tonight? How much longer could they keep coming?

The slide locked back as the Colt ran out of bullets. Adam reloaded as slugs from the enemy's guns whined around him. When he looked up, one of the Japs was right over him, standing on the brink of the foxhole, rifle poised for a downward thrust with its attached bayonet. The Jap screamed something. Adam shoved the barrel of the Colt in his belly and started pulling the trigger. The enemy soldier screamed again, in agony this time, and folded up as the .45 caliber bullets blew his insides out. He toppled into the foxhole, thrusting the bayonet toward Adam with the last of his strength. Adam twisted aside and felt the tip of the blade rake across his ribs. Then the body hit him and knocked him down, and the man's intestines slid out into Adam's lap. Adam shoved the corpse off him and rolled onto his side to retch into the mud. Then, weak, stunned, he started crawling upright again. The Japs were all around the foxhole now, overrunning it. Leo fired his rifle up into them as he crouched over Ed, protecting his friend's body with his own. Adam lifted the Colt and squeezed off the last two rounds in it, sending one of the Japs spinning to the ground. Another man stopped and swung his rifle toward the foxhole, ready to empty it into the three Americans. Before he could pull the trigger, a burst of fire from a BAR ripped him apart.

The crescendo of death rose even higher as defenders on both sides of Adam's position poured a cross fire into the momentary Japanese breakthrough. Adam slid to the ground and pulled Leo with him. They huddled there next to Ed. Adam fumbled another clip into the butt of the Colt and lifted it. Above them, the Japs began to retreat, their highwater mark reached and lost. Adam fired into them as they stumbled past, not caring that he was shooting them in the back. He didn't care about anything anymore. He wasn't even aware of anything except the feel of the automatic as it bucked against his palm. He seemed to drift away on a sea of noise and blood and fire.

When he came back to himself an unknowable time later, the battle was over. He was still pulling the trigger of the Colt, even though the gun was empty.

# THIRTY-NINE

"Man, isn't that a beautiful sunrise?" Ensign Roy Kirkland asked from the rear cockpit of the Douglas SBD Dauntless dive-bomber.

Phil Lange just grunted. He was scanning the horizon for any sign of Japanese ships, as well as watching the sky around them. Kirkland ought to be doing the same instead of mooning over some damned sunrise.

A faint smile tugged at the corners of Phil's mouth. Not even twenty-three years old, and he was turning into an old curmudgeon. He turned his head to the east, toward the spot where the blazing orange ball of the sun was climbing out of the endless blue green waters of the Pacific. A few clouds floated high above, and the arrival of the sun made them seem to be aflame as well. The kid was right. It *was* a pretty sight. Phil wished he could have been watching it with Missy Mitchell.

Instead, he was scouting for Japs near the Santa Cruz Islands, several hundred miles east of the Solomons. From the scuttlebutt he'd heard, the Marines over there had their hands full trying to hang on to the beachheads they'd established during their landings back in August. Here it was late October and the fighting was still going on. One thing you could say for the Japanese: They were stubborn. Phil hoped that Catherine Bergman's husband was all right.

For the most part, Phil was glad to be back in action, even though he hadn't seen any combat since the *Enterprise* had rejoined the *Hornet* and the rest of the task force a few days earlier. The time he'd spent at Pearl Harbor while the *Enterprise* was undergoing repairs had been all right. He'd had a chance to catch up on writing letters to his folks and his brothers and sisters. He was sure they would be glad to hear from him and know that he was all right. He

331

certainly was happy to receive all the letters they'd sent that finally caught up to him at Pearl. For a few hours as he read those letters over and over, he had been transported back to the small town in western New York State where he'd grown up, to a simpler time when the world hadn't been at war. That had been nice.

And so were the letters from Missy. She couldn't go into specifics because of the military censors, of course, but he had been able to tell by reading between the lines that the *Solace* was still docked at Tonga Tabu. She was fine, she said, and so were Catherine and the other nurses who were her friends. Tonga was a backwater of sorts, a good place for a hospital ship to be moored, since the Japanese hadn't shown any interest in it. But that could change without much warning, and Phil knew it. Hell, no one had dreamed that the Japs would dare to attack Pearl Harbor, and everybody knew what had happened there last December.

The United States had been at war for nearly eleven months, at least here in the Pacific. Over in Europe, it was a different story. Phil had read in *Stars & Stripes* how people were clamoring for our boys to get in on the fighting over there too, but so far it hadn't happened. Maybe soon that second front would be opened.

In the meantime, Phil had this early-morning patrol to fly, and he didn't need to let his mind wander. That was difficult, especially when he wanted to think about Missy, but he forced his attention back on the water. He was getting as scatterbrained as the kid, he told himself.

"What's that?" Kirkland asked. "Look over there at nine o'clock, Lieutenant!"

Phil heard the excitement in Kirkland's voice. He turned his head and saw some indistinct shapes on the horizon. Might be ships, he thought. But he was too far away to say for sure. He picked up the radio microphone and called the Dauntless that was flying off his right wing in a two-man formation.

"Possible enemy vessels at nine o'clock," Phil said. "We're going to take a look."

The reply came back from Lieutenant Alex Dougherty, the pilot of the other dive-bomber. "Okay, Phil, we'll be right behind you."

Phil swung his Dauntless into a long turn that sent it winging northwest of the Santa Cruz Islands, which were visible in the distance to the east. In a matter of minutes, the shapes Kirkland had spotted were taking on more definite forms. Facing backward in the rear cockpit as he was, Kirkland couldn't see their quarry anymore. Impatience was in his voice as he asked, "What about it? Are they Japs?"

Phil felt his heart rate accelerating as he recognized the shapes. "It's them," he said. "At least three flattops and some cruisers."

"Are we going in?"

"Might as well," Phil said. "Get on the horn to the *Enterprise* and let them know what we've found."

On scouting missions such as this one, the Dauntless carried only a single 500-pound bomb, so that its speed would be greater. If a target was spotted, however, the pilots were expected to attack it if possible. It certainly looked possible here. Phil checked the sky—no Zeros in sight, just some puffy white clouds high above. The Japanese carriers should have had some fighters up, just in case. That oversight was going to cost them.

When Kirkland had finished radioing the position of the Japanese ships to the *Enterprise*, Phil keyed the mike again. "We'll make a run at them, Alex," he told Dougherty. "I'll go in first."

"Aye, aye," the other pilot responded. "Good luck, Phil."

Phil looked over at the cockpit of the other plane and gave Dougherty a thumbs-up. Then he eased the stick back and started to climb. He would need plenty of altitude to start his dive toward the enemy ships.

The two planes were almost high enough, ascending into clouds that had begun to thicken, when Kirkland yelled, "Zeros, Phil! Two o'clock!"

Phil's head jerked around. Sure enough, a flight of eight Japanese fighters was emerging from the clouds and roaring toward them. The Japs had been flying high and hiding in the clouds, maybe hoping that a couple of stray American bombers would come along and try to attack the carriers. Now the Dauntlesses were the prey instead of the hunters.

Phil's hand tightened on the stick as he looked at the Zeros rushing through the sky toward him. If he and Dougherty threw the planes into their dives right now, they might be able to release their bombs before the Japanese fighters caught up to them. But they would never be able to escape. When they pulled out of the dives, they would be sitting ducks for the Zeros.

Acting with a combination of instinct and command sense, Phil kicked the left rudder and sent the Dauntless swooping toward some thicker clouds. He snatched up the microphone and called, "Forget it, Alex! Let's get out of here!"

Dougherty followed Phil's example and veered his plane into the clouds too. Phil advanced the throttle, making the engine of his Dauntless scream as he urged more power out of it. From the rear cockpit, Kirkland shouted, "They're coming after us, Phil!"

Phil hadn't expected any less. Shooting down a couple of dive-bombers would be a nice morning's work for that flight of Zeros. He said to Kirkland, "Get ready for a fight!"

For a bomber, the Douglas SBD was a fast plane—but it wasn't fast enough to outrun a fighter. Phil knew they were depending upon two things for survival: his flying skill and Roy Kirkland's talent as a rear gunner. Phil was confident in his own ability, but he would have felt a hell of a lot better if he'd had Jerry Bennett back there in the rear cockpit, manning the gun.

But that was never going to happen again. For better or worse, Phil thought, his fate was partially in the hands of the young, inexperienced ensign.

He headed for the thickest clouds he could find, weaving in and out of the puffy white banks. Maybe they could lose the Japs in the clouds. It was a slim hope, but better than nothing.

The rear gun opened up, spewing a stream of .50-caliber machine-gun bullets toward their pursuers. Phil turned his head and looked at the second Dauntless, now flying alongside him. Flames spurted from the rear gun of Dougherty's plane too. Phil couldn't hear the Zeros shooting over the sound of Kirkland's gun, but he felt the tiny shudders that ran through the Dauntless and knew that it had taken some hits. He put the nose down and dived a couple of hundred feet through the clouds before leveling off. Kirkland's gun went silent.

Fearing that the kid had been hit, Phil said over the cockpit radio, "Roy, are you okay?"

Kirkland's voice came back without hesitation. "Yeah, I'm fine. But a couple of those Zeros are still on our tail! Here they come!"

The rear gun started blasting again. Kirkland's voice had sounded strong, Phil thought. As long as the ensign's nerves held out, they stood a chance.

An explosion tore through the sky behind them. Phil heard the blast, then the next instant, Kirkland let out an excited whoop. "Got him! I got the bastard, Phil! He blew up in midair!"

"Good job. Watch out for the other one."

Phil looked around, searching for any sign of Dougherty's plane. The second Dauntless was nowhere to be seen. That didn't mean it had been shot down. It could be almost anywhere in the clouds.

Those clouds were getting thinner, though, indicating that Phil's plane was approaching the bottom of the layer. He had been letting the SBD drift generally downward, but he thought that maybe he should climb a little. If he did that, though, the airspeed would drop and the remaining Zero would be right on top of him. Damned if he did, damned if he didn't, he thought.

"Here comes that other Zeke!" Kirkland warned.

Obviously, he wasn't going to be able to shake the Japanese pilot, Phil thought. So one way or another, it was going to be a fight. Might as well get out of the clouds so that he could see what was going on. He dropped the Dauntless's nose even more and swooped down into the open sky. The sun was up now and the golden light washing across the ocean was beautiful.

The hammering from Kirkland's gun started up again. Phil saw tracer rounds from the Zero whip past his right wing. The Japanese pilot probably expected him to veer left in an attempt to get away from the bullets. Instead, Phil hit the right rudder, trying to time the move so that the Dauntless would slide in that direction between bursts from the Zero's machine guns. As he banked right, he also started to climb.

Behind him, Kirkland twisted the gun back to the left. Phil looked over his shoulder and saw that the Zero had overshot them slightly in his zeal to close in on them. It gave Kirkland enough of an angle for him to be able to stitch a line of fire down the side of the Zero's fuselage. Black smoke began to drift from the fighter.

The Zero was damaged but not out of the fight. The pilot peeled away, then threw his plane into a tight loop. Phil was still banking to the right. The Zero came in at him, flying a course almost perpendicular to the Dauntless's. Phil dived again. The Zero tried to follow him, and for one horrifying instant, Phil thought the planes were going to collide in midair. Then he was under the Zero, which zoomed past overhead. Kirkland fired again. Phil didn't think Kirkland's gun would be able to reach the Zero from this angle; the elevation couldn't be raised that high. The bullets caught the Zero's tail, though, blasting away both stabilizers. The Japanese plane, already in trouble due to the fire inside it, was now out of control as well. It spiraled down toward the ocean as Phil felt a fierce exultation go through him. He and Kirkland had not only survived the dogfight, but they had shot down two Zeros as well. He kept his eye on the plummeting plane, expecting to see the pilot bail out. No one emerged from the cockpit, and a second later the fighter plowed into the waves with a huge splash. Either the Japanese pilot had been hit, or he had been unwilling to abandon his plane, preferring to go into the drink with it.

Kirkland yelled happily and slapped his palm against the skin of the fuselage beside the rear cockpit. "Slow but deadly, baby, slow but deadly!" he shouted, using the nickname given to the SBDs by some of their crews. Phil had never thought the Dauntless was all that slow, but deadly . . . yeah, they had pretty much proven that, going all the way back to the dive-bomber's successes at Midway. Phil felt himself grinning.

"Good shooting, Ensign," he told Kirkland. "We'll have to start calling you Hawkeye."

He was joking, but Kirkland said, "Really? Gee, that would be great! Hawkeye Kirkland, ace of the air."

"Slow down, mister. You'll have to shoot down a few more planes before you start calling yourself an ace."

"Three more, right?" Kirkland asked. "I got two today, so I need three more."

"Yeah, I guess so," Phil agreed. He wished he had kept his mouth shut. The kid would probably go on and on about that Hawkeye business . . .

"Any sign of Dougherty?" Phil went on. He was scanning the sky below the clouds himself, looking for the other Dauntless or the rest of the flight of Zeros.

After a moment, Kirkland asked, "Is that him? About ten o'clock?"

Phil turned his head and looked, and sure enough, he saw the distinctive outline of a Douglas SBD. He angled in the same direction, and within minutes, he and Dougherty were flying alongside each other again.

"What happened to the rest of those Zekes, Alex?" Phil asked his fellow pilot over the radio.

"We shot down one of them, and the rest headed back toward those Jap flattops. I suppose they didn't want to stray too far from them."

"No, probably not," Phil agreed. "It won't be long before they have more company." He knew that back on the *Enterprise* and the *Hornet*, the report Kirkland had radioed in of the Japanese carriers' location would have resulted in strikes being launched from both American carriers. Flights of Dauntlesses, Avengers, and Wildcats would be on their way already.

"What about us, Lieutenant?" Kirkland asked, using Phil's rank again now that he wasn't so excited. "Are we going to get in on the attack?"

"Not until we've headed back to the roost, refueled, and taken on a full load of bombs," Phil replied.

"But what if all the Japanese ships have been sunk by the time we get there?"

Phil chuckled. "Haven't you been shot at enough already today, Ensign? You want a taste of ack-ack too?"

"Yes, sir, if it means we get to blow up a Jap carrier!"

Phil shook his head as he flew on toward the *Enterprise*. With an attitude like that, Kirkland would probably make heroes of them both.

Either that, or get them killed.

*   *   *

By the time Phil's plane reached the *Enterprise*, the strike aimed at the Japanese carriers had already taken off, just as he had thought. As soon as the tailhook caught the arresting cable and jerked the Dauntless to a halt, the flight deck crew chocked the wheels and then swarmed over the plane. Phil and Kirkland climbed out and took off their flight helmets while the airedales checked the damage. One of the sailors looked down at Phil and asked, "How'd you get back here, Lieutenant?"

"What do you mean?"

"You've got a busted oil line. Didn't the gauge redline?"

Phil shook his head. "The needle stayed right where it was supposed to be."

"You must have a bad gauge too. We'll have to go over this baby with a fine-tooth comb."

Kirkland gripped Phil's arm. "Does that mean we can't go join the attack?"

"That's what it means, Ensign."

"Damn!"

With a pointed expression, Phil looked down at Kirkland's hand on his arm. "Don't worry, you'll get more chances to grab some glory. In the meantime, I'd appreciate it if you'd stop grabbing me."

"Oh." Kirkland let go in a hurry. "Sorry, Lieutenant."

"Don't worry about it," Phil told him. "Let's go. They'll want to ask us about what we saw out there."

They made their report in one of the ready rooms, along with the crew from the other Dauntless. When that was finished, they had nothing more to do except clean up and change into fresh uniforms. That done, Phil went to the CIC to find out what was happening with the raid on the Japanese task force.

He knew several of the officers on duty in the Combat Information Center, one deck below the bridge. One of them, a lieutenant named Richmond, gave Phil a friendly nod as he stood next to one of the plotting tables. A sailor with a pair of earphones on his head listened to the reports coming in over the radio and relayed the information to Richmond, who used a stick to push around markers that represented ships and planes on the plotting board. Several higher-level officers stood by watching.

"At least four directs hits on the *Shokaku*, sir," the radioman said to Richmond. "Heavy damage to her flight deck. The pilots say there's no way it's usable."

"Is she going down?" Richmond asked.

The radioman listened to the chatter in his earphones. "No indication of that, sir. She's turning back north, though."

"Running away because of the damage," one of the other officers said. "Her planes will have to be diverted. Either that or ditch in the ocean."

Suddenly the radioman burst out, "The *Hornet*'s been hit! She's taken two torpedoes, and two of the Jap planes have crashed into her!"

Kirkland came up beside Phil in time to hear that report. "That's bad, isn't it?" he asked in a half-whisper.

Phil's jaw tightened in irritation at such a dumb question. "The *Hornet* is a good ship," he said. "She can take a lot of punishment." He knew even as he spoke, though, that things didn't look good for the other aircraft carrier, nor for the U.S. Navy in general. The *Saratoga* was undergoing repairs at the moment, much as the *Enterprise* had earlier. If anything happened to the *Hornet*, that would leave the *Enterprise* as the only American flattop in the South Pacific that was fit for duty.

"More bomb strikes on the *Hornet*," the radioman reported. He swallowed hard. "She's on fire and dead in the water. No radio communication at the moment."

Phil shook his head. If the firemen on the *Hornet* were unable to bring those blazes under control, the ship probably was doomed. What had started out looking like a promising morning was turning sour.

"Enemy aircraft approaching *Enterprise*," the radioman said, his voice hollow now.

Moments later, the booming of the ship's antiaircraft guns began to sound. Phil knew that the crews up there in the gun tubs would be working feverishly to erect a screen of AA bursts that would protect the carrier. In addition, the cruisers and destroyers that flanked the *Enterprise* would pitch in with their guns.

It wasn't enough. Something slammed into the ship several minutes later. Phil heard the explosion and felt the deck vibrate under his feet. His hands clenched into fists as he listened to alarm klaxons sounding throughout the ship. He wished he were in a plane, doing something to try to fight off the waves of Japanese bombers. The Wildcats that hadn't gone along with the Dauntlesses and Avengers to hit the enemy flattops would be up there harrying the Vals and Kates. Those pilots knew their jobs, and they were a lot better at it than he would be, Phil thought. But still, he wished he could do something besides just stand here.

He felt the ship begin to turn sharply. A few moments later, it started to swing back in the other direction. The captain was trying to avoid torpedoes launched from the Japanese torpedo bombers. Phil waited tensely for another explosion that would signify the effort had been a failure. It didn't come.

"Enemy planes are withdrawing," the radioman reported as he heard the news from the bridge. "At least half a dozen of the enemy were downed by our fighters and antiaircraft fire."

Kirkland leaned closer to Phil and whispered, "Is it over?"

"For now," Phil answered with a nod. He felt relief coursing through him. The *Enterprise* had survived this battle. But as the damage reports began to come in to the CIC, he grew worried again. One of the Japanese bombs had destroyed a main turbine bearing. The flight deck was damaged as well, and several small fires were still burning in the ship. The planes that had flown off to attack the Japanese flattops would be able to land when they got back, but from the sound of things, the *Enterprise* was going to need a lot of work before it was fully functional again. Phil just hoped the damage wasn't so bad that the ship would have to return once more to Pearl Harbor.

"Man," Kirkland said, shaking his head, "I'm not sure things can get any worse."

Phil just looked at him. He wished like hell Kirkland hadn't said that.

*   *   *

It seemed that the Battle of the Santa Cruz Islands was over. All three of the Japanese carriers had been damaged, one of them quite heavily. But planes were still able to take off from the other two, and though many of the enemy fighters and bombers had been shot down already today, enough Vals and Kates were left so that attacks could be launched again that afternoon. Ignoring the *Enterprise*, the bombers homed in on the already stricken *Hornet*, attacking it as a predator in the wild will single out the weakest prey. In mid-afternoon, a torpedo bomb slammed into the *Hornet*'s aft engine room, crippling the ship even more and causing it to take on so much water that it developed a severe list. Two more torpedo strikes did little to make the situation worse, but it was already bad enough. The *Hornet* was going down, like the *Lexington* and the *Yorktown* before it, and the order was given to abandon ship. With the sinking of the *Hornet* and the damage to the *Enterprise* and *Saratoga*, for the first time since the beginning of the war, the United States Navy had no usable aircraft carriers in the South Pacific. For now, the enemy had a chance to turn the tide of war in the Pacific once more.

# FORTY

Catherine sat at the desk in one of the *Solace*'s wardrooms, writing a letter to her mother. She didn't have much free time, and when she did, she preferred to spend it either writing to Adam or reading the letters he wrote to her. But she wanted to stay in touch with the rest of her family too, so she made an effort to write home on a regular basis. It wasn't as much as she should have done, she knew, but it was the best she could do right now.

The last letter Catherine had received from her mother lay open on the desk beside the sheet of paper on which she was writing. That letter talked about the new clinic, as all of Elenore Tancred's letters did these days. It was hard for Catherine to believe that her father was devoting so much time and energy, not to mention money, to a charity effort. She loved her father, of course, but she was objective enough to know that no one would ever accuse Gerald Tancred of being full of the milk of human kindness. He had to be doing it because of Catherine's mother. For a long time after Spencer's death, Elenore hadn't written, and Catherine had been able to tell from her father's infrequent letters that her mother was in a bad way. Losing Spencer had caused her to have a breakdown. But she had come back from it, and Catherine suspected the clinic had had a lot to do with that. Quite possibly, it had had everything to do with Elenore's recovery.

*Tell Daddy I think he is doing a wonderful thing by trying to help those people at the clinic*, she wrote, but before she could go on, Missy came hurrying into the wardroom.

"Patients coming aboard," Missy announced. "I heard one of the doctors say they're Marines from Guadalcanal."

Catherine's head jerked up. Adam was on Guadalcanal now, after having spent a couple of months on the island of Tulagi. She'd had only one letter from him recently, and although he hadn't been able to come right out and say that he was now on the largest island in the Solomons, that was the conclusion she'd drawn from hints that he dropped. He had mentioned being visited by their old friends Louie and Charlie, and by asking around among some of the patients already on the *Solace*, Catherine had found out that the Marines referred to the types of Japanese planes that bombed Guadalcanal as Louie the Louse and Washing Machine Charlie, the former because it was so annoying and the latter because of the thumping, unsynchronized sound of its engine.

The nearly constant bombing and shelling from enemy vessels made day-to-day existence on Guadalcanal a living hell for the Marines who were trying to hang on to their part of the island. Catherine knew that too, although Adam had sounded cheerful and optimistic in his letter. That was Adam's way, though. He wouldn't want her to worry about him . . . even though anybody with any sense would know that she was worrying about him anyway.

She hadn't received any word about him being wounded, but stuck here at Tonga Tabu, she might not. So she folded both the letter from her mother and the reply she was writing and stuck the pieces of paper in one of the pockets of her white uniform. Even though she was off duty, she stood up and said to Missy, "Let's go."

Patients were brought in through a hatch in the side of the ship and processed in a large open area just inside. The medical officers assessed their condition here, and they were sent to various wards according to the type and severity of their injuries. That was where Catherine and Missy headed now. Catherine's heart was beating rapidly in her chest, and she seemed to have something stuck in her throat. She was having trouble swallowing.

There was no reason to think Adam would be one of the patients, she told herself. Probably she was getting all worked up over nothing. On the other hand, if he was wounded, he might be sent home, back to the States where he would be safe. It was a horrible thing to think, she told herself, but the thought crossed her mind anyway. She felt a little disloyal, because she knew that Adam would not want it that way, but still . . .

They entered the big room where doctors and nurses were moving around from stretcher to stretcher. The hatch was open, letting in sunlight and warm air. A few of the wounded men were moaning in pain, but most were quiet, either unconscious or doped up with painkillers. Catherine scanned the faces of the men as she came to them. Some of them were heavily bandaged, but she knew she would recognize Adam if he were among them, even if his face was covered.

Doc Johnston, the *Solace*'s chief medical officer, straightened from where he had been kneeling beside one of the wounded men. When he turned and saw Catherine, he said, "Nurse Bergman, I didn't think you were on duty this afternoon."

"I'm not, sir," Catherine said.

Johnston's weathered face creased in a grin. "But you heard that these men were brought here from the Solomons, so you came to see if that husband of yours was one of them." He held out a clipboard that he had in his hand. "He's not. I have a list of them right here. No Bergman, Lieutenant Adam J. I think I would have noticed."

Catherine closed her eyes for a second as a feeling of overwhelming relief washed over her. But it was followed almost instantly by more worry. If Adam wasn't here, that meant he was still on Guadalcanal being bombed by the Japs.

Or on Guadalcanal—dead.

"There is someone here asking for you, though," Johnston went on.

Catherine opened her eyes and looked at him in confusion. "What? I mean, what did you say, sir?"

Johnston pointed. "That Marine right over there. He says he knows your husband. He was hoping you'd come along so that he could say hello."

Missy tugged on Catherine's sleeve. "Come on, let's go take a look at this mystery Marine."

"Thank you, Doctor," Catherine said to Johnston as Missy led her away. They went over to the patient the doctor had indicated. Even lying down, he was a large man, built so solidly that he gave the impression of being almost as wide as he was tall. His left shoulder and arm were swathed in bandages. His eyes were clear and alert, though, as he looked up at Catherine and said, "Hello, ma'am. You must be Nurse Bergman. I reckon I'd know you anywhere, I've heard Adam talk about you so much."

"Ed?" Catherine asked as she knelt beside him. "Ed Collins?"

He laughed. "Adam must've told you about me in his letters. What'd he say, that I was a fat, ugly, ol' farm boy from Iowa?"

Catherine clutched his right hand as he lifted it toward her. Smiling, she said, "He told me you were one hell of a Marine, Ed."

Missy knelt on his other side. "How are you, Private?"

Ed switched his gaze to her and let out a whistle of admiration. "Ma'am, I'd say you're as pretty as a speckled pup, but to tell you the truth, I ain't never seen no pup, speckled or otherwise, that could hold a candle to you."

Missy laughed and said, "Yeah, and I'd flirt right back at you, big boy, if I wasn't already spoken for."

"Well, if that ain't bad luck, I don't know what is. It ain't enough that the Japs shoot me in the shoulder and mess up my arm, but just when I'm surrounded by pretty gals, one of 'em's married to one of my best friends and the other one's already got a fella." Ed sighed dramatically. "Might as well go back to the war, I guess."

"Not for a while," Catherine told him. Then she couldn't hold back any longer. "How is Adam? Is he all right?"

The grin on Ed's round face disappeared, to be replaced with a more serious expression. "He was fine when I saw him last, ma'am. We had us a big ol' battle with the Japs, and for a little while they overran the foxhole I was in with Adam and Chopper Sikorsky. You know who Chopper is?"

Catherine nodded.

"Well," Ed went on, oblivious to all the hubbub around them, just as Catherine was, "I got hit and knocked out of the fight, but Adam and Chopper took care of me. Our boys threw those Japs back across the line, and our corpsmen got me out of there, patched me up as best they could, and shipped me off down here as soon as they could. What you really want to know, though, is that Adam didn't get hurt much at all during that battle."

"Much?" Catherine repeated.

"He got a bayonet scratch across the side, but that's it. Like I said, he was fine when I left the 'Canal."

"Thank God," Catherine breathed.

"Yes, ma'am," Ed said. "I thank God every day. I thank Him that I didn't get hurt worse than I did, and that I got friends like ol' Chopper and Adam Bergman."

Catherine squeezed his hand and smiled, and she stayed with him until he was taken to one of the wards. She would just have to wait to finish that letter to her mother.

\* \* \*

Elenore Tancred walked into the tiny office that her husband used in the South Side clinic and went to the desk, where he was seated making notes on patients' charts. She wore a short fur jacket over an expensive charcoal gray suit and white silk blouse, and a gray hat with a small feather in it perched on her short dark hair. She said, "Hello, dear," and when Tancred looked up, she bent over and kissed him on the forehead. He took her hand and squeezed it for a second as he smiled at her, then he went back to his work.

From the corner where she was putting charts in manila folders and filing them in a steel cabinet, Karen Wells smiled at the couple. Elenore turned to her and gave her a pleasant nod. Karen said, "You look very elegant tonight, Mrs. Tancred."

"Thank you, Karen. Dr. Tancred and I are going out to dinner, then to the symphony."

"Yes, I know. He told me about the evening the two of you have planned. It sounds wonderful."

"I'm sure it will be quite nice. What about you, dear? Do you have any plans?"

Karen shook her head. "Not really." Mrs. Tancred didn't know she was a singer. Dr. Tancred had never mentioned that fact to his wife, and Karen dressed conservatively here at the clinic, of course. This was no place for some slinky cocktail gown.

At first it had bothered her that Tancred hadn't said anything about her real profession to his wife. She didn't like even the appearance of secrecy and possible wrongdoing. But over the weeks as she had volunteered here at the clinic, she had come to understand that the doctor simply was concerned about his wife's mental and emotional state. Spencer's death had left her in a bad way, and it had taken her a long time to recover as much as she had. Tancred didn't want to do anything to jeopardize that recovery, so he didn't bring up the circumstances of Spencer's life during the final few months he had spent in Chicago. Like it or not, Karen was part of that whole sordid mess, because she had known both Spencer and Joscelyn.

So she was content now to play the part of the innocent, the wholesome ingénue who was volunteering at the clinic purely out of the goodness of her heart. Singing was like acting in a way; you had to communicate an image to the audience. It really wasn't all that difficult.

Dr. Tancred finished with the last chart, added it to a stack of several others, then stood up and handed them to Karen. "Thank you, Miss Wells," he said.

"Will this be all for the day, Doctor?"

"Not quite. There's one more thing." Tancred turned to his wife. "Why don't you step back out into the waiting room, and I'll be with you in a moment, Elenore. I'm almost ready to go."

"Of course, dear." If she saw anything unusual in the request, Mrs. Tancred showed no sign of it.

Karen, on the other hand, wondered what the doctor wanted to say to her that he didn't want his wife to hear. This was a bit worrisome. She filed the last set of charts and waited while Mrs. Tancred left the office and shut the door behind her.

Tancred turned toward Karen, a frown on his face. "I am not sure how to go about asking this of you . . ." he began.

"Why don't you just come right out and say it?" Karen suggested. Her tone was a bit curt with annoyance. She had believed, based on everything she had seen of him, that Tancred was a real straight arrow, the sort who would never play around on his wife. Tancred had been moralistic enough in dealing with his son, that was for sure. He hadn't cut Spencer a break on anything. But Karen knew that was the way some people were: unable to forgive anyone else's faults while being totally blind to their own.

"All right," Tancred said. "There is a man I want you to go and see. His name is Merrill, John Merrill."

Karen frowned in confusion. That wasn't what she had been expecting. "Who is he?"

Tancred turned back to the desk and picked up a pen to write something on a prescription pad. Then he tore the sheet off the pad and handed it to Karen. "He works for a pharmaceutical company."

Karen took the paper and looked at it. An address in Evanston was written on it. She said, "You want me to go all the way out here? Tonight?"

"I should have spoken to you earlier concerning this matter. I'm sorry, Miss Wells. I wasn't expecting my wife to make arrangements that would occupy my evening. I planned to go see Mr. Merrill myself."

Karen shook her head. "Look, Doctor, I don't mind running errands for you if it has to do with helping here at the clinic—"

"It does, I assure you. It has everything to do with the clinic."

"But I need to know what's going on," Karen continued.

To her surprise, Tancred sank down in his chair and put his head in his hands for a moment. With his shoulders bowed, he looked older than he really was, and very, very tired. "I have done a thing I should not have done," he said.

Karen really was starting to worry now. "Doctor? What's this all about?"

"You know it has been difficult here, getting the drugs we need for the clinic?"

"I heard Mrs. Walsh say something the other day about medicine being in short supply," Karen said.

"So much goes to the military now. It is not just gasoline and tires and things like that. I have known John Merrill for many years, through my medical practice. When he came to me and made his proposal, I should have refused, but . . . the needs here are so great."

Karen's eyes widened as she began to understand. She lowered her voice to little more than a whisper as she asked, "Dr. Tancred, are you talking about buying medicine on the black market?"

Tancred spread his hands. "I have no choice. Otherwise, I must send patients away untreated. I can tell them what is wrong with them but cannot help them." He sighed. "It is important to my wife that this clinic make a difference in these people's lives."

"But you're already doing that," Karen argued. "You don't have to break the law. Our boys overseas need those drugs."

"They will still have an ample supply."

"If that's true, then you could buy the medicines you need legitimately, openly. Why deal with the black market if there's a plentiful supply?"

Tancred leaned back in his chair and looked at her for a moment, then he said, "Miss Wells, do you have money?"

"I make a good wage at the club. Why?"

"Have you ever been poor?"

She hesitated. "Not really."

"Nor have I. In fact, for much of my life, I have been quite well-to-do. Considering the economic situation in this country during the past dozen or so years, I believe I have been extraordinarily lucky."

Karen couldn't argue with that. The depression hadn't hurt Tancred. It hadn't hurt her, either. She'd been just a kid when it started, of course, but her father had owned several successful hardware stores in Wisconsin and was a partner in a bank. Sure, things had been a little dicey for a while after the stock market crash, but the family had come through all right. Looking back over her life, Karen had to admit that she had never really known want.

"What are you getting at, Doctor?" she asked.

"Just that people such as ourselves have the resources to obtain what we need. Yes, the pharmaceutical companies have to supply whatever the military requires. But the medicine that is left over is available to hospitals and medical practices at a premium price. Despite rationing, those with enough money can get what they want. It is as true with sulfa powder as it is with gasoline."

"Then buy it for the clinic."

A grim smile played across Tancred's face. "My funds are not limitless. I must make the most of what I have. So when John Merrill offered to supply me with medications at less than the regular price, I did not hesitate before agreeing to his proposal."

"Wait a minute," Karen said. "In the black market, you always pay more than the going rate for what you're buying."

"It is an unusual situation," Tancred said.

"I'll say. What's Merrill's angle?"

"He wants to help support this clinic. He and I have known each other for many years." Tancred shrugged. "And I did him a kindness several years ago when his daughter was in . . . a delicate situation."

"She was pregnant?"

Tancred shook his head. "No. Addicted to drugs. With my help, she was able to conquer her addiction. Now she is married and has a young child. Her husband is a decent sort who knows nothing of her past troubles."

"So you're blackmailing this guy Merrill into supplying you with cheap medicine?"

"Blackmail?" Tancred looked deeply offended by the very idea. "Of course not! As I said, Merrill is grateful to me and wants to help the clinic. That is all."

For a moment, Karen didn't say anything as she thought about what he had just told her. Then she took a breath, nodded, and said, "All right, Doctor, I'll help you out. What do you want me to do?"

Tancred nodded in relief. "Simply go to that address. Take a taxi. Merrill will meet you there. It is a warehouse belonging to his company. A truck will be waiting. You and Merrill will bring it back here."

"Can't he just bring the stuff here himself?"

"No, he insists that either I or my representative be with him at all times during the delivery. I believe he hopes that if he is caught, the presence of one of us will make it seem more like a legitimate arrangement."

"Good luck," Karen said under her breath. The whole thing sounded fishy to her. If she had to guess, she would have said that Merrill wanted Dr. Tancred there so he wouldn't have to take the fall by himself if anything went wrong. "Are you sure he'll agree to me taking delivery of the goods?"

"I'll call him. He'll have no choice but to agree if he wants the deal to be consummated. I'm sure it will be fine."

Karen wasn't that convinced. Crooks didn't like it when their plans got changed at the last minute, and no matter how much of a noble face Tancred wanted to put on it, this sounded like a crooked deal to her. Maybe the doctor was telling the truth about his part of it, but Karen was willing to bet that somebody, somewhere, was going to make some illicit bucks off of this arrangement.

So maybe she was the right one to handle it after all, she thought. She knew plenty of guys who operated on the shady side of the law. She had been around them for years. She had even fallen in love with one of—

She forced that thought out of her mind and said, "All right, make the call. I'll get my coat and start over there."

"Thank you, Miss Wells. I can't tell you—"

He didn't get a chance to tell her anything else, because at that moment Mrs. Tancred opened the office door again and stuck her head in to say, "Are you about ready, Gerald? We're going to be late for our dinner reservation."

"Yes, dear, I'm coming," Tancred said. "I just have to make one telephone call first."

"All right," Mrs. Tancred said. She looked at Karen, who was getting into her coat. "I hope you have a pleasant evening, Miss Wells."

"Thank you, Mrs. Tancred," Karen said. "I hope so too."

But for some reason, she had her doubts.

# FORTY-ONE

Mike Chastain leaned forward and cranked down the roadster's window as a burly figure in a plaid cap and a thick sweater loomed up out of the darkness. "Hello, Billy," he said.

The man touched a finger to the short brim of the cap. "Evenin', Mr. Chastain. How you doin'?"

"Fine," Chastain replied. "You ready?"

"Yes, sir." Billy pulled up the sweater to reveal the butt of a revolver stuck in the waistband of his trousers. "The guy won't give us no trouble."

"Lay off that unless you have to use it," Chastain cautioned.

"Yes, sir, I unnerstand."

Chastain nodded, and Billy turned to walk back up the alley toward the truck. He had left the engine running while he came over to check in with Chastain, and on this autumn night, with a chilly wind blowing in from the lake, the truck's exhaust made puffs of steam belch from its tailpipe.

Chastain left the car window down for a moment, enjoying the coolness. Then it got to be a little too much, so he closed the window and turned up the collar of his overcoat. That was the trouble with life, he told himself. All too quickly, too little became too much.

He had thought he was getting back into the rackets on a limited basis when he first threw in with Roger Hale. But it hadn't taken long until he was a full-blown criminal again. Whether he wanted to admit that to himself or not, deep down he knew it was true. There had been moments along the way when he could have pulled out, gone back to the way of life he'd been enjoying with Karen before he'd gotten involved with Hale. But each time he had hesitated, and the moment was gone like a snap of the fingers.

What was the old saying? In for a penny, in for a pound? Must've come from England, Chastain thought. The English called their money *pounds*. Whatever, he supposed it applied to him now. He was a crook again.

He turned the key and pressed the starter. The roadster's engine turned over and caught. It was a good car with plenty of power. Not armor-plated, but heavy enough to stop at least some bullets. All the serial numbers on it were long gone, and the license plate was clean, a phony that bore the same number as a similar vehicle that belonged to a priest over in Rockford. Chastain pulled out of the alley, Billy following behind him in the truck.

Normally, somebody else would handle this part of the job, but since it was the first one like this they'd pulled, Hale insisted that Chastain himself be there for it. "I'd do it myself, Mike," Hale had said when they got together at Chastain's penthouse for a drink. "But just in case there's any rough-and-tumble, I think you'd better go. I'm not as handy as I once was."

It was true that Hale still hadn't regained all his strength after being wounded in the belly. The doc who was taking care of him warned him that he might never be the same. But the doc was a lush who'd lost his license. If it had been him, Chastain often thought, he would find a real sawbones and pay the guy enough to keep quiet about treating the aftereffects of a bullet wound. If Hale would do that, then maybe he could get well.

But why should he bother when he had Chastain to do the dirty work for him? Chastain had asked himself *that* question often enough too.

He put that worry out of his mind as he followed the cones of illumination cast by the headlights toward Evanston. This would be a good haul tonight. He and Hale would make plenty of dough off the truckload of medicine. It had taken Hale a while to find a suitable mark and set up the job. He always said it was best to steal from other crooks, because they were less likely to go to the cops. This guy Merrill wasn't a real crook—he worked for the drug company—but he was mixed up in something underhanded. Chastain didn't really have the straight of it, but he knew Merrill wouldn't be in a hurry to go yelling to the law about how he'd had a whole shipment of medicine heisted. And since he wasn't a pro, he probably wouldn't put up a fight, either. According to the information Hale had gotten from a guy who worked in the warehouse, Merrill and some doctor were going to meet there tonight so that Merrill could turn the goods over to him. The doctor probably planned on soaking his rich patients plenty for the illicit drugs. He wouldn't squawk, either. Chastain grinned as he drove along the highway. Yeah, it was a sweet deal all around.

Except that when he approached the warehouse, a truck was already pulling out through a gate in the fence that enclosed the yard. Chastain looked at the warehouse. No other truck was there, so the one that was leaving had to have the goods on it. He grimaced as he checked the time. Still five minutes until eight. That bastard Merrill had moved up the deal.

Chastain grinned, his lips pulling back from his teeth. He could still salvage things. No way that truck could outrun the roadster. All he had to do was swing around and follow it. The road was pretty empty between here and Chicago. Just pull up alongside, flash a gat at the driver, and motion for him to pull over. That was all it would take.

The truck that had just left the warehouse rumbled past. Chastain couldn't tell anything about who was in the cab, but there couldn't be more than two guys. Billy had his cousin Dennis with him. Merrill and whoever was with him, probably that doctor, wouldn't be any match for Billy and Dennis.

Chastain hit the brakes and spun the wheel. The roadster wheeled around, leaving the highway for a second and bumping across the rough shoulder. Chastain wasn't worried about alerting the driver of the truck. He pressed on the accelerator and sent the car leaping after his quarry. A glance in the side mirror told him that Billy was turning the second truck around. That would take longer, since he'd have to back up, but it didn't matter. By the time Billy caught up, Chastain would have the other truck stopped. Chastain was sure of it. He was filled with confidence tonight.

The roadster surged ahead, knifing through the night. The truck ahead of it seemed to be lumbering faster now, as if its driver had noticed that he was being followed and wanted to get away.

Chastain poured on the speed. The highway was nearly empty. Only an occasional car passed going in the other direction. People who were going into Chicago for the evening were already there.

Chastain swung out into the other lane. He edged the roadster up alongside the truck. Keeping his left hand on the wheel, he reached under his coat with the right and produced a short-barreled revolver. He leaned forward and extended the gun across the seat toward the passenger side window. His eyes darted back and forth between the road in front of him and the cab of the truck beside him. He could see a man behind the wheel of the truck but couldn't tell if the guy was alone or not. The man turned a frightened face toward him, and Chastain knew he had seen the gun. He made a curt gesture with the weapon, waving the truck driver toward the shoulder.

Instead of complying, the driver suddenly swung the truck toward Chastain's roadster. Instinctively, Chastain jerked the wheel to get the car out of the way. That made him slow down too, and the truck surged ahead. Lights topped a rise in front of Chastain. He cursed and hit the brakes, dropping back and swerving behind the truck, out of the way of the oncoming traffic. The car going the other way whipped past.

Furious that the driver of the truck wasn't cooperating with him, Chastain fed more gas to the roadster. Its front bumper tapped the back of the truck. That'd shake up the son of a bitch, he thought. He pulled out again and sped up.

The truck driver must have had the foot feed floored, but he couldn't get away. Chastain drew alongside him again, and this time he didn't bother brandishing the gun. In fact, he laid it on the seat beside him and used both hands to grip the wheel. If the guy wanted to be cute about this, he was about to find out just how cute Mike Chastain could be.

Chastain turned the wheel to the right. The roadster was lighter than the truck, of course, but it was still a heavy car and had a powerful engine. Its right front fender slammed into the truck's left front fender. Chastain knew that by the time he was able to force the truck off the road, his car might sustain quite a bit of damage. But in a few hours it could be fixed up good as new in any of the garages across the city that were run by the boys in the mob. Just take a fender off a hot car of the same model and slap it on. It would be expensive, of course, but Chastain could afford it.

After tonight, he was going to be richer than ever.

He backed off, and then rammed the truck again. He saw the wheel spinning in the driver's hands as the guy fought to control it. The truck's right front wheel went off the pavement and into the gravel. It skidded, and then the driver managed to haul the truck back onto the road. Chastain hit it again. This time both wheels left the pavement on that side of the road. The truck slid farther off the pavement. It started to tip. Chastain slowed down a little to watch as the truck skidded along the embankment next to the road and then went over onto its side. Dust and gravel flew into the air. The truck's rear end tried to swap places with the front end. It came to a stop lying on its side, twenty feet off the pavement, perpendicular to the road.

It occurred to Chastain that medicine usually came in glass bottles. He hoped the stuff was well packed and hadn't gotten all busted up in the wreck. He felt a surge of irritation at himself as he braked the roadster to a stop. He had let his temper get the best of him.

He left the roadster half on and half off the highway. A hundred yards or so behind him, the truck being driven by Billy was still struggling to catch up. With the pistol gripped tightly in his hand, Chastain ran toward the overturned truck. Merrill probably wasn't armed, but Chastain wasn't taking any chances. He had already been foolish once tonight, when he decided to run the truck off the road.

"Climb out of there! Now, damn it!" he shouted as he came up to the truck. The cab seemed to be intact, just crumpled some on the passenger side where it had landed. If there had been someone riding over there, they might have gotten hurt, but the driver ought to be okay. Chastain circled the front of the truck, keeping the gun trained on the cab as he did so. Steam shot up from the busted radiator and blocked his view for a second, but then it cleared and he could see the shattered windshield. He came closer and ordered again, "Get out of there!"

Somewhere not far away, a siren whined into life.

Chastain's head snapped up at the sound. That was a police siren, and it wasn't more than half a mile distant. What the hell were the cops doing out here? That was just his luck, to have a patrol come along to investigate the wrecked truck. He glanced at the highway and saw the other truck easing to a stop behind his car. Billy opened the door, stepped out on the running board, and called, "Cops coming, boss! What do we do?"

Just like that, everything was shot to hell, Chastain thought. His mouth filled with bitterness. The night had started out looking so good, and now it had turned to shit.

He waved his free hand at Billy. "Get out of here! Move!"

Billy nodded and got back in the truck. With a grinding of gears, it pulled around Chastain's roadster and took off toward Chicago.

Another siren howled in the night, coming from a different direction this time. Chastain looked around, saw flashing lights coming toward him from half a mile away. He felt panic nibbling around at the edge of his mind. He was going to be trapped here with this wrecked truck, pinned down by cops coming from both directions at once. He needed to get back to the roadster and get the hell out of here. Maybe he could find a side road somewhere close by and get off the highway before the cops spotted him. He thought there was a road not too far ahead that turned off to the left.

But something drew him on toward the wrecked truck. He wanted to know what had happened to the driver and anybody else who was in there. He bent down to get a better look through the shattered windshield. "Hey!" he called. "Anybody in there?"

A muffled groan answered him. He moved closer. A man's voice, weak and thin with pain, said, "H-help . . . help me . . ."

Chastain wished he had a flashlight. The truck's headlights were still burning, and that threw some reflected glow into the cab. So were the dashboard lights. He saw a man reach up and grab the steering wheel. The guy pulled himself into view. His face was dark with blood.

"H-help," he said again.

"Should've pulled over, buddy," Chastain said.

"There's . . . a woman . . ."

Chastain stiffened. A woman? There was a woman in the truck? That made things even worse. The truck might catch on fire, and if it did, the gas tank could go up. A part of him wanted to get the guy and the woman out of there before that happened, but there was no time. Those sirens were closer now.

He had to see. He took another step and put his left hand on the top of the cab, leaning forward to get a look through the broken windshield. By the faint greenish glow of the dashboard lights, he saw the crumpled shape of the woman as she lay on the passenger side door. Her hair was around her face, thick curly hair that hid her features. Even in the bad light, Chastain could tell that it was a dark, lustrous red. His insides flopped over and turned cold as he realized there was something familiar about the woman.

The man with blood on his face reached down and gripped her shoulder and yelled, "Miss Wells! Miss Wells!"

Mike Chastain could only stand there and stare at the motionless form of the woman and listen to the screaming of the police sirens as they came closer.

# FORTY-TWO

Pete Corey's foot jabbed from the gas to the brake and back again as he fought to keep the car on the road but still get all the speed he could out of it. He whipped around the curves and almost lost control a couple of times, but he managed to keep the vehicle rocketing toward the scene of the crash up ahead. In the passenger seat, Carl Bowden cranked the siren with one hand and held the microphone of the police radio with the other. "Be careful!" Bowden shouted into the microphone. "They'll be armed and dangerous!" He lowered the mike and glanced over at Corey. "I gotta hand it to you, Pete. You got a nose for trouble."

Pete's hands tightened even more on the wheel. "Yeah, but I don't know if that's Chastain up there. I don't even know what's in that truck."

"Something worth hijacking, that's for sure."

Yeah, there was no doubt of that, Pete thought. What in blazes had the Wells woman gotten herself mixed up in?

The chief of detectives had given Pete hell for continuing to run frequent stakeouts on Karen Wells. "She broke up with that louse Chastain," the chief had said. "You told me yourself, Corey, that she ain't been to his penthouse in weeks. Forget about her."

Pete hadn't been able to forget, though. Every instinct he possessed told him that sooner or later, Karen would lead him to something he could use to get Chastain. He had even tailed her some on his own time, since he and Bowden had other cases to work and not that many hours to spare on something the department no longer considered a high priority. They weren't able to get the goods on every racketeer in the city, so why try? Chastain had had his moment in the sun, so to speak, and when Corey and Bowden hadn't been able to turn up anything to justify an arrest or even enough to pull Chastain in for questioning, the chief of detectives had decided to move on. Chastain's folder went in the inactive file.

But tonight, in the absence of anything more pressing to occupy their time, Pete and his partner had staked out the medical clinic on the South Side where Karen Wells worked one day a week. It was some sort of charity operation. After tailing Karen there the first time, Pete had looked into it enough to know that it was run by some doctor named Tancred, a swanky Gold Coast pill pusher. Guy must have a guilty conscience over something, Pete decided, and he was trying to make it feel better by helping the poor.

When Karen left the clinic tonight in a taxi, Pete figured she was headed either to her apartment or to the Dells. Instead, she had taken the taxi 'way the hell out and gone to Evanston. It had dropped her off at a warehouse, where she met some guy in a suit. Bowden had called in the address and discovered that the warehouse belonged to a pharmaceutical company. In the meantime, Karen got in the truck with the guy, and they drove off.

Pete had been about to tail them when he spotted the long, heavy roadster turning around to follow the truck along the highway back toward Chicago. Right after the roadster turned around, another truck came along and did the same.

Curiouser and curiouser. Pete didn't know where that phrase came from, but it sure as hell applied to what he was seeing tonight.

He joined the convoy, staying so far back from the second truck that it would be just a fluke if anybody spotted him.

Then, from the top of a rise, he had seen the roadster trying to run the first truck off the highway. At that moment, the possibility that Chastain might be involved in this leaped into Pete's head. Maybe the girl hadn't really broken up with Chastain after all. Maybe she was acting as a spotter for him, and that was him up there trying to hijack whatever was in the truck. But that would mean Chastain was risking Karen's life too, and that didn't seem right. Pete didn't know. All he was certain of was that he had to catch up. That need became even more pressing when he saw the truck go off the road and crash onto its side.

Bowden had called in the pursuit, and a patrol car a couple of miles up the road toward Chicago was responding. They had the roadster and the second truck bottled up, Pete thought. This was pure luck instead of a planned trap, but they had to take advantage of it anyway.

"C'mon, baby, c'mon," Pete murmured to the car as he urged more speed out of it. Another eighth of a mile and they'd be there.

\*　\*　\*

Billy saw the flashing lights up ahead and started to move his foot from the gas to the brake, but then he tromped down harder on the accelerator. Not that it did any good. The truck was already running full out. It wouldn't go any faster.

"Oh, shit, Billy!" Dennis said from the passenger side of the seat. "There are cops up there!"

"I see 'em," Billy said. "Just because they're there don't mean they're lookin' for us."

"Why else would they be out here?"

"Hell, I don't know!" Billy said. "Chasin' some goddamn jay-walker, maybe?"

"All the way from Chicago?" Dennis said, as if he took Billy's suggestion seriously. Dennis always had been a pretty dim bulb, Billy thought. Not smart like him.

Now Billy started to brake. He had to think, had to do the smart thing. As he brought the truck down to a normal rate of speed, he said, "We'll act like we don't know anything's wrong. If we just drive along like we ain't got a care in the world, maybe the cops won't even stop us."

"But what if they do?" Dennis insisted. "This truck don't belong to us."

Billy frowned. Dennis should've been too dumb to think of that. Maybe he wasn't the smart one after all. He said slowly, "We'll tell them it belongs to a friend of ours who's just lettin' us use it. Yeah, that oughta work."

"But what if it don't?"

"But but but!" Billy exploded. "Shut the fuck up with the buts!"

Dennis started to say something else, then thought better of it.

Pouting, he leaned back in his corner of the seat, putting as much distance as possible between him and his cousin.

Billy couldn't see the cop car's lights anymore, but a flashing glow played across the clouds in the sky, telling him that the cop was still up ahead. The truck lumbered around a bend in the road, and suddenly, there was the cop. The car was pulled across the road at a slant, blocking part of both lanes.

"It's a roadblock, Billy!" Dennis burst out, unable to control himself at the sight of the patrol car. "They got us!"

As his heart pounded with fear and excitement, Billy forgot all about his plan to try to bluff their way through. Instead he floored the gas pedal and shouted, "I can get around 'em!"

Dennis clutched at his right arm. "No, Billy, the road's too narrow!"

Billy shoved him away. There was enough room behind the patrol car to get around it on the shoulder. He was sure of it. He twisted the wheel to send the truck bumping and rolling in that direction.

A couple of blue-uniformed cops waved their arms to try to get the truck to stop. When Billy ignored them, they pulled their guns and ran behind the patrol car. Billy saw muzzle flashes winking in the darkness as the cops opened fire.

Glass flew in every direction as bullets shattered the truck's windshield. Billy threw up his left arm to try to protect his face, but he was too slow. A fierce pain stung his eyes, as suddenly he couldn't see anymore. Hot wetness trickled down his cheeks like tears, but he knew he wasn't crying. The steering wheel slid through his hands, spinning wildly out of control. Dennis screamed as the truck swerved back toward the police car.

Billy could no longer see what was about to happen, but somehow he wasn't surprised when the truck slammed into the patrol car. He was thrown forward. His head went through what was left of the windshield. Jagged glass shredded his flesh and ripped his arteries. He was wetter than ever, but cold now instead of hot. And something was wrong with his insides. It took him a second to realize that the steering column had snapped off and the broken end had punched right through him, pushing his guts out the huge hole in his back.

The gas tanks of both vehicles blew up then, so he didn't have to worry about any of it anymore.

\*   \*   \*

Mike Chastain had no idea how long he had been standing there staring at Karen. All he knew when he snapped back to himself was that the cops were close now, too damned close.

He stood there for a moment longer, torn between the desire to go to Karen and see how badly she was hurt, and the instinctive need to run from the cops. Seeing her here like this was so unexpected, he thought at first he must be dreaming. But the guy had called her Miss Wells. There was no doubt it was really her.

Somewhere down the road toward Chicago, there was a crash and then an explosion. That was enough to tip the scales. Chastain's indecision vanished. He turned and ran toward his car.

One of the sirens had stopped, but the other was close now. Chastain made it to the roadster and threw himself behind the wheel. A hundred yards away, back toward Evanston, a car came into view. Chastain knew from the sound of the siren and the way the headlights swerved as the driver wrestled the vehicle around the curve that it was a police car, even if it didn't have any flashing lights on it. He threw the roadster into gear, tromped on the gas, and let out on the clutch. The roadster leaped ahead so abruptly that Chastain feared for a second it would stall.

The engine kept running with a smooth purr, though. Chastain glanced in the mirror. The cops were about fifty yards behind him, but already he was beginning to pull away from them again. The roadster had a lot more power than their car. They wouldn't be able to catch him.

He swung around a curve and saw flames leaping into the sky ahead of him. He knew instantly the fire was the result of the crash and explosion he had heard. It was difficult to look right into the inferno, but he thought he saw the outline of a truck. That would be the truck Billy was driving, he thought. Dumb son of a bitch was probably roasting in there right now, along with his cousin.

The worst part of it was that the flaming wreckage blocked the whole road. Chastain wasn't even sure if he could get around it on the shoulder.

He wasn't going to get the chance to try. A couple of uniformed cops were up there close by the burning wreck. They turned toward him as his headlights caught them, and their hands came up with guns in them. He had no doubt that if he tried to get past, they would open fire on him.

The thought of maybe someday having to shoot it out with the cops was something that everybody in his line of work had to live with. But not tonight, Chastain told himself. Not with Karen lying back there in that other wrecked truck, maybe hurt bad, maybe already dead. And it was his fault. He wasn't sure yet how he felt about that, but he knew it was bad. He knew he didn't want to die until he had sorted it all out, until he was certain what her condition was.

He jammed on the brakes and spun the wheel.

The roadster responded, the rear end sliding around in a controlled skid that left the car facing back the way it had come. Facing the police car that was rushing toward him with its siren still howling. The roadster's tires were smoking a little from the sharpness of the turnaround.

Chastain sat there for a second while he rolled down the window beside him and switched the pistol from his right hand to his left. Then he gripped the wheel with his right and hit the gas.

"Shit!" Bowden yelled. "The bastard's coming straight at us!"

Pete saw the roadster's headlights loom up in front of him, so bright that they almost blinded him. But he could still see well enough to pick up the muzzle flashes as the driver of the roadster stuck a gun out the window and blazed away at them. He heard one of the bullets smack into the front of the car. He was thinking about trying to get his own gun out so he could return the fire when the left front tire blew out with a loud bang. Pete didn't know if the guy in the roadster had hit it with a lucky shot or if the crappy rubber had just given out. Didn't matter. Either way, the car was slewing around the road, out of control and threatening to roll over. Sparks shot into the air as the tire shredded off the rim and metal dragged along the pavement. For a second, Pete thought they were going to crash head-on into the roadster. That'd serve the guy right for blowing out their tire. Then, in a flash, the roadster jerked aside and shot past them. The police car careened on down the road for another fifty yards before it came to a shuddering stop.

Pete was out of the car before it stopped moving completely. He saw the red taillights of the roadster speeding away and jerked out his service revolver. He emptied the gun after the roadster, but he knew he wasn't doing a damned bit of good. The roadster was too far away and going too fast. Pete slowly lowered the revolver.

He turned to see Bowden talking to a couple of harness bulls, probably the guys who had been closing in from the other direction. Pete figured they had blocked the road, and the truck had run into their car and exploded. Bowden turned and trotted over to him, puffing from the exertion.

"We better go back to that other crash, see how bad they're hurt," Bowden said.

Pete nodded as he reloaded his gun. "Yeah, I hated to just drive on by, especially knowing the Wells woman was in there, but I wanted to catch that roadster."

Bowden jerked a thumb over his shoulder at the uniformed cops and said, "These guys will use our radio to call for an ambulance. I guess the radio still works."

"Don't see why it wouldn't," Corey said.

He and Bowden started running back up the road. Neither of them was in the greatest shape, nor were they built for running. Between puffs, Bowden said, "I thought for sure that guy . . . was gonna hit us."

"So did I." Pete was thinking about the first wrecked truck. Karen Wells had been in the cab; he was pretty sure of that. He had seen her climb in back at the warehouse, and the truck hadn't stopped anywhere so that she could get out. That meant she'd been in the crash. He hoped she was all right.

They jogged around the curve and headed along the straightaway toward the overturned truck. As they came closer, they saw that the guy who'd been driving had crawled out of the wreckage, and he must have pulled the woman out as well because she was sitting up at the edge of the pavement while the guy paced around nervously. Pete felt a surge of relief. Karen didn't look like she was hurt too bad.

She and the man with her both looked scared as Pete and Bowden hurried up to them out of the night. Bowden called, "Take it easy, folks, we're cops."

"It's Pete Corey, Miss Wells," Pete added. He wished he wasn't breathing quite so hard as he came up to her and knelt beside her. "Are you all right?"

She nodded and lifted a tentative hand toward her head. "I just hit my head and got knocked out for a while. I've got a real goose egg."

"What about you, buddy?" Bowden asked the driver. "You're bleedin' pretty good."

"My head's cut," the man said. "I'm not sure when it happened. But it looks worse than it is. Scalp wounds always bleed a lot."

"Well, there'll be an ambulance on the way in a few minutes, if it's not already." Bowden looked past them at the wrecked truck. "What the hell happened?"

"This . . . this lunatic came up beside us," the man said, waving his arms for emphasis. "He pointed a gun at me and gestured like he wanted me to pull over. I . . . I didn't want to, so I tried to get away from him. He ran into us, forced us off the road."

"Why didn't you just stop like he wanted?" Bowden asked. He frowned as instincts honed by years of dealing with suspicious characters kicked in. "You got something in that truck you didn't want to give up?"

"N-no, that's not it. I was just afraid—"

"Afraid of what?"

"That he was a thief or a killer! He looked like a madman, I tell you."

"What *did* he look like?" Corey asked. He turned his attention back to Karen Wells. "Did you see him, Miss Wells?"

She looked up at him and nodded. "Yes, I did. I got a very good look at him while he was trying to get Mr. Merrill here to stop."

"And did you recognize him?" Corey asked, his voice taut with tension.

"No," Karen Wells said, looking straight at him as she shook her head. "I never saw the man before in my life."

*   *   *

Chastain's hand was shaking so badly that the key rattled in the lock as he slid it in the door of his penthouse. He didn't like that. Hale was supposed to be waiting for him inside, and Hale had good hearing. He would know now that Chastain was coming in.

The hell with it. Hale would know soon enough anyway.

Chastain turned the knob with his left hand. It was shaking too. But as he slid his right hand under his coat and closed his fingers around the butt of the gun, that hand became rock steady. All he needed to do was hold a gun, and his jittery nerves started to smooth out. He took a deep breath as he stepped into the apartment and eased the door closed behind him. He was as smooth now as fine whiskey and a smoky blues number.

*Don't think about that,* he told himself. *Not yet.*

As he moved through the foyer, Hale called out, "That you, Mike?"

Chastain forced his voice into some semblance of normalcy as he answered, "Who else would it be?" He reached the top of the two steps down into the sunken living room. The lights were dim, but he could see Hale on the other side of the room, sitting in a chair near the windows that overlooked the sparkling panoply of the Loop. The cities on the coasts might be blacked out because of the war, but here in the middle of the continent, nobody was worried about being bombed or shelled by the Japs or the Nazis.

369

Hale took a drag on his cigarette, making the coal glow red in the half-darkness. He set the cigarette aside and lifted a glass to his lips. When he had taken a sip of the drink, he said, "How did it go? Easy, right? And now we're the proud owners of a whole truckload of medicine that's going to make us a small fortune."

"No," Chastain said. "Not quite."

Hale leaned forward and set the drink on a small table. "What happened?"

"The job went bad. We didn't get the drugs. And Billy and Dennis are dead."

"My God." Hale shook his head. "Are the cops after you?"

"I don't know, but if they're not, they will be soon. That guy Merrill got a good look at me. He can describe me."

Hale came to his feet, unfolding his body from the chair. "You'd better get out of town for a while, until this all blows over."

"I plan to, just not yet. I've got something else to do first."

Hale took a step toward him. "What could be more important than getting out of a jam like this?"

Chastain took the gun out of his pocket and said, "Killing you."

Hale stopped where he was, staring at Chastain across the living room. It was hard for Chastain to see his face, but he could tell from the way Hale stood so stiff and straight that he was surprised. After a moment, Hale said, "What are you talking about, Mike?"

"Merrill wasn't alone," Chastain said as he peered at Hale over the barrel of the gun. "Karen Wells was with him."

That was so unexpected that it jolted a "What?" out of Hale. After a second, Hale went on, "I don't understand. What does she have to do with this?"

"You got me," Chastain said. "But she was there, all right, in the cab of the truck with Merrill when it turned over and crashed between here and Evanston."

"Oh." Hale hesitated and then shrugged. "What can I say, Mike? It was a tough break. Was she killed?"

"I don't know yet."

"I'll find out and get word to you." Hale was trying to distract him, trying to act like everything was normal. It wasn't going to work.

"You've forgotten that I'm going to kill you."

"I was hoping *you'd* forgotten. Why do you have a grudge against me, Mike? I didn't have anything to do with her being there. Hell, it doesn't even make sense to me."

"I can't explain it, either, but I know if I hadn't gotten mixed up with you, Hale, Karen would be all right now. She'd probably be here, with me."

Hale's voice was sharp as he said, "You made your own decisions, buddy boy."

"And you lied to me," Chastain snapped back at him. "That first job we ever pulled together, when we heisted that load of meat, you said everything was arranged. And then you shot the guy in cold blood."

Hale lifted his cigarette to his mouth, took a drag on it. "Best way to shoot somebody. They can't make trouble when they don't know it's coming. That's the way you should have shot me tonight, if you really meant to do it."

He flicked the cigarette right into Chastain's face and threw himself sideways, clawing under his coat for a gun.

Chastain didn't budge. He let the cigarette hit him in the left cheek as he tracked the gun to the side, following Hale. His finger squeezed the trigger. The gun gave a wicked crack. Hale jerked and fell in an awkward sprawl on his face next to an expensive divan.

"Yeah, I'm to blame for what happened to Karen," Chastain said, "but you are too, Hale. If you hadn't come along, I'd have stayed out of the rackets."

Hale groaned and tried to push himself up on hands and knees. He lifted his head and turned to look at Chastain. His lips were drawn back in a grisly mockery of a grin. "You would've . . . gone back . . ." he said. "If I hadn't . . . come along with a deal . . . somebody else . . . would have."

"You're wrong."

"The hell . . . I am." Hale moaned again and swayed, then toppled to the side. But as he fell, he picked up the gun that had dropped out of its holster and landed underneath him. He raised his arm and fired twice. Chastain felt the wind of the first bullet lash at his face. The second one tore through his left arm, halfway between the elbow and shoulder, missing the bone. The slug's impact turned him halfway around. He staggered, caught his balance, and fired two more shots at Hale. Hale twitched as the bullets struck his body, but he didn't feel them. He was already dead.

Chastain stumbled a couple of steps closer. He wanted to empty the pistol into Hale's head, but there was no need. And he didn't have any time to waste, either. This apartment house was a ritzy place. Somebody would have heard the shots and called the cops, and they would respond in a hurry when they found out the address. He had to get back downstairs. He'd left the roadster in the alley and come into the building through the basement entrance, so the doorman wouldn't see him. He could get out the same way. Then he'd have to get his arm patched up and see about leaving town. Chicago wasn't a safe place anymore.

Without even looking around, he turned and stumbled toward the door. There was nothing here in the penthouse he wanted to take with him. None of it meant anything without Karen. He knew now what he had lost, knew as well that it could never be regained.

Leaving the penthouse door open behind him, he went to the service elevator. By the time it arrived, he was feeling light-headed. He knew it was from loss of blood. The left sleeve of his coat was soaked. He fumbled with the elevator controls, finally got the lever moved to the right position. The door clanged shut, and with a lurch the elevator started down.

With any luck, Chastain thought as he slumped against the wall of the little chamber, he wouldn't bleed to death before it got to the bottom.

# FORTY-THREE

When the orders came at last in late October for the Americans to leave England, no time was wasted putting them into effect. Joe and Dale were told one afternoon to be ready to leave that night. As they packed their gear, Dale said, "I wonder where we're going. I've been hearing a lot of talk lately about Russia. You think we're going to help out old Uncle Joe, Joe?"

"Uncle Jo-Jo? We don't have an Uncle Jo-Jo. You mean Jo-Jo the Dog-faced Boy in the circus?"

Dale grinned and threw a rolled-up pair of socks at Joe's head. "I'm talkin' about Stalin, lamebrain."

Joe caught the socks and threw them back at Dale. "I don't know where we're going," he said. "I'm just glad to be going."

Only the second part of that statement was true. Thanks to Arthur Yates, Joe had a pretty good idea of their destination. But ever since his visit to the house near Kensington Park, he had kept that knowledge to himself. He didn't want it getting out that Arthur had revealed information he shouldn't have. The last thing Joe wanted was to jeopardize Arthur's job at the ministry. He was convinced that the work had saved Arthur's life.

Besides, he didn't want to do anything to separate Arthur from Yeoman Gretchen Ames. Having her around probably had done Arthur a lot of good too.

Their duffel bags were packed by the time a truck came around the camp to collect them. They would carry with them only knapsacks, helmets, weapons, and the uniforms on their backs. The duffel bags wouldn't be returned to them until they reached their destination. More trucks arrived, and the men were loaded on them and driven to the train station. A thin, cold rain had started to fall, and as the truck carrying Joe and Dale pulled away, Joe looked back at the camp that had been his home for a couple of months. He didn't feel any nostalgia or regret about leaving the place.

He was on his way back to the war, and this time, he would be serving under the Stars and Stripes.

*      *      *

The train carried them to Southampton, and in the predawn hours, it lurched to a stop beside the docks. As Joe and Dale climbed down from the car into which they'd been packed like cattle with scores of other soldiers, Joe could see the sides of transport ships looming high above the docks. The men marched through a long shed where clerks checked them off endless lists. It was still raining. The moisture in the air created a glowing nimbus around the few lights that were burning. The heavy atmosphere seemed to muffle sound too, so that the normally hard-edged *tramp, tramp, tramp* of feet became instead a soft murmur of movement leading aboard the ships. It was a solemn occasion as thousands of men climbed steep ramps and went onto the ships in near-silence.

So many men were being moved onto so many ships that it took a couple of days to load them all, along with their gear, which was taken aboard in huge cargo nets. Joe began to realize just what an awesome undertaking this mission was. It had taken a long time— too damned long in the minds of many—for the United States to take an active part in the war in this part of the world. Now that was about to be remedied with a vengeance.

As usual, the enlisted men and noncoms were quartered in the cargo holds below decks. These were big rooms filled with long wooden tables that had benches on each side. Instead of the cramped, built-in bunks that Joe and Dale had suffered in on previous ocean voyages, the quarters on these transports were equipped with canvas hammocks that could be slung on hooks above the tables at night. It was an odd sleeping arrangement, but from the first night, Joe found that he preferred it to regular bunks. The hammocks were taken down during the day so that the men could eat, play cards, read, write letters, or otherwise pass the time at the tables. Big-band music was piped over the ship's public address system, as well as news from the BBC, most of it concerning the fierce battle going on in the deserts of North Africa as the British Eighth Army broke out from El Alamein and tried to force Rommel to retreat.

Joe and Dale thought about their friends who probably were in the middle of that effort and hoped that they were all right. Joe couldn't help but wonder if soon he and his brother would be in the middle of the fight too.

When the time came for the ships to sail, the troops were allowed up on deck. What looked like the entire population of Southampton had turned out to bid farewell to them. Joe and Dale stood at the railing and looked at the throngs of civilians that packed every available inch of the docks. Flags waved, including quite a few American ones, and cheers rang out. Dale watched for a few minutes, then asked with a grin, "Are they happy because we're going off to fight the Nazis, or because we won't be around here drinking their beer and chasing their women anymore?"

Joe laughed. "A little of both, probably."

With slow, stately majesty, the ships of the convoy pulled away from the docks. As they moved out into the Channel, corvettes and cruisers fell in around them as an escort. Most of the transports were British ships, but they were manned now by American crews, Joe had heard. The warships forming their protective screen had their original British crews, because the Brits knew the waters of the Channel and knew how to navigate past the Rock of Gibraltar into the Mediterranean. That familiarity could come in handy, because German U-boats were still prowling all along the convoy's route.

Battle drills were held starting on the first day of the voyage. Other than those who served in the ships' crews, the Americans had nothing to do during those drills. Orders were clear: Everyone was to stay in their quarters. No going on deck during a drill, or especially during a real battle.

Dale groused about that. "Hell, I saw a torpedo nearly hit the ship we were on when we went to Egypt. I know how to handle myself when there's trouble."

"You'd just be in the way up top," Joe told him. "Or would you rather they'd assign you to a gun?"

"Damn right. That's a good idea."

Joe just shook his head and went back to writing on the sheets of paper he had spread out in front of him on one of the tables in the cargo hold that served as the quarters for their company. He'd been scribbling on them for hours, writing an espionage story set in the shadowy back alleys of Cairo, featuring a stalwart American hero and a slinky Egyptian femme fatale who was on the hero's side— maybe. Or maybe not. The hero wasn't sure, and at this point, neither was Joe. He'd hesitated when the idea came to him, thinking that maybe his memories of Melinda were still too recent and too painful to be mined for fiction. But maybe writing something loosely based on what had happened to him would help him get over the anger and sadness he still felt when he thought too long about her. Anyway, he was hoping he could sell the yarn to Kenneth White at *Adventure* or Dorothy McIlwraith at *Short Stories*. When he was finished, he would bundle up the pages and send them home, along with a letter telling his mother where to submit the story. She could type it up and send it in. Best to keep plugging away, Joe told himself. That way the editors wouldn't forget about him by the time the war was over.

For the first couple of days, the convoy didn't get in any hurry as it made its way along the French coast. The crews test-fired all the guns, so the roar of artillery went on almost all the time. Rumors flew as fast and furious as the shells from the guns. Some of the men, like Dale, were convinced that the convoy's ultimate destination was Russia. Others thought the ships were bound for Norway or Iceland or even—wishful thinking—back home to America. Joe didn't hear much talk about North Africa. That had been popular speculation at one time, but not anymore.

However, men who were good at telling what direction the ships were traveling began to notice that their route led generally southwestward, around the curve of the French mainland. Sure, they could always turn and head back north once they reached the open sea, and that would get them to any of those other rumored destinations. But Africa lay this way too, and on a more direct route than the others.

More ships rendezvoused with the convoy. Word got around

quickly that they were transports that had steamed here straight from the States. That seemed to be what everybody had been waiting for. The convoy put on more speed, and soon the ships were cutting rapidly through the waters of the Atlantic, with the Iberian Peninsula off to the east.

On the fifth day out from Southampton, officers showed up in the cargo holds and began passing out leaflets to the men. When Dale got his, he looked at it and then raised his eyes in surprise to Joe. "Africa?" he said. "We're going to Africa?"

"North Africa," Joe said as he took one of the leaflets. He had never seen one like it before. It gave a quick rundown on the geography, peoples, and customs of Morocco, Algeria, Tunisia, and Libya. As Joe looked at the map printed inside, he recognized the names of some of the places in Libya because they had been frequent subjects of discussion among the British soldiers in Cairo. That was the area where Rommel had been operating over the past year. Farther west, Morocco, Algeria, and Tunisia were controlled by France—or rather, by the Vichy government of France, which was nothing more than a puppet of the Nazis.

After the German occupation of the northern two-thirds of France during May and June of 1940, Marshal Philippe Pétain had arranged an armistice that allowed France to retain nominal control over the southern part of the country, with the government centered at the town of Vichy. Even so, the Nazis were really running things, and to the Allies, Vichy had become a dirty word, and so had *collaborator*, especially when applied to Pétain, once a French hero of the First World War. Joe knew that as long as that was the case, the French would be their enemies, albeit maybe reluctant ones, in North Africa.

The rest of the leaflet consisted of advice—meaning thinly veiled orders—on how members of the United States Army were expected to conduct themselves in foreign countries. There was to be no looting, no commandeering of goods or services unless necessary, no unwanted advances made to the local women. Those were typical instructions, Joe supposed. They probably wouldn't be followed to the letter, but at least they would help keep some of the men in line.

"You think we'll ever get back to Cairo?" Dale asked.

"Why?" A thought occurred to Joe. "Are you worried about that girl, what was her name—"

"Betty," Dale said. He shrugged and looked vaguely uncomfortable. "Betty Rawlinson. I went out with her a few more times after that blind date, you know. She's a nice kid. Not much of a looker, mind you, but pretty smart."

"You seem to have forgotten about her fast enough once we got back to England."

"I got a letter from her—" Dale shook his head. "Ah, hell, forget it. We got other things to worry about."

Joe nodded. "Like an invasion."

Dale sat down on one of the benches and studied his leaflet with a frown. "If we're going to one of these places, does that mean we'll be fighting Frenchies instead of Krauts?"

Joe straddled the bench and said, "Could be. Remember when we saw General de Gaulle in London?"

"You saw him. I still don't know the guy from Adam. The one in the Bible, I mean, not Bergman."

"Well, de Gaulle's heading up the Free French movement, but most of the French military is still following orders from Vichy, and those orders start out in Berlin."

Dale shook his head. "I don't get it. Why would the French want to fight us? We're trying to help them."

"You know how they feel about the British. They can't stand 'em. That goes all the way back to Napoleon, maybe even farther. Things got worse a few years ago when France fell to the Nazis and the Royal Navy sunk four French battleships so Hitler wouldn't get his hands on them. That just made them more determined than ever not to get along with the British. And who's our partner in this operation?"

"Yeah, the Limeys," Dale said, nodding. "And with that nutty little Austrian paperhanger runnin' things back in France, the French have gotta be scared to cross him."

"Add all that up, and it means if we go ashore in Morocco or Algeria, the French forces there will try to stop us."

"That's a damned shame. I'd whole lot rather kill Krauts."

"Hang around for a while," Joe said. "I expect you'll get your chance."

378

*　　*　　*

Over the next few days, the American troops learned more about their mission. It was called Operation Torch, and when Joe heard that, he recalled a cryptic comment Colin Richardson had made about a torch being lit. He realized then that this joint American-British invasion must have been in the planning stages for months. Now it was finally coming to fruition as the massive convoy, which would split into three separate task forces, steamed toward North Africa.

The Western Task Force, under the command of General George S. Patton, was bound for Casablanca, on the Moroccan coast a hundred and fifty miles south of the Strait of Gibraltar.

The Central Task Force, composed mainly of the U.S. II Corps under the command of Major General Lloyd R. Fredenhall, was to land at Oran, in Algeria. Joe and Dale, as members of the U.S. First Armored Division, were part of this task force. Neither of them knew anything about Oran except that it was a major seaport, and that it was expected to be defended heavily by the French.

The Eastern Task Force was more of a mixture of American and British forces and was bound for the port of Algiers. Major General Charles W. Ryder of the U.S. 34th Division would be in overall command of this part of the invasion, but once Algiers was in the hands of the Allies, command would be turned over to one of the British generals, Sir Kenneth Anderson.

The whole thing made sense to Joe. The Allies were trying to make it look like Operation Torch was primarily an American effort, in hopes that the French defenders wouldn't put up as much resistance when the troops came ashore. Putting together an invasion like this must have taken a huge amount of work, not only the logistical task of getting the men and machines of war from one place to another but also figuring out what the responses of the enemy were likely to be. Especially when the U.S. really wanted that enemy—the French—on the same side with them.

One thing certain was that the Allied forces on these transports would not be joining the British Eighth Army under General Montgomery. The news from that front was inconclusive. The battles were still going on and seemed to be at a stalemate.

Joe spent some time pondering the situation, as well as working on his story. Dale frequented what was called the "wet canteen" because it sold hot tea and soft drinks. They sold no liquor, though, and Dale was bitterly disappointed about that.

About a week into the voyage Joe had the pages of his story spread in front of him when Dale came hurrying up. "Some of the guys are gettin' together a variety show," he said as he sat down at the table. "You want to be in it?"

With a frown, Joe stared at his brother. "What? Why would I want to be in a variety show?"

"I figured maybe we could do a brother act. You know, sing a few songs, maybe do a little soft-shoe, tell a joke or two."

"Are you out of your ever-lovin' mind? I'm no singer or dancer! Hell, I never even went to the vaudeville shows very much."

"Aw, come on! It'd be fun."

Joe shook his head. "Forget it. If you want to get up in front of a few thousand GIs and make a fool of yourself, go right ahead. But you'll have to find another partner."

Dale glared and said, "Maybe that's just what I'll do."

"Go right ahead. Knock yourself out."

"Yeah, yeah." Dale got to his feet. "You're just an old stick-in-the-mud, Joe, you know that?"

Joe turned his attention back to his story. "I've been called worse."

"You just wait until I've got everybody on the damned ship clapping for me. Then you'll be sorry."

"Yeah, that's just what I'll do. I'll wait."

Muttering curses, Dale stomped off. Joe lifted his head and watched him go. He supposed that Dale missed the applause. On numerous brilliant sunny afternoons, Dale had roared around the dirt tracks of the Midwest in the old jalopy he and Harry Skinner had souped up into a race car, and most of the time he had won. He had heard the applause and the cheers, seen the excited faces of the people who were rooting him on to victory, and that acclaim had been like food and drink to Dale. Then, suddenly, all of it was gone. Instead of being in the spotlight, he was just one of countless, faceless thousands in olive drab. His serial number meant as much or more than his name, and nobody gave a damn about all the races he had won. Yeah, it was probably tough on him, going from being a some-body to being a nobody. Joe couldn't say for sure, since he'd never been a somebody, but he figured that was why Dale had developed a sudden interest in being in the troops' variety show.

With a shake of his head, Joe went back to his writing. This was one time he couldn't give his brother a hand, whether he wanted to or not.

* * *

Still grumbling, Dale made his way to one of the higher decks where an area had been cleared in a cargo hold for rehearsals by the men who were going to take part in the show. Joe was always such a damned old fogey. He always had been. Always had his nose stuck in a book when he was a kid, and then when he got older he was either studying or reading or writing stories. It probably hadn't been a good idea in the first place to ask him to partner up for the show. Dale had heard Joe sing. Joe couldn't carry a tune in a tin bucket.

He'd just have to find somebody else, Dale decided. Either that or go it alone. A solo act. He lit a cigarette and grimaced as the thought crossed his mind. He didn't like that idea. He wouldn't have admitted it, but the thought of going out on stage by himself scared the shit out of him. Maybe he just wasn't meant to be a performer.

He stopped just inside the door of the cargo hold as he heard somebody singing. The voice was rich and deep, pure and powerful. The guy, whoever he was, had a good set of pipes, that was for sure. Dale couldn't see him because he was at the other end of the hold and there were too many men in the way. A few moments later, when the singer finished the song, the men standing around broke into applause. Several of them whistled their approval.

When the clapping died down, a man in the front of the crowd said, "Okay, March, you're in the show. Good job."

"Thanks, Al." The knot of men was breaking up now, and Dale could see the singer. He was a big, handsome, dark-haired GI. The man who had spoken to him was shorter and stockier, with close-cropped blond hair and a strong jaw. He had a corporal's two stripes on his uniform sleeve, and he was holding a clipboard. He turned and surveyed the men in the room.

"Anybody else want to audition?"

This was it, Dale thought. Do or die. Put up or shut up. Fish or cut bait. Shit or get off the—

"Okay," the blond corporal said. "That's it, then. We got the lineup for our show. I'll figure out the running order and then post it."

Well, so much for that, Dale told himself. He had waited too long. Sure, he could still speak up and say that he wanted to audition, but that would make him look like a jerk. He had never really wanted to be in show business, anyway.

With a sigh and a smile of secret relief, Dale turned and left the cargo hold. He was a driver, not a crooner. Better to leave that to the guys who were actually good at it, like Private March.

# FORTY-FOUR

He had seldom seen a bigger, more beautiful moon, Captain Neville Sharp thought as he sat in the open hatch of his tank. As he looked to the right and left, he saw tank after tank, a long line of General Grants and General Lees and Matildas that stretched into the distance. Behind them were armored cars, supply trucks, and speedy jeeps. Then came the infantry, seemingly endless ranks of men in khaki shirts and shorts, desert boots, and flat brown helmets. For weeks, both men and supplies had been flowing into Eighth Army headquarters at El Alamein. The Germans had tried but failed to cut the lines of supplies and reinforcements. Churchill had wanted an attack back in September, but somehow Montgomery had put him off. Good old Monty, Sharp thought. The beret and sweater Monty always sported were theatrical touches, designed to make the soldiers feel more of a kinship with him, and they worked. Even the men who were smart enough to know they were being manipulated responded to Monty's presence. They wanted to fight for him, wanted to win for him.

And that was a large part of any battle, right there.

Now, after weeks of preparation, the Eighth Army was ready to move. Rommel had thought he had the British bottled up at El Alamein, but in truth they had been biding their time and getting ready for a strike of their own. There was nothing Rommel could do about it. In fact, Rommel was no longer a factor in North Africa. He had fallen ill and gone to Austria to recuperate. That left General Georg Stumme in command of the Deutsche Afrika Korps. Sharp didn't know much about Stumme, but he would have been willing to wager that the German commander had no idea what was in store for him and for the army he commanded.

Over the past weeks, the British had carried out an elaborate deception. To make it appear that any attack they might launch would come along the southern part of their line, they'd had men out digging what appeared to be a water pipeline but was really nothing except empty gasoline cans placed end to end. This supposed pipeline led to an area in the desert where hundreds of supply crates had been stacked up, evidently in preparation for an attack. Those crates were empty, just like the cans that formed the "pipeline." Monty and his staff knew that the Germans were keeping an eye on them with scout planes and reconnaissance patrols and knew what they would think when they saw all those preparations. Trying to fool the enemy this way was a calculated risk, but one that stood a good chance of paying off.

Around El Alamein itself, where the troops were concentrated, all was calm. An air of suspended expectation hung over the desert. The tanks sat untended in the rear areas. At least, that was what it was hoped the Germans would believe. Earlier today, canvas covers had been rigged over the tanks to make them look like nothing more than innocuous supply trucks. Then they were moved to the front. To complete the deception, dummy tanks made of lightweight wooden frameworks and painted canvas were rolled into place where the real tanks had been. Montgomery and the chief architect of this plan, Lieutenant Colonel Charles Richardson, were doing everything possible to lull the Germans to sleep.

They would need that element of surprise, Sharp thought as he looked across the desert toward the German lines. Between the British and German fronts was a deadly minefield that the Germans called the Devil's Gardens. Over half a million mines were laid out there, ready to maim and kill. A devilish crop indeed, Sharp told himself. It would be up to the British sappers, armed with long-handled mine detectors, to find and defuse as many of those mines as they could. And all the while, British artillery and air forces would be laying down a barrage the likes of which had not been seen for decades. Soon, the desert was going to be transformed into a scene straight out of some medieval artist's vision of Hell.

Right now, however, it was one of the most peaceful places

Sharp had ever seen, with a warm breeze blowing and that gorgeous moon floating over it all.

"How much longer, sir?" Bert Crimmens asked from below.

Sharp looked at his watch. Almost 9:30. "It shouldn't be much longer now," he told Bert. He knew that his crew was getting anxious. They were shut up down there in the tank with nothing to do but wait. At least up here he got to look around and see what was going on, even if it wasn't much right now.

"I'll be bloody glad when this night is over," Bert muttered.

"As will we all," Sharp said.

He lifted his head a moment later as he heard a distant throbbing. The sound came from above and to the east. After a few seconds, Sharp identified it as airplane engines. The bombers were on their way from RAF aerodromes at Cairo and Alexandria. The bombs they carried in their bellies were part of the first deadly combination that Monty planned to throw at the Germans.

Sharp tugged on his leather helmet and settled the goggles over his eyes. Right behind the sappers would come the water carts, which would sprinkle water on the sand in an effort to hold down the dust, but it was inevitable that clouds of the fine, gritty stuff would be thrown up. Hundreds of tanks and trucks and thousands of men couldn't be moved across the desert without kicking up some dust.

"Here we go, lads," Sharp called down to Bert, Jeremy Royce, and Tom Hamilton. From his position in the driver's seat, Royce muttered something about it being bloody well time. Sharp grinned. The British army had known successes along the way as they contested the Germans' march across North Africa, but in the final analysis, they had lost more battles than they had won. They had been pushed back again and again, almost to the breaking point.

Tonight all that would change. Sharp felt it in his bones.

The bombers flew past, high overhead. Sharp held his breath. He listened close and thought he could hear the high-pitched keening of falling bombs. That was probably just his imagination, he told himself.

But when the bombs landed and the thunderous roar of their explosions rolled across the desert, that was no figment, no flight of fancy. Nor was the blast of artillery from the rear of the British position. Suddenly it was like being on the edge of the greatest thunderstorm in the world. Even in the heavy tank, Sharp could feel the ground shaking from the force of the blasts. Down below, Bert burst out with an awe-stricken "Blimey!"

The golden light of the full moon was now eclipsed by the fiery glow of exploding bombs, artillery shells, and mines. The whole sky took on a reddish-orange tint that was shot through by clouds of black smoke. Some of the barrage was directed toward the German lines, but many of the shells fell deliberately in the Devil's Garden. The explosions set off as many as a thousand mines at once, and those earth-shattering blasts threw uncounted tons of dirt and rock and dust into the air.

In the open hatch of his tank, Sharp leaned forward, impatience gripping him. He was ready to move up and get into the action, and he knew his crew felt the same way. But they had to hold back until the sappers cleared a path for them. It would be impossible to neutralize all the mines, so the sappers weren't even going to try. Instead they would concentrate on opening lanes wide enough for the tanks and trucks to advance. As the big guns in the rear were elevated, the shells stopped falling in the minefield. All the artillery fire was now directed at the German positions. With that, the sappers moved forward, thrusting their mine detectors in front of them, listening as if their lives depended on it—because they truly did—for the telltale ping that would tell them a mine had been located.

He wouldn't have had the nerves for that job, Sharp thought. There were two types of mines out there in the Devil's Gardens, antitank mines packed with high explosives and antipersonnel mines that fired a spray of deadly shrapnel. Once a sapper located either type of mine, he had to dig down in the sand to expose its triggering mechanism—carefully, carefully. The igniters on the antitank mines could be removed without setting off the charge. On the shrapnel mines, nails could be inserted into the tiny holes where their safety pins had been, and that rendered them harmless. Both procedures were tricky and dangerous, and as Sharp saw more explosions out on the desert, he knew that some of the sappers were giving their lives to open the way for the rest of the army.

Orange and green lights began to flicker into life. Sharp felt a thrill go through him as he spotted the markers. They delineated the areas that were cleared of mines. He moved the interphone mike closer to his mouth and said, "Let's go."

The tank lurched into motion. All along the line, others followed suit. Royce kept the rate of advance slow. The tank rolled down a slight incline and then started across the open desert. From up above, Sharp had a better view of the lights and the strips of white tape that marked the safe areas, so he directed Royce into the proper path. If they strayed, they risked death from an unexploded mine, of which there were thousands still littering the vicinity.

Progress was slow and nerve-wracking. What seemed like hours passed, and the tanks had advanced only a few hundred yards. The artillery barrage continued, though all the bombers had dropped their loads and turned back toward home. It had been planned that the armored divisions would lead the attack, but it was taking too long to clear the mines. Units of infantry were moved up around the tanks. The foot soldiers didn't need as much room and could advance faster. But without the protection of the tanks, would they be advancing into certain death?

That possibility didn't seem to worry them. Sharp saw them trotting forward, their steps crisp, their bayoneted rifles held high. The machineries of war were awe-inspiring things, but at the heart of any army were its men. And these were men he was proud to call his brothers-in-arms, Sharp thought.

The battle plan had called for an armored front to be punched all the way through the minefield by dawn. As the sky lightened in the east, Sharp realized that effort was going to be a failure. The advance had not penetrated nearly that far. From the chatter he had heard on the radio, he knew the Germans had been taken by surprise and thrown into chaos by the bombardment, but by now they were getting themselves organized again and were starting to fight back. Several tanks had been knocked out by enemy artillery fire. The British infantry was meeting fierce resistance from German ground troops. And the Luftwaffe was beginning to take a hand in the battle as well. Stuka dive-bombers and Messerschmitt fighters were wreaking havoc in parts of the British line. So far none of the planes had attacked Sharp's tank, but he had seen and heard them roaring through the sky overhead.

The sappers were still at their perilous work. Many of the mine detectors had malfunctioned or been destroyed, so some of the men were reduced to using bayonets to probe in the sand for buried mines. That slowed down the advance even more. Sharp could sense the initial momentum of the attack slipping away.

The worst of it during the long, hellish day was that he and his men couldn't really fight back against the enemy. Their part of the battle had been reduced to creeping forward a few feet at a time. Out here in this no-man's-land there was no one with whom to do battle. With a rattle and clank of treads, the tank moved up, then stopped, moved up and then stopped, again and again until it seemed there would never be an end to it. They would be trapped out here for all eternity, Sharp found himself thinking wildly. Forever and ever, amen.

He gnawed rations, swigged water, blinked dust from eyes that were heavy with weariness. Somehow the day passed and night began to fall again. They had been out here almost twenty-four hours, and they had advanced less than five miles. The tank's guns were unfired. Sharp called the 3RTC's commander on the radio and asked, "For God's sake, why won't they let us go ahead? We have to *do* something!"

"Patience, Captain," the imperturbable voice came back. "Our time will come."

Perhaps, Sharp thought. But would they all be dead by then?

\*   \*   \*

The heat and dust during the day had been incredible. Sharp thought he must have swallowed at least a pound of grit. At least darkness came as a little relief. The air cooled slightly, though it was still full of the odors of exploded powder, burning rubber, and burning flesh.

Nightfall brought another sort of relief as well. It brought the order to advance at full speed.

*At last!* Sharp thought as Bert Crimmens relayed the order. "All ahead, Sergeant Royce," Sharp said over the interphone. He felt the wind in his face pick up as the tank gained speed.

He knew they were risking death from the mines and that they were charging into a German resistance the strength of which was unknown. But anything was better than creeping along as they had been doing since the attack began.

Mines detonated to either side. German artillery shells whistled in around them. But they kept rolling forward. To the rear, bombs from German planes fell on a supply column and set several trucks afire. German artillery targeted the area around those blazes and added to the inferno.

Sharp saw flashes up ahead and realized they were coming from German artillery batteries. "Tom!" he called to Hamilton. "Can you hit those guns?"

"I can try, Captain," Hamilton replied.

"Don't just try. Do it, lad!"

Hamilton took that to mean he should fire whenever he was ready. A few moments later, the Grant's 75mm-gun roared and belched fire. Hamilton fired again as soon as he had reloaded. Royce kept the tank moving forward. In the darkness, it was impossible to tell what effect the shots were having, but the tank continued to lay down a barrage as it advanced. All along the line, the other British tank commanders were following Sharp's example.

Sharp's M3 lumbered up a rugged slope. Remembering the maps he had studied, Sharp thought it might be the Miteirya Ridge. If that was the case, it meant the British advance, at least this part of it, had finally penetrated past the German minefield. The front lines of the German positions were just over the ridge.

Bert Crimmens grabbed Sharp's boot and gave it a tug to get his attention. When Sharp looked down, Bert called up to him, "We're to hold our current position! No more advance!"

"Bloody hell!" Sharp burst out. "We're just about to crack their line!"

"GHQ says we don't have adequate support. We're out here almost by ourselves, Captain!"

Sharp heard the worry in Bert's voice. He looked around. It was true that only a few of the British tanks had come this far. Most of them were still bogged down back in the minefield.

The tank was still clanking toward the top of the long ridge. "Cap'n?" Bert asked anxiously. "What are we goin' to do?"

Sharp took a deep breath. They were close to the Germans now. He could sense the presence of the enemy. But if they charged over the top of the ridge, they might find themselves in the middle of a suicide mission that would fail to accomplish a thing. He wasn't going to throw away his life or the lives of his men like that.

"Stop!" he called over the interphone. "Hold your position until further orders, Royce."

"Aye, Cap'n," Royce replied.

Sharp got on the radio with headquarters again. The orders he received were clear and more detailed than the first flash Bert Crimmens had got. They were to pull back to a distance of half a mile from the base of the Miteirya Ridge and hold that position until directed otherwise. It was a frustrating but probably wise course of action.

"All right, Jeremy," he said to Royce. "Get us out of here."

"But the bloody Jerries are right up there!" Royce protested.

"I know, Sergeant. We're going to have to wait to take our turn at them, though." He clapped a hand on Royce's shoulder. "Look at it this way. When the time comes, we'll be right here, ready and waiting."

Over the next several days, however, Sharp began to wonder if the time would ever come. All along the line of battle, which stretched for over thirty miles across the desert, the British forces had advanced so far and then stopped, either because they were ordered to do so or because the Germans had dug in and stopped them. That halt didn't mean the fighting came to an end as well. The Afrika Corps launched a number of counterattacks in an effort to push back the British lines. Sharp and his men fought several battles with squads of Panzer tanks that rumbled down the ridge and started

across the flats toward them. Each time, they were able to turn back the German attack. The British offensive had begun on the night of 23 October 1942. By the time October changed to November, the desert in front of Sharp's position was littered with the burned-out hulks of destroyed German tanks.

The British had taken their own losses, of course. One entire squadron of tanks, more than two dozen in all, had been destroyed by a massive artillery barrage. Others had been blown up by Luftwaffe bombers. Infantry regiments were decimated by hard-fought battles with their German counterparts. Supply lines were always imperiled. Rations of water and food were short. Sharp hoped that the Germans were in just as bad shape; otherwise he and his companions were doomed to certain failure and probable death.

Not everything was a stalemate. At the northern end of the front, units of Australian armor and infantry had broken through the German lines and pushed almost all the way to the highway that ran along the coast. If they could capture that road and advance along it to the west, Rommel would be isolated at last, completely cut off from any supplies or reinforcements—assuming that he had anything left in reserve. Rommel himself was back in command, Sharp heard, having returned from Austria after the first couple of days of battle. His subordinates who had been left in charge had failed, but the Desert Fox might be a different story. So far, he had always found a way to triumph, to turn seeming defeat into victory. If he managed that now, the war in the desert would be over. Egypt, indeed the entire Middle East, would belong to the Third Reich.

"What's Monty goin' to do, Captain?" Bert asked during a lull one evening. They had been fighting for over a week, hard as it was to believe. The days and nights had all blended together into a blur of smoke and flame and death.

"I'm not sure," Sharp replied. "What I've heard is that he's going to shift most of our forces to the north and try to push on through there."

Royce said, "That'll leave us sittin' down here on our hands, I'll wager."

"It's all right with me if our part's over," Hamilton put in. "We've been bloody lucky so far."

That was true enough, Sharp thought. Most of the tanks had suffered damage or casualties among their crews or both. All four of them were all right, and the tank hadn't been hit except by small-arms fire that had done it no harm. That had come during an ill-advised German infantry charge that had been ripped apart by machine-gun and cannon fire.

"I don't know what's going to happen," Sharp said, "but we'll do what they tell us."

Royce snorted. "That doesn't sound like the famous Hell on Treads Sharp to me."

Sharp felt a surge of anger and was about to lash out verbally at Royce when Bert Crimmens saved him the trouble. In a flash, Bert was across the crew compartment, thrusting his jaw in Royce's face and saying, "Shut your bloody yap, Royce!"

Royce stared at him in surprise. "What the hell's this? The mouse has grown fangs?"

"I'll show you fangs, you sodding lout." Bert swung a punch that caught Royce flush on the jaw and knocked him back against the hull of the tank.

Royce rebounded. His face was dark with fury. He started to swing a blow at Bert, but before he could launch it, Hamilton grabbed his arm and threw him back.

"That's enough!" the gunner snapped. "You deserved that, Royce, and you know it. Insult the captain again and you'll answer to me too."

Royce mouthed a curse and clenched his fists. Sharp said, "That's enough. Sergeant, if you don't like the way I command this tank, take it up with me after the battle. I'll be glad to discuss it with you man-to-man, without any ranks involved. But until then you do as you're ordered."

"Have I ever done otherwise, Captain?" Royce demanded.

"No," Sharp admitted. "You're a good soldier, Royce. A right bastard when you want to be, but a good soldier."

Royce nodded. "We'll leave it at that, then. Sir."

"All right, Sergeant. Carry on, all of you."

Bert put his earphones on again, and not ten seconds had passed before he stiffened and said, "Message from GHQ, Captain! The colonel wants to talk to you."

Sharp took the earphones and microphone. "Sharp here." He listened intently, and the others saw a slow grin spreading across his face. He said, "Understood, sir. We'll be ready." He took off the gear and handed it back to Bert. Seeing the expectant looks on the faces of his men, he said, "The attack in the north along the coast is a feint. Rommel has shifted his Panzers up there to meet it. So we're going across the line here, up the ridge and all the way to the Rahman Track!"

The Rahman Track was a road that led out of the desert north to the village of Sidi Abd Rahman, on the coast. If the British tanks could reach it and strike north along it, they would be able to fall on the rear of Rommel's forces that had been moved to counter the expected attack along the coastal highway. It was a brilliant maneuver, Sharp thought, and one with a good chance of succeeding. If it did, Rommel would have to either retreat or see his forces totally destroyed.

But the whole thing hinged on reaching the Rahman Track.

Tensions ran high as the British forces facing the Miteirya Ridge waited for the order to attack. It came that night, and infantry and armor surged forward. Sharp dropped down from the hatch and buttoned it up. Lead would be flying tonight. Rommel might have moved his Panzers, but there was still plenty of artillery and dug-in machine-gun nests and hardened German troops to oppose the British advance.

Guns began to roar as the tank clanked and clattered across the open ground to the ridge. On previous nights, German soldiers had slipped out from their lines and laid more mines. Some of those mines began to erupt now. The artillery came into play. "Lob some shells up there, Tom!" Sharp ordered, and Hamilton got busy. The tank's 75mm-gun slammed again and again. Sharp himself loaded and fired the smaller 37mm-cannon.

He felt the tilt of the ground when the tank started up the ridge, knew as well when it reached the top. The going was slow as they advanced toward the Rahman Track. When the firing hit a lull,

Sharp climbed into the turret and opened the hatch. When he looked to the east, he saw that the sky was gray with the approach of dawn. He turned to gaze to the west and saw the road. They were almost there. But waiting on the far side of the road was the heaviest concentration yet of German artillery.

The big guns spoke in their booming voice, scattering dozens of explosions through the advancing British tanks. To the right and left both, Sharp saw tanks burst into flames as shells struck them. The stricken tanks lurched to a halt. Some of the crew members were able to make it out, most of them with their clothes burning. Many others never emerged from what had become metal pyres.

Machine-gun bullets spanged off the front of the tank. Royce steered straight for one of the trenches where gunners had dug in with their weapons. Sharp heard the screams of the German soldiers as the tank rolled over them. They had stayed at their posts rather than running, and they had paid for that devotion to their duty with their lives.

Then the tank was among the artillery batteries, crushing more stubborn Germans. Sharp gripped the handle of the .30-caliber machine gun mounted on the front of the turret and depressed the trigger, scything down some of the fleeing German gun crews. One man ran toward the tank, brandishing a grenade shaped like a potato masher. Sharp knocked him backward with a burst of fire before he could toss the grenade.

In the midst of such chaos and carnage, time had no meaning. The sun rose, but its light was choked off by dust and smoke. The British tanks, those that had survived the initial assault, reached the Rahman Track and turned north, toward Rommel's rear. They had to fight for every yard they advanced, however. The Germans knew this was the end for them. Victory or death . . . and it was the same for the British.

The tanks rolled on, and sometime during that endless day, Captain Neville Sharp felt a sudden stab of pain in his chest as he loaded a fresh belt of ammunition into the turret machine gun. He looked down and saw the dark red stain spreading on the front of his shirt, and a great cold emptiness began to expand through him. He gritted his teeth and fought to hang on as he finished loading the gun. Then he said through the interphone, "Bert . . . carry on."

His hand clutched the trigger of the machine gun. It spurted flame and lead and cut down three more Germans who were firing rifles at the tank. Sharp slumped forward, but his finger never left the trigger of the machine gun. It kept jumping and snarling until the belt was empty. As if from a far, far distance, he heard Bert's frantic shouts of "Captain! Captain Sharp!" but those faded away along with the other sounds of battle.

Sharp opened one eye and found himself looking to the west, toward the fiery red ball sinking toward the horizon. The sun had arisen in the morning, and now it was going down in the evening, and for Sharp, that was enough.

General Erwin Rommel, his forces battered and bloodied beyond his belief, his supplies of petrol and ammunition almost exhausted, ordered a retreat on the evening of 3 November 1942. An urgent message from the Führer himself countermanded that order. Being a good general, Rommel hesitated while he pondered the situation.

Then he ordered the withdrawal to resume. By the next day, Hitler grudgingly had agreed with Rommel's decision. The British breakout at El Alamein was complete. The Deutsche Afrika Korps, the pride of the German army, was on the run, heading west across Libya toward Tunisia.

Their troubles were far from over, as they would soon discover.

# FORTY-FIVE

Gene March hummed to himself as he went back to his quarters. He had been confident that he would get a place in the variety show's lineup, but it was always good to have that confidence in himself confirmed. Some people thought of him as arrogant, but they just didn't understand that he knew what he could do and how well he could do it. He had learned early on, when he was still Gino Marchetti, the son of a candy-store owner in Trenton, New Jersey, to play to his strengths and try to minimize his weaknesses. That was why he had changed his name. It would be a hell of a lot easier to get on the radio with an All-American name like Gene March. No point in advertising that he was actually the son of a guinea immigrant. Especially after that fat, oily bastard Mussolini came along and gave Italians everywhere a bad name.

Before the war, Al Satterfield had run a booking agency that put talent in a string of clubs along the Atlantic seaboard. He was a good man to know. When Gene had heard that Satterfield was in charge of the variety show that had made up his mind for him. If he impressed Satterfield now, the chances of Al remembering him after the war was over were that much better. And Al had seemed impressed after the audition. Yeah, everything was looking up, Gene thought as he entered the cargo hold that served as quarters for his infantry company. All he had to do was keep his head and his ass down until the war was over, and he'd be singing in some swanky nightspot.

He found an empty spot at one of the long tables and sat down. Paper crinkled as he reached into his pocket and pulled out several folded envelopes. They contained the last letters he'd gotten from home before the First Division pulled out of England. One from his mother—written in Italian, of course, and she still called him Gino—one from his sister Rosalie, and one from Peggy McCafferty. Gene smiled to himself as he sniffed the faint scent of perfume that still lingered on Peggy's letter. At school, the nuns had tried to keep the two of them apart, but nothing had been able to do that. From the first time pretty, redheaded Peggy McCafferty had laid eyes on Gino Marchetti, she'd wanted him to be her man. And what Peggy wanted, she usually found a way to get. Gene, of course, had cooperated as much as possible. That Peggy, he thought with a sigh, she was one hot gal.

A hand came down on Gene's shoulder. "Put away those letters and stop your daydreamin', March," Sergeant Hollis said. "Don't you hear those alarms?"

Gene looked around, hearing the klaxons that hadn't penetrated his perfume-induced reverie until now. His eyes widened as he asked, "Is it an attack? Are the U-boats after us?"

"Nah, it's a drill," Hollis answered. "But get on your feet and get to your station anyway." As Gene got to his feet and moved to join the other men lining up along the walls of the cargo hold, he heard Hollis mutter under his breath, "Damn goldbrick."

Gene's hands clenched into fists. He didn't like Hollis, never had ever since he'd been assigned to the man's squad. Hollis wasn't much more than a kid and was probably younger than Gene himself, but he had moved up quickly through the ranks because he was a sap and did everything the brass told him to do. He even volunteered for jobs he didn't have to do. Plus he was from down south somewhere, and Gene knew how stupid all those yokels were. It wasn't fair that Hollis got to boss everybody around.

With an indrawn breath, Gene controlled his anger. He had to pretend to be as big a chump as Hollis was. He would follow orders, mind his manners, and try to get along. If he got too much on the sergeant's bad side, then once they were in combat, Hollis would give him all the dangerous jobs, Gene was sure. He didn't want that. He had to be careful, had to bide his time until this crazy war was over. Then, when he broke into the good clubs, fame and fortune would await him.

Fame, fortune, and dames a hell of a lot ritzier than Peggy McCafferty.

*　　*　　*

The convoy split up on schedule, the Central and Eastern Task Forces heading on to Gibraltar and the Mediterranean while the Western Task Force moved south toward Casablanca. The news of the British victory at El Alamein had reached the ships, prompting wild cheers when the distinguished tones of the BBC commentator announced that Rommel was in full retreat, was piped over the loudspeakers.

Even Dale was caught up in the excitement. "Once we get ashore, the Krauts will be running right toward us," he said to Joe as they sat in the cargo hold after listening to the announcement.

"I think that's the general idea," Joe said.

"Yeah, well, when did you get to be such a great strategist?"

"I could be, if I ever got the chance."

"Yeah, sure."

But there was some truth to that claim, Joe thought. Sure, he'd never been to West Point and he'd never even thought about being in the Army until the time came when he and Dale had to get out of Chicago in a hurry. He had imagination, though, and that helped. To win a war, you had to do things the enemy didn't expect you to do. He remembered some Civil War general who had said that the commander who wins the battle was the one who got there "the fustest with the mostest." That made sense to Joe. You had to be decisive, had to think and move quickly.

Of course, he was just spinning his wheels by thinking such thoughts, he told himself. Because of his hard work, he'd made sergeant. That was probably as high in the ranks as he would ever rise.

The Nazi wolf pack was known to lurk in the vicinity of the Rock of Gibraltar. Stuka dive-bombers flew missions over the area too, from airfields in occupied France. So the ships faced possible danger from both sea and air as they cruised past the massive Rock under moonlit skies. This was the third time Joe and Dale had passed the landmark, and it was no less impressive now than it had

399

been the first time. The Rock of Gibraltar had been called one of the Seven Wonders of the World, and Joe couldn't argue with that.

Tension was high on board all the vessels in the convoy. Radio reports said that as many as fifty German U-boats were waiting up ahead. Joe tried to work on his story but gave it up when he couldn't concentrate. Dale was playing solitaire at one of the other tables. Joe slid over beside him and said, "How about dealing a hand or two of poker?"

Dale grinned. "Sure. What'll we use for stakes, though? We're both broke."

"I guess we'll have to use IOUs."

"Good enough for me." Dale's smile widened. "By the time we get back to Chicago, you'll owe me all the money you make for the next ten years, big brother."

"Shut up and deal," Joe said.

Despite the apprehension felt by everyone on board, the night passed quietly, with no attacks from the Germans. Now that the convoy was in the Mediterranean, it would take only a few more days to reach its destination. The next night, the variety show put on by the troops took place, even though rehearsal time had been short. This would be the last chance for any sort of entertainment for a while.

The enlisted men crowded into the cargo hold where rehearsals had taken place. A couple of men who had been carpenters before the war had found enough planks to nail together a stage of sorts at one end of the room. The audience members were crammed together on the benches that ran along the tables, and the tables themselves were full of men sitting cross-legged. No officers or war correspondents were allowed. A pair of noncoms were stationed at the door to keep them out. This show was put on by enlisted men, for enlisted men only.

As the time approached for the performance to begin, the audience got impatient. Joe and Dale clapped their hands and stomped their feet along with everyone else. Finally, the corporal Dale had seen with the clipboard during the auditions stepped up onto the stage and raised his arms over his head, signaling for quiet. When that didn't work, he put a couple of fingers in his mouth and let out an ear-piercing whistle. Finally, all the racket began to die away.

"That's better," the corporal said, his voice carrying to all corners of the big room. "I'm your master of ceremonies for the evening, Al Satterfield, and I want to welcome you boys to the GI Follies of 1942! And that's just the war I'm talking about!" He paused as if waiting for a rimshot, but there was no drummer to give it to him. After a second Satterfield went on, "We got a lot of great acts to entertain you tonight. The first one is a juggler from Oshkosh, Wisconsin—no joke—named Chuck Brinker. Take it away, Chuck! Let's give him a big hand!"

Satterfield led the applause as he moved out of the way and the show got started. For the next hour, the troops were entertained by the juggler, a trio of banjo players from Arkansas, a plate spinner from North Dakota, a singer from Oklahoma who yodeled just like Jimmy Rodgers, a couple of operatic tenors, a guy who played hot jazz licks on a saxophone, even a birdcaller. Al Satterfield kept the show moving along briskly, peppering it with bad jokes between acts. The audience had a fine time, adding plenty of whooping and hollering of their own. Even Joe, never a fan of vaudeville, got caught up in it and found himself grinning and laughing and applauding. During one break, he leaned over and said to Dale, "Maybe you were right. Maybe we should have gotten an act together."

"Too late for that now," Dale said. "You should have thought of that when I asked you."

"Yeah, well, maybe next time. I notice you're not up there doing a solo act."

Dale shrugged. "I wouldn't want to embarrass the other guys by showing them up with my talents."

"Yeah, right." Joe began clapping again as one of the men started playing a piano that had been wheeled out onto the makeshift stage. Joe had no idea where they had gotten a piano. Appropriated it from one of the officers' wardrooms, probably.

Satterfield came on stage to introduce the show's final act. "We've saved the best for last, guys," he said with his hands raised again. "You'll think we got Frank Sinatra on board when you hear this private sing. Let's hear it for New Jersey's own Gene March!"

The handsome, dark-haired GI Dale had seen and heard at the

audition came out. Satterfield cranked a record player for accompaniment, and the scratchy strains of an instrumental version of "I'll Never Smile Again" came out. All evening long, the audience had never been completely quiet, but as Private March started to sing, a hush spread through the crowd. Within moments, there was no sound to be heard except March's voice, the music from the record player, and the breathing of hundreds of men who were caught up in what they were hearing. Even some of the hard-bitten noncoms began to sniff and grimace as they tried not to wipe away the tears that had formed in their eyes. As they listened to March sing, it was almost like they were back home.

When he finished, the roar of approval from the audience was so loud and sustained it sounded almost like an artillery barrage.

Dale clapped and whistled and cheered, then turned to Joe and exclaimed, "Man! That guy's good!"

"Yeah," Joe agreed. "What's he doing in the Army? He ought to be on the radio, or in Hollywood making pictures."

"He probably got caught in the draft like everybody else."

"Well, if he doesn't get shot, he'll be famous someday," Joe said. After listening to Gene March sing, he felt pretty safe in making that prediction.

*     *     *

But before anybody could get famous, there was a little thing called Operation Torch to get through, Joe reminded himself the next day as the ships in the convoy steamed closer to Oran. There was one brush with a German submarine, but it fired only a single torpedo that missed all the ships and then fled as British corvettes dropped depth charges.

The convoy had been moving due east through the Mediterranean in an attempt to make the Germans think they were bound for Malta or perhaps the Libyan coast. However, on the night of 7 November 1942, the ships turned to the south. The Eastern Task Force had pulled well ahead of the Central, so that on this night 250 miles separated them as they lay offshore north of their targets, Algiers and Oran respectively.

The level of tension was high, but it was a different sort than the one that had gripped the troops earlier in the voyage. Then they had been holding their breath, waiting to see if they were going to be attacked by U-boats or dive-bombers. Now they were waiting to strike a blow of their own, and anticipation and excitement mingled with the nervousness they felt. Before the night was over, American troops would be setting foot on enemy-held soil for the first time in this theater of war.

The gear that had been carried in storage for the entire trip was now passed out to its owners, along with new supplies such as dust masks and water purifying apparatus. Joe stowed his dust mask in his pack, knowing he would need it after the coastal towns were secured and the American forces moved out into the desert. Dale hefted his and said, "Sort of like the goggles I used to wear when I was racing."

"You won't be doing any racing here," Joe told him.

Dale grunted. "Don't I know it. Tanks never get in a hurry."

As soon as beachheads were established, landing craft would start bringing ashore supplies and tanks and trucks. Joe and Dale were both assigned to a support company of the First Armored Division, a rear echelon company that would follow along behind the advance and make sure the tanks were kept in good running order. It wasn't a glamorous assignment, and that bothered Dale, Joe knew. Dale would have rather been out front, taking the point in the attack. But Joe told himself that what they were doing was just as important.

If he repeated that often enough, he thought he might actually convince himself of it.

They moved on deck with the rest of the company. The assault craft were already full of infantrymen who had clambered down rope ladders that hung from the sides of the transports. The night seemed quiet and peaceful, but suddenly the darkness was split by flashes of light from somewhere on shore. A second later Joe heard the distant booming, almost like waves crashing on rocks. He knew it was the sound of big guns being fired. He listened to the artillery for a moment and then said, "The French are putting up a fight."

Dale's lips tightened on the cigarette in his mouth. He said around it, "You didn't really expect anything else, did you?"

Joe sighed and shook his head. "I guess not."

Trailing sparks, French artillery and mortar shells arched high in the sky and splashed down in the warm Mediterranean waters. Most of them missed, but a few struck Allied ships and exploded. The landing craft surged toward the shore, not slowed in the slightest by the bombardment. Watching from the transport, Joe and Dale saw flickers of light that marked machine-gun fire from the men going ashore. Faint sounds of battle drifted over the waves.

Dale caught hold of Joe's arm and pointed. Joe looked and saw a dark shape cutting through the water, slicing into the convoy like a wolf into a flock of sheep. Cannons roared from the decks of the newcomer.

"That's a French destroyer!" Joe said.

The French vessel lived up to its name, slamming shells from its guns into one of the Allied ships until it erupted in flame. The other ships in the convoy were fighting back by now, but the French destroyer was fast and elusive. Joe didn't know much about naval combat, but as he watched, an unwilling spectator to the battle, he had to admire the skill of the French captain. Vastly outnumbered, the destroyer was not only avoiding Allied fire, it was dealing out considerable punishment. Another ship in the convoy soon was ablaze as the result of hits from the destroyer's guns.

Shouted orders told Joe and Dale and the other members of their company to move to the rail. If they were getting ready to go ashore, that meant at least some of the division's tanks had been landed safely. When the next order came, they climbed over the rail and started down toward the waiting landing craft. Joe tried not to look down. He had never cared much for heights. Climbing down the side of a huge ship on a swaying rope ladder in the middle of the night wasn't his idea of fun. Especially when explosions were still bursting not that far away, the brilliant flashes illuminating the night like a lightning storm.

When he was close enough, he let go of the ladder and dropped. A second later, Dale landed beside him. They knelt in the bottom of the boat as more troops crowded around them. With a growling of engines, the boat swung away from the ship and headed toward the shore.

This was it, Joe thought. When he jumped out of the boat, he would be in Algeria, in enemy-held territory. It didn't matter that the French were reluctant enemies. Their bullets and artillery shells were just as deadly as those of Nazis.

The Mediterranean might be warm, but the spray that came over the bow of the landing craft and soaked Joe and Dale and the other soldiers was cold. The trip covered several hundred yards, and Joe's teeth started chattering before the landing craft reached the shore. Or maybe he was just scared, he thought, and that was the reason his teeth were chattering. Either way, he clinched his jaw to try to stop it.

A mortar shell burst close by the boat, throwing even more water into it. Joe ignored the discomfort and stared toward the shoreline. Oran was a large city, but to look at it, you'd never know it was there. The French authorities must have ordered a blackout tonight, he thought. That meant they had finally figured out the real objectives of Operation Torch. He wondered if the same things were going on at Casablanca and Algiers. The attacks in all three places were supposed to be timed so as to occur simultaneously. Joe doubted if that was the way it had worked out. Nothing in the military ever went exactly the way it was supposed to. He had been a GI long enough to know that.

"Look out!" the man next to him yelled, and a hand on top of Joe's helmet pushed down hard. He ducked as bullets whistled through the air around the boat and smacked into its sides. The firing stopped after a couple of seconds. Joe risked a glance over the side and saw a motor launch circling back toward them. The small boat had a machine gun mounted on it. As it swept past, the gunners opened fire again. Joe dropped as low as he could, just like all the other troops in the landing craft. "Dale!" he hissed. "Dale, are you all right?"

"Yeah, I'm fine," Dale replied. He was next to Joe on the other side from the man who had pushed him down. "Those Frogs are sure puttin' up a fight."

Joe wiped the back of his hand across his mouth. "Yeah, I was afraid of that." He tightened his grip on the M1 Garand and wondered if he and the other men should have been shooting at that motor launch instead of ducking. Probably not, he decided. Their real work was on shore, not here in the harbor. On the other hand, they had to reach the shore before they could get started with their mission.

Dawn was lightening the sky in the east. The morning of 8 November 1942, was about to break. Joe was looking at that sky when he heard the sound of the landing craft's engines change. They were idling down, and as they did, the bo'sun's mate at the controls shouted, "Go! Go!"

The troops pulled themselves up and rolled over the sides of the landing craft, dropping into water that was no more than three feet deep. In the gray light, Joe saw a long beach littered with rocks and clumps of brush about fifty yards in front of him. Holding his rifle high, he started splashing toward it. The water and the sand on the bottom tugged at his booted feet and slowed him down. He felt like he was never going to reach the shore. Looking around, he saw Dale a few yards away, charging inland just like he was. Dale was yelling, and Joe realized that he was too.

As he splashed ashore, Joe saw clods of mud being kicked into the air to his right and realized that machine-gun fire was chewing up the beach in that direction. He veered to his left and from the corner of his eye saw Dale go the other way. The line of machine-gun fire went between them and stitched into the water. Somewhere behind Joe, a man cried out in pain, hit by one of the flying slugs. Joe angled toward some rocks and threw himself behind them. He got mud in his mouth when he landed. He spit it out and raised his body enough so that he could thrust the barrel of his carbine over the rocks. Spotting the flickers of muzzle flashes in another group of rocks that marked the location of the machine-gun nest, he aimed at them and opened fire, squeezing the trigger of the Garand as fast as he could work the bolt and throw a fresh cartridge into the chamber. All along this section of beach, other men were doing the same thing, as the American troops tried to knock out the machine gun that had them pinned down.

A couple of minutes later, somebody threw a grenade that sailed into the rocks where the French gunners were huddled. It blew up with a sharp explosion, and the machine gun fell silent. Several men charged the rocks and leaped among them, firing their rifles from the hip. A moment later they turned and waved the all-clear. The gun was knocked out, and so were the defenders who had been manning it.

Joe scrambled up and looked for Dale. He didn't see his brother anywhere, and for a few seconds he was afraid that Dale had been hit. Then the sky grew even lighter, and Joe spotted Dale among the men who had rushed the machine-gun nest. Dale was grinning, and as Joe watched, he took a soggy cigarette from his pocket and put it in his mouth. He waved at Joe and then pointed seaward. Joe was angry with Dale for taking part in that risky charge, but they could talk about that later. Right now Joe turned and looked where Dale was pointing, and he saw a sight he would never forget. With the machine gun knocked out, more landing craft had closed in and were unloading their passengers. A long line of soldiers trudged out of the water and onto the beach, and one of the GIs was carrying a pole with an American flag on the end of it. The Stars and Stripes fluttered in the morning breeze as the sky turned gold and orange with the rising of the sun on this new day.

Joe swallowed hard, turned inland, and said to the men near him, "Let's move out. We've got work to do."

# FORTY-SIX

Several tanks had rolled ashore off landing craft, and their crews drove them up off the beach onto the roads leading into Oran. Before noon, Joe had been summoned to repair three radios that weren't working properly. Two of the jobs were pretty easy, but the third one had to be carried out while the tank was engaged in knocking out a French 75mm-cannon located in a blockhouse that overlooked one of the beaches where Americans were landing and still coming up from the water. The cannon was protected by several machine-gun nests, so while Joe was bent over the radio with the tank's radioman, he could hear bullets smacking into the General Grant's armor only a couple of feet from him. He had confidence in that armor, but still, the racket made it difficult to concentrate on the exposed guts of the radio. After a few minutes, Joe found a bad capacitor and replaced it. With the radio still mostly apart, the tank's radioman tried it out and found it working again. He and Joe put the set back together while the tank rolled over a machine-gun nest and used its own 75mm-gun to batter the French blockhouse into rubble. Joe had to wait until they'd subdued all the resistance before he could climb out of the tank.

As soon as he was on the ground again, he went looking for his squad. His main assignment was to see that field telephones were put into operation between the front and the unloading areas along the beach, so that frontline commanders could call for more supplies or men, as they needed them. That meant stringing wire, lots and lots of wire. Joe had a corporal, Bill Curry from Indianapolis, and three privates in his squad. As they hurried toward the front, all of them carried large rolls of telephone wire wrapped around wooden spindles.

Joe had no idea where Dale was. They'd gotten separated once they were ashore, as they knew they probably would be. Dale was off somewhere dealing with tank engines that had decided to act balky.

The command post for this section of the landing was located in an abandoned warehouse near the beach. Joe and his squad started there. Corporal Curry hooked up the field phones with the wire he was carrying, and then began unrolling it as the squad moved up. When Curry's wire ran out, they would splice it into the next roll. The five men trotted up a narrow street toward the center of Oran. The street was dirty, the gutters clogged with filth and debris. Most of the buildings they passed were shut up tight, as the civilians laid low while the battle was going on. But some of the Frenchmen inside the buildings called out to the GIs as they passed. Joe looked up in surprise the first time he heard a strident shout of *"Vive les Americains! Vive les Americains!"*

The citizens were cheering for them, he realized. No matter what the official position of the Vichy government was, many of these Frenchmen knew that the Americans were their friends and wanted to lift the Nazi yoke off their shoulders. That made Joe feel a little better about the whole thing.

But there was resistance too. After they had unrolled all of Curry's wire and were working on the second spool, shots rang out and bullets kicked up dust from the cobblestone streets around their feet. "Take cover!" Joe yelled, and the squad split up. He dived behind an old car parked half on the street and half on the tiny sidewalk. Bullets thudded into the car's body. Joe risked a look through the car's windows, searching for the sniper. From the sound of the shots, only one man was firing at them.

Joe saw puffs of smoke coming from a second-floor window in a building in the next block. He crawled to the rear end of the car and watched the window for a minute. When he saw the pale blur of a face inside the room and the barrel of a rifle poking over the sill of the window, he felt justified in returning the fire. The butt of the Garand kicked against his shoulder as he squeezed off two shots. The face jerked back and disappeared, and a second later, the rifle slid over the windowsill and dropped to the street below. "Come on!" Joe called to his squad as he scrambled to his feet. "Anybody hit?"

The other four men emerged from their hiding places. All of them were unhurt. "Let's go," Joe said, "but keep your eyes open. Not everybody here is glad to see us."

By midday, they had strung the wire for the field telephones and the front lines were in contact with the rear. Joe and his men pulled back, listening to the sounds of the fighting that was still going on in scattered pockets throughout the city. There seemed to be a lot less fighting now than there had been early that morning.

They were able to take a break in the command post near the beach, and while they were there, Joe learned that the strongest resistance by the French had been directed at the landing craft and the ships in the Central Task Force's convoy. Once the Americans were on the ground, the going had gotten easier. It hadn't been without cost, however. Quite a few men had been wounded, and several had been killed. A couple of American tanks had been destroyed. Now American infantry and armored units were going from street to street and house to house cleaning out the last stubborn French defenders.

"We estimate that by tomorrow night, the city will completely under our control," one of the captains hanging around the command post told Joe.

"What about the landings in Casablanca and Algiers?" Joe asked. "Have you heard anything about them, sir?"

"We've had a pretty easy time of it in Algiers, judging by the radio reports I've heard," the man replied. "But Casablanca . . ." He shook his head. "That's been a tougher nut to crack. General Patton's got his hands full over there."

Joe didn't know General Patton, but from what he had heard of the man, he suspected Patton would be able to handle whatever the French in Casablanca threw at him.

"Better get a cup of coffee while you've got the chance, Sergeant," the captain went on, gesturing at a pot that had been set up on a field stove. "Things haven't been too bad so far, but there's still a lot of work to do."

"Yes, sir," Joe said. That was always true of the Army. Whenever one job was finished, another was waiting.

\*    \*    \*

411

Gene March had never been so scared in his life. Not as a kid, when on a dare he had hooked a watch out of Hefferman's Jewelry Store and a cop had chased him for six blocks before giving up, and not as a young man when Emily Jenkins's husband had come home early and caught him and Emily in the sack and come after him with a butcher knife. Those times had been bad enough, but getting shot at was the worst.

He was hunkered on his heels with his back pressed against the bullet-pocked stucco wall of a house on the outskirts of Oran. A few yards away from him, one of the guys from his squad lay sprawled in a pool of blood. The wounded man was still breathing—Gene could see the back of his jacket rising and falling—but he had passed out and probably would bleed to death before too much longer if he didn't get some help.

And Gene was the man closest to him, the only one who could give him that help.

The French machine gun was silent now, but a few minutes earlier it had opened up as the squad advanced down the street. The bullets had chopped through the air around the men and sent them scurrying for cover, all except the man who was hit. His name was Bittersohn, George Bittersohn. He was from Delaware or Rhode Island, somewhere like that, Gene recalled. He didn't know the guy well at all. In fact, the five minutes or so he had just spent staring at Bittersohn's bloody form was the most he had ever looked at the man.

The rest of the squad was in an alley across the street, more than twice as far away from Bittersohn as Gene was. Gene was the only one who had gone left instead of right when the machine gun started firing. In the mouth of the alley, just behind the protection of the building, Sergeant Hollis knelt and called across to Gene.

"March! Grab Bittersohn and get him out of there, March!"

Gene swallowed. "The machine gun—"

"We'll give you covering fire! Just do it!"

Gene still hesitated. If he didn't go out there to get Bittersohn, he would be disobeying a direct order. But if he did leave the meager shelter of the building, that French machine gun might slice him to pieces even before he could take the two strides he would need to reach Bittersohn. The guy was going to die anyway, Gene told himself. Anybody who lost that much blood had to be mortally wounded.

"March!" Hollis yelled again.

Then Hollis burst out of the alley, firing his Thompson toward the French machine-gun nest, which was located in the next block behind a pile of rubble. "Now, March!" Hollis screamed as the MG opened up on him, sending dust and chunks of stone flying from the building on that side of the street.

Without thinking about what he was doing, Gene threw himself out from cover and fell to his knees beside Bittersohn. His hands reached out and clawed at Bittersohn's jacket. He got a good hold and hauled back, his feet scrabbling against the cobblestones as he tried to pull both himself and the wounded man to safety. Across the street, Hollis hit the dirt but kept firing the Thompson. The other members of the squad got into the fight, firing around the corner of the building with their carbines. The machine gun fell silent as the heavy fire forced the gunners to duck.

Gene flopped back behind the corner, taking Bittersohn with him. Bittersohn groaned as both of them fell hard on the cobble stones. But at least they were out of the line of fire now. Panting from fear and exertion, Gene looked across the street as Hollis rolled up next to the building. The French MG was chattering again, and it would have meant Hollis's life if the sergeant stood up to try to get back in the alley. All he could do was huddle against the building and hope the Frenchies ran out of ammo before their bullets found him there.

On his knees, Gene crawled to the corner and risked a look around it. From this angle, he could see a little of one of the men working the machine gun. His hands were shaking, but he tried to steady them as he poked the barrel of his M1 around the corner. The French were still directing their fire at the alley and at Hollis. The sergeant was lying behind a low concrete stoop, and that was the only thing that had saved him so far.

Drawing a bead on the tiny target, Gene waited a second for the shakes to pass. They did, and as the sights on the carbine steadied, he squeezed off a round. The Garand kicked against his shoulder. He saw blood fly, and a guy fell out from behind the rubble that shielded the machine gun. The man jerked and writhed in pain. Gene had shot him through the right side of the body, just above the waist. Gene ignored him, worked the bolt of the carbine, and fired two more shots through a small opening in the rubble. He didn't know if he was going to hit anything or not, but at least there was a chance.

Then he pulled back as the slugs from the machine gun clawed the air around him. With his pulse hammering crazily inside his skull, he looked over and saw Hollis ducking back around the corner into the alley. He had given the sergeant the chance he needed to get under cover. Hollis glanced over at him, and their eyes met across the street. Hollis gave him a curt nod.

A couple of minutes later, a General Grant tank came rolling along and blew the hell out of the machine-gun nest with its cannon. The street was clear. Bittersohn was dead, though. Just as Gene had thought would happen, he'd bled to death before anybody got a chance to help him. The whole thing had been for nothing.

The squad left him there and moved on. As they did, Hollis said to Gene, "Good work back there. Maybe you're good for something besides singing after all."

Gene just nodded, not trusting himself to speak. He was thinking that if Hollis ever put him in a spot like that again, sergeant or not, he would shoot the son of a bitch himself.

*   *   *

True to the prediction of the captain in the command post, by nightfall on 10 November, Oran was firmly under control of the American troops that had landed there. So was Algiers. And so too was Casablanca, because a cease-fire order had gone out from Admiral Jean Francois Darlan, commander in chief of all the Vichy French forces in North Africa. A member of the Vichy regime and a former supporter of the Nazis, Darlan was a shrewd man who knew when to switch allegiances and go with a winner. The cease-fire issued by Darlan was one of the last orders given in the name of Vichy France. Never more than a facade of a real government, Vichy ceased to exist that same day as German and Italian forces invaded the unoccupied areas of France, putting the entire country under Axis control.

With the first phase of Operation Torch successful and Casablanca, Oran, and Algiers in Allied hands, the attention of the Americans and British turned to Tunisia. The city of Tunis was the next objective. But the German forces in North Africa that had not been involved in Rommel's attempt to crush the British Eighth Army were moving toward Tunis too, in hopes of preventing the Allies from capturing it.

It was a race, with the fate of the Nazi war machine in North Africa as the stakes.

# FORTY-SEVEN

On the other side of the world, the rest of the Second Regiment Marines had been transferred to Guadalcanal by early November 1942, leaving behind only a small garrison on Tulagi. It was a good time for them to get there, because having been denied in their every effort to expel the Americans from the island, the Japanese were getting ready for a showdown, preparing to pour as many men and supplies onto Guadalcanal as it took to achieve victory. The Marines would need all the men they could get to hold off the inevitable attack, including the 164th Infantry Regiment of the United States Army. Dogfaces or not, the Marines were glad the 164th was there. The American forces were also augmented by the arrival of the Eighth Marine Regiment from Pago Pago. These men had yet to experience jungle combat firsthand, but they had been in the South Pacific for months and were accustomed to the climate and the surroundings. General Vandegrift put them to work right away, sending them to the east across the Tenaru River to deal with a sizable Japanese force that had come ashore there several nights earlier, landed by the fast transports of the Tokyo Express.

In the other direction, to the west of Henderson Field, beyond the Lunga River to Point Cruz, a combined force of Marines and Army infantrymen had pushed forward and dug in, and side by side they were holding the line against enemy efforts to drive them back beyond the Matanikau. The days were hot, steamy. Heavy rains sometimes moved in and flooded foxholes and campsites. The nights were the worst, though. That was when the Japanese came, appearing out of the darkness like unearthly spectres with screams and cries of "Banzai!" and "Marines die!"

Adam leaned against the wall of the foxhole he shared with Leo

Sikorsky and closed his eyes. It was morning again, slender rays of sunlight slanting through gaps in the tall trees, and that meant he and Chopper had survived another night on the line. In fact, it had been one of the quietest nights so far for them: only one attack by half-a-dozen Japs, and they had been able to kill all of them. The bullet-riddled bodies still lay out there, about fifteen feet in front of the foxhole. By midday, the stink would be pretty bad, but nobody noticed that much anymore. All over Guadalcanal the air smelled like death.

The fighting had been worse on both sides of the position held by Adam and Chopper. Several attacks had been beaten back during the night. The leathernecks and doggies had had their hands full, so much so that nobody had paid much attention to the shelling and bombing going on to the east, as the Japs hit Henderson Field again both from sea and air. Like the maniacal attacks from the jungle out here on the front, the pounding back at Henderson Field was an every-night occurrence.

Chopper lit a cigarette and let out a long, shaky sigh. He and Adam and their companions had been out here for over a week, though it seemed longer. The expeditionary force had been larger when they started out, but the new Japanese threat off to the east had caused General Vandegrift to withdraw some of the men who had been sent beyond the Matanikau. Some of the men felt that they were being hung out to dry, and Chopper voiced that sentiment now.

"They've forgotten we're out here," he said between short, savage puffs on the cigarette. "They ain't sendin' us any relief."

"We're doing okay," Adam said. "The Japs haven't gotten past us, have they?"

"Yeah, but we lose a few more guys every night. Sooner or later they're gonna overrun us. It's just a matter of time." Chopper pinched out the butt and put it carefully in his pocket. "And the brass don't give a damn."

"That's not true," Adam insisted. "I talked to the captain just yesterday, and he said General Vandegrift promised us more men as soon as they get the Japs cleaned out on the other side of the Tenaru."

"Yeah? When's that gonna be?"

Adam had to shrug. "Your guess is as good as mine."

418

"My guess is we're gonna die out here. Ed's the lucky one. Mark my words. That was a million-dollar wound that fat farm boy got."

Adam wouldn't have called Ed lucky for being wounded. He'd been hit pretty bad, had lost a lot of blood and had quite a bit of muscle torn up by the bullet. But Ed was alive and was nowhere near Guadalcanal anymore, having been taken off the island with some of the other wounded. Adam liked to think that Ed had been sent to the *Solace*, so that he could see Catherine and tell her that he was all right.

It would be worth a million dollars if he could see Catherine, he thought. At least that much, and more if he could hold her, feel her warmth in his arms, taste the sweetness of her mouth. Adam sighed. It was never good to think too much about such things out here in the jungle. Getting distracted at the wrong moment could cost a guy his life.

Adam lifted his head as he heard the growling of a jeep somewhere close by. When the Second Marines had come out here, they had hacked a crude road out of the jungle, just wide enough for a jeep to get through it. The road was muddy, with ruts so deep the men joked than an entire jeep could disappear into one and never get out. Adam raised up, hoping there were no snipers around, and peered toward the point where the road emerged from the jungle. The sound of the jeep's engine grew louder, and a few moments later, it bucked and jolted into view.

"Whatta we got?" Chopper asked. "VIPs?"

"A doggie colonel," Adam replied as he looked at the man seated beside the jeep's driver. Whatever had brought the colonel out here, it had to be important if he had come personally, instead of just calling on the radio. "I'll go see what he wants."

By the time Adam had climbed out of the foxhole and walked over to the jeep, the Army colonel had gotten out. Adam saluted and said, "Lieutenant Bergman, sir. What can I do for you?"

"At ease, Lieutenant," the colonel said as he returned the salute. He must have just come out from Henderson; he looked spit-and-polish, especially compared to the haggard and bearded men squatting in the foxholes. He went on, "I've come to do something for you and the rest of these men. I suspect you've been sitting around here long enough?"

"We're being relieved, sir?" Adam wasn't going to let himself believe it until he heard the words for himself.

"No, but this holding action is over. We're going to be advancing again."

"Sir?" Adam said. His voice sounded hollow to his own ears.

"We're moving up. Advise your men, Lieutenant. Your platoon will be leading the advance."

Chopper was listening, and at that revelation, he came up out of the foxhole. "Leading the advance?" he exclaimed. "We been out here for a week, fightin' off the Japs every night, and now we're leadin' some sort o' damn advance—"

Adam swung around quickly and grabbed Chopper's arm. "Get back in that hole, Marine!" he snapped. "Now!" He had seen the look of anger on the colonel's face and knew that Chopper was just a scant few words away from big trouble.

Chopper hesitated, and Adam said again, "Now!" With a grimace, Chopper turned away, trudged back to the foxhole, and dropped into it. He still glared at the colonel, though.

"That man is insubordinate," the colonel said stiffly.

"Yes, sir," Adam said. "I'll see that he's disciplined."

"You do that, Lieutenant." The colonel relented a little. "But I suppose it can wait until after we've cleaned out some of those Japs."

"What are our orders exactly, sir?"

"Advance to the west and eliminate enemy opposition as you encounter it. It can't get much simpler than that, Lieutenant."

"No, sir. When does the advance begin?"

The colonel looked at his watch. "Oh-nine-thirty. That's thirty minutes from now. Can you have your men ready that quickly, Lieutenant?"

"Yes, sir," Adam answered without hesitation. "They're Marines, sir. They'll be ready."

"Is that a veiled comment about the readiness of the United States Army, Lieutenant?"

"No, sir. The men of the One-sixty-fourth, they'd make good Marines, sir."

The colonel nodded. "All right. I'll take that as a compliment." He saluted. "Carry on, Lieutenant."

Adam returned the salute. "Aye, aye, sir," he said, using the Marine affirmative and not caring if the colonel noticed or not.

The colonel climbed back into the jeep, and Adam turned to his platoon. All four of his sergeants had come through the fighting so far, and they were waiting for his orders.

"You heard the man," Adam said. "Get ready to move out. We're going hunting."

*　　*　　*

The advance began on schedule and with no problems. The danger of snipers was always greater during the day. As the men chopped their way through the jungle with knives and bayonets, the thought was never far from their minds that a bullet could come out of nowhere and end their lives with no warning.

And yet despite that constant danger, despite the hardships and deprivations they had endured, they still cracked jokes and talked about home. The pride Adam felt in them before only grew stronger during that long day.

It was late afternoon before they encountered resistance. The terrain had gotten a bit more rugged, and the platoon was moving along a grassy ridge between two stretches of jungle. The ridge led toward a small hill. Adam kept his eye on the hill, which was dotted with rocks. That was just the sort of place the Japs would hide, especially if some of those rocks concealed the entrance to a cave or two.

Those thoughts were going through Adam's head when a sound like ripping paper suddenly split the air. He knew it was one of the Japanese light-caliber machine guns. "Down! Down!" he yelled at the men as he motioned for them to hit the dirt. He threw himself forward, landing in the tall grass. The stalks were high enough to completely conceal him, but they wouldn't stop a bullet. And if he tried to move, the telltale waving of the grass would give away his position to the Jap machine gunners. The same was true of the other men. They had to just lie there motionless as the machine-gun fire searched along the ridge for them.

Adam pressed the front edge of his helmet into the dirt as he lay there listening to the gun. When it stopped, as it would have to do eventually while the Japs reloaded, he would leap up and dash forward for a few yards before dropping to the ground again. It would make for slow and perilous progress, but to charge the gun in the open would be tantamount to suicide.

Sure enough, the machine gun fell silent. Adam surged to his feet and yelled, "Follow me!" He launched into a run, but he had gone only a step or two when bullets began to whistle past his head. A second machine gun had opened up, he realized as he dived earthward again. The bastards had two guns, and they were taking turns trying to kill the Americans.

That was going to make things a lot more difficult, Adam thought. Moving slowly so as not to stir the grass any more than he had to, he lifted his head and shoulders and risked a quick look at the hillside. He saw flame spurting from the muzzle of one of the machine guns as it poked out from behind a rock. Fixing the location in his mind, he dropped flat on the ground again. The machine gun was at least thirty yards away and at an angle uphill. It would be a difficult throw with a grenade. That was the only way to take out the gun, though. The rocks provided too much cover for rifle fire to be effective.

A volley or two might make the gunners duck for a few seconds, and that was all Adam needed. Sergeant Vardeman's squad was the closest to him. He called, "Vardeman!"

"Yeah, Lieutenant?"

"When I give the word, you and your boys rear up and open fire on that machine gun."

"Yes, sir," Vardeman replied.

Adam plucked a grenade from his belt and pulled the pin. "Now!"

He waited a split second, just long enough for Vardeman's squad to start throwing lead at the Japanese machine gun. Then he came up on his knees, drew back his arm, and heaved the grenade toward the hillside. He aimed for a spot several yards above the location of the machine gun he had noted.

Both of the Jap MGs were firing now, and Adam heard men cry out in pain as he watched the grenade sail through the air. If he had thrown it right at the machine-gun nest, the gunners might have been able to grab it and toss it far enough away to escape the worst of the explosion. As it was, though, the pineapple hit a rock farther up the slope and bounced back down. Adam heard screams from the Japs just before the blast rocked the hillside.

Dust billowed up, sweeping along the slope. Adam lunged to his feet and sprinted forward, firing the Thompson as he ran. He hoped the dust was enough to throw off the aim of the men using the second machine gun. Behind him, the rest of the platoon was charging as well. More grenades were tossed through the dust and smoke. Adam went to the ground, shouting, "Hit the dirt!"

The grenades went off, one after another in a sustained roar. They had been thrown blind, but with the way they were scattered across the hillside, there was at least a chance one of them had gotten the second machine gun and its crew. As the echoes of the explosions rolled away across the jungle, Adam scrambled to his feet and ran forward again, slapping a fresh magazine into the Thompson as he charged. Dust and smoke were everywhere. A figure loomed up out of the chaos and flung itself toward Adam, screaming curses in Japanese. The man's face was already streaming blood from shrapnel wounds. Adam put a burst into his chest, the bullets flinging him backward. Adam jumped over the corpse and kept moving forward up the hill.

Gradually, the shooting died away. Adam had reached the top of the slope. He stood there and scanned the surrounding jungle as the hot wind cleared the clouds of dust and smoke from the hillside. Chopper came up to him and reported, "All the Japs are dead, Lieutenant. I counted eight of 'em, four with each of those machine guns."

"What about our men?"

"Three wounded, none of 'em so bad the corpsmen can't patch 'em up."

Adam nodded in satisfaction. "All right. Tell the sergeants to have the men take five while the wounded are being cared for, and then we'll move out again."

"Sure, Lieutenant," Chopper said. He hesitated before adding in a quieter voice, "They're sendin' us out like lambs to the slaughter, you know that, don't you, Adam?"

Adam hefted the Thompson. "Lambs never had one of these," he said.

Not even Chopper could argue with that.

\*     \*     \*

For the next twenty-four hours, the combined force of Marines and infantrymen pushed west, well beyond Point Cruz. It was hard going. Adam lost track of the number of caves he and his men cleaned out, always at great personal risk. Most of the caves were man-made, and they had been dug so that they turned at sharp angles just past the entrance. Pouring rifle and machine-gun fire into the mouths of those caves did little good. The best way to deal with them was to get close enough to lob grenades inside. More than half the time, the blasts caused the caves to collapse, burying any survivors under several tons of dirt and rock.

A few Japanese soldiers were captured because they were too sick to fight. When Adam saw how ill and undernourished these men were, he realized that the Japs had their own problems with supplies. In every case, the prisoners expected to be summarily executed and were always surprised when their lives were spared. Adam knew if the situation had been reversed, American prisoners would not have been treated so decently. And there was a part of him that remembered Wake Island and all the fighting here in the Solomons. A quick bullet through the head was more mercy than the Japanese soldiers deserved. But that was just the sort of thinking they were fighting against, and the men seemed to have an instinctive understanding of that. He had no trouble keeping his platoon under control, though there were rumors that not all the prisoners elsewhere were so lucky.

By mid-afternoon of the second day, a radio message caught up to Adam, relayed from platoon to platoon. The radioman, a guy named Timms, came trotting up to Adam and held out a walkie-talkie toward him. "CO wants to talk with you, skipper," Timms said.

Adam took the radio. An officer named Spaeth had taken the place of Captain Hughes after Hughes was killed by a sniper. Adam pressed down the send button on the walkie-talkie and said, "Bergman here, Captain."

The captain's voice came from the little speaker with a crackle of static. "New orders, Lieutenant Bergman. Discontinue your advance and pull back."

Adam frowned in surprise. "Say again, sir?"

"Pull back," Spaeth said. "That's an order, Lieutenant."

"How far?"

"The eastern bank of the Matanikau River."

That was more than surprising. Shock made Adam's eyes go wide. He hit the button and said, "Did you say the Matanikau, sir?"

"Affirmative, Lieutenant. Effective immediately."

Adam hesitated, then said, "Aye, aye, sir. Understood." He handed the walkie-talkie back to Timms and motioned Chopper over to him. "We're falling back to the Matanikau."

"What? Really? Why?"

Adam shook his head. "I don't know. Pass the word, will you, Chopper?"

"Sure. But it's a shame. We were just gettin' the hang of this rat-killin'."

"I thought you said we were sacrificial lambs."

"Yeah, but like you said, these lambs got teeth." Chopper shrugged and turned to trot off in search of the platoon sergeants.

By nightfall, the Marines and the Army infantrymen were moving at a smart pace through the jungle, leaving behind the territory they had won by spilling their blood and risking their lives. It wasn't a good feeling, Adam discovered, and he hoped the brass had a good reason for what they'd done.

That reason was being called the Superchief, Adam and the other men discovered when they reached the Matanikau and made camp on its eastern banks. Word had reached General Vandegrift and the other commanders that the Japanese navy had put together the largest convoy yet of men and supplies bound for Guadalcanal. It was expected to come roaring down the Slot like a runaway train, hence the name. With the Marines and the men of the 164th spread out over such a large area of the island's northern coast, it was believed that they would not be able to repel the inevitable Japanese assault. So they had been pulled back from both east and west to strengthen the defenses around Henderson Field. Hanging on to the beachhead there might be a losing battle, but the defenders were going to give it their best shot. It would help if the Navy could do something to derail the Japanese Superchief.

But so far here in the Solomons, the Navy had been able to do very little to prevent the Japs from accomplishing whatever they wanted.

Adam's platoon was posted not far from the coast, so they were able to see the flashes from the channel that night as the Japanese convoy approached. But they couldn't make out the details of the battle, so it was the next morning before they heard the news: A small force of American cruisers and destroyers had met the Japanese off the coast of Savo Island and through the sheer audacity of their commanders had dealt a punishing blow to the enemy. Taking the Japs by surprise, the American vessels had steamed right among the convoy, guns blazing, and sank two Jap cruisers and four destroyers. The Superchief had to throw on the brakes and back up out of range.

The spirits of the men on Guadalcanal got a definite boost when they heard about the sea battle. They were not out of danger yet, though, and they knew it. This time the Japanese weren't going to give up until they had thrown every punch in their arsenal.

The next night, Adam stood with Chopper on a small hill and watched as guns began to flash again out in the Slot. This time, the Japanese held the upper hand, and shells from their big guns began to fall on the island. Chopper let out a yelp and dove for a foxhole as an explosion less than a hundred yards away made the ground jump under their feet. Adam didn't lose any time following Chopper into the meager shelter.

That went on all night as the enemy ships pounded the beachhead. As usual, the Marines couldn't do anything except huddle in their foxholes and dugouts and pray that none of the shells landed right on top of them. When morning came, some of the Wildcats were able to get aloft from Henderson Field, but the Japanese ships were already heading back north, their night's work done.

"That was just to soften us up," Chopper predicted. "You wait and see. Tonight they'll try to land more men to finish the job."

Adam was afraid he was right.

As it turned out, both of them were wrong about the enemy's timing. All day long, Wildcats and Dauntlesses roared overhead, and word reached the camp on the Matanikau that a dozen Japanese troop transports were steaming toward Tassafaronga, where an enemy beachhead had been established a few weeks earlier. Cheers rang through the camp as reports came in over the radio. One transport was sinking, then another and another. By the end of the day, the American fighters and dive-bombers had sent eight of the Japanese transports to the bottom of the channel. Some of the men had started calling it Iron Bottom Sound because of all the ships that had been sunk in it, and today that name was more appropriate than ever. That evening, the four transports that had gotten through to Tassafaronga were hit by American artillery set up around Henderson Field. So far, though outnumbered and outgunned, the Navy and the Marine fliers from Henderson Field and the Marine and Army gunnery crews had managed to turn back everything the Japs had thrown at them.

But supplies were running low, and the enemy seemed to have no end of men and ships. Sooner or later, if nothing changed, the defenders on Guadalcanal were going to be pounded into submission.

The next night—15 November 1942—a warning reached the camp where the Second Marines and the 164th Infantry were dug in. Two Japanese battleships along with a multitude of cruiser and destroyer escorts were on their way into the Slot. "I know what that means," Chopper groaned. "They'll be droppin' rotten eggs on us all night long."

Adam figured it the same. The nightly bombardment had taken a heavy toll. Several men in Third Platoon had been killed, many were wounded, and casualties were even higher in some of the other platoons.

"I've heard all we got left from the Navy are three or four PT boats," Chopper went on. "You know that handful of swabbies can't stop the Japs."

Adam shook his head. "It doesn't sound like it."

Chopper paced back and forth on the edge of the foxhole. "I got a bad feelin' about this, Adam. I ain't sure I'm gonna make it through the night."

"Damn it, don't talk like that, Chopper. It doesn't do any good."

"I can't help it," Chopper insisted. "Some guys just know when their number's up."

"You've been convinced your number was up before every other battle we've been in," Adam pointed out. "And you're still here. That seems like a good omen to me."

Out in the Slot, big guns began to boom in the darkness. Chopper dropped into the foxhole, knowing quite well by now what that sound meant. Both he and Adam waited tensely for the first shells to fall among the American camps scattered along the Matanikau.

Instead, the explosions continued out in the channel, but no artillery shells came crashing down on shore. After a few minutes, Chopper asked, "What the hell's goin' on? I hear all that shootin', but we're not gettin' hit."

One possibility occurred to Adam, and it made his hopes surge. "Maybe those are our guns," he said. "Maybe we're hitting the Japs."

"But we don't have anything that big on our PT boats."

"We do on our battleships," Adam said.

Chopper just stared at him in the darkness, as the flashes of a huge battle at sea reflected off the clouds floating overhead.

Conventional wisdom had it that battleships could not operate effectively in the shallow waters of the Slot. That was why the captains of the Japanese vessels that came steaming around Savo Island that night expected to find no opposition waiting for them except the little American PT boats.

The PT boats were there, all right, but suddenly they peeled away, and like leviathans slicing through the waves the U.S. battleships *Washington* and *South Dakota* came charging toward the startled Japanese. The 16-inch guns on the battleships opened up with a thunderous salvo of fire that rained down on the Tokyo Superchief. Like lightning bolts from on high, the volleys wreaked destruction from one end of the Japanese convoy to the other. The enemy had sailed right into a trap, the Marines on Guadalcanal learned the next day, a trap set by Admiral William F. Halsey—"Bill" to his friends, "Bull" Halsey to those more colorfully inclined—and Vice Admiral Willis "Ching" Lee. Lee, Commander, Battleships, Pacific, had personally led the attack from the bridge of the *Washington*. The Japanese ships that survived the destruction ran north again, and this time they would not be coming back. The Tokyo Express had been permanently knocked off its tracks.

This was the best news Adam and the other men on Guadalcanal could have heard. The next day, after much excited rehashing of the scuttlebutt concerning the sea battle, Adam found himself standing on the eastern bank of the Matanikau, gazing across that sleepy, winding river at the jungle beyond. Leo Sikorsky came up beside him and said quietly, "We got a chance now, don't we?"

Adam nodded. "The Japs won't be landing any more reinforcements. We'll have to clean up the ones that are left on the island, but they know now just as well as we do that they'll never get us off of here until we're ready to go."

"Go?" Chopper repeated. "Go where?"

Adam didn't look at his friend but kept his eyes on the jungle instead as he said, "There are still a lot of islands—between here and Tokyo."

# FORTY-EIGHT

Ed Collins tried to flex his arm and winced at the pain that shot through it. But he said, "See? Good as new. No reason I can't go back to the 'Canal."

Catherine shook her head and said, "I'm not convinced that arm is ever going to be the same, Private Collins, and neither is the doctor. You may have bought yourself a ticket home."

Ed looked up from the bunk in one of the *Solace*'s wards, a miserable expression on his face. "But I got to go back," he said. "Adam and Chopper need me."

Standing on the other side of the bunk, Missy patted Ed on his good shoulder and said, "I'm sure they can get along without you, Marine. We got word this morning that all that's left on Guadalcanal is the mopping up. The Japs aren't even trying to land men and supplies there anymore."

"Yeah, well, moppin' up can be dangerous too," Ed said, a sulky expression on his round face. "I promise you right here an' now, ladies, that before this war is over, I'll be back with my unit."

"If that's what you want, I hope you're right," Catherine said. She picked up Ed's chart from the bottom of the bunk, made a few notations on it, and then she and Missy moved on, continuing their rounds.

Later, during a break, they stepped out onto the fantail. Missy leaned against the railing, sighed, and said, "Do you really think Ed will ever get back to the action?"

Catherine shrugged. "It's hard to tell. Dr. Johnston says he suffered significant nerve damage in his shoulder and arm. That's why he doesn't have full use of them yet. Maybe the damage will heal itself, and maybe it won't."

"It wouldn't stop him from leading a pretty normal life back home, though, would it?"

"I wouldn't think so."

"The million-dollar wound," Missy said. "It gets you home but it doesn't ruin your life."

"I don't know," Catherine said. "If Ed feels like he let his friends down, he might consider that ruining his life. Especially if something happens to Adam or Leo."

"But they're all right. At least Adam is. It's been a couple of weeks since the last naval battle up there. You would have heard by now if anything had happened to Adam."

"Maybe. And maybe the word's still making its way through channels."

Missy shook her head. "Look, kiddo, you're assuming your man is all right and I'm assuming my man is all right. That's all we can do."

"The *Enterprise* has been moved back to the Central Pacific. Phil's not in any danger right now."

As soon as the words were out of Catherine's mouth, she was ashamed of them. There was no competition between her and Missy to see which of the men they loved was more in harm's way. At least there shouldn't be. She put out a hand toward Missy and said, "I'm sorry. I know how that sounded. I know how quickly things can change."

"Yeah," Missy said as she looked out over the railing, a faint, sad smile on her face. "That's the way it is with war, I guess. Nothing ever stays the same, and it usually gets worse before it gets better."

Dr. Gerald Tancred already had his hat on and was about to slip into his overcoat when the office door opened and Mrs. Walsh said, "You have a visitor, Doctor."

Tancred was about to ask who it was, but before he could do so, Karen Wells stepped past Mrs. Walsh into the office. "Hello, Doctor," she said with a smile.

Tancred returned the smile as he put his overcoat back on the hook. "Miss Wells!" he said. "How are you?"

"Better. My knee is still giving me some trouble, but I can handle it."

She certainly looked wonderful, Tancred thought. The contusions on her face from the wreck had healed well, leaving such small scars that they could be covered easily with makeup. The sprained knee had been the more serious injury. When Tancred had first gone to see her in the hospital and consulted with her physician on the case, the man had said that he feared a torn ligament that would require surgery. Tancred had looked at the X-rays and disagreed with the diagnosis. It had felt surprisingly good to him when he got in there and argued—civilly, of course—with the other doctor. He had been able to win the man over to his side too. In the end he had agreed that the ligaments in Karen's knee were only severely strained, not torn.

"It may take several more weeks before the soreness goes away," Tancred told her now. He dropped his hat on the desk. "Please, sit down. What brings you here this evening, Miss Wells?"

Karen sat down in the chair in front of the desk. She wore a fur jacket and an expensive green dress that hiked up a bit over her silk-clad knees as she crossed her legs. She said, "I wanted to find out how the clinic is doing."

"Excellent. We're treating more people than ever."

"There wasn't too much trouble over the drugs in that truck?"

Tancred's expression became more solemn as he sighed. "There were no criminal charges filed. But I'm afraid Mr. Merrill lost his job with the pharmaceutical company. And a pair of thoroughly unpleasant policemen came here and asked me all sorts of questions about a man named Chastain."

"That would be Detectives Corey and Bowden," Karen said. "I've come to know them quite well the past few weeks."

"Who is this . . . Chastain?"

"Someone I used to know," Karen said. "But he didn't have anything to do with this, Doctor."

"That's what I told those detectives. I told them I didn't even know the man. They seemed quite displeased with my answers. They said something about a . . . a homicide. A man named Hale." Tancred shook his head. "A very unpleasant business. I've learned my lesson. No more shady deals."

Karen laughed.

"I said something amusing?" Tancred asked with a frown.

"Not at all, Doctor. It was just that comment about shady deals. You seem much too dignified and distinguished to have even heard of such a term, let alone be using it."

"Well . . . perhaps the neighborhood is rubbing off on me. I'm becoming more . . . earthy. That might not be such a bad thing."

"No, it might not," Karen agreed with a smile. "Anyway, I just wanted to be sure everything was all right down here before I left town."

Tancred's eyebrows arched in surprise. "Left town?" he repeated. "My dear, where are you going? I assumed that when you were recovered sufficiently, you would return to your singing as well as continuing to volunteer here at the clinic."

"That's sort of what I planned to do, all right, but then I got a call from a man I know who used to play piano for me at the Dells. He's putting together a troupe of musicians and singers for the USO. They'll be going overseas to put on shows for our soldiers and sailors. I thought . . ." Karen smiled. "I thought that might be something I'd like to do. I wouldn't mind getting out of Chicago for a while. And somehow I don't think Spencer would mind."

Tancred leaned back in his chair, his face serious. "Spencer was always a boy who . . . liked a good show. I remember once, when he was nine or ten, we went downtown to one of the theaters where they put on vaudeville performances. He laughed and applauded and had a wonderful time. . . ." The words trailed off as Tancred was lost for a second in the mists of memory. Then with a little shake of his head, he came back to himself. "We should have done things like that more often, gone on more such outings. But for what it's worth, Miss Wells, I agree with you. Spencer would applaud your decision. We'll miss you here at the clinic, of course, but we'll manage."

Karen leaned forward, reached across the desk, and caught Tancred's hand in her own for a moment. "Thank you, Doctor. I was hoping you'd say that."

She got to her feet, and Tancred stood up as well. "When do you leave?" he asked.

"Sometime next week."

"Good. Then you'll have time to come and have dinner with Elenore and me before you go." He held up a hand to forestall any protest. "I insist, and so will Elenore when I tell her you're leaving town."

"All right, Doctor. Thank you." Karen hesitated and then asked, "How is Mrs. Tancred these days?"

"She's doing splendidly. Many of the ladies from our social circle are donating stockings—silk for parachutes, you know—and Elenore is coordinating the effort. Plus she has been coming down here nearly every week to help in the clinic since you were injured." Tancred paused. "She still has bad times, of course. Bad memories. But at least now she knows they are memories, and the pain is fading a little day by day. She can deal with it now instead of retreating into a world of fantasy. There's not much room for fantasy in a world at war."

"No, I suppose not." Karen stepped around the desk and gave him a quick hug. "But there's always room for hope."

Kenneth Walker and Jacob Ellinger wheeled the cart along the underground hallway toward the abandoned squash court where the nuclear pile was being constructed. The cart was loaded with blocks made of a gray, slippery substance. The blocks were "dead" graphite, graphite that contained no uranium and no radioactive charge. They would form one of the several sets of walls around the pile.

"Seen Emily lately?" Jake asked over the squeaking of the cart's wheels.

Ken frowned. "What brought that up?"

"I was just curious. Back during the summer, I couldn't shut you up about her. Now you haven't mentioned her for weeks."

"We had a . . . disagreement." Ken's frown deepened at the memory. After that unpleasant conversation at the restaurant, he had waited a week to call Emily, and when he finally did, she was cool to him and begged off when he asked her to go out to dinner and a movie with him, saying that she was too busy. After getting the same answer a couple more times, Ken realized it was time to give up. He might be a lot brighter when it came to science than he was about women, but even he could get the idea through his thick skull sooner or later.

"Yeah, well, it's less than a month until Christmas. This is a good time of year for making up. Get her a present, you'll see."

"Maybe," Ken said, but he didn't really mean it. Emily's views on the war were just too far from his. With friends like Joe Parker fighting somewhere overseas, Ken had to do whatever he could back home to help the war effort. If that included helping to build a super-bomb, then so be it.

If Ken had ever harbored any thoughts that the work being done at the Met Lab would not have military applications, that idea had been quashed during the autumn by the appointment of Brigadier General Leslie Groves to oversee the project. Before that, a connection between the work going on under Stagg Field and the Army had been assumed, but now it was out in the open. The Metallurgical Laboratory was now part of the Army's Manhattan Engineering District— though what any of it had to do with Manhattan, Ken didn't know. Rumor had it that once the construction of the pile had been completed here in Chicago—assuming everything was successful—the rest of the work on the Manhattan project would be moved to different locations. Ken didn't know if that was true or not, but if the rumors turned out to be correct, he was ready to go wherever and whenever they needed him.

In that case, he didn't need to be trying to rekindle things with Emily Faraday. He still felt a pang of regret whenever he thought too much about her, but he could live with that.

"Your mind's drifted off again," Jake said. "I can tell by looking at you. You're thinking about her, aren't you?"

Ken shook his head. "I'm thinking that if we don't get this graphite in there, Dr. Fermi and General Groves are going to have our hides."

"I guess you're right," Jake said. "War doesn't wait for the lovelorn."

\*       \*       \*

The December wind was icy as it howled off the lake. Mike Chastain pulled down his hat and turned up the collar of his overcoat as he walked along the street. Department-store windows decorated for Christmas cast bright pools of light on the sidewalks. It was late afternoon, but the season and an overcast sky made it dark already. That was one reason Chastain was out this early. For the past several weeks, he hadn't left the dingy apartment in the rundown building under the El except at night. Today, though, he had something to do and he had to get there before the place closed.

He had been cold ever since the night Roger Hale had shot him. When Chastain made it to the doc's place, the old man had patched him up and assured him that the wound was messy but not that serious. Chastain would have put more faith in that diagnosis if the doc had been sober any time during the past ten years, which was pretty damned unlikely. But he had to admit that he had healed well, except for the fact that he could never seem to get warm.

He'd had enough cash in his pockets to get a room in the dive where he'd been staying. They didn't ask questions in a place like that, as long as they liked the color of your money. While he was recuperating from the gunshot wound, he had food sent in from a deli down the street and never showed his face unless he had to. The thing of it was, Hale had friends in this town, more friends than Chastain did, and they didn't like it when they heard Hale was dead. The fact that his body had been found in Chastain's penthouse didn't leave much doubt as to who was responsible. Chastain hoped the fact that his blood had been found there too would convince Hale's buddies that they'd gunned each other and that Chastain had gone off somewhere else to die. Hell, if they wanted to think that he'd stumbled into the river and drowned, that was all right with him. All that really mattered was that they not come after him to even the score for Hale, because Chastain knew he couldn't deal with that while he was laid up.

And now that he was better, he didn't *want* to have to deal with a bunch of vengeful mobsters. It would be better to get out of town, to go someplace where nobody knew him.

Some place where he could do penance for what had happened to Karen.

Over the years he had pushed his Catholic upbringing so far into the background of his life that he never even thought about such things. The idea of having to be punished, of having to pay back God for the bad things he'd done, just never occurred to him. Thinking like that was for saps.

But now he knew he could never face Karen and ask for her forgiveness. He never wanted to look into those green eyes and see the pain that he had caused. Oh, he knew she was all right. The doc still had enough contacts in the medical profession so that he was able to ask around and find out her condition while she was in the hospital. She'd hurt her knee in the wreck, but that was the worst of it. All the other cuts and bruises would heal. Chastain was relieved to hear that—but it wasn't enough. For days he had struggled with the need to go see her. He could slip into the hospital through a rear entrance, at night, and make his way to her room without too many people seeing him. He thought it would be safe enough.

He had made it as far as the street a block away from the hospital, and then the coldness that had gripped him ever since the night of the crash had intensified until his teeth were chattering and he could hardly move, as if his limbs were frozen.

That cold, he knew now, was fear. Fear of what he would see in her eyes and on her face. . . .

No, he couldn't ask her forgiveness, so he had to try to earn it through some higher power. Working through the doc again, he'd gotten a guy to make him a new set of identification papers, all the way back to a phony birth certificate. That wasn't too difficult. Figuring out what to say about the gunshot wound was harder. Finally, Chastain and the doc had agreed it was the result of an industrial accident. "I saw a guy who looked like that once," the doc had said. "Worked in a steel mill, he did. He got a red-hot metal rod jammed through him. Left a hole just like a bullet."

Maybe the doctors who examined him would accept that explanation. Chastain hoped so. Anyway, even if they were suspicious, the cops were looking for Mike Chastain, not Bennett McKendrie. That name wouldn't mean a damned thing to the flatfeet.

Chastain turned off the sidewalk and started up the steps of Chicago's old main post office. It was a federal office building now.

More people were coming out than going in, and he hoped he hadn't timed this visit too late. If the place he wanted was closed, he would have to come back again some other day, and that would just increase his risks. Besides, he had made up his mind what he was going to do, and he wanted to get on with it.

He went inside, steam heat wrapping around him but failing to penetrate the sheath of coldness that gripped him. As he made his way through the crowded lobby, he heard a guy call, "Merry Christmas!" and another guy said, "Merry Christmas to you too!"

Chastain found the office he wanted, read the words painted on the pebbled glass upper half of the door, and tried the knob. Lights were still on inside, and the knob turned. He was in luck. He opened the door and stepped into the office, and as a guy dressed in an olive-drab uniform looked up from a chair behind a desk, Chastain put a grin on his face and asked, "Hey, buddy, is this where you go to join the Army?"

# FORTY-NINE

Joe settled down in the chair behind the desk, pulled a sheaf of papers from the pack he had lowered to the floor beside him, and set them beside the typewriter. He took a sheet of blank paper from the stack on the other side of the typewriter, rolled it into the platen, and took a deep breath as he poised his fingers over the keys. Then he looked at the handwritten text on the papers to the right and started to type.

He had lucked into this opportunity, and he wasn't going to waste it. His unit was stationed here in this coastal village east of Oran, and he had discovered that one of the clerks on the CO's staff was a fan of the pulps. The guy had offered to let Joe use the typewriter in his office, which was located in a commandeered house on the edge of the village. Joe had to do the work at night, though, when no one else was there.

The fact that the office wasn't occupied at night was a reflection of the casual attitude here in this part of Algeria. The Western and Central Task Forces had been left where they were, around Casablanca and Oran respectively, to serve as a rear guard in case any of the Germans tried an end run back to the Atlantic coast. The Eastern Task Force, now under the command of General Kenneth Anderson, was the one doing the work these days. They were pushing on into Tunis, their objectives the port cities of Tunis and Bizerte. The advance had been slowed considerably by the weather. Heavy rains had moved into the region, and combined with the mountainous terrain of northern Tunisia, that had caused the tanks and trucks to bog down. Still, several battles had been fought between the Allied and Axis forces—and the Allies had come off second-best in most of them. The first part of Operation Torch, the landings at Casablanca and Oran and Algiers, had been a smashing success. The task of pushing the Germans out of the rest of North Africa was going to be a lot longer and harder job, though.

Joe's fingers moved faster and faster as he typed up the espionage story he'd been working on for weeks now, polishing and revising as he went along. He had planned to ask his mother to type it when he sent the pages to her, but this was better. This gave him a chance to go over the story one more time and make sure it was the best work he could do. As usual, he got caught up in what was happening on the pages, and he failed to notice that he was no longer alone in the office until a man cleared his throat. Joe's head jerked up in alarm. He saw a colonel standing there, tall, gray-haired, his back ramrod-straight, a severe expression on his lean face.

Joe shot to his feet and brought his hand up in a crisp salute. The colonel returned it and said, "At ease, Sergeant. Are you on duty here tonight?"

For a fraction of a second, Joe considered lying and trying to pass himself off as somebody who was supposed to be here. But then he looked at the colonel's keen gray eyes and decided that a bluff wouldn't stand a chance. He said, "No, sir. I was just, ah, borrowing the office."

"And using up the Army's typewriter ribbons and paper for exactly what purpose?"

Joe felt like he was dangling over an abyss and would be dropped into it at any second. He swallowed and said, "I'm, ah, writing a story, sir."

"A story?" The colonel's tone was hard, flinty.

"Yes, sir."

Suddenly, a smile tugged at the corners of the colonel's mouth. "Then I've come to the right place. You must be Joe Parker."

Joe blinked in confusion. This officer knew who he was? Knew that he wrote stories? How was that possible? Joe managed to say, "That's right, sir."

"I'm pleased to meet you, Sergeant. My name is Gault. Bradford Gault. I'm attached to General Eisenhower's staff, in the G-Two section."

G-2 was Intelligence. Joe let that soak in, along with the fact that

Gault worked for Ike, and as they did, he began to feel a sense of unease creeping through him.

"You know a British officer named Colin Richardson, don't you?" Gault went on.

"Yes, sir." As before, Joe knew it wouldn't do any good to lie.

"So do I. He's the one who told me I ought to look you up." Gault picked up a straight-backed chair and turned it around, then straddled it and waved Joe into the chair behind the desk. With a hint of a southwestern drawl in his voice, he continued, "Sit down, son. I know you're not really supposed to be here, but don't worry about that. I'm concerned with more important things than type-writer ribbons and paper."

Joe sat down. He was on shaky ground here and knew it. He was going to cooperate with Colonel Gault as much as he could.

"I guess you know what Captain Richardson told me about you."

"No, sir, I wouldn't venture to guess."

"He said you were a smart young man." Gault's tone hardened. "Don't prove him wrong, Sergeant. I'm a man who likes to put his cards on the table, and I like to deal with men who feel the same way."

"In that case, sir, I imagine Captain Richardson told you that I helped him out on a certain matter in Cairo."

"That's exactly right."

"And did he tell you, sir," Joe went on, "that he duped me into it and nearly got me killed?"

Gault looked at Joe for a couple of seconds and then laughed. "When I said to put your cards on the table, you took me at my word, didn't you, Parker?"

"Yes, sir."

"All right, I'll do the same. I've spoken to your superior officers, and they tell me you're a damned fine radioman. You did good work after the landings. But it's my opinion, and the opinion of the other officers I've consulted, that the United States Army could make better use of your talents in another capacity. To put it bluntly, Sergeant, I want you to come work for me."

"In Intelligence?"

"That's right."

Joe's head was spinning. He wasn't sure what to say. After the debacle in Cairo, he had sworn that he would never have anything else to do with spying. He was content just to be a simple soldier and do whatever was asked of him.

And yet, something was being asked of him now, and he didn't know how to respond. He had told Dale that he thought he would make a good strategist, and working for G-2 would put him closer to that than ever before. Of course, he'd be just a very low-level cog in the machine, but still . . .

"If my CO is agreeable, you could just have me transferred, sir," Joe pointed out to Gault. "You don't have to ask for my agreement."

"That's right, I don't. But in the work we do, everyone has to be trustworthy, from the top of the chain of command all the way to the bottom. That's why I want people working for me who want to be there." Gault's hands gripped the back of the chair. "Some people thought we'd just waltz in here and take over, that Rommel and all the rest of the Afrika Korps wouldn't be able to run back to Germany fast enough. But I knew better and I suspect you did too, Parker."

"I saw the way Rommel fought the British Eighth Army over in Libya and Egypt, sir," Joe said. "I never figured it would be easy to get him out of Africa."

"That's one reason I want you on my staff. You've been here in this part of the world for a while. You know what it's like, you know how the people think. Hell, you probably know Rommel better than some of our generals. So what do you say, Parker?"

Joe realized he didn't have to think about it after all. He came to his feet and said, "I'm in, sir."

Gault stood up, shoved the chair aside, and stuck out his hand. "I'm glad to hear it, Sergeant. I can promise you you won't regret your decision."

Joe clasped the colonel's hand.

"If you live through it, that is," Gault added with a grin.

\*   \*   \*

"I'm telling you, we can't beat the Panzers with General Grants," the sergeant from Detroit said. Dale couldn't recall his name for sure—it was Melvin or something like that. The guy went on, "You saw what they did to us at Chewey-Gooey. The Krauts blew the hell out of our M-threes, and we barely scratched them."

From the other side of the table, Sergeant Henry Garmon said, "The Grant's a good tank, a damned good tank. They're a hell of a lot faster than the Panzers."

"Yeah, but what good does it do to run circles around them when we can't hurt them?" Melvin asked.

Dale picked up his beer and took a sip. "An M-three can knock out a Panzer," he said, his voice quiet.

Melvin glared at him. "How the hell do you know?"

"I've seen it done," Dale said. "Twice. I even did it myself once." He ignored the warning look that Garmon sent at him. "You just have to know where to hit them."

Melvin pointed a finger at Dale. "That's bullshit." He was a little drunk. So was Dale, for that matter. They were in what had been an Arab tavern until the Army had come in and taken it over, transforming it into an unofficial enlisted men's club. The guy behind the bar was a master sergeant from the motor pool.

"Whattaya mean, bullshit?" Dale said, leaning forward and cupping his hands around his mug of beer. "You weren't there. You don't know a damned thing about it."

Melvin snorted in derision. "I know no sergeant has ever knocked out a Panzer. We don't have any tanks commanded by sergeants."

"I never said it was an American tank."

"That's enough, Parker," Garmon said. He had been Dale's sergeant ever since basic training at Camp Bowie, Brownwood, Texas, and as a master sergeant he still outranked Dale.

"Did I ever tell you the story, Sarge?" Dale said. "All 'bout how I went out in the desert and—"

"I don't want to hear about it," Garmon cut in. "I've heard rumors about you, Parker, but I don't want to believe 'em because I don't want to have to do my best to see you busted back down to private. So just shut your yap, all right?"

Melvin said, "He might as well shut up. He's lyin' anyway."

"You shut up too," Garmon snapped. "In fact, why don't you get the hell out of here, Melvin?"

"Why don't you make me?" Melvin asked, thrusting his jaw out.

Good, Dale thought. There was going to be a brawl. It would feel good to hit somebody again. The Army had been sitting around for weeks now instead of going after the Krauts like they ought to.

At least that was true of this part of the Army. The Eastern Task Force, composed of a mixture of British and American troops, was pushing eastward into Tunisia. Dale wanted to get in on that. He didn't like sitting around in the rear, never had liked it. But he didn't expect to get in on the action any time soon. The commander of the Central Task Force, General Lloyd Fredenhall, was a cautious man. So cautious he'd had the engineers dig out an underground bunker for his command post, just in case the Germans tried to bomb him or attempt some long-range shelling. With a guy like that in charge, Dale didn't figure they'd be dashing out to attack the Krauts any time soon.

At least some of the American tankers were getting in on the action. An entire tank battalion commanded by Colonel John K. Waters—the son-in-law of General Patton, the commander of the Western Task Force—had run into a bunch of Panzers near the village of Chouigui, a place which had had its name Americanized to Chewey-Gooey. Unfortunately, the Panzers had shot the hell out of the American M3s, destroying half-a-dozen of them while sustaining only minor damage themselves. It was true, Dale reflected, that a heavier American tank with better armor would be a good thing, but until that came along, they had to make do with the General Grants.

Sergeant Garmon hadn't responded to Melvin's challenge. He didn't get a chance to because at that moment, Joe came in and looked around, spotted Dale sitting at the table, and raised a hand in greeting. Joe looked excited about something, Dale thought as his brother came across the room toward him.

"I need to talk to you, Dale," Joe said as he came up to the table.

"Sure, go ahead."

Joe glanced at Melvin. The burly noncom shoved to his feet, glared, and said, "I know where I'm not wanted."

"Then why the hell are you still here?" Garmon asked.

Melvin poked a finger at him. "One of these days, cracker, you and me."

"Whenever you want."

Melvin glared for a second longer, then turned and made his way out of the bar. He was a little unsteady on his feet.

Garmon looked at Joe and said, "You want me to leave too?"

Joe hesitated, but only for a second. Then he sat down in the chair Melvin had vacated and said, "No, that's all right, Sarge. I've known you longer than anybody else in the Army except my brother. I guess I can trust you."

"Thanks," Garmon said dryly.

Joe leaned forward, pitching his voice low so that only Dale and Garmon could hear what he was saying. "I just found out that there's some sort of German convoy moving through the desert south of here."

Dale's eyebrows went up. "Where'd you hear that?"

Joe shook his head and said, "I can't say. I've got contacts, though."

Dale grunted. Joe had been acting as mysterious as all get-out lately. A couple of weeks earlier, he'd been transferred to another part of the outfit, working for some colonel named Gault who was in charge of supplies or something. Dale sensed that there was something not quite on the up-and-up about the whole deal, but he didn't press Joe for the details and Joe didn't volunteer anything.

Now, though, Joe was bringing him some very interesting information. "What are a bunch of Germans doing 'way over here?" he asked. "I thought they were all in Tunisia and Libya."

"Maybe they were on some sort of long-range patrol and got cut off. Now they're just running for the coast. Or they're some sort of commando group out to make trouble in our rear. Whatever, I think we ought to look into it."

"Wait a minute," Garmon said. "Do the brass know about this, Parker?"

"Well . . . not yet. I was just told about it by an Arab informant."

" 'An Arab informant,' " Dale repeated. "You know what you're starting to sound like, Joe? A spy, that's what."

"A spy?" Joe laughed. "That's crazy."

Dale frowned. He wasn't so sure the idea was crazy. He wouldn't put much of anything past his brother, especially if it meant Joe got to act like he was in one of those pulp stories he wrote. Of course, Dale told himself, he was a fine one to talk, since he liked action and adventure even more than Joe.

"All right," Dale said. "What do we do?"

"Wait just a damned minute," Garmon said. "*We* don't do anything. Parker, go tell someone in authority about what you've learned."

"But I'm not sure the information is reliable," Joe said. "I thought I'd check it out myself first."

"So you're going to go tearing off into the desert to look for a German convoy, and you're going to drag your brother along with you?"

"Damned right he is," Dale said with a grin. "He's not goin' without me."

Garmon looked back and forth between them and then sighed. "All right. You're both nuts. But I'll go with you, just to make sure y'all don't get into trouble."

"You, Sarge?" Joe asked, surprised. "I didn't think—"

"That's the truest statement I've ever heard." Garmon pushed himself to his feet. "I wouldn't be doin' this if I wasn't a little drunk. And I'm sure I'm going to regret it in the morning."

Dale stood up and said, "I know where I can get a jeep."

"We need some weapons," Joe said. "Maybe a couple of Thompsons."

"I can put my hands on those," Garmon said.

Dale clapped a hand on his shoulder. "Hell, Sarge, you're a regular guy after all."

"A damned fool, that's what I am."

Less than half an hour later, the jeep went bouncing over the sand dunes south of the village with Dale at the wheel, Joe sitting beside him, and Garmon perched in the back. Joe and Garmon held

Thompson submachine guns cradled in their laps. Dale drove without lights. The desert sand was bright enough in the moonlight for him to see where he was going.

Garmon leaned forward and said, "Listen, if we find these Krauts, we hotfoot it back and report them, right? We let the artillery and the Air Corps take care of them?"

"Sure, Sarge," Joe said. "That's all I had in mind."

What he really had in mind was showing Colonel Gault that he was good for something besides pushing papers, which was all he had done so far since going to work for G-2. He was developing his own contacts among the natives, his own sources of information. Nosing out a secret German convoy would make Gault pay attention to him. The colonel had seemed to be so eager to have Joe assigned to his command, but then he hadn't given him anything meaningful to do.

Of course, if this backfired, Gault would probably ship him off to the real quartermaster corps, instead of the phony unit G-2 was using as a cover for its intelligence work.

Dale was steering by the stars, heading due south from the village. After they had gone several miles, he said over the sound of the engine and the rush of wind in the open vehicle, "How do we find these guys?"

"We ought to intercept their route in maybe ten more miles. If they've passed that point already, we'll have to trail them."

"How do we tell their tracks from all the other tracks out here?"

Joe frowned. He hadn't thought of that. "Maybe we'll come across them."

"You're trusting an awful lot to luck."

Joe supposed that was true. But all of life was a gamble, wasn't it?

Twenty minutes later, from the top of a long ridge of sand and rock, they spotted dark shapes moving against the desert ahead of them.

Dale eased the jeep to a stop. "Son of a bitch," he breathed. "You were right."

"You doubted me?" Joe asked. Dale just looked at him, and Joe laughed. "Yeah, I wasn't sure we'd find anything, either."

"That's a Kraut armored car with those trucks," Garmon put in.

"How can you tell?" Joe asked.

"I know an armored car when I see one," Garmon said with a sniff. "I know every armored vehicle the Krauts have got, as well as the Italians, the Brits, and us. I study these things, Parker. Maybe you should too."

"You're right, Sarge. I guess we head back now. Our flyboys can bomb them as soon as it's light."

"Maybe we should get closer," Dale suggested. "You know, it would be even easier for our bombers to hit those trucks if they weren't moving. I'll bet we could shoot their tires out so they couldn't go anywhere."

"Yeah, and what would that armored car be doing while we were doing that?" Garmon asked.

Dale grinned. "The trick is to move fast enough that the Krauts can't do anything to stop us."

"Parker . . ." Garmon said warningly.

Joe caught his breath, knowing what Dale was about to do. He braced himself against the seat, so that when Dale threw the jeep in gear and hit the gas, he wasn't thrown back too hard. Garmon let out a yelp and had to grab the back of the passenger seat to keep from being jolted from the jeep.

"Parker! Have you lost your mind?"

Joe didn't know which one of them Garmon was talking to. It didn't really matter, since they were both crazy tonight.

Dale swung the jeep to the left, heading down a valley between sand ridges. "We'll come up behind them," he shouted over the wind. "They won't know we're here until it's too late. Joe, aim for the tires as we pass the trucks. Sarge, you hit the cabs and knock out the drivers."

There was a tone of command in Dale's voice that Joe had never heard there before. He wondered if that was what Dale had sounded like when he took over that British tank and used it to blow up a German Panzer.

Dale sent the jeep through a narrow pass and then turned back to the west. He sped up, and in a moment the German convoy came into view again, moving in the same direction they were. Dale's foot came down hard on the accelerator, getting all the speed out of the jeep that he could. "Get ready!" he called to Joe and Garmon.

450

Joe's hands tightened on the Thompson. He had used one of the submachine guns before, but it had been a while. The important thing was to keep the recoil under control and keep the barrel from riding up. The arming lever was back, there was a full clip attached, and the gun was ready to go. The jeep was coming up quickly on the left side of the convoy. Joe could see the trucks a lot more clearly now. There were five of them being led by that armored car. These Germans weren't commandos, he realized. Commandos wouldn't travel in slow-moving trucks. Chances were they were supply vehicles that had gotten cut off from their unit in the aftermath of Operation Torch. As the jeep drew almost even with the last truck in line, he could see the black Iron Cross painted on its side, a German icon.

"Let 'em have it!" Dale shouted.

Joe twisted in the passenger seat and lined the Thompson on the tires of the last truck in line. He pressed the trigger and fought the recoil as noise and flame erupted from the muzzle of the weapon. Right behind him, Sergeant Garmon was firing as well.

Joe found that he could best control the submachine gun by firing short bursts, one after another. He saw sparks fly as the slugs smashed into the wheels of the truck. The jeep was moving so fast that it was even with the truck for only a few seconds, just enough time for Joe to fire three or four bursts, and then it was past and closing in on the next truck. Joe and Garmon sprayed it with fire too.

At first the Germans had no idea they were under attack, but they caught on pretty quickly. Joe saw muzzle flashes from the cab of the third truck, but then the bursts from Garmon's gun smashed into it and the truck swerved violently to the right. One of Garmon's bullets must have found the driver. Joe twisted his head to look back over his shoulder. The two trucks they'd hit first were no longer moving. The third one careened to a halt as well. The jeep rocketed past it. Joe and Garmon kept firing.

Up ahead, the Germans in the armored car knew something was wrong by now. It swung to the left in a sharp turn, looping around so that the crew of the machine gun mounted on its back could open fire. Flashes spewed from the muzzle of the gun. Dale jerked the jeep to the right, veering even closer to the trucks. Joe's eyes were wide with excitement and fear. Shots were still coming at them from the cabs of the trucks. Dale was driving right into a cross fire.

But he was too fast for the gunners in the armored car. Their bullets missed the jeep and tore into the motor of one of the trucks instead. The truck lurched to a stop as flames burst out of its engine compartment. The two men in the cab piled out and ran for their lives, barely escaping before the fire reached the gas tank. The truck blew up, lifting from the ground and breaking in two.

Garmon swiveled around and laced the armored car with submachine-gun fire. Joe concentrated on the last of the trucks, blowing out its tires with well-aimed bursts from his Thompson. The armored car was the only German vehicle still able to move. Dale spun the wheel, sending the jeep into a skidding turn. Joe hung on for dear life, thinking they were going to turn over. But Dale knew instinctively just how much he could ask the jeep to do, just as he had known how fast he could push a racecar around those dirt tracks back home.

Joe gripped Dale's shoulder and shouted, "We can't knock out an armored car with Thompsons!"

"He's right, Parker!" Garmon added.

"Hit him again on our way out!" Dale urged. He twisted the wheel, sent the jeep squirting past the armored car. The German gunners fired again, but Dale was still too fast for them. The jeep spurted ahead, clear of the burst of lead.

Joe and Garmon fired their Thompsons, emptying the clips at the armored car. Then Dale sent the jeep up the side of a shallow dune so fast that when the speedy little vehicle reached the crest, it went airborne for a second before coming down on the other side. Joe let out a startled yell. Then the wheels hit the ground and caught, flinging sand out from under them, and the jeep shot ahead into the night, safe now from any fire that the armored car might send after them.

"Yowza!" Dale whooped as he tromped the gas pedal. "We shot the hell out of those Krauts!"

"And nearly got our own asses shot off doin' it!" Garmon said.

"Nah, Sarge, they never had a chance at us. We were movin' too fast. Faster than a speeding bullet, just like Superman!" A grin stretched across Dale's face. He slowed down a little as he drove north toward the village. "You know, if you had a jeep with a heavier machine gun mounted on the back, say a Browning fifty caliber, you *could* knock out an armored car. Hell, you could knock out anything the Krauts've got, short of a Panzer."

"Oh, Lord," Joe said. "You're probably already trying to figure out a way to do *that*."

"Maybe," Dale said. "You might have something there, big brother." He looked over at Joe. "And a jeep like that would make a damned good vehicle for a spy to race around in, wouldn't it?"

From the back, Garmon said, "I don't want to hear this. I don't want to know anything about it. You Parker boys are the craziest sons o' bitches I ever saw!"

The sarge might be right, Joe thought, but there was a war on, a war waiting to be won, and a little craziness might not be such a bad thing. Joe grinned back at Dale and the jeep raced on into the night, the glare from the burning German truck lighting the sky behind them.

# FIFTY

Christmas had come and gone, and so had the New Year. It was 1943 now, and chilly, wet, and miserable in North Africa. The port cities of Tunis and Bizerte, in the mountainous country of northeastern Tunisia, were still the primary objectives of the Allied forces, but they seemed far away. Sure, more men, machinery, and supplies were pouring into the region all the time, but the Allied soldiers had to ask themselves a vital question: While they were resting, reinforcing, and resupplying, were the Germans doing the same thing?

More than some, Joe had an idea that wasn't true, at least not to the same extent. The rumors floating around in intelligence circles seemed to indicate that while the Germans were still sending supplies to their troops in North Africa, the supply lines were stretched thinner than ever. Looked at from a purely logistical standpoint, the outcome of this conflict seemed clear. Eventually the Allies would triumph.

But there was nothing logistical about the way the German soldiers fought, no way to quantify their stubbornness or draw up a chart that reflected their spirit. The Allied forces would have to be equally determined if they were going to emerge victorious.

There had been no repercussions for the daring raid on the German convoy in the desert, though Colonel Gault had looked at Joe a bit suspiciously as the colonel mentioned the anonymous tip that had led a flight of American planes over the crippled convoy the next day. The trucks had been set on fire and abandoned. The Germans that had been with them were gone. Some might have died of thirst as they tried to flee through the desert; others, no doubt, had escaped. Only two were ever picked up, spotted by a reconnaissance plane, and when they were brought in they told a crazy story about being attacked by a lone American jeep with three men in it. No one took the yarn seriously, except perhaps Colonel Gault.

All Joe knew for sure was that when he brought up Dale's idea of mounting a .50-caliber machine gun on a jeep and using it for intelligence purposes, Gault threw his weight behind the plan. The colonel even suggested that Joe would be the perfect man to try it out, and since he would need a driver, Dale could be transferred over to G-2, as well.

That idea gave Joe pause. Dale, working in intelligence? Somehow, that just didn't seem right. And yet, Joe knew that nobody was better behind a steering wheel than his little brother. Dale was a good mechanic—damned good, in fact—but there were plenty of guys who could work on tank engines. Joe wound up agreeing with Gault's suggestion. The Parker brothers were going to stay together, at least for a while longer.

Which was how they came to be driving without lights across the nighttime desert just west of Tunisia's Eastern Dorsal mountain range, near the village of Sidi Bou Zid. In the village, General Dwight D. Eisenhower was conducting an inspection of the American command post located there. American forces held this area, the southern sector of the defensive line established in Tunisia.

The line ran north and south and split the country almost in half. The Axis forces, pushed up into Tunisia by the steady advance of the British Eighth Army, occupied the eastern half of the country. In the south, the Mareth Line, a cluster of fortifications built long before by the French, closed off a bottleneck between the Mediterranean and a range of hills. The Germans, now under the joint command of General Rommel and General Jurgen von Arnim, had dug in along the Mareth Line, which could be defended with a relatively small portion of their troops. The rest of the Axis forces could turn their attention to the Eastern Dorsal, and if they were able to push across those mountains, drive the Allies back across the plains and over the Western Dorsal, the way would be open for a massive counterattack into Algeria. If the Germans reclaimed Algeria and smashed the Allied supply lines, they would be almost impossible to dislodge from North Africa. During the bad weather of the winter months, the momentum of Operation Torch had slipped away.

Though the Germans were still at a disadvantage, they were poised to become the aggressors once again.

Joe had discussed all of this with Colonel Gault and knew what the Allies were facing. So did Dale, because he had talked about it with Joe. As both of them looked toward the rugged, rocky heights of the Eastern Dorsal, they could almost sense the Germans over there, biding their time, waiting for just the right moment to strike.

Dale slowed the jeep to a halt and rested his hands atop the steering wheel. "What time is it?" he asked.

"I'm not sure," Joe replied. "After midnight, I'd say."

Dale turned toward his brother and grinned. "Then it's February fourteenth. Valentine's Day."

Joe just stared at him for a second, then laughed. "Here we are in the middle of a war, and you point out that it's Valentine's Day."

"Hey, romance is still important. Not that either of us have a gal right now. But one of these days . . ."

Dale's voice trailed away into silence. After a moment, Joe asked, "Do you ever think about Elaine?"

"I try not to," Dale said. "How about you? You think about Melinda?"

"Like you said, I try not to."

Again silence reigned, until Dale laughed. The sound was edged with bitterness. "That's us, the hard-luck Parkers." He reached for the lever to put the jeep back in gear.

Joe stopped him. "Wait a minute. Cut the engine, will you?"

"What's the matter?" Dale asked as he turned the key, shutting off the jeep's engine. Joe held up a hand, motioning for quiet. That was what he got, the nearly complete silence of the desert at night. The only sounds were the faint whisper of sand as it moved under the ceaseless prodding of the light wind, and the ticking as the metal in the engine cooled in the chilly night air.

Then Dale heard it too, a growling that came and went with no regular pattern. The noises were brief and fleeting and so faint that both Joe and Dale thought they could have been imagining things. But they knew they weren't.

"Engines," Dale breathed after a few moments. "Big ones, 'way up there in the passes through the mountains. That's gotta be—"

"Panzers," Joe finished for him. "The Germans are coming. To-night."

"And Ike's back there in the village."

Dale didn't have to say anything else. His hand shot to the ignition and twisted the key. His foot tromped the starter. The jeep's engine ground and whined as it tried to start.

"Come on, damn it!" Dale burst out. "If the Krauts get to the village while Ike's still there—"

Joe didn't want to think about that. The failure to take Tunis and Bizerte before winter set in had been a bitter disappointment to all the Allies, but Ike had held things together. Nobody was giving up, but rather, they were just waiting for the right moment to try again. Coordinating everything between the various British and American commanders was a tricky business, and so was keeping all of them relatively happy. General Eisenhower had done a masterful job of that so far. Joe wasn't sure if anyone else could do as well.

The engine caught with a roar. Joe leaned back against the passenger seat and blew out his breath in a sigh of relief. Dale shifted gears smoothly, wheeled the jeep around, and sent it racing across the sand toward Sidi Bou Zid.

*　　*　　*

A sandstorm blustered up behind them before they reached the village. The flying grit stung their faces as they leaped out of the jeep, which Dale had just brought to a rocking halt in front of the command post. Joe looked around. The staff cars and armored cars that made up General Eisenhower's convoy were gone. Ike had pulled out already.

Colonel Gault was still here, though. He stepped out of the CP to meet them. "You drove in like a bat out of hell, Sergeant," he said to Dale. "What's wrong?"

Joe jerked a thumb over his shoulder toward the Eastern Dorsal. The wind that had whipped up the sandstorm was strong and loud, and he had to raise his voice to be heard above it. "Panzers, sir!" he shouted. "Sounded like they were coming over Faid Pass!"

Gault stiffened, but before he could say anything else, another sound rose above the wind. It was a cross between a roar and a howl, with a high-pitched whine thrown in for good measure. Dale grabbed Joe's arm and flung him to the ground next to the jeep, diving down beside him as he yelled, "Stukas!"

Gault hit the dirt too. A second later, a huge explosion made the ground shake beneath them. More German dive-bombers swooped down out of the swirling dust and dropped their deadly loads. The earth rocked and heaved, and water from the pool that formed the oasis of Sidi Bou Zid was thrown high in the air as one of the bombs detonated in it. Drops of the precious liquid showered down like rain around Joe, Dale, and Gault as they scrambled to their feet.

"They're trying to soften us up with the bombers!" Gault said as he urged Joe and Dale into the jeep. "The Panzers will be along soon. Let's get out of here, boys."

"But, sir," Joe objected, "shouldn't we stay and help the men stationed here?"

"The three of us won't turn the tide here," Gault snapped. "If the German push has started, there'll be plenty of work for us elsewhere. Now come on, Sergeant Parker. That's an order!"

Joe and Dale piled into the jeep, which was still running. Joe climbed onto the back as Gault took the front passenger seat. The rear seat had been removed and a .50-caliber machine gun bolted to the floorboard in its place. From where he sat, Joe could handle the Fifty if he had to. Both he and Dale had been given a crash course in firing the heavy machine gun when they were assigned to the jeep.

With Dale behind the wheel, the vehicle squirted away from the command post. All over the village, American GIs were scrambling to their posts. Antiaircraft guns began to bark. In the dark, in the middle of a sandstorm, it was impossible for the gunners to see what they were shooting at, though. It would be sheer luck if any of the Stukas were shot down.

In the jeep, Joe leaned forward and shouted in Gault's ear, "We were afraid General Eisenhower was still here!"

Gault shook his head and looked back over his shoulder. "He left two hours ago! He was pretty upset with General Fredenhall's defense preparations!" The colonel gave a bark of grim laughter.

"Looks like we'll get a chance to see just how ready Two Corps really is!"

*   *   *

Not ready at all. That was the answer. By dawn on 14 February 1943, the Tenth Panzer Division had stormed through the mountains and overrun Sidi Bou Zid, trapping a considerable number of American forces on two nearby hills. A relief column of American tanks was turned back with heavy losses. The surrounded Americans had no choice but to try to break out on their own. They were unsuccessful. The Germans captured most of those who were not killed. Out of 2,500 men, only 300 escaped.

Disheartened by this, the Allied brass ordered their remaining forces to pull back to the Western Dorsal. This range of mountains was some fifty miles away, and every step of the retreat caused American spirits to sink lower.

But the Germans could still be stopped at the Western Dorsal. The main route through these mountains was a narrow gap known as Kasserine Pass. Beyond the pass lay a main road that led into Algeria. This was the place Allied resistance had to stiffen.

This was the pass that must be held.

# FIFTY-ONE

Gene March leaned against a rock that was taller than he was and wiped sweat off his face. It was winter and should have been cold, but the sun beat down this afternoon with an unseasonable fierceness. Or maybe it was just nerves, he told himself. Any reasonable guy would be a little skittish in a situation like this.

After all, right over there on the other side of Kasserine Pass were thousands of bloodthirsty Krauts, and the main thing each and every one of them wanted to do was kill Private Gene March.

That was the way it felt to him, anyway. The Germans were bearing down on his position. He'd been put out here like a sacrificial lamb, all by himself. He blinked sweat out of his eyes and wished he were back in Oran. Those days, the opening days of the Allied invasion of North Africa, seemed far, far in the past now. And the relative comfort of Algeria might as well have been a million miles away.

"Stop daydreaming, March," Sergeant Hollis said. "If you're bored, the Krauts will be here soon enough to occupy your time."

Gene gave a little shake of his head. He wasn't alone out here, of course. His company was only one of many that had been shifted here to Tunisia to try to stop the Germans. Hollis and the rest of the men were scattered through these rocks that littered the plain in front of the mouth of Kasserine Pass. Behind them, the road split, one branch heading north to the village of Thala, the other going on west to Tebessa. Artillery emplacements were spread out along both branches of the road. The muzzles of the cannons all pointed toward the mouth of the pass, waiting for the Panzers to poke their snouts out.

Gene wasn't sure why the infantry was even up here on the front line. What good could carbines and tommy guns do against tanks, after all? It was a waste of manpower, that's what it was. The damned brass didn't know how to carry out a war. Why, if he were in charge—

"Hear that?" Hollis's voice cut into Gene's thoughts. "Here they come."

Gene tightened and retightened his grip on the Garand. He could hear the rumbling of the tanks too. Sure enough, a minute later, he saw movement in the shadows at the mouth of the pass. Here they came, clanking and clattering and growling like massive metal beasts that wanted to gnaw his bones.

With a roar like thunder, the American artillery launched a volley toward the Panzers. Hollis yelled, "Now!" and started firing his Thompson. Gene still didn't see what good small-arms fire was going to do against the lumbering behemoths, especially at this range, but he lifted the carbine to his shoulder and squeezed off a shot toward the Krauts. His cheek nestled against the smooth wood of the stock. Without lifting his head, he worked the bolt and fired again, then again and again.

Though it was still winter, the weather had been warm enough in recent days to prompt the blooming of wildflowers on the plain before the pass. Now those flowers were whipped back and forth by the explosions and the bullets that passed among them. The Panzers roared out of the pass, their heavy cannons belching fire. Shells whined overhead, making Gene crouch involuntarily. The shots from the tanks exploded behind the infantry positions, among the American artillery. The Panzers kept coming as the volleys from the Allied big guns decreased.

The tanks were about a thousand yards away. Gene could see men walking between them, German infantrymen. He switched his aim to them and saw a couple of the Krauts drop to their knees and then pitch forward. He didn't feel much at the thought that he had just killed those men. Better them than him.

The cannons began to pound again behind him. The Germans had shaken up the American gunners for a few minutes, but now they were back at work and were in fact redoubling their efforts. They rained down fire and lead on the Panzers and German troops emerging from the pass. After a while, dust and smoke filled the air and it was hard to see much. The artillery kept up the bombardment, even though orders went along the line of infantry to cease fire.

Gene slumped to the ground and rested his back against the rock. His shoulder ached like blazes from the recoil of the carbine as he'd fired countless shots over the past hour. Hollis trotted over and hunkered beside him. "I think we're going to turn them back," the sergeant said.

Ever since Gene had saved his bacon back in Oran, Hollis had acted like he thought they were buddies or something. Well, not buddies, exactly, but it was clear Hollis didn't regard Gene as the same sort of goldbrick as he had before. Hollis always seemed a little disappointed when Gene didn't respond much. Gene didn't want to get too friendly with the sarge. Hollis might get some crazy idea in his head, like making him a corporal or something.

"How long do we have to stay out here, Sarge?"

"Until they tell us to do something else. You ought to know that by now, March."

Gene took a chocolate bar out of his pocket and started to unwrap it. He didn't smoke—bad for the ol' pipes. He took a bite of the candy bar as the artillery continued to blast away at the Krauts.

Hollis laughed. "You're a cool customer, aren't you, March?"

"No, Sarge, I'm not. But if we're going to be out here for a while, I figure I'd better keep my strength up."

"That's probably a good idea." Hollis gazed off toward the pass. "I don't think the Krauts are going to give it up any time soon."

Sergeant Hollis's words proved prophetic. Though the Axis forces were bottled up in Kasserine Pass that afternoon, 19 February 1943, by the next morning Afrika Korps infantry patrols had infiltrated the Allied lines and caused havoc during the night. The Germans renewed their attempt to break through the pass, spearheading a massive infantry assault with a rocket attack. This time the American and British forces had no choice but to pull back. By late in the afternoon of 20 February, Rommel was watching his men march unhindered through Kasserine Pass.

But then, with uncharacteristic caution, the Desert Fox called a halt to the advance. Suspecting that an Allied counterattack was in the offing, Rommel decided that his troops needed some time to rest and be resupplied before continuing toward the Western Dorsal. What he failed to take into account was that the delay also gave the Allies time to regroup and an opportunity to move up reinforcements. At the first sign of a German advance, the Americans near the village of Thala launched a huge artillery barrage that stopped the Panzers and the Afrika Korps in their tracks. Rommel, knowing that his supply lines already were stretched perilously thin and knowing as well that an attack on the Mareth Line by the British Eighth Army was inevitable, decided that the Reich would be better served if he abandoned his thrust into western Tunisia and turned back to meet the British threat.

Though Rommel's thinking was sound, his execution was not. On 6 March, near the village of Medenine, the Deutsche Afrika Korps and the British Eighth Army clashed again for the first time since the already legendary battle of El Alamein. Rommel's assault was turned back time and again by the deadly, coolheaded firing of the British antitank gunners. He had no choice but to call off the attack and let the stalemate settle down again.

Rommel himself had reached the end of his run. Convinced that the Axis could no longer hold North Africa, the general flew to Berlin to advise the Führer of this fact. Rommel's suggestion that the troops in North Africa could be used to the better advantage of the Reich elsewhere met with a furious response from Hitler. Rommel was relieved of command, though Hitler tried to soften the blow somewhat by announcing that the general was going on sick leave. From now on, General von Arnim would be the supreme commander of Axis forces in Africa.

That wasn't the only change of command going on in that part of the world.

\*　　\*　　\*

"You know anything about this guy Patton?" Dale asked as he and Joe lounged in the jeep parked alongside the road just outside Tebessa.

"Not much," Joe said, though he had heard quite a few off-the-record comments about General George S. Patton from Colonel Gault and some of the other intelligence officers. "He was some sort of hero in World War One. Supposed to be pretty much spit'n'polish and by the book. I figure he's got to be better than Fredenhall." Joe pointed down the road toward an approaching convoy. "At least he's not sitting underground in a bunker."

Dale let out a whistle. "You can say that again."

Indeed, General Patton was making himself conspicuous by standing up in the rear seat of the convoy's lead car, a heavy Ford convertible with the top down. Dressed in an immaculate uniform, his helmet strapped down tightly, Patton could have stepped right out of a recruiting poster. As the line of scout cars and half-tracks swept past the jeep where Joe and Dale sat, they got a good look at the new commander of II Corps. And Patton got a good look at them. Joe caught his breath and felt a tingle go through him as the general's eyes locked on him for a second before the convoy rolled on.

"Son of a bitch!" Dale exclaimed. "Did you see what he was wearing?"

"A general's uniform," Joe said weakly, still a little shaken by the scowl Patton had sent his way.

"No, I mean the six-guns. Pearl-handled cowboy guns, just like Buck Jones or Hoot Gibson!"

Joe looked over at his brother and said slowly, "I wouldn't let him hear you comparing him to movie cowboys if I was you."

Dale started the jeep's engine and put it in gear, pulling out to fall in behind the convoy. "I wonder where I could get some pearl-handled six-shooters like that," he mused.

Joe just shook his head.

By that evening, word of how Patton was going to shake things up had gotten around. Being out of uniform was no longer permitted, no matter what the circumstances. Military discipline and protocol would be observed at all times. It remained to be seen whether the men would fight any better because of these new measures, but by God, at least they'd be spiffier!

Joe and Dale had been carrying out night patrols ever since Rommel and the Germans had pulled back, just to make sure the Krauts didn't send any sorties toward the American lines. They pulled into camp a few mornings after Patton's arrival just as dawn was breaking, covered with dust as usual. As Dale brought the jeep to a stop, he gazed over at a line of tanks that hadn't been there the night before when he and Joe left. They were bigger and more heavily armored than the General Grants. Dale hopped out of the jeep and said excitedly, "Those are the Shermans, Joe! I told you we were going to get some of them sooner or later. Look at those babies! What I wouldn't give to take on a Panzer in one of them!"

A sharp voice came from behind them. "Soldier, I wouldn't let a slovenly bastard like you anywhere near one of those tanks!"

Joe and Dale both stiffened to attention. The tone of voice was enough to tell them that an officer had spoken. Joe's heart seemed to sink right into the pit of his stomach as the officer walked around them and he recognized the sharply creased uniform, the pearl-handled guns, and the belligerently jutting jaw.

"What the hell is that on your head, Sergeant?" General Patton asked Dale.

"My helmet, sir," Dale replied after swallowing a couple of times.

Patton leaned closer and shouted into Dale's face. "That's not a helmet, goddamn it! That's a helmet *liner!*"

That was true. Dale had removed the heavy steel helmet, as usual when he and Joe were on patrol, and was wearing only the lightweight liner. The actual helmet was in the jeep, lying in the floorboard next to where the .50-caliber machine gun was mounted. As Joe watched Patton bawling out Dale, he was glad that he was wearing his helmet.

The general concluded his obscenity-laced tirade by saying, "That's a twenty-five-dollar fine, Sergeant. Next time you're caught out of uniform, it'll be worse. Do you understand?"

"Yes, sir," Dale said.

Patton leaned in, lashing out verbally in the time-honored tradition that went all the way back to boot camp. "What was that, soldier? I can't hear you!"

"*Yes, sir!*"

"That's better." Patton gave a curt nod. "Don't forget what I told you, Sergeant. And get that dust cleaned off."

"No, sir. I won't forget, sir. And yes, sir, we'll get cleaned up right away."

Patton started to turn away, but Dale stopped him by saying, "Sir?"

Joe suppressed a groan. The general was finished with them. What in blazes did Dale think he was doing, drawing Patton's attention back to them this way?

"What is it?" Patton asked gruffly.

Dale nodded toward the tanks. "Those General Shermans, sir? They're ours? We're going to use them against the Krauts?"

"That's the idea, son. Once we've greased the treads with enough Nazi guts."

"They'll knock out the Panzers, sir. They're just what we've been needing. The M-three is a good tank, but from what I hear, the Shermans are a lot better. You can kill a Panzer with a General Grant, so I know the Shermans can handle 'em."

Patton regarded Dale curiously. "You sound like you speak from experience, Sergeant."

"Yes, sir. My brother—I mean, Sergeant Parker and I were assigned to the Royal Tank Corps, assisting the British."

Joe held his breath, hoping that Dale wouldn't start bragging to Patton about how he had taken command of a British tank and used it to destroy a German Panzer. The story about how Dale had attacked a whole group of Panzers in a jeep probably ought to stay untold too. On the other hand, if Patton really was the wild man everybody said he was, he might appreciate those yarns.

Patton stared at Dale for a moment with narrowed eyes. "What's your current assignment, Sergeant?"

"G-Two, sir," Joe answered before Dale could say anything. "We work for Colonel Gault, who's attached to General Eisenhower's staff."

Patton grunted. "I know Gault. A good soldier." The general

was still looking at Dale. "But if you get tired of doing that, Sergeant, you come to see me. I can always use a man who knows tanks. They're the weapon that's going to win this war for us."

"You mean the tanks, sir?" Dale said.

Patton shook his head, his lips pressed together in a grim line. "No. I mean the men. The killers. Down through the ages, they're the greatest weapons ever put on the face of the earth."

# FIFTY-TWO

With the German forces still concentrated in southeastern Tunisia in defense of the Mareth Line, something had to be done to draw some of them away so that the British could break through the line. That job—what some might see as little more than a glorified distraction—fell to General George S. Patton and the American II Corps.

The strategy was to drive southeast through the mountains at passes located near the villages of El Guettar and Maknassy. This would put the Americans on the northwest flank of the Axis forces bunched behind the Mareth Line. The mountain passes were held mostly by Italian troops. II Corps moved out on the night of 16 March, heading toward the rocky slopes of the Eastern Dorsal where it curved into a rough fishhook shape.

Joe and Dale were out in front. G-2 sent several patrols ahead of the main advance to scout out the strength of the Axis defenses. The first possible stronghold was the tiny village of Gafsa. A month earlier, it had been in American hands, but then the Germans had pushed across the Eastern Dorsal, forcing the Yanks to fall back. Now, Joe perched on the back of the jeep with his hands tight on the handles of the .50-caliber machine gun. He didn't know what they were going to find up ahead. Reconnaissance planes had reported no Axis activity around Gafsa, but sometimes the Krauts were good at hiding what they were up to. Anything could be waiting at the oasis.

Dale was running without lights, as usual. As the jeep approached the village, Joe's eyes scanned the small cluster of buildings for any sign of a threat. Gafsa appeared to be sleeping. No lights were visible. If the Germans were there, they would be able to hear the jeep's engine by now. The skin on the back of Joe's neck crawled as he waited for a sudden burst of machine-gun fire or a belch of flame from the mouth of a cannon.

Somewhere up ahead, a dog started to bark.

Dale let out a laugh as he wheeled the jeep between the buildings. "There's nobody here, not even the natives," he called back to Joe. "The place is deserted."

Except for the dog, which ran after them, yapping. If any of the Arab inhabitants of Gafsa were left in the village, they were lying mighty low tonight. Joe didn't blame them. The people of Tunisia, indeed all the citizens of the countries that made up North Africa, had been caught up in a conflict not of their making. All they could do was try to stay out of the way as best they could.

Dale drove all the way around the village. No Germans or other Axis forces anywhere. Joe leaned forward and tapped his brother on the shoulder. "Head back to the column," Joe said. "We'll let General Allen know the way is clear." General Terry Allen was the commander of the First Infantry Division, the outfit heading up the column that was bound for the mountain passes.

Dale wheeled the jeep around and roared off in the direction he and Joe had come from.

The Americans passed through Gafsa without any opposition. They moved on through the village of El Guettar and into the broad, grassy basin beyond it. To Joe's eyes, the landscape looked a lot like what he had seen in various Western movies over the years: plains and mountains, deserts and rocky ridges. He halfway expected to see a stagecoach or a troop of mounted cavalry moving along the road that led from El Guettar to the passes, instead of Sherman tanks and armored cars and troop carriers. Whenever he looked at a hill, he thought that John Wayne might ride over it at any moment. If General Patton was a cowboy at heart, as his pearl-handled six-shooters implied, then he had come to the right place.

Gafsa and El Guettar were undefended, but the same was not true of the high hills on the other side of the basin. Only two narrow passes led through those hills. On the afternoon of 20 March, from the back of the jeep, Joe trained his binoculars on the passes and saw the ugly snouts of machine guns and antitank guns poking out from behind the rocks that littered the walls of the openings. Studying the passes themselves, he spotted twisted rolls of barbed wire coiled on the ground. He lowered the glasses and said to Dale, "I'll bet there are mines in there too."

Dale was sitting behind the wheel of the jeep, a Lucky Strike dangling between his lips. "Maybe they're trying to fool us," he suggested. "Maybe those aren't real guns up there."

Joe looked sharply at him. "You think so?"

Dale blew a smoke ring and said, "The Krauts have used that trick before. For that matter, so have we."

Joe nodded, remembering stories he'd heard of how the British had built phony tanks out of boards and canvas to make the Germans think they were building up their forces in one place while in reality the concentration was taking place in another area. The Germans could be pulling a variation of that now, making it look like the passes were too heavily defended to be passable so that the Americans would waste their time looking elsewhere for a way to cross the hills.

"Only one way to find out," Dale said, looking back over his shoulder and grinning at Joe. "Hang on."

With that, he put the jeep in gear and sent it spurting forward, raising a cloud of dust behind it. Joe barely had time to grab hold of the Fifty to steady himself as the jeep bounced over the rutted road.

His mouth was dry with tension as they approached the passes. Soon they were close enough so that he could see the guns without the binoculars. Dale kept the jeep at a steady speed, as if he intended to drive right on through the northernmost pass.

Suddenly, geysers of dirt spouted up in the road about ten yards ahead of the jeep. Dale jammed on the brakes and spun the wheel. "I knew it!" he shouted. "I knew the sons o' bitches would get trigger-happy!"

Joe hung on as the jeep slewed around. He hunched his shoulders as more slugs from one of the machine guns in the pass chewed up the road around the vehicle. Dale tromped on the gas. The jeep shot ahead, going away from the passes now. The machine-gun fire fell behind as the jeep raced out of range.

"If that Kraut gunner had waited ten more seconds, he would have shot us to pieces!" Joe shouted over the wind whipping past them.

"Yeah, but I figured he wouldn't!" Dale flung back over his shoulder.

"But you couldn't *know* that!"

Dale glanced back at him. "Hell, big brother, in this world, nobody really *knows* anything! You just take your shot and wait to see what happens!"

*     *     *

In this case, what happened was that the American column ground to a halt in front of the passes, well out of range of the Axis guns positioned there.

The geography of the area dictated the next move. Close observation of the northernmost pass showed that it might be possible for a small group of men to climb to the top of a hill that overlooked the pass. If a force was able to get up there, then they would have the high ground and would be able to fire down into the Italian defenders holding the pass. The men selected to lead that assault were Army Rangers under the command of Lt. Col. William O. Darby.

Darby's Rangers wouldn't be the only ones going on this night strike, however. Colonel Bradford Gault found Joe and Dale, who had gone to the rear of the column to grab some chow after giving their report to Gault earlier, and informed them of the plan.

"G-Two is going to be part of this operation," Gault said. "In this case, that means the two of you."

Dale was sitting on the jeep's running board, eating some rations from a tin. He stayed there, Gault having waved him down when he started to stand up and come to attention. He swallowed and said, "Aw, Colonel, we already did the reconnaissance this afternoon. You mean we gotta let the Krauts shoot at us again?"

"What do you think, the war's over?" Gault snapped. "Anyway, those aren't Krauts in that pass. They're Italians."

"They can still shoot," Joe pointed out.

"Yeah, that's why they call it war," Gault said. "You've got your orders, both of you. Report to Colonel Darby at twenty-two hundred hours."

"Yes, sir," Joe said. Dale echoed the response.

When the colonel was gone, Dale asked, "Does this make us commandos now?"

"Commandos are British," Joe said. "Americans are Rangers. And anyway, just because we're going with Colonel Darby and his men doesn't make us Rangers. We're still attached to Intelligence."

"I think they got the name wrong," Dale muttered. "I'm not sure how smart it is to get shot at all the time."

"You were the one who drove right up to the pass this afternoon and dared them to stop us."

Dale grinned. "That was different."

"Sure it was."

Just before 2200 hours, the two of them reported as ordered to Colonel William O. Darby, who said, "I guess I can understand why Colonel Gault wants you to come along. Just stay out of my boys' way."

"Yes, sir," Joe agreed. "We intend to."

"Don't think you're going to just be observers, though," Darby warned them. "I expect things to be pretty hot up there."

"Yes, sir, I expect so too."

Darby turned them over to one of his noncoms, a sergeant named Patterson. He gave Joe a little round tin of burnt cork. "Get your faces blackened up good," Patterson said. "Don't want those fellas in the pass spotting us too soon."

Joe and Dale rubbed the stuff on their faces. "I feel like I ought to be in a minstrel show," Dale cracked. "What do you think, Mr. Bones?"

Joe just ignored him and kept blackening his face with the cork. Sergeant Patterson was right about not being spotted too soon.

A short time later, the group of Rangers moved out, heading across the basin toward the hills. Joe had a little trouble keeping up with the squad he and Dale had been assigned to. Dale was breathing hard too by the time they reached the bottom of the slope they soon would ascend. These Rangers were in peak condition. They began moving in single file up a gorge that slashed through the side of the hill.

The going was hard, and the need for near absolute silence made it harder. Joe struggled to control his breathing so that he wouldn't be puffing and panting. He stepped carefully to avoid loose rocks that might roll down the gorge and cause a clatter that would alert the pass's defenders. At the head of the gorge, a nearly sheer cliff rose. The Rangers had to climb it one by one, searching out footholds and handholds. Joe and Dale pulled themselves up, knowing that if they couldn't make it on their own, the Rangers would leave them behind.

The ascent of the hill took most of the night. Joe was drenched in sweat by the time he pulled himself over the last ridge and stood atop the hill with Dale and the other men. The lowering moon shone down on the far side of the slope where the Italian soldiers charged with holding the pass crouched behind rocks, blissfully unaware that the enemy was now above them. Darby gave his men only a few minutes to catch their breath, and then a bugle call rang out stridently in the predawn darkness. That was the signal for the attack to begin.

With a yell, Sergeant Patterson leaped down the slope, firing his carbine toward the Italian positions. The rest of his squad, along with Joe and Dale, followed suit. Dale bellowed and howled, throwing himself into the spirit of the thing. Joe bounded from rock to rock in silence, stopping each time to steady himself before he squeezed off a shot.

Like devils, the Rangers swarmed down the hillside. Within minutes, they were among the Italians, shooting some at close range and bayoneting others. The battle was fierce but short in duration. The firing died away as the sky turned orange and the sun began to peep over the hills. Many of the defenders had surrendered as they were startled out of sleep by what must have seemed like a horde of howling maniacs. Most of the ones who had put up a fight were dead.

Joe and Dale came through the clash unscathed. They were standing nearby when Colonel Darby, who had led the attack personally, got on the radio to General Allen and reported that the pass was clear. Standing on the heights, the black-faced Rangers waved carbines and submachine guns over their heads as down below the American column started through the pass. Joe grinned tiredly but proudly at the sight.

Beside him, Dale said, "I guess we're honorary Rangers now. Maybe once we link up with the British, we can go along on a commando mission, so we'll be able to call ourselves commandos too."

Joe laughed. Dale was never going to grow up . . . and a part of Joe hoped it would always be that way.

# FIFTY-THREE

One of the passes was clear, but the other one, the one that actually led in a more direct route to Mareth, was still held by the Axis forces. Early on the morning of 23 March, a German Panzer division came storming through this pass, taking the fight to the Americans.

Gene March was startled out of sleep by the sudden booming of cannons and the brisk rattle of small-arms fire. He rolled over and came to his feet, getting tangled in his bedroll for a few seconds before he was able to kick free of it. Sergeant Hollis ran by, shouting, "Fall in! Fall in! Tank attack!"

Gene stumbled after the sarge, clutching his carbine in one hand while he felt along the front of his jacket with the other. Four grenades were still clipped to his jacket.

Not that he wanted to get close enough to those damned Panzers to start tossing grenades at them. But at least he had them, just in case. It was a safe bet the Garand wouldn't do him any good. Carbine rounds would bounce harmlessly off the armor on the German tanks. Might as well be throwing rocks at them, Gene thought.

The sun was just below the peaks to the east, already high enough to scatter a considerable amount of reddish-orange light over the scene. Gene heard a roar and looked up to see German fighter planes coming over the mountains and diving toward the basin. He thought they were Messerschmidts, but he was no expert on such things. All he knew was that the planes were swooping down toward the American infantry positions. Slugs screamed through the air.

Gene dove toward a foxhole as bullets whipped around him. One of them hit so close to his head that it threw dirt in his face, blinding him for a moment as the gritty stuff got in his eyes. He yelled in sheer, involuntary terror and pawed at his eyes. Other than the discomfort, he didn't know why the dirt in his eyes bothered him so much. If one of the Nazi slugs found him, he would never see it coming anyway.

He hunkered lower in the hole. Somebody dropped beside him. Hollis yelled, "March! Are you hit?"

Gene finally got enough of the dirt out of his eyes so that he could see again, even though his vision was still pretty blurry. He looked over at Hollis and shook his head. "No, I'm okay!"

"Then get your head up! Here come some more of the bastards!"

Gene looked up and saw more fighters angling down from the dawn sky. He wedged the butt of the Garand against his shoulder and started to fire at them. Beside him, Hollis's Thompson began to chatter. It was almost impossible to shoot down a plane with small-arms fire, but with a lot of luck, it *could* be done.

*I've been around the world in a plane,* Gene thought, seeming to hear the smoky tinkle of a late-night piano in the back of his head. *Settled revolutions in Spain.* Damn, but he loved to sing that song. *But I'm brokenhearted . . .* He wished he was in some club right now, with a beautiful girl at a table down front, watching him with soulful eyes as he cradled the microphone stand and sent his voice out to her and her alone, making love to her with the deep, rich tones.

*. . . 'cause I just can't get started with you . . .*

Sergeant Hollis screamed and something hot and wet splashed over the side of Gene's face. He flinched away and looked over to see that at least one bullet had torn through Hollis's left arm. Blood spurted from the wound. The slug had hit an artery. Gene dropped his gun and reached over to grab Hollis. The sarge was twitching and shaking, and he might bleed to death in a matter of minutes if the wound kept pumping like that. Gene reached down and fumbled with Hollis's belt. After a moment he got it off and wrapped it around Hollis's arm just below the shoulder. He pulled it as tight as he could. The scarlet flood slowed down to a trickle. Hollis sighed and sagged back against the side of the foxhole. He had either passed out or died, Gene thought. He heard the rasp of breath in Hollis's throat and realized the sarge was still alive, just unconscious. No telling how long it would be until a medic came along. That would all depend on how the battle went. Gene dug out a field dressing from the first-aid kit in his pack and pressed it to the wound, then used tape to bind it in place. The bleeding had slowed a lot. Hollis might make it if he got some proper medical attention in time. Gene loosened the makeshift tourniquet on the sergeant's arm.

He picked up his carbine again. The Germans were still coming. He lifted his head and peered over the top of the foxhole. The line of tanks still ground inexorably toward the American positions. Behind them came the infantry, as usual. Gene didn't know if the foot soldiers were German or Italian. It didn't really matter. As they swarmed closer, he began trying to pick them off.

An American jeep with a machine gun mounted on the back raced past. The GI manning the Fifty had it spouting lead and flame toward the attackers. A shell burst just behind the jeep, throwing a cloud of smoke and dust into the air. When it cleared, Gene couldn't see the vehicle anymore. It was up ahead somewhere, careening toward the very front of the battle.

Gene sang softly, "Just can't get started . . . with you . . ." and settled his cheek against the stock of the Garand. It kicked hard against his shoulder as he squeezed off another round.

Joe clapped a hand to the back of his neck, but when he took it away a moment later, there was only a little blood on his palm. His neck stung like blazes, but obviously, the bit of debris or shrapnel that had hit him when the shell went off right behind the jeep had only nicked him. He had bled more than that from shaving cuts.

"Wahoo!" Dale yelled from the front seat. "Let's find one of those damn Panzers!"

His brother had gone nuts, Joe thought. They couldn't take on a tank with just a jeep and a .50-caliber machine gun. But then, recalling some of the things Dale had done in the past, Joe was convinced that was exactly what he meant to do.

The American artillery and antitank guns pounded the advancing line of Panzers, but the Germans kept coming. In fact, two of the tanks were only about a hundred yards away, lumbering toward an Allied command post. That was General Allen's CP, Joe realized, his eyes widening. And there was the general himself, yelling orders and stalking back and forth out in the open, heedless of the urgings from his staff officers to get back under cover.

The jeep shot past the command post. Dale had the gas pedal floored. Like it or not, Joe thought, they were going to be right in front of those Panzers in a few seconds. Might as well feed them a few .50-caliber snacks. He squeezed the machine gun's triggers.

The bullets scythed through a line of German infantry and then stuck sparks as they ricocheted from the thick armor of one of the tanks. The machine-gun fire must have drawn the attention of the Panzer's commander, because the big .75mm-cannon started to rotate toward the jeep as the tank lumbered forward. Joe was about to lean over, tap Dale on the helmet, and yell for him to get the hell out of there, when the front end of the Panzer suddenly seemed to lift a couple of feet into the air atop a ball of fire. Black smoke billowed as the tank crashed back to earth. It had hit a mine, Joe realized.

All along the advancing line of German tanks, more explosions roared out. The Panzers had blundered into an area thickly sown with powerful mines by American engineers. The attack shuddered to a halt, but it was too late. In a matter of minutes, more than two dozen of the tanks were burning furiously. Their way blocked by these blazing hulks, the other Panzers had to stop, and that made them sitting ducks for the American artillery and antitank guns. As fresh rounds screamed in and exploded, the German officers did the only thing they could.

They ordered the tanks to turn tail and run.

Dale let out an excited whoop at that sight. "Look at 'em go!" he said. "That'll teach 'em to mess with us! Give 'em a good-bye burst, Joe!"

That seemed sort of pointless to Joe, since the Germans were already retreating, but then Dale's enthusiasm proved infectious. With a grin, Joe elevated the barrel of the Fifty a little and squeezed off a long burst. He didn't know if any of the bullets hit anything, but right now, it didn't matter one way or the other. The burst of fire was a show of defiance, nothing more. But it felt mighty good anyway.

The enemy pulled back all the way through the pass, but they didn't stay gone. That afternoon, the Germans were back, this time with even more infantry. The tanks that had survived the morning's debacle led the way as the soldiers came pouring out of the pass. They charged across the basin, right into heavy fire from both the American artillery and from the new Sherman tanks as well. During the lull, General Patton had moved up the Shermans to support General Allen's infantry and artillery.

That fiery resistance broke the momentum of the German attack. The Panzers retreated again, and the infantry fell back right behind them. Two hard strikes at the Americans in the El Guettar basin had failed utterly. Even the most optimistic of German commanders had to realize by now that the Americans were not going to be dislodged.

But the Axis forces still held the main pass at El Guettar, and also the one farther north at Maknassy. Those passes would have to be cleared before II Corps could go any farther. With typically stubborn determination, Patton settled down to batter his way through them.

*   *   *

Gene March didn't want to be here. He hated hospitals, hated the smells and the noises and everything else about them. Hospitals were for sick people. He had no business being there. He was as healthy as a horse.

But Sergeant Hollis had sent word that he wanted to see him, and Gene couldn't figure out any way to refuse without looking like a real jerk.

The medical corps had taken over several buildings in the village of El Guettar and made wards out of them. Gene walked down the aisle between two rows of beds that were full of wounded men. Some of the men moaned in pain, some cursed, and some just lay there, silent and motionless, staring at the flyspecked ceiling. Others, who weren't hurt as bad, sat on the sides of their bunks and played cards or shot the bull with other patients. The place reminded Gene a little of a barracks, only the antiseptic smell that hovered in the air threatened to make him sick to his stomach.

He was looking for the sarge, but he heard a different voice call his name. He stopped and turned around and saw Al Satterfield coming toward him. Al was in his skivvies and had a bandage wrapped around his right thigh. He grinned and stuck out a hand, saying, "Hey, March, good to see you, buddy."

Gene shook Satterfield's hand. "Hello, Corporal. I didn't know I'd run into you here."

"Yeah, one of the filthy Boche winged me."

"Are you going to be shipped back home?"

"For this little scratch?" Satterfield slapped his thigh, then winced. "Nah, it'll be fine. But I *am* getting a transfer. Just found out about it. I'm going over to Special Services to work with the USO." He jerked a thumb toward the ceiling. "It's about time those lunkheads up the totem pole figured out where my real talents lie. I'm wasted shootin' at the Krauts when I could be putting together shows for the rest of you boys."

The USO . . . that meant Satterfield would be far away from the front lines. The Army wouldn't want any celebrities getting anywhere near the shooting.

"That's great, Corporal," Gene forced himself to say, even though he was thinking, *You lucky son of a bitch.* "I'm sure you'll do a great job. Guys still talk about the show you put on on that troop transport while we were coming over here."

"Yeah, seeing you reminded me of that show. You were a big hit, March. You ever think about singing professionally?"

"Just every day of my life for the past few years!" Gene couldn't stop the words from tumbling out of his mouth.

Satterfield laughed. "Spoken like a true entertainer. Tell you what, kid. How'd you like me to pull a few strings, see if I can take you with me over to Special Services? I think it'd be great for the GIs to see somebody like you in the shows. One of their own, you know what I mean?"

Gene's head was swimming. He couldn't believe the turn that fate had taken. He had a way out of combat now, and it was legit. Honorable, even. Hell, everybody respected the USO. And none of this would have happened for him if Hollis hadn't gotten hit and Al Satterfield hadn't picked up that so-called scratch on his leg.

"Well, whattaya say?" Satterfield prompted.

"I say sure, Corporal. Thank you." There was no hesitation in Gene's reply now.

Satterfield clapped him on the arm. "Call me Al," he said. He leaned closer and lowered his voice. "We gotta keep up with the military discipline and all that crap whenever any brass are around, but you and me, kid, we know the real score. We speak the same lingo, savvy? Showbiz, baby, showbiz."

Gene felt like he had come home.

A curious expression came over Satterfield's face. "Say, what are you doing here, anyway?"

"I came to see my sergeant," Gene replied. "He was hit a couple of days ago, when the Krauts attacked through the pass."

"Devoted to your old sarge, eh?"

"He sent word to the squad that he wanted to see me." Gene felt a little uncomfortable now. "I guess he's got it in his head that I saved his life or something, just because I tied up his wound before he could bleed to death. But that's all there was to it."

Satterfield's eyes widened. "You saved your sergeant's life?" He punched Gene on the arm. "Why, hell, you're a hero, kid! That's even better! The sweetest baritone this side of Sinatra, and a hero to boot! We can really play this up." He made shooing motions with his hands. "Go see your sarge, and then come back and talk to me some more. We got lots of plans to make."

"All right, Corporal. I mean, Al."

A little dazed, Gene walked on through the ward until he spotted Hollis lying on a cot on the left hand side of the aisle. Hollis's arm was heavily bandaged, and he had sort of a dopey look on his face, like the doctors had pumped him full of morphine. His eyes grew more focused, though, when he spotted Gene approaching.

Hollis lifted his hand. "March," he said. "Thanks for coming."

"Glad to, Sarge," Gene said as he clasped Hollis's hand. A few minutes earlier, that would have been a polite lie. Now, it was the truth. Gene was glad he had come to the hospital, even though the reason for his happiness had nothing to do with seeing his wounded sergeant.

"How's the squad?"

"Doing okay, I guess. Corporal Owens is running things."

"What about the Krauts? They still have the passes?"

Gene nodded. "Yeah. We haven't been able to shake them out yet."

But that wouldn't be his worry for much longer, he thought. He was getting out of here and going someplace a lot better.

"We'll get through," Hollis said. "It's just a matter of time."

Gene forced himself to make conversation. "What about you, Sarge? How long are you going to be laid up?"

Hollis frowned and shook his head. "I don't know. The docs are worried that there may be some kind of nerve damage or something in this arm. They don't know if it'll ever be right again." He gave a hollow laugh. "I may be through with the war, March. Washed up."

For the second time in the past few minutes, Gene thought, *You lucky son of a bitch.* He said, "That's okay, Sarge. You've done your part."

Hollis's eyes blazed with anger. He looked anything but doped-up now. "The hell I have!" he exclaimed. "This fight's got a long way to go yet, and I want to be part of it. I *need* to be part of it!"

"Why?" Gene asked without thinking. "There are plenty of other GIs."

"Yeah, sure, but we all have to carry our share of the load. It's up to all of us, March. Each and every American who's over here trying to . . . to make the world what it used to be. What it ought to be."

Gene pressed his lips together. He had to restrain himself from asking where Hollis had picked up such a load of hokey, cornball sentiment.

The sergeant looked away. "Sorry, March," he muttered. "Didn't mean to get carried away like that. I just wanted you to come by so that I could thank you."

"There's nothing to thank me for," Gene said. "I just did what anybody else would have done."

Hollis turned his head so that he was looking up at Gene again. "You saved my life," he said. "What's more, this is the second time. I owe you more than I can ever pay back, March."

Gene shook his head. "Forget it. You don't owe me a thing."

"Yeah, I do," Hollis insisted. "And I'll find a way to pay it, at least part of it. If they ship me out of here and I don't come back,

March, I want you to know that in my heart I'll be right beside you the rest of the way. You remember that when you're fighting the Krauts. You may be fighting for both of us."

Hollis didn't understand. As soon as Al Satterfield could get him the hell out of here, he wouldn't be fighting the Krauts anymore. He wouldn't be fighting anybody, and as far as Gene was concerned, it could stay that way from now on. If he never heard another gun go off, that would be just fine.

But for some reason, he couldn't say that, couldn't explain it to the guy lying there on the cot with his arm swathed in bandages. The arm that might be useless for the rest of his life.

"You gotta promise me you'll remember, March," Hollis said. "You gotta promise me that you'll carry on, that you'll fight for the both of us if you have to."

"Sure," Gene said. "Sure, I promise, Sarge." The lie came easily. It was what Hollis wanted to hear. The sergeant looked relieved. His head sagged back against the thin pillow underneath it.

"Give 'em hell," he murmured. The drugs he had fought off in order to talk to Gene were taking control of his system again and making him groggy.

Gene leaned over and patted Hollis on the shoulder. "So long, Sarge. You just take it easy."

Hollis nodded and closed his eyes, and Gene took advantage of the opportunity to get out of the hospital before Hollis woke up and started preaching at him again. He didn't feel bad about making a promise he had no intention of keeping. There was no room in his thoughts for that.

All he could think of was that before much longer, he would be on stage, singing for a bunch of entertainment-starved dogfaces. Talk about your captive audiences!

# FIFTY-FOUR

For the next three weeks, the American forces under Patton pounded at the Axis-held passes with no success. More German Panzers were shifted from the Mareth Line to defend the passes, and the Americans were unable to dislodge them.

However, that shift in Axis forces was the key to the entire operation, and the resulting weakening of their defenses along the Mareth Line enabled the British Eighth Army under Field Marshal Montgomery to break through and force the Germans to start retreating up the coast toward Tunis and Bizerte. The Germans and Italians who had been holding the passes against the Americans received orders to pull back as well, in support of the Axis retreat from the Mareth Line.

With the way clear at last, Patton started his men and tanks dashing east toward the sea. On the afternoon of 7 April 1943, Joe and Dale were scouting ahead of the main column in the jeep. Dale licked his lips and said, "I can taste salt. We must be getting close to the coast."

Joe looked around. The hills had been left far behind them. The terrain had flattened out into a plain. The ground was still rocky in places and sandy in others. The jeep raised a small cloud of dust behind it as it rolled along. Joe spotted a similar cloud up ahead and to the right.

He said to Dale, "Look over there," and pointed. Dale saw the dust and leaned forward a little in anticipation, gripping the steering wheel tighter as he veered the jeep to the right. Joe saw that their new course would intercept that of whoever was raising the other dust cloud.

"We'll head 'em off," Dale said. "Maybe it's some Kraut stragglers."

"Or a British patrol," Joe suggested. "Colonel Gault said they were coming up the coast like gangbusters."

"Yeah, well, I'd rather it was Krauts. We haven't fired that Fifty in a couple of weeks. I'm gettin' bored."

Joe smiled. Leave it to Dale to get bored just because nobody was shooting at him.

They sped on toward the dust rising in the distance. Joe noted that the cloud had changed direction a little too. Whoever was over there wanted to intercept him and Dale. They were coming together in a hurry now.

A few minutes later, Joe saw several things at the same time. Some large rocks loomed in the distance, and beyond them was a sweep of blue that could only be the Mediterranean. A vehicle appeared at the base of the dust cloud coming toward them. It was a truck of some kind, too large to be a jeep but not big enough to be a tank. As the truck came closer, Joe recognized the Union Jack flying from a radio mast on the back of it. He let out a whoop of excitement.

"It's the British!" Joe pounded Dale on the shoulder and looked over at his brother. Dale was grinning too. He might be a little disappointed that there wasn't going to be a battle today, but he was glad to see the British too.

Dale brought the jeep to a stop about twenty yards from the truck, which also came to a halt. Desert fighters from the Eighth Army, in khaki shorts and shirts and bush hats, jumped down from the vehicle and trotted over to the jeep as Joe and Dale were getting out. The Englishmen were tanned to a dark shade of brown except around their eyes, where they wore goggles. They were covered with dust. One of the men pulled his goggles down so they dangled around his neck and grinned broadly at the Americans.

"Hello, Yanks!" he called out in a cheery voice. "Fancy meeting you here!"

Joe stuck out his hand and shook with the Englishman. "We expected to see the Nazis," he said.

The Brit waved his hand toward the north. "Oh, no, they're all running away. Probably wishing they could scurry back to their dear old Uncle Adolf, I daresay. But the bloody Mediterranean is in the way. They'll have to stop at Tunis and Bizerte."

"Then that's where we'll get 'em," Dale said as he shook hands too, with the leader of the British patrol. "General Patton's right behind us with the whole American Two Corps."

"And Monty's coming up with the rest of the Eighth Army. It'll be a bit of a race to see who gets to the Jerries first, eh?"

"Maybe," Joe said. "But I think we're both going to win."

The Germans might be retreating, but they were hardly ready to give up. By the middle of April, they had established a defensive line that encompassed both of the port cities of Bizerte and Tunis, as well as the peninsula south of Tunis known as Cape Bon. They laid mines, set up artillery emplacements, and covered the ridges and hillsides with trenches and foxholes. There was no doubt in the mind of anyone among the Allies that the Germans would fight for as long as they possibly could. In Berlin, Hitler was making speeches proclaiming that the Axis would maintain their presence in North Africa. The German soldiers would do their best to make the Führer's pronouncements come true.

Now that the Americans and the British had linked up, the next step was to decide who would go after which target. The original plan called for the British to carry most of the load, relegating the American II Corps to support and mop-up duty. Vehement protests by General Patton and his second-in-command, General Omar Bradley, prompted General Eisenhower, as supreme Allied commander, to overrule the British generals who had designed the scheme. The British First Army, which had come ashore with the Americans as part of Operation Torch the previous autumn, would close in on Tunis, supported by Montgomery and the British Eighth Army. The American II Corps was given the job of capturing Bizerte on its own.

II Corps would attempt that, however, under the orders of a new commander. Bradley was elevated to overall command of II Corps, while Patton was transferred back to England. Rumors ran rampant about the reason for the departure of Old Blood and Guts, as Patton had begun to be called, but through his contacts in Intelligence, Joe Parker knew the truth. Patton had been recalled to help with the planning for an invasion of Sicily. The Allied High Command was thinking already about the next step in the war, once the Axis had been driven from North Africa.

The American drive toward Bizerte began on 23 April. The first obstacle in the way was a rugged height known as Hill 609, because that was the way it was designated on the French maps the Americans were using. The Arabs called it Djebel Tahent. By any name, it was an important piece of real estate. The German artillery on top of the hill controlled the Tine River Valley, through which the American forces would have to pass to reach the coastal plain around Bizerte. Until II Corps took the hill, any real advance would be stalled.

Infantry attacks against Hill 609 were ineffective. Conventional military wisdom indicated that tanks should not be used against an enemy on higher ground. The soft-spoken General Bradley, who was quite a contrast to the loud, profane Patton, proved to be capable of daring maneuvers just like his predecessor. Bradley ordered the Sherman tanks of the First Armored Division to lead the attack on Hill 609. The tanks rumbled up the slopes, 75mm-cannon booming, followed closely by waves of infantry. The unexpected tactic worked, and the Axis forces atop the hill were forced to retreat. The high ground now belonged to the Americans, who began streaming up the valley toward Bizerte.

Dale was asleep, slumped behind the wheel of the jeep, when a hand grasped his shoulder and started shaking him. "Wake up!" a voice said urgently. "Wake up, Dale!"

Blinking bleary eyes open, Dale looked up into the face of his brother. Joe's features were set in tense lines. Dale sat up straight. "What is it?"

"Colonel Gault just got word that the British are closing in on Tunis. We have to get to Bizerte."

Dale's mouth stretched in a grin. "We gotta get to the finish line first, is that it?"

"You ought to understand that feeling better than anyone," Joe said. "After all the times you drove around and around a dirt track just to see if you could do it faster than some other guy, you know what it's like. Only this time it's important."

"Hey, the races I was in were important too!" Dale protested. He raised a hand as Joe opened his mouth to argue. "But I know what you mean. Hop in. We'll be in Bizerte before the Limeys waltz into Tunis."

The way hadn't been all easy after the capture of Hill 609 on 26 April. A week and a half of intense fighting had followed as the Americans advanced toward the coast and the road that ran between Tunis and Bizerte. Many tanks had been lost, but many more Panzers had been destroyed than Shermans. But earlier today, 7 May 1943, advance units from II Corps, including Joe and Dale, had reached the coast road. They had pulled up there to await orders, and as usual, Dale had taken advantage of the opportunity to snatch a nap.

Now he tromped the jeep's starter as Joe climbed in the back, settling down to man the .50-caliber machine gun if needed. The engine caught with a roar, and Dale put the jeep in gear. The little vehicle spurted down the road toward Bizerte.

Dale glanced back and saw that none of the rest of the American forces were following them. He said over his shoulder to Joe, "Are you *sure* we were supposed to head for Bizerte?"

"That's what the colonel said."

"Looks like somebody forgot to tell the rest of the army," Dale muttered.

He didn't mind, though. The road was open in front of him, clear of any enemies as far as the eye could see. And on this coastal plain, that was pretty far. He pressed down harder on the accelerator, enjoying the response of the jeep's engine. It spoke to him like a thing alive, and the wind was alive too, singing a siren song to him as it whistled past his ears. Going fast was the best thing in the world.

Afternoon sun beat down on the two young Americans in the jeep. To the southeast, around Tunis, large black clouds clogged the sky, and Dale wondered if it was raining down there. Here there was no storm, only the road that unwound before them, leading them on toward their goal.

Joe suddenly tapped Dale on the shoulder and called, "What's that?"

Dale had already seen what Joe was talking about. He saw what seemed to be a dark hillock to the right of the road, and as the jeep sped closer, Dale realized it was a canvas cover erected to give shade. A truck was parked underneath it, and beside the truck a machine gun had been set up on a tripod. Dale grinned tautly. There were no Allied forces up here, so that machine-gun post had to be manned by Germans.

"Hang on, Joe!" he shouted. "We're goin' through!"

He floored the gas and sent the jeep leaping ahead. Figures tumbled out of the back of the truck and scrambled to reach the machine gun as they heard the roar of the approaching vehicle. The jeep shot past before the German gunners could get set up. Joe twisted his head around to stare back at them. The Germans were standing around, apparently confused by the sudden appearance of the speed demon that had raced past them.

"If they've got a radio, they'll alert the next post!" Joe called.

"Doesn't matter!" Dale replied. "They can't lay a finger on us, big brother!" His laughter pealed out over the rugged, arid landscape, trailing away behind the jeep. He knew he probably sounded like he had gone nuts, but that wasn't the case at all. He had never felt more sane in his life, or filled with more confidence.

This day belonged to him, by God. To him and all the other Americans behind him, all the GIs who had come ashore months earlier to join the big fight at last. To the guys who were still fighting, to the ones who lay in hospitals and aid stations recovering from their wounds—and to the ones who lay in graves either back home or here in a foreign land, who had given everything they had in the effort to take back the world from the barbarians who threatened to overrun it. . . .

Dale blinked rapidly. The whole damned Third Reich could get between him and Bizerte, and it wouldn't matter. Not today. He and all the other Americans would not be stopped.

"Comin' up on your left!" he shouted to Joe, and the Fifty began to chatter as Joe opened fire on the German machine-gun post up ahead. These Krauts were ready for them. Fire lanced from the barrel of their machine gun. Bullets kicked up dust in the road in front of the jeep and alongside it as well. Joe hung on to the Fifty and swung the barrel and kept firing. Bodies tumbled away from the German machine gun as the jeep flashed past it. Dale didn't know if the Krauts had been hit or were just hopping for cover. It didn't really matter. One more obstacle was now behind them.

He let out a whoop and turned his head to look back at Joe. Joe leaned forward, bracing himself against the Fifty. His face was ashen, and blood showed on his shirt. Dale cried out incoherently. His foot stabbed toward the brake.

"No!" Joe's voice rang out, clear and strong. "Keep going! It's nothing! Just a scratch!"

"Joe!" Dale said brokenly, not knowing if his brother was telling the truth about the wound or not.

Joe's hand came down on Dale's shoulder and squeezed. There was strength in the grip, more strength than Dale had ever felt before. "Drive," Joe said. "Drive like you've always wanted to. As fast as you can. The people in Bizerte are waiting for us." Joe's hand tightened even more on Dale's shoulder. "All over the world, they're waiting for us. We can't let them down because of a little scratch. . . ."

Dale swallowed hard and punched the gas. Joe was right, and he knew it. The race had to be won. Not the race to see whether the British or the Americans would reach their objective first. That didn't really matter. The true finish line wasn't in Tunis or Bizerte.

It was in Berlin.

They drove on, leading the way, two faces wreathed in fighting grins, two sets of keen eyes peering into the future with hope and determination.

On the afternoon of 7 May, Allied forces captured the Tunisian port cities of Tunis and Bizerte. The Italian soldiers who had opposed them surrendered in droves. The German forces tried to retreat and fought on in isolated skirmishes for nearly another week. Finally, outnumbered, surrounded, and with no way to replenish their ammunition and other supplies, the last of the once-proud Deutsche Afrika Korps surrendered. The Allies were now in complete control of the entirety of North Africa.

And the eyes of the Allied High Command could now turn north, across the Mediterranean, toward Sicily and Italy.

# ABOUT THE AUTHOR

James Reasoner has been a professional writer for the past twenty years, writing dozens of novels in a variety of genres, including several Wagons West historical novels (as Dana Fuller Ross) and nearly a hundred short stories. He lives in Texas with his wife, award-winning mystery novelist L. J. Washburn.